DEVIL'S TEMPLE

GOD'S CHAIN

Book two
in
GOD'S CHAIN

Nikolaus Baker

DEVIL'S TEMPLE

Published by Mikey Books [2020]

First Edition, 2020

ISBN: 978-1-9162589-0-7

Dedicated to
My mother Jessie (Cissi) Thom and father Michael.
Provost George and Marjory Murray

THE PROPHECY

They will come first and smite.
All will shake in terror.
Cold is the land.
Nowhere to hide.

The cursed will come and bite.
All will run in terror.
Pained is the land.
Nowhere to hide.

Devil's will come and spite.
All will fall in terror.
Dead is the land.
Nowhere to hide.

Darkness will come and blight.
All will bow in terror.
Black is the land.
Nowhere to hide.
Souless and suffering in the land of nowhere.
Nowhere to hide.

DEVIL'S TEMPLE

INDEX

PROLOGUE

DEVIL'S TEMPLE

DEVIL'S TEMPLE is the sequel to GENESIS in GOD'S CHAIN.

DEVIL'S TEMPLE is a story of fate and legend, of feared words spoken in whispers of power and mystery. A Shaman's grim forewarnings tell a tale of a temple that appears every five hundred years deep inside the jungle, and this is such a year! On the other side of the world, a civilian expedition becomes lost inside one of the most unforgiving places on earth, Amazonia. Does the truth lie within this remorseless rainforest?

GOD'S CHAIN is an epic story that begins a dark mystery, its ancient origins are in the west coast of Scotland and span the world with a black veil. A diary of deceit from centuries past hints at a primordial struggle for power that continues in Devil's Temple and now continues inside Amazonia.

Bio-piracy is big business and the cost of developing new drugs is soaring with over two hundred companies involved in bio-prospecting in Brazil. The ONCOL Scientific Corporation is one such conglomerate, which finances scientific research of natural resources and can potentially net the corporation billions of dollars in patents and royalties. This is an elaborate smokescreen as the Vatican has other interests, not just the religious indoctrination of indigenous tribes.

The expedition does not believe the tribal leaders who foretold of an ancient bloodline and magical temple. A few in the team had heard of a secret Shaman's myth that told tales of a treasure named Eldorado. Defying failure and cutting a torturous path through the jungle, the explorers head deeper into unexplored green hell. In the coming months, before the earthquake that sent waves rippling as far as Scotland, they uncover ancient walls not seen since the days of the Portuguese Crusades. What priceless wealth would lie inside?

Suddenly, horror strikes when a scientist is killed in an act of human sacrifice. The death toll continues to rise, and nothing makes sense anymore as friendships stretch to breaking point and religious tensions begin to tighten. Who or what is killing them? Inside the temple, a tapestry of death traps lay waiting. If these don't get them then horrific life-forms from another world surely will. Would anyone be found alive to rescue? Be warned, that only a dreadful enlightenment awaits those who search for Devil's Temple.

CHAPTER I

THE CARDINAL'S FOLLY

Cardinal Giovanni Dalla Gassa looked uneasy, watching across the landscape from his lofty villa heights. Daylight was leaving, chased away from its sandy coloured walls and draining life from its warm pastel tones. The sun departed his affluent domicile-like water in sand while long shadows began to stretch and elongate across the country. Lukewarm light had already captured the nearby rural village of Acilia and now travelled towards his high vantage point. Country folk would wonder with trepidation about the far-off turrets of his shadowy villa above the serene valley.

It was late evening in October and the electric lights down in the village began switching on in symphony, orchestrated like constellations in the heavenly sky. Distant, dark blue hills began silhouetting against a wonderful translucent orange and cherry red ambience. Transient coloured tones travelled along the length of a low skyline horizon and rose high and skywards, becoming the deep blackness of space beyond. Night would dominate again.

The cardinal sat on his outside veranda and measured the stars with a stare, his gaze held frozen for a moment, suspended in time while ominous shadows moved gradually across the land. His iron brown eyes were a final witness to the fading sunlight in the early eve while darkness swept over the high ridges and rim of his land, and married to the sounds of the night. Some noises were like music to his ears and others lonesome and wild, primeval.

A sudden cold breeze swept through the air disturbing the leaves in the nearby oak trees, which rustled nervously. The darkness was a bearer of bad memories and a conduit signalling a change Giovanni could not see but felt. His face froze into an icy grimace. For comfort, the Cardinal switched on his side lamp and looked again at his laptop to review a vital email containing secret correspondence sent at the beginning of the year from the Vatican External Affairs Office (VEAO). The Vatican External Affairs was a special branch of secret agents who dealt with all sensitive and classified foreign policy issues for the Holy Pontiff.

`"Your Grace,`

`We have received an urgent communication from the Food Agricultural Organisation regarding sweeping changes beyond the signed agreements from 1994. These changes prohibit the Vatican government and any other governments in the world to claim legal ownership or intellectual`

property rights over any 'gene plasm'
discovered or synthesised from
indigenous flora and fauna within the
Amazon, or anywhere inside Brazil.

Self-satisfied once again, the well-informed cardinal read through this confidential email but was not worried and enjoyed his wine, sipping it and savouring its fine taste. His recursive eyes eagerly moved back and forth along the text, planning his next tactic.

"In terms of bio-piracy and
agreements made with FAO in Rome, and
the Consultative Group on
International Agriculture Research
(CGIAR) in Washington DC, the
unauthorised extraction and use of
widespread resources is now illegal.
Penalties will be more than punitive
and will carry the possibility of
imprisonment and heavy financial
sanctions for those caught.
Signore, as you will understand,
these are very serious implications
to our theatre of operations in this
locale."

Dalla Gassa shrugged and smiled, he knew how to keep the fat cats happy, the stakeholders, the shareholders and all those further up the food chain. These people on the Board of Management, right up there inside the European Commission Bank in Luxembourg.

"Oh Si! They were rich, *very rich.* There were plenty of ways to fund his private mission." Unknown to everyone, there was an inner circle of people, a secret group of key individuals who made up a *shadow board,* people that kept hidden agendas and dark dreams, seeing far and beyond simple greed. An exclusive secret society moving their puppets ruthlessly from afar. It was they who really held the purse-strings of these performing marionettes. Driven by a greed for power, this sinister sect would never meet in person. Instead, they preferred the illusion of movement that dwelt in their own virtual worlds to achieve their ultimate ambitions. Written in the Bible, their day of judgment like all others was coming.

Raising another glass of wine steadily to his stained red lips, the cardinal polished off his bottle of wine sourced from his personal vineyards. Reaching for another slim necked bottle from his side table, the cardinal clicked the PURGE button on his laptop and shredded the email marked as *extremely classified.* He blasted it into cyber-space; there would be no trace anywhere on the system.

Dalla Gassa was confident there would be *no backup* of this surreptitious information because of the *Ventessi* tapeworm, a vicious in-house computer program he knew had been unleashed and left to wander freely unchecked throughout the Vatican computer systems.

The main computer systems administrator was in hospital suffering from her recent trauma.

Francesca De Rose was under close medical supervision being treated for cracked ribs and severe stress having survived an attempt on her life. She was now helping police in the brutal murder investigation of her work colleague Massimo and the disappearance of a close friend named Michaelangelo. The Curia insisted that the young woman have time off to stay in hospital for observation with all expenses paid; it was the least the Vatican could do to help her recovery.

His Grace's mouse-hand had developed a peculiar shake. He had seen it before. Staring at it made it worse. Dalla Gassa could not understand where his gravid fears were coming from.

Lord, I cannot control it. His posture began to change and quite unexpectedly, his hand stopped trembling.

Swallowing hard, he quickly redirected his thoughts to protect his sanity onto more rewarding successes, patting his own back and praising himself once again. Perceptive enough, the cardinal had successfully acquired businesses and niche scientific companies specialising in Biotechnology. These acquisitions and investments would help supply and boost his personal Peter's Pence, skimming vast monies for his *holy mission.*

A new industry was worth billions. The extrapolation of the seemingly endless natural resources found inside Amazonia were exponential and would open vast wealth. These riches would provide everything he would need. He could not fail.

Being a financial wizard and superior intellect, Dalla Gassa could acquire massive monies from unsuspecting shareholders. This expertise and knowledge enabled his plans to continue. His ethics were immoral but were justified to him because they were in the name of the lord. Giovanni Dalla Gassa absolved himself, convinced that the mission was true and a holy crusade. He did not think his actions were wrong because the outcome of a greater world was *just* and *right* and proof of his love for an almighty God.

The cardinal was also very well versed in the procurement of companies. He knew how to labour through European legalisation and award contracts sent for publication. He was not alone in this intimate practice of exploitation, there were other men, more ruthless and every bit as clever. Dalla Gassa would have to be careful.

Some *contracts* were intentionally not sent to the governing body, which employed hired killers and would prove fatal to those who stood in the way of progress. People would disappear. Some were purged or rescinded. It all meant the same thing: assassination.

Inopportune, unseen events had already taken place and the cardinal's communication with the expedition had been severed. Unfortunately, his plan was now in serious jeopardy of failing as the exploration of the green continent was the key to power.

Growling epithets under his breath, he had not expected this setback. However, he thanked God for his forethought, having made a meticulous and well-organised contingency plan, and then nodded calmly to himself knowing that his rescue mission had already reached its target. Soon he would be in possession of one of the three fabled Reliquae.

The Holy Pontiff is ignorant and knows nothing of any of my ingenious plans, he thought, *and this is the way things will remain.* Dalla Gassa contemplated further at the Brazilian government's unexpected insertion, *the rainforest is a very dangerous place. The inclusion of a Brazilian D.E.A. personnel is indeed a hindrance to my mission. Accidents are always a risk; when so far away, things can happen.*

Suddenly, his smile turned stony and grave, and his whole persona changed without transition. A heaviness pushed on him and made his body appear older, and his frame became hunched and he felt unwell. It was a warning or premonition that occurred just as an icy cold breeze blew across the veranda. Cold bitter air that had channelled its way up from the lower valley. Its touch affected his whole being, and yet, the cardinal's skin beaded quickly with sweat. *Fear.* A long shiver shot up his spine, with a secret dread wiping across his worn-out face. Jerking abruptly, his crooked back straightened. Giovanni instantly felt his body become a wooden plank.

It will be an early winter, he thought, while trying to ignore the fear inside him. Giovanni believed there are more precious things to lose than money and felt a pang of self-retribution, trying to push away his inner dread. He had sanctioned Operation Aequinoxium. Failure was not an option. *Much greater things are at stake.*

Something deep and terrible had started to disturb him. His self-confidence evaporated and waned while gagging back nausea at the unspeakable horror invading his psyche. It was not his conscience or his resolve to finish the mission that was making him feel this way. His willpower was already set firm and unshakable in his *holy mission*. This feeling of a coming evil was something else.

He gulped his wine quickly and filled it up again with an erratic and unsteady hand. Annoyed, he gripped the glass harder and overfilled it; it went over the lip and spread out like blood, running red onto the table. His shakes returned as they always did at night.

Yes, the darkness was with him again and his dreams would soon begin. They were becoming increasingly worse. The wine became sour to his palate despite its unsavoury taste not bothering him much. Preoccupied, the cardinal stretched carelessly and tipped a small bottle of pills that scattered helplessly across the small stone table. Moaning unceremoniously, he began to scramble vaguely like a drunk. Unfortunately, he was not drunk enough. The mighty Cardinal,

Giovanni Dalla Gassa, Secretary of State to the Vatican, was a man reduced to a mere shadow of himself. He stared intensely while his iron gaze rusted at the tiny white objects peppered on the table, mixed in red fluid. He swallowed them one by one, helped over with more wine.

Keep me awake God, oh please keep me awake!

****

CHAPTER II

PRAYING MANTIS

The dense rainforest of the Amazon inhibited most of the sunlight's struggling rays, filtering some of them into its component parts and displaying them as a myriad of colourful frequencies. To all creatures that saw it, what wonder, what beauty! God's spectrum shone throughout the canopy layers. Indeed, it was a miracle. This was a forest of different tints of green and brown, that sometimes lit up into beautiful tones of blue, yellow, and red. Thriving and teaming with life of all colours were countless creatures, all with one thing in mind, survival.

Deafening sounds came from within and there were many strange noises. Buzzing insects were everywhere, all uncountable and uncontrollable, crawling and flying. Crazy birds chattered together, all competing with their distinctive sweet songs and calls of panic set against the jittery din of monkeys. These screeching primates jumped suddenly, boasting skilful acrobatics to their mates while swinging from treetop to treetop.

In the upper canopy forty-six metres high, many maddened monkeys seemed inconsolable about something different and out of the ordinary. All were screeching and leaping out of the way, each protesting with renewed alarm and agitation which soon turned into enraged anger and panic. A large patch of colourful butterflies tried to leave as well, but it was too late for them, when large heavy objects came crashing through the greenery accompanied by what appeared to be giant nets from the air.

Without warning, these wide green sheets spread out and captured them at once. Confused, the monkeys watched like a gang of pickpockets taking advantage of a new opportunity. The intruders' parachutes quickly settled onto the treetops and smothered everything. Man had arrived.

Birds flew in blind panic in every direction, disturbed by the unnatural predators. Other keen eyes looked curiously at the commotion and numerous vines and branches rustling above. A tropical storm had formed a fine mist around the beast waiting below.

It was a large jaguar that lay calm and concealed, hidden in the moisture. It had been waiting for a very long time for this moment, for mankind to arrive. With watchful eyes that never rested, wise and noble this beast snarled in a low growl. It seemed almost as if it knew what was about to happen as the mist completed its disguise. It could hear them. It could smell them.

A change had come to the forest. The intrusion was unwelcomed by all in the forest, scarlet macaws flew off in fright and squirrel monkeys jumped like springs to escape entrapment as more manmade sheets fell from the sky.

Through the branches, bare face howler monkeys scattered in every direction. Their dark pigmented skins and copper red faces with large swelling beneath roared deep noises of protest. They grabbed cheekily at some of the torn parachutes, stealing the cloth material and ripping it away while avoiding capture. Not all feared these new intruders, from anaconda to ant, or tree sloth to lively cricket; they went about their normal business of survival with complete indifference to the human intruders.

****

The scientists had gone missing and were lost somewhere in this dense region. They had found something secret and quite remarkable, an ill omen that came as a spawn from another world, flying out from the embroiled black clouds high above the canopy. An enormous creature, huge and black, burst from *nowhere* without warning, flying and swooping in the nitric air as if chased by the Devil.

Born unto the wing high in the air featherless, completely bare, it uttered an unearthly and high-pitched scream that would make a man quake. It swooped down quickly from darkness and its massive beak shrieked loud and guttural. Appropriately, DEATH was the beast's name and it had come to seek the dead and dying and pay homage to its awful master. In flight, the creature opened to full wingspan, wider than an aircraft, as it navigated over this new land mass with ease.

The carrion effortlessly utilised the atmosphere's warm currents, gliding naturally and smoothly in the brooding skies. Excited, the monster had come from a place called *Nowhere,* and rabid for blood. There was nothing natural about the creature called DEATH.

The huge brute was released from its evil bonds and with its sad and apologetic eyes, soared high as the last parachutes settled on the treetops below. Like a hybrid between pterosaur, a flying reptile with razor teeth lined beak and vulture, it defied all-natural law. Soon it would grow feathers as it matured and mutated. It gave out an almighty screech that defied resistance as it began lowering in altitude and encircling the soldiers below. The men in the landing zone were completely unaware of its foul arrival.

****

Synchronized noises of rustling and human sounds spread from the trees, as numerous ropes began dropping down to the forest floor. Boots and bodies suddenly appeared, all wearing camouflaged battle gear. The rescue mission was ready to go.

Relieved to have reached the safety of the ground, this type of drop always runs the risk of breaking bones. On reaching the forest floor, the soldiers steadied themselves as best they could. Standing on an uneven surface, sudden immediacy forced them to adjust unsteadily on a steep and slippery slope as their legs disappeared into a light ground mist. Below their feet, a light and watery blanket held hidden treachery. Some unfortunate soldiers fell unceremoniously onto the wet decomposing foliage.

Obvious to everyone was the random pitter-patter of belated heavy rain drops smacking off the large thick leaves, their wet sounds echoing all around them that kept running off the turgid vegetation since the recent down pour; the water heated and changed into a more gaseous state where the men regrouped. As planned, everyone assembled at their designated drop zone. The drop zone was named *Jesuit* after the priests who bravely practiced Christianity with untamed head-hunters in South-America long ago.

The jungle would be an intimidating place by nightfall, proving difficult to traverse; every yard would be a battle. The soldiers' primary destination was located much higher in altitude, normally hidden under a blanket of cloud that kept the place hidden and secret.

They were about seven miles or so below the cloud forest. It was essential to close in from a safe distance. Operation Aequinoxium had arrived.

****

In the cover of darkness, the men had landed into an eerie and lonely spot in the early morning at 0400A.M. of late October. Unfortunately, some soldiers had to climb down through the high trees where their ropes could not penetrate the lower forest layer. Other men made a quick, unimpeded abseil straight to the floor.

Colonel Greco Rossi of the 9th Degree Paracadutista (Parachutist) Assault Regiment, Special Forces, was far from his base in Tuscany. His mission orders were direct from a four-star General of Commando Forze di Difesa 1 also known as COMFOD One.

Rossi answered to General Benedetti, who resided in the north eastern city of Vittorio, oversaw operations and commanded most of the specialised brigades in the Italian army. They shared the base with the American USAF Administration. His small and very specialized group of soldiers were all Swiss guardsmen who used the Italian army to cloak their own inimitable existence. Their presence was secret and was politically unacceptable outside Vatican City; elsewhere in the world the Popes guard did not exist.

The colonel's cropped haircut matched his short grey stubble. He stood about five feet nine with a model-like body, solid muscles sculptured to perfection through twenty years of covert sorties and specialized campaigning. His piercing steel blue eyes scanned the intimidating environment and he heard his sergeant coming up a murky slope. The soldier arrived and saluted smartly.

As commander of the unit, he was a respected officer and a natural leader. He knew how to rule the most ruthless of soldiers and get the most out of them.

All guardsmen wore the coveted crossbow insignias on their outer combat jacket shoulder pads. On their short sleeved inner shirts, there was a badge with a brown crossbow, red scribing and gold edging with the words "Croce di Luce" or *Cross of Light*; immortal words, proudly displayed on a green shield with gold black edging. The word "elitist" was also tattooed on each soldier's right bicep just above a one by two-inch Swiss flag.

The colonel focused, speaking quickly and earnestly to his subordinate, Sergeant Davide Romano, a reliable soldier who had served with him for the past five years. The men in this privileged unit were all Swiss guards, a prerequisite for their commission to this part of their fighting division. Each soldier was a Swiss citizen and Catholic faithful, having trained at military school in Switzerland. Each country has its own security and the Vatican was no exception. They were a long way from home and itching to get started. Special sorties like these kept them at their best fighting edge.

The Swiss Guard has a maximum of 110 guardsmen and sixty remained back home to continue their normal duties and protect the Holy Father, as his personal security had done for many centuries. His agents were pre-assigned to other duties elsewhere in the world.

In a strong commanding voice Colonel Rossi spoke, "Report Davide" as he observed the sergeant's facial scar as he came through the dense trees. The leader's eager eyes continuously roved left then right around the blackness of the night. With parental alert, he watched over his men and tuned to any danger that the forest might hold. His assembling command began organizing around, standing close to him on the slimy gradient.

Before this mission, five of the guardsmen had been decorated by the Pope for showing utmost courage under fire and for displaying complete disregard for their own safety. These men were himself, his sergeant with the call sign *Scorpion,* and ahead of him was Major Trentino on an exploratory spearhead mission known as *Mantis.* Two other soldiers had been killed shielding civilians from certain death at that time.

The *Apostle of God* was the most highly awarded medal given by the Holy See and a personal accolade from the *Emissary of God.* Each Swiss guardsman proudly displayed a small fabric ensign that was a replica of the medal stitched into the forehead of their purple Berets. It was a special ensign made of cloth material and a rich weave finished into an image of a golden bird of prey, a different species depending on whichever tactical unit each man assigned. Each bird was sharp eyed and riveted on prey, held in a dive with its wings upturned and elevated like cupped hands with fingered feathers enclosed around an internal shield on a blue background. Inside the shield it held an upturned enflamed dagger with an open parachute inside. The colonel's unit was named after the Osprey, the bird of prey that fiercely gripped its fixed claws in immortal combat with the following proud words, "Silendo Libertatem Servo Mobil," the Brigades motto meaning "Serving Liberty Silently in Motion."

The sergeant's camouflaged face, furrowed with urgency they needed to get moving,

"Signore, Mantis's unit are already routed on reconnaissance as planned, I estimate three hours before our arrival. He should be halfway to our prime objective already." The soldier indicated the direction Trentino's unit had departed and shined his torch to find signs of machete hacked undergrowth. "No injuries in our descent. All our men are accounted for and in good health. We are ready to go, signore!" He paused in ready stance holding his loaded weapon, "Colonnello, are we expecting trouble on this one?" His rhetorical eyes seemed excited, "The men and I want to kick some ass again, signore!" His over enthusiastic sergeant completed his update and awaited further instructions from the colonel.

"This is a rescue mission sergeant. I hope it is a small sortie, in and out, surgical." His tone was clinical. "However, it is not a standard rescue mission." His voice defying failure. "It's important that these civilians are found alive," the commander stated firmly.

"The men will be frustrated my colonnello. Hand holding is not what we soldiers are about, signore." He said in a less respectful tone. "Do you not remember Iraq?" The man's macho censure at his superior officer warranted an immediate response.

"Sergente," the Officer spoke calmly, "Remember yourself. I do mean that, soldier. I of all people know what we did there. We lost valuable men on a so-called rescue mission," the colonel stated briefly, "All the men were his responsibility, their safety and lives were in his hands. On that occasion we both know well, the Islamic insurgents were given something else to pray about that night."

The sergeant had been referring to a previous and highly successful rescue mission of the ambassador's delegation, saving them from the executioner's knife.

"Signore, my apologies!"

"Sergente, you are right, those people would certainly have been brutally murdered. That was down to the men and your own bravery," Colonel Rossi acknowledged with utmost admiration of his tall sergeant.

"Si signore!" He felt better within himself, for his colonel had recognised his own individual contribution. Standing to attention, all six-foot six of his massive muscular frame, the man remembered it was his colonel who played a vital part in that sortie.

The colonel would not take credit for his part, the officer had saved the whole squad and all civilians from massacre reflecting his past events, he thought, *Si, we rescued the civilians, but it was the colonnello, who saved everyone!*

On that night, a few years before and in a daring combined mission between Italian and Swiss Special Forces of the ninth Degree Paracadutista Regiment, they had managed to neutralize all the insurgents inside the Italian embassy.

Outside the large embassy building the enemy was dug in, there was no escape. As planned, the rescue teams had quickly organized the civilians for evacuation by air. The enemy had surrounded the building when their rescue had been uncovered. Unfortunately, one insurgent lay concealed during the operation, the terrorist hid in the building and managed to raise the alarm.

The enemy knew that the fate of their comrades inside the embassy were by now all dead. Instead of capture for political ransom, the insurgents outside decided to gain a bigger headline by obliterating the building and everyone inside it. They began blasting and shooting at the building like maniacs. The arrival of more enemy reinforcements meant more RPG rocket propelled grenades to target the embassy.

Out of the igniting darkness, men were screaming orders and yelling obscenities between blasts as total mayhem ensued. The sound of Soviet made RPG-7 explosions and Chinese built Type 88 automatic belt-fed machine gun fire completed the chaos. The Type 88s were used as bipods for easy, lightweight operation. Everywhere the arsenal of weaponry steadily demolished the walls bit by bit, in other places, blasting out chunks of masonry. Piles of rubble and dust erupted everywhere. The building in a very short period would be nothing more than grains of sand and dust once again, just like the surrounding desert dunes not far away. It was frightening.

Under the cover of hellish devastation, shaking off the light of sporadic fire fight flashing in the explosions, the colonel hid on the ground near the embassy; creeping and moving quickly in silent motion. In and away like a shadow, he ignited their own explosives stash which caused a massive diversion. The man created complete disorder. This signalled the arrival of the rescue choppers.

One by one, with the hands of a skilled surgeon, he coldly slit their throats; many lone snipers and machine gunners stationed around the embassy knew nothing. Not one of them uttered a single sound. All it took was a quick twist of their heads and the pull of the sharp blade across their throats, easily opening their bloody tracheas. A hand over their mouth just in case, then a life was over in a pitiless second amid a gushing and gurgling mess. Against the immediate noise, the chopper's roaring engines and main rotors whirled up sand and debris all around the embassy. This turmoil completed his cover.

One helicopter hovered above the burning building, creating a tornado-like whirlwind in a mega dust storm. Landing tentatively on the buildings flat roof with all lights off, the crew completely committed.

The chopper was completely vulnerable when suddenly, two other helicopter gunships appeared humming quickly past and banked fast in either direction, going around the building blasting at anything on the ground.

Gunship firepower quickly kept the heads down of the startled enemy with the latest night vision, as the aircrew found easy targets pinpointing each with deadly accuracy. The insurgents screamed up suicidal abuse moments before flesh and bone blasted mercilessly from them.

Tiny grains of sand flew everywhere to the sounds of gigantic fans whipping up dust that added to the general confusion. Small arms fire rained up with screams of the dying, their crying voices mixed with bloodied vapour in all directions.

Under this turmoil, the stunned embassy staff were being hustled and airlifted off the rooftop by soldiers, quickly leaving the danger zone against sporadic gunfire. It was over in a few minutes, done and dusted.

Due to the colonel's disregard for his own safety and natural killing instincts, he was able to secure this mission. There were a few casualties on the airlift as all soldiers bravely acted as human shields for the civilians.

A keen survivor with his rescue complete, he was able to make it back undetected. His disguise was identical to insurgent attire and the enemy knew nothing; he moved like a ghost.

Colonel Rossi, known as the *Chameleon*, had been amongst them. The scattered bodies and silenced RPG's rocket activity told of his trail of death. At a safe distance outside the city, a camel waited. With resolve and dogged determination, Chameleon shifted safely away under the cover of deep dune shadows, his face covered from those twisting cold desert winds. This was all in the past.

****

Back inside the Amazonian Rainforest, standing in front of his colonel, Sergeant Davide Romano's memory of events were accurate, he loved it. The excitement was something both men had in common. Wearing green and brown camouflaged uniforms from head to toe, the men were difficult to see inside the tropical forest. They were equipped with lightweight high pack rucksacks that held everything needed for such a short sortie. Well trained in survival techniques and jungle warfare, each man could endure unaided in this inhospitable terrain.

Staying alive is all about making the most of what you have and what you find in the surrounding environment will save a man's life; never the less, everyone was equipped with first aid kits, malaria pills and emergency rations, along with a flint stone to make fire.

This odd-looking search and rescue party packed Mk. 48 British MOD.0s and NATO 7.62x51mm calibre machine guns fitted with optical scopes, pistols and bayonets plus hand grenades, incendiaries and flash bangs. Each guardsman was complete with a machete to hack a path through the relentless jungle.

Water would not be a problem in this habitat as it was in great abundance. It channelled up the large woody xylem plants, mosses absorbed it and soaked up moisture like sponges, and running streams or rainwater could keep them well hydrated.

Food was also in great quantity inside the forest, where there were many edible plants. The soldiers knew how to identify these, like certain sweet tasting begonias, recognised by their fleshy red flowers and green leaves. Identifiable too, were the brown spotted yellow orchids with their uneven leaves. Even the numerous insects of the forest, big and small, were potentially on the menu for a hungry survivalist.

The current Brazilian regime was used to having foreign troops on its soil for whatever legitimate reason, whether on manoeuvres, training or military consultation inside the jungle. Tracking down the ruthless drug Barons were not uncommon, providing government officials were well paid. New rules had come into place earlier in the year but this did not affect the cardinal's plans. This Operation was already well under way.

Corruption in all countries was commonplace and Brazil proved no exception. The reasons did not matter because everything boiled down to money. New laws had been imposed by a new government aimed to limit the reliance on foreign countries and curtail exploitation of the rainforest. The government was more accountable and less exploitable to those profiteering foreign organisations. However, those types of covert activities were always difficult to thwart and military ops did go on with and without their knowledge.

It did not seem to matter inside the dense interior. Here was a place where no men had been for centuries. This was a primitive and primordial mass, a colossal country and if people were foolish to get into trouble, then who really cared? All were classified as tourists. Explorers who became lost, died. Disappearances happened every year in this green place with nothing said; no rescue mission sent, out here you were all alone.

****

With Brazil's main religion being Roman Catholic, a variety of Catholic priests were allowed to routinely pass over the borders with only perfunctory checks, if any. Brazil and all other South American countries had seen many missionaries stay for years and build their own missions, with their own diocese located here as a host country that helped its poor people by giving them hope and salvation.

Many priests had brought education and stability to many communities of the wilder parts of the country, even to the dangerous places where no one else would venture. Some never returned. Most holy men were good people, and some missionaries had come from as far as Scotland to live in isolation or set up homes in those uncharted territories to teach these fine doctrines.

The gospel was so widespread, as were its moral riches taught by the papal church. It gained much wealth by doing good. Occasionally some unscrupulous clergyman, like Cardinal Dalla Gassa, planned many things behind the Vatican walls; eager to siphon this continual monetary and soulful tap for his personal crusade. Deep inside the jungle and so far away from the Vatican, this place was not God's dominion.

Here others lived, not for hundreds but thousands of years; natives and indigenous tribe's people hid quite secretively, keeping as far away from any so-called *civilization.*

Centuries ago, these quiet people had been brutally exposed to corrupt Spanish and Portuguese predators. This brief and spiritual encounter with white men that was around four or five hundred years ago had been enough. For them, this short contact with Europeans was only a blink in the green primordial eye. Head hunting and human sacrifice was thought to be a thing of the past, but sometimes, old habits die hard. And yet, in this year of the Prophecy, other unnamed things, horrible obscene things, things not of this world awaited them inside these thick forests.

****

"A group of scientists are lost," advised the colonel, "They belong to an important company called ONCOL Scientific Corporation. It is partly funded by the Vatican, and as God only knows, the Vatican needs that extra money." He smiled sarcastically. "Their work is very important to his holiness and no doubt has many benefits which we will never see, let alone ever understand." He turned to face his men. "We have no need for this now do we signores?"

"On holiday then are we, colonnello?" a soldier began chuckling.

Eagle unit consisted of twenty soldiers, Osprey twenty-one and the initial scout detachment Phoenix unit having nine, with fifty specialists in Colonel Rossi's total command.

The men stood in readiness and began laughing along with him. Everyone in high spirits as the colonel continued with his mission orders.

"These people, who are lost, have been out in this part of the world for many months looking for wild herbs to make drugs for medicines. Our top priority men, is to find them, alive."

With no expression on the soldiers' blunt face, he spoke "Signore, come on, we all thought the unit was here to find lost Inca gold! We could easily help them with that."

To the men, this seemed like a big operation just for a few lost people and a military one at that. Why not ask for aid from the Brazilian government? Something did not ring true to them. The men laughing at the soldiers' frivolous response and with his vague suggestion, of light-hearted dishonesty.

"Si, and that is why we need these machine guns is it not my colonnello," another soldier joined in with good-humoured banter, tapping the side of his weapon.

"No such luck soldier, many treasures were hidden far from the Conquistadores and any gold or treasure that is found in any case belongs to the Vatican. We are not mercenaries."

"Excuse me signore, but that does sound like we are mercenaries."

"Shut up Lucchese!" the sergeant's voice boomed.

Some of the men's faces changed a little in submissive disappointment. Others saw this as a free opportunity quickly slipping away, but who really knew what lay ahead of them. The colonel finished off his tactical résumé.

"Recent discoveries make it essential that we secure the target and evacuate these scientists out of the area, ASAP. Stealth is required" he explained. "A week ago, all contact was lost from the scientists. We need to quickly locate their camp and get them. In and out, back to civilization and I'll show you how." Looking at Sergeant Romano, "Very well sergente, now that all the men are accounted for and in reasonably good shape, let's get cracking on," pausing briefly, "Oh and one last item men, the nature of our job has changed over the years and as you know, most people see us back home, as brightly dressed ornaments, showpieces, or pretty boys for the ladies."

"Not in sergente's case!" Lucchese butted in laughing with an innuendo of homosexuality.

"Secure that shit, Lucchese." Nothing could be further from the truth as Sergeant Romano moaned. The men could see the sergeant's discomfort and began laughing.

"The ladies like looking at him too Lucchese." The colonel supported the men and smiled at the awkward sergeant imitating bisexuality, before smiling back suggestively to the officer. The immediate response was instant gun rolling laughter from all the men.

'Swiss guardsmen!' he straightened up to attention, the colonel stared at his command bolstering his troops, "We all know our pedigree, our honour, our oaths of devotion and to the safety and loyal protection of our Pope. Croce di Luce!" he called.

"Croce di Luce!" The men chorused in respect, saluting their commander, their bond and brotherhood.

Colonel Greco Rossi grinned back in admiration at their salute, considering thoughtfully and at the last moment said to his men, "Here we are again and Si, there will be trouble. So, stay alert." A short moment passed, "Any questions men?"

"What kind of trouble signore?" Sergeant Davide Romano was holding his Beretta SCP 90/100 Assault C rifle. His weapon had a detachable barrel adaptor to launch rifle grenades. "Signore?" he respectfully prompted the superior officer for more information.

"In one of our last communications, the scientists reported local tribes in the area." His voice implying peril, "We have been informed they are head-hunters," the soldiers faces changed. Their mission had just taken on a new and deadly dimension, only hearing blowpipes before dying was not at the top of their *to-do lists*.

"Merda," one of the men cursed silently.

"You will not see these tribesmen." The colonel explained, "Two years ago and five hundred miles from here, some missionaries disappeared. If there are any natives living in this locality maybe they or another tribe were responsible. Quite simply, we do not know. Treat them as hostile."

Sergeant Romano was adding more camouflage to his face with dirt, looking around speaking to the soldiers, "The colonnello is right, Head hunters are silent and lethal. So, don't be heroes and stay close to each other. This is a hostile environment. *Never drop your guard.*"

"Scorpion." The colonel was ready to give orders.

"Signore!" he responded instantly.

"Take your *Eagle* unit and follow the trail made by Major Trentino's smaller exploratory team. Time is of the essence. Once I have all the kit assembled here then my own *Osprey* unit will cover your rear. We will catch up later. You should reach them by tonight, late evening."

"The time signore?"

"I will rendezvous with your Eagle and Trentino's Phoenix unit tomorrow morning at 04:00 hours. Exactly twenty-four hours from now. We will reinforce you with our heavier weapons and complete this exercise."

"Christ signore, you really are expecting trouble," he stated in a lower voice, Scorpion was staring sharply at Chameleon.

"We must be ready for anything. Right signores, let's synchronize our watches and on my mark. This mission is probably not going to be as easy as our holy overseers have anticipated. I am not sure what we will find when we get there but one thing is for certain, all our instincts will play a big part before we are through. You are highly trained and well prepared," his tone conveyed confidence and sincerity.

"Si signore." Scorpion replied with complete trust in his commander, the sergeant knew only too well that his good friend and long-term comrade, Greco Rossi, was holding something back, there was something else the colonel was not telling them. The men prepared to leave.

"Do you smell the air Davide?" the colonel whispered unspoken thoughts while his sergeant turned to face him. He took another deep breath of the clean filled air and held it inside for a moment, saturating his blood, and spoke again, "It's the atmosphere Davide, full of oxygen, you can almost eat it."

Colonel Rossi appeared elated, ready and energised for the mission. To his friend, his eyes expressed that devilish excitement. Scorpion recognised that slightly crazy look of his before; it was always the case seen in his friends' gaze, an eager glint before mortal combat.

Scorpion was thinking of what must be ahead. *It's that look of his again, Merda, Si, there is going to be trouble all right. Rossi must get off on this kind of trip, I'm sure of it. The mad Bastardo.* Davide smiled affirming his readiness for action.

"It is so humid, look at us signore." The sweat was pouring off both men's foreheads.

The sergeant took out a cigarette and began smoking trying to fend off the blanket of insects buzzing around them. This pestering would be much worse later during the evening, when the mosquitoes would come out, blood at the top of their menu.

The sergeant rolled up his sleeve exposing his arm to a weird looking flying insect, it was right on target, the soldier slapped at it and missed. It went buzzing off towards the next man.

"Little Bastardo!" he smashed at one again, another horrible and larger green type of parasite which landed on his hairy forearm just where the other had lifted his skin.

The Croce di Luce or *Cross of Light* tattoo clearly visible on his right bicep, it stood out over his other tattoo, a one by two-inch Swiss flag just where his own call sign image of a tiny red Scorpion tattoo was poised, and ready on the sting. It was then that a glimpse of sunlight began shining through a break above the Canopy.

"Better get used to that kind of thing Davide, it looks like we will be on the menu here for the foreseeable future, eh?" Each man smiled, they had come out safely from many dangerous situations before, and this one would be no different.

Colonel Rossi was every bit as cold blooded as a reptile, the *Chameleon*. Like the remaining men of his command, he began rubbing green brown mud and streaking it down and across his face. He stared into the jungle and gave its hidden warning serious consideration.

Unexpectedly he then held the sergeant firmly by both shoulders sensing something.

"Davide, look after yourself." as his third in command glanced awkwardly, Colonel Rossi had never done this before.

"Arrivederci, Greco." Sergente Romano had observed that insane glint of the colonel's which had lasted only for a moment. He knew it so well. It was there and gone, affirming once again to himself, *there is something else, he is not telling me everything.*

Silence spoke louder than words, Romano felt it in his bones, it was all wrong. Turning, he and his men moved quickly and vanished on their way into the dark Forest.

The sergeant's affectionate nickname *Scorpion* had proven to be indeed a venomous stinger, the soldier an expert in hand to hand combat, Rossi knew that Scorpion was more than a match for most, an asset to any fighting unit.

Scorpion soon picked up Phoenix unit's trail, freshly trampled vegetation from the previous morning's trek. A narrow green channel had been cut earlier and had already overgrown even after this short time. Ravaging vegetation already eager to cover trampled tracks, soon nothing would be left of their passing, no evidence.

Osprey unit stayed at the drop zone *Jesuit,* and all men actively engaged in locating and assembling several heavier 58kg with tripod Browning M4HB Machine Guns. Unplanned, one was in a tangle of trees nearby and the other was lost. The weaponry was set with automatic heat targeting and night vision systems, firing about 950-1200 armour piercing rounds/minute with a 4Km range. Yes, there was going to be trouble all right, Chameleon sighed.

****

A distant rumble of thunder could be heard quickly growing in magnitude, it was soon above them like energetic Chinese drums. The noise deafening, cataclysmic. Then came the rain. At first with a few heavy drips, then the heavens opened with a crash of thunder and lightning flash. The darkened forest burst with light for a long second when rainwater ran in quick torrents and smashed off thick leaves.

The deteriorating conditions, unnerved the primates who screeched and crazily jumped again, pulling and tearing more at their already tattered parachutes. Their noises soon reached fever pitch. Suddenly they went off swinging through the overhead canopies like a chasing game.

The soldiers of Eagle and Osprey were unaware of the monkey games high above in the canopy, or the large jaguar that was still watching them since their arrival. The cat had waited long and seen enough. In a black mood it departed with feline cunning, concealed inside the gloomy night and trailing mist, following the Eagle.

Some Europeans had ventured into these parts centuries ago; they too had come into this remote place. The forest had not forgotten them. Ill fated, none had ever returned. The next day, the remaining soldiers of Osprey would follow the same trail and very soon they too would be gone. The jungle seemed cursed.

****

Inside the thick forest the Eagle unit slowly moved, visibility next to nil. Gradually undefined noises could be heard further on, it seemed at first like a distant gurgle coming to them every now and again. Eventually the trickle of sound morphed to more than a murmur, almost like the sea creaming the rocks. The sounds gradually increased into an unstoppable clamour in a mad rush of ferocious wild water.

These huge streams and rivers were the natural highways of the forest thrashing its way through the heart of the jungle. The men did not talk much but the noise had built up as they drew closer and closer until it became impossible to hear anything else. The water absorbed everything as it crashed on echoing raw power.

In the forest, fast water rapids often meant that treacherous falls were close by, hidden from immediate view by the dense undergrowth.

"It must be a river rapid!" the sergeant competed to be heard. Rivers formed quickly in the Amazon basin, another flash flood would appear and then vanish almost as quick after a sudden downpour. These would become increasingly sporadic and more dangerous during the monsoon season.

Morning moved on and the light arrived, dim and dour. Through the forest floor, some patches of brightness appeared speckling brilliantly onto the path, reflecting over the stippled green brown faces of the Eagle unit.

Looking up they could not quite see the sky. The men passed through swiftly. Everywhere shades of light formed shadows of dappled darkness as daylight struggled down through the canopies, opening amazing views, and displaying more beautiful forest tones.

Looking down from the sky was the green canopy stretching on and on forever, the rainforest broken up only by the winding entrails of twisting river masses and waterways. Dark thunder crashed again, and the men were completely gone.

****

One day earlier...

A small detachment of soldiers had already departed from the Jesuit drop zone, and at this point approximately twenty-four hours ahead of the colonel's main force.

An impenetrable jungle moved little before the men of Phoenix, they all furiously swung their machete blades left and then right, hacking the easiest route through a green hell. Managing to slice out a narrow zigzag bandwidth into this punishing wilderness was the best they could do.

Pushing hard against a mixture of sixteen-foot long dense grasses, masses of thick bamboo, large ferns and masses of variable dense foliage, this rescue was a mammoth undertaking, in parts, water rose up to their knees.

The intense humidity and high altitude made life like a pressurised autoclave. Their march felt unbearable. Eventually a gruelling path continued through this merciless milieu. Bit at a time, breaking their ultimate target into manageable pieces, checking their distance and direction periodically by climbing high trees to see the skyline. The mission was a race against the clock.

Numerous animals and birds were scattering in every direction as Phoenix approached their habitats. A thirty-foot anaconda with its long body was completely still and wrapped around a large branch, and roughly four feet above when the men passed underneath. With this din, how on earth could they ever hope to appear at their target unannounced?

With each step taken, insects indefatigably dived at them. The soldiers continually cursed at the unremitting and excruciating pests, they could put up with anything, anything at all; except the flies, they were the worst.

In this, the initial reconnaissance, Phoenix made very little progress, especially after a five hundred foot cliff and a treacherous waterfall. Each man was lighter equipped than the larger force and packed less weaponry to make movement faster paced.

How the other units would fair here, with this obstacle and others like it, the major did not care. His mobile unit's objective was *MalisIblis* and set in the far north Vale of Iblis. This was the name given to an ancient temple by a long dead civilization.

The unrealistic *smart target* made by the Vatican military, time to reach their objective was an over ambitious eighteen hours from their drop zone Jesuit. Seven o'clock in the morning and there were still miles to go. The Vatican had badly underestimated the density. The soldiers knew by now that it could take a day to travel a mile.

I told Chameleon, there was not enough time planned for this sortie. Merda. The major wiped his frustrated face, as more sweat ran down his furrowed forehead, *nothing else for it, a few miles more*, scolding his superior's tight deadline. It was imperative that they reach and secure his destination by evening.

"Keep at it men. Come on." He pressed his soldiers. He knew that complete silence and secrecy in this part of the mission was critical. The major had strict orders to have no contact with base or his immediate commander. Rossi's fighting force on route by helicopter to the drop zone Jesuit. He understood that more units of Swiss guardsmen would be following his own trail next morning.

The major did not underestimate anything, experience taught him that it would be easy to get lost inside this giant greenhouse. With little to guide them, and unless they stumbled across a small opening in the forest, then there seemed to be next to nothing to aid their navigation. Desperate to find new defined features, this proved very difficult because each stream or tree looked much like another. The trees were growing so high and overhanging that daylight seldom made it to the floor. Conventional navigation by map and compass were proving inaccurate and unreliable because this terrain was hidden and completely unchartered.

The men had one advantage, using a combination of a counter-intelligence Satellite Navigation Systems and the use of good, old-fashioned human resourcefulness. Tried and tested techniques of climbing massive trees at times became essential for observation, spotting key contours of their immediate terrain.

Most predators hunted during the night at the Equator. Being close to it meant roughly twelve hours daylight and twelve hours darkness. Evening was when things would become much more hazardous. Danger lurked everywhere!

****

"Maggiore Trentino, signore! This place is like a fucking sauna." A young corporal cursed, stopping briefly to rest next to the major. The soldier with tightness in his throat spoke out of breath to the officer in charge. "Look signore, what are those strange shaped hoppers over there?" Both men watched hundreds of funny looking frogs jump near a fast-flowing stream. The Phoenix unit found themselves again at another narrow rapid.

Their eyes were opened by the sight of hundreds of species of brilliantly coloured butterflies on top of the moist riverside sandbanks. Yellow-banded poison spring-loaded frogs hopped about from bank to bank as the men approached. The frogs quickly jumped out the way of the soldiers' heavy boots as they made short work of another white water stream, this time only ten feet wide.

Watching like a father from behind them, the major observed his men who were also hopping about like the same little frogs evading them. The men began precariously leap frogging from one large stone to another across the deep water.

"Si, soldier, more like a steam room I think." The major answered, "This place is worse than a minefield. See those little buggers over there? They are green and black poison. Dart frogs." "A good cure for *any* hang-over." Mantis joked, screwing his eyes and scanning quickly around. "We cannot see further into that mire."

The officer was referring to the thick fog beyond the far bank; knowing that his men were in danger and could become easily separated.

"Once over the stream, get the men to come closer in together and tighten up, be quick about it." he commanded the corporal.

"Si signore," the soldier quickly crossed the water and disappeared into the murky grey cloud. Inside they were all still quite close and able still to pass on the word for the squad to keep within eye contact of each other.

A cloud of butterflies flew off in fright as a fluttery cloud began swarming surprisingly towards the major and the rest of his men still to cross over.

"Careful men, how would that look back home if the holy father found out that the demise of his elite soldiers was by a bunch of butterflies!"

The insects obscured their view and made it much more dangerous for the men to see where the stepping-stones were lying below their feet. Everyone knew that one wrong step, slip or touch of something unusual might prove fatal.

Survival was all about living by your wits, and the men progressed passing close to numerous clusters of lovely mixed yellow and red plants, beautiful varieties at three or four feet in height with large star shaped light petals. At the petal's edges and within its stems were very fine almost invisible tiny needles, murderous mortal points waiting to inject its toxic hydrocyanic acid or alkaloids into any unsuspecting animal's blood and nervous system and poison or paralyze them.

Decay in the forest occurred so quickly, especially in this oxygen rich atmosphere that in no time at all, a body would rot in a few days to a few weeks. The men mentally noted another decomposing carcass, what may have been a sloth which was partially hidden under the thick undergrowth, giving everyone a grim reminder of the jungle's deadly deceits.

Reaching the other side of the sandbank safely, the atmosphere felt muggier and muffled, the air was so heavy and saturated with moisture that it had become cloudy, reducing visibility next to nothing.

Gradually climbing higher in altitude and as the unit continued moving through into a patchy *cloud forest* it seemed like an alien world. The trees in this part of the forest were massive. Tree trunks increasing in size and girth and distance between each of them, growing as high as tower blocks. They would appear at first to the men as vague grey white shadows and then materialize instantly into focus, standing sharply right in front of them, threatening the men with their huge and intimidating stature.

Wiping his brow, the major's piercing green eyes scanned everywhere for danger. Taking off his beret remarkably revealed his dark hair style in perfect condition. Resembling a Wall Street financial whizz kid, gelled and neatly swept back. Vanity, he knew it. No one was perfect. He always kept those follicles in good condition, no matter how arduous the journey, and always maintained a well-groomed, smart appearance. There seemed little point out here for most men putting back on his beret. His green eyes became red with annoyance as the bugs pestered his scalp. The Amazon certainly posed him with many problems in that department.

A devout Catholic, he always kept a small bible in his top right pocket. Once every now and again he would touch it and pray to himself. That was one reason at least for part of his nickname, *Praying Mantis*. The other, his reputation as a top-class sniper, waiting motionless and with saintly patience, before a kill.

The major spoke to his sergeant, "Sergente, we will follow the valley down towards the east and traverse around the base. From there climbing up again north-wards into the vale, and sergente," he paused, "that is our objective. Ok men!" he shouted, "Have a rest for a minute while I check our direction of travel."

He opened his ultra light-weight electronic satellite map, flexible and thin as a polythene sheet; sitting it down and positioning it between the large base roots of a huge tree. Data had already been pre-programmed into it; information about his route to the vale that was supplied by one of the scientists in a previous communication.

The prototype mapping system was powered by a solar battery transmitting environmental data to a geocentric orbiting satellite far above the earth.

Cloaking was pre-set *on* for the security of the unit. The system could potentially map the immediate terrain in finer detail if the security screening had been set to *off*. Each man was electronically dog-tagged for recognition on the map for any localized area, which would be seen generated as numerous green blips on the map's surface. Their individual movements, positions and group formations precisely plotted; each soldiers' physical condition and logical profiles were accessible by touch screen to any commander relative to a *layering topography*, which seemed to build around them as the unit progressed towards their target.

The commander could use this tool and magnify into each man's online personal profile and then interrogate his real-life sensors like heart rate and brain patterns by electrodes implanted inside their hats, watches and electronic dog-tags around their necks. A central computer contained within each man's specific *e-dog-tag*, linked an electronic soldier to the commanders digitized map. Data like serial numbers within the dog-tag, were encrypted and stamped with their own digital certificate. This data could be uploaded to a master computer satellite system on a later date or when required, storing the information within the map chips as a backup, giving the commander some form of security and remote control of his unit.

Occasionally, a new technological advance comes along that is truly significant, and especially for the military. This was it! It is called a VT3DMS System for short and correctly called the Ventessi Terraform 3D Modelling System.

There was an unknown problem, a few design faults, one due to impairing solar batteries and chip set susceptibility to electromagnetic interference, which resulted in malfunctioning within its application microcode.

Additional multiple overlaying capability could be supplied by on the ground operatives by keying input data and environmental sensors. This *layering effect* was able to divide-up the surrounding canopy. This way, battle groups' movements were tagged displaying their electronic data periodicals.

The military generals loved this little toy. Appealing to their sense of power and displayed to them on demo by the Ventessi Salesmen and Software Engineers, as a complete spying gadget, they could use and observe changing events from a safe distance. The battlefield arena seemed to unfold as it happened. Even so, the major was still old fashioned at heart, instead relying on his survival instincts, keeping his men near. He did not like gadgets.

The major and colonel both were completely unaware of an electronic override switch, allowing for remote and secure surveillance.

A computer software company recommended and trusted by the military, and those with vested interests like the Cardinal and shareholders, planned to make the data commercially available in the future, for the entertainment industry. Sad to think his men's lives meant so little to people with purse strings. Entertainment and death were bed-fellows as they had been once long ago. Brutal gladiatorial events of old, where everyone had become desensitised and dehumanised to the real and cold-blooded murder. Some things never change.

Ventessi had many fingers in many pies, especially as a purportedly neutral software house, providing business computer applications software for their e-tendering services to different governments and private companies.

This navigation system could provide an immediate financial profit in the marketplace, the Italian Army was ripe for the picking but then, maybe this was going just a bit too far for the generals. However, commerce was very powerful and there were a few unscrupulous businesspersons in high circles, who wanted more. Here in the jungles their system was tested for real.

****

An hour later, and yet another deluge, water fell as God's hands twisted the cloud like a sponge, squeezing them even tighter, emptying its wet contents from the heavens. Trudging on, rain bounced off their shoulders, and the Phoenix unit was by this time well hacked-off, and any eagerness for the mission completely and utterly dampened, all except for Mancini Bellucci.

Bellucci was a man who loved anything the others hated. The rainier, dirtier and tougher the conditions, the better. Twenty-four years old with fine features. He had the mind of a complete psychopath; an expert killer at an early age, whereas the others were trained to kill. Mancini Bellucci, in his case never needed any training in that department. It was rumoured that his father was a policeman who was murdered by the Sicilians. So, he joined the regular Italian Army at a much younger age. Being part Swiss and unmarried he was eligible to join the Guard. He was deeply religious about his passion; that is, his passion for killing. He enjoyed it. Revenge was always in his mind.

Bellucci slashed cruelly at the vegetation with pent up anger inside his head, *the devil must be driving him on* thought the major. Only he knew what Bellucci was thinking.

Cutting away with a fury at the unending foliage, thunder booming everywhere, reverberating its anger through the forest and the continual crackling sounds were heard like gigantic light switches shorting out the sky.

Yet they could not see the sky, only the brightness from incessant detonations flashing through the foliage showing them like enigmatic energetic ghosts. There for a moment and then gone.

These savage conditions seemed unstoppable and were getting worse. The canopy was not giving much cover from the rain. Clenching their teeth, the men kept going.

Another narrow trail made from the jungle, the effort needed was taking its toll by the time they reached the bottom of a hillside. The rain stopped as quickly as it had arrived, the thunder rolling away. Nothing stopped their dogged determination continuing to beat a path through the thick walls of woody vines.

Sometimes the men found themselves clambering over the vines or twisting their bodies under or through a flexible resistance, escaping sharp barbs with the skill of Houdini. Under the cover of the canopy, their antagonized battle with the land continued. A punishing place.

Another hour passed. The rain quickly replaced by intense heat, humidity and unrelenting sunshine. Their discomfort increased as the forest steamed up all around them, the men swearing at the constant insect attacks. The mosquitoes were becoming more persistent as time went on, then glimpses of light became brighter when a large area surprisingly appeared in the foliage. It was a clearing!

The men began looking up to the blue sky. Walking on they began passing green ragged termite mounds, about the height of a tall man, some old and broken, displaying internal honeycomb structures.

It looked more open further on. At that moment, they became aware that the forest had become unnaturally quiet, transforming to a dead nothing. No sound at all.

Fanculo, this place is going against nature, the officer swore in his head uncertainly. Then the major's face suddenly twisted. Instinctively Trentino's eyes widened because there was nothing in the forest to laugh about. So, it was with a sense of dread, the alarm bells were already ringing in his head.

The major could not see the soldiers, they were ahead when a queer apprehension ran down his spine, he sprinted harder and stopped suddenly skidding to a halt. He entered the large forest clearing and saw his dirty and bedraggled men staring as he did too with complete incomprehension.

Oh Merda! He thought.

"Ants!" A soldier shouted a warning. His men stood paralysed; their Machetes had no use and hung limply by their sides as they stared at something quite unbelievable.

The tightly packed lines of ants were swarming rapidly across everything in the wide opening, and what was once, a lush green forest, was now massive trees and forest floor that had been picked to the bone. Everything was covered completely by their writhing bodies. Stripped bare in minutes, these tiny creatures left nothing, bustling red and black bodies moving as one massive organism. A ghastly and yet awesome sight, they ate everything in their path.

Everywhere, they could see ants, billions organized into many highways. Multitudes of small bodies moving like rivers. The ants naturally sensing the men when suddenly, the miniature army wheeled and started coming their way like fast flowing lava in undulating waves. Smothering everything as they came at them.

Eating everything that lived in their immediate vicinity, crawling inside every hole and onto every leaf, nothing was safe. The ants were hunting for food. Now it was their turn.

"Arriadoracid ants!" He gasped. "Much bigger than normal ones signore!" Shouting, in his panic-stricken voice to his paramedic, "I have never seen anything like this! We had better get out of here right now!"

"No wonder there are no animals around!" Another worried soldier stared, his voice wobbling at the site.

Major Trentino instantly knew the danger his men were in. The ants' poison would affect the nervous system and, in such numbers, would quickly paralyze any man or beast in their path.

It looked like these forest demons were covering an area of at least twenty or thirty metres square, spreading much wider beyond their view. Now his men were right in their path.

"Lucchese! Get the hell out of there man, now!" The major screamed. Lucchese was affectionately known as the *Big Stallion*.

The man on point had been laughing only a minute earlier and was taken by surprise seeing this mass of undersized insects. Bravado stood his ground, jeering loudly at this odd spectacle.

Deaf to his commander's voice, the minute insects began madly crawling closer towards them. The tiny bodies began scattering widely from his crushing boots.

Strangely, the ants began creating a large empty surface area around him. The first avoiding his tramping feet, most moving too fast to be believed. The huge rippling mass surrounded him in seconds and flowed quickly beyond him.

Suddenly Lucchese could see above him, to the left and right they were everywhere! A mixture of black and red headed directly towards the other men. Panicking, he looked all around.

Lucchese's humour transformed from nervous hilarity to nauseating horror, like a trapped animal he wanted to escape. Too late, there was nowhere to run. The trap was now complete.

With not a second thought for his big comrade, Private Hernán Narváez, who had been with him a moment ago, had been standing at the side, was off. He had not waited as long as the big man; he saw the danger and his feet took wings.

Yelling and still slapping his stinging body, the private ran for his life. He headed towards his gob smacked comrades and behind him was the hapless Lucchese.

The Stallion already was swiping wildly across his large frame, a dance with death; he shook his body madly and grabbed handfuls of the tiny insects from his encased body, throwing them away.

In seconds, the ants were all over Lucchese before he understood what had happened.

Merda, these little buggers are not going to chase me. Defiance sparked through stubborn pig headedness. Revolt lasted a fleeting second and quickly vaporised as ants crawled across his blurry eyes and partially blinded him.

Stinging and biting into his bloodshot conjunctiva, looking over he could hear his major calling him which helped him refocused his thoughts.

The major was like a Pied Piper and Lucchese began to follow his commands. Lucchese shouted and screamed uncontrollably.

"Help! Help me!" He attempted to look for an exit, any escape. "Come back, don't leave me! Do something! Maggiore, please help Maggiore! Ah, get them off! Get off! Eee... Aaagrh!"

Everything had gone crazy and in seconds from hearing the man laughing, the major and his men witnessed the full horror of his bravado.

From head to toe, the man was engulfed by wave upon wave of driving black and red bodies. Lucchese could not see anything. His vision completely paralyzed him making him stagger about like a drunk.

The soldier desperately tried to find the direction of his comrades, who were retreating further back, when suddenly in one final terror Lucchese veered away and right off track.

Twisting awkwardly, everyone could see his black and red frame headed blindly towards nearby bark bare trees, but there was no sanctuary for him there either. Lucchese disorientated, ran further and deeper into the waves of the devilish masses. He was thrashing around wildly, and his arms were flailing uncontrollably when Lucchese had suddenly stumbled. He fell into the blackening ground where his body dropped underneath the thickening mass. It was too hard to breathe; they were smothering him.

Dogged determination, he attempted to lift his massive frame out and upwards. But it could not be done. He fell again and rolled around screaming and coughing up blood.

Inside his ears, up his trousers and sleeves; there was no part of his skin untouched. Feeling them scrambling up his nostrils, his mind agonised and his mouth opened to release a drowning gut-felt scream.

"Ok men, back here!" Trentino instructed his soldiers, "Come back this way to me! Forget Lucchese, it is too late for him." The stark reality prompting his guidance, "This way men!" he ordered smartly. *Poor Bastardo,* the major watched the man's agonizing death. "Back up the trail men. We will flank them over that hillside!"

Waving his arm back towards him, the major signalled his troop to come. Immediately they were in full retreat, passing the major to the sounds of the screams of the trapped man.

"Save me maggiore! They are eat— eating me!" The wretched man stammered knowing what was happening. His skin began peeling off him.

Coughing more, he slurped uncontrollably and swallowed more and more. The giant man reduced into a heap as he began drowning in millions of little hard bodies scurrying down into his numb throat. His oesophagus began to swell, jaws and teeth crunched at their hard bodies, but the masses kept going in. They entered every part of his mouth, biting, sticking and began eating from inside out. Breathing was not possible and soon they were crawling into his lungs.

Still twisting around underneath in panic and horror, his body suddenly stopped moving. The horrid creatures were rapidly crawled up his nose too, no place was sacred. He coughed up blood hysterically. Lucchese laid down, still alive, laying powerlessly as the ants devoured him.

All this, and it had only been a few minutes, death unfolding in front of Trentino and his men. He could not save his fallen comrade. The major felt cold, pushing his feelings back. His prime responsibility to his men and the rest were in retreat.

Death came suddenly in the jungle and regrettably, for poor Lucchese, it looked like death would not come fast enough.

The squad was now running full pelt down the trail. When far enough away, the men cut an alternative trail giving the small killers a wide berth.

****

Watching the man's hideous torment, the major's mind was ice cold and calculating while holding back for a moment longer until his men were safe. His own position was not so safe. The ants were getting seriously close to him too.

Steadying his resolve, he would not move, *Not yet. Wait,* frozen like his determination to see it through. The ants would soon outflank him in less than thirty seconds. They were already beginning to trap him. *Stand firm,* he calmly commanded to himself.

A natural soldier, he had been trained as a sniper as a young Swiss guard and learned his trade in action. Having studied the way of his enemy, he understood their individual killing techniques of past and present deadly assassins. Their differing methods of concealment before their fatal acts of atrocity and the knowledge of how past Popes had been killed or had come close to death, Major Trentino was ready. Mantis and the assassin alike; were one. Always watching and always waiting in silence for that one moment of opportunity. It was now.

At home, in Vatican City, the Swiss guards standing apparently on parade, unknown to most people in St. Peter's Square, there were just as many plain-clothes security guards and policemen than were visitors or, so it seemed. His holiness travelled around the world and he was always more vulnerable even with his personal security. God's works must be done, at all costs. The Pope knew the risks and God's word would prevail. Major Trentino's keen surveillance had already worked; silently he neutralized two attempts in recent years.

His mind frozen, hearing Lucchese's gurgling scream, it was his last humiliation that the man had left to give. The major would never forget the dying sounds of Lucchese. His blood running cold. Major Trentino waited a second longer, *knowing your enemy is part of being a guard*.

The ants were completing their entrapment, encircling the waves outflanking his position, quickly closing their trap and encircling their next prey—him.

Taking a steady and deep breath in that fleeting last moment, did he see Lucchese's eye, was his comrade staring out of that hideous mass, for mercy? There was no more time to lose. He must leave. Making no mistake with Lucchese, he pulled the trigger.

****

One of their team dead, a tiger of a man, huge in body and spirit. Death was always a risk and something each soldier knew. With their own thoughts no one could really believe how quickly it all had happened. Lucchese was gone.

Taking a wide detour, they scrambled and climbed with vengeance, trying to forget what had just happened. They kept on going, soon making it over the top of a steep slippery hillside, descending into a much different valley and leaving the ants; their voracious appetite never fulfilled. The ant area had covered more than a mile square at that time. Luckily, the unit had only skirted the edge of the *Ant Highway* leaving the place bone dry and bare. The ants ate only a tiny part of the forest's life-cycle and would soon grow back.

The detour took them far off their planned route when the company followed a fast-moving river, twisting down the slope from the other side of the tree-covered hills. The men trekked further and came across another forest clearing.

This time a sigh of silent relief, it was not a clearing made by ravaging ants and they soon began discovering where they were. This time they appeared to be on top of a naturally made high point, quite open with less undergrowth. All around sounds of buzzing insects competing against noisy crickets. The forest was a crazy place where danger lurked everywhere.

Green viper snakes seemed common in this place, lying hidden and lurking in trees. Ready to inject haematoxic venom into any animal coming too close, poisoning them and attacking their red blood cells, soon leading to complete organ failure within hours. No wonder they were on the edge.

From this green window, the place below them seemed still and uncanny. Underneath they saw a view of much lower terrain, the contours nearby were easy to distinguish, and just below them was a saddle like area. It was what they had been searching for, the entranceway to the secret vale.

Staring downwards from this high vantage point into the surreptitious basin beyond, it appeared grey and misty. Clouds drowned the green-brown expanse underneath.

The major studied the convoluted grey white scene floating before them as clouds tried to smother other green hills. The vale looked ominous and foreboding. Some enormous trees would not be smothered, cutting their solitary presence through the cloud cover for air. When they heard a queer noise it made them flinch, the call of some wild animal and yet it seemed out of place, unnatural.

His attention turned immediately to observing something barely visible, far off in the sky. He lifted his telescopic glasses. At this great distance, the man observed something large, that was gliding lazily in the warm air. It would be dark soon.

Major Trentino watched and said nothing. His eyes narrowed with revulsion. The foul creature floated effortlessly at first and then moved towards the highest hill. It looked like a huge bird, and yet not quite; ugly and ill formed.

My god, what the merda is that, shaking his head in disbelief, the military man felt he was going crazy. Screeching as if in pain like an out of tune mating call. Whatever it was, this flying creature gave out more hellish noises.

Trentino's hairs stood out on the back of his neck hearing the mutated scream of *DEATH.* Arrhythmically it called out into the vale. His men looked uncertainly to the far-off sounds.

The perspicacious major did not mention what its grotesque head looked like. The carrion, to him only a distant spec. It began circling an isolated hill down through the valley before disappearing all together into the cloud forest. He lowered his telescopic glasses and let out a sigh. He held an unspoken fear, realizing quickly that what he was looking at was not a hill. It was the temple!

"Phew!" The commanding officer pointed to the distant object and directed their view towards this solitary structure. It was a huge flat-topped pyramid, and Trentino pointed out "The temple men."

Not waiting any longer, the soldiers began their steep descent into the vale and were soon under the canopy once more and heading for the saddle dipped landscape.

A mist began to rise through the forest, visibility dropping to no better than poor. Soon everything transformed into a strange, inhuman and featureless place. Their trudging seemed to flatten with claustrophobic sentiment, entering a motionless world mixed with hazy grey moisture. The smell of rotting wood, strong and musty hung in the air as if the whole place was decaying. It was a cloud forest.

Pushed hard by Trentino, the men did not talk, each mile won at a high price and sapping every ounce of endurance, they would need rest soon. The officer knew that extra care was required closer to the temple.

To him, the place did not feel right; with the heaviness of death-watch dread already working on their minds. The place seemed cursed.

The unit had lost a fellow. It happened. They had suffered casualties before, but this was not the only reason for a forborne mood, the temple seeped into their exhausted psyche. A heavy and intense oppression weighed on them, an irrational fear. The vale had that effect on everyone, all who were foolish enough to enter.

****

Just out of Trentino's earshot, the men eating their paltry rations, Corporal Bianchi spoke in a guarded tone.

"This place is bad Merda," reflecting the horrific memory of their comrade's slow death.

"His screaming, it was terrible. What a way to die, and what for?" Gritting his chipped front tooth, "Why are we really here? Does anyone know?" He took off his beret and wiped off the sweat from his bald head, his hair replaced by a zigzag patterned tattoo. He wanted answers!

"Nothing we could do about it son," the sympathetic Sergeant Moretti replied. "Only God knows what this sortie is all about, and of course the major, well he is keeping stump on anything else. I will tell you what, it is not normal to send our division anywhere without there being real trouble. Even I am not sure anymore. A rescue mission, Si, it is, but I think it is likely to be more than just a church reunion, *Eh Bianchi?*" He smiled back into the man's nerve riddled eyes.

Observing that his words had helped, made him smile broader. He hoped to bolster the man's low morale with a genuine warm grin. Moretti's inner thoughts were cold and sober, his instincts knew better.

"Church business, yeah right," another guardsman raised his voice.

"I wouldn't be surprised if we were fighting some tribe of damn Head-hunters with their dinky little poison darts or maybe a drug cartel, or an army of mercenaries!"

"The mercenaries I can deal with, fine, bring them on. The little Bastardo's with their darts are something else. No hope for the scientists being found alive if Head-hunters have them," another added.

"The Pope has sent us out here and that is good enough for me son. There is always hope," Moretti finished their speculation.

Bianchi could not shake the horrendous vision of Lucchese's wriggling body under a mass of heaving ants.

"The Pope does not know we are here, that I am sure." Bianchi stated bluntly. Trentino came over and joined the men.

****

The Pope never knew of these little excursions abroad even though he decorated them for obedience, gallantry and courage. Their dedicated service and love for him and God was enough.

It was the others, they were the ones really calling the shots and sending them off on crazy holy missions. The Swiss guards were the Pope's personal bodyguards and for generations remained loyal, but unknown to him were being used unofficially, to search for holy treasures or artefacts when normal diplomatic means were of little use.

In the service of the Pope, they were his sworn guards of allegiance until death. On this mission, they were as usual under the direct orders from the Cardinals. They had become quite literally like a modern day *Knight Templar*, and this mission was their holy grail. For some, it would be a grail quest to the grave.

Finishing their light meals, the men were ready and hacked mercilessly at the unyielding jungle again and quite by chance, they saw strange-shaped mounds. If the men had time and stopped to examine these humps, underneath the vegetation was speckled, red Brazil sandstones cut into large blocks. A type of building material that was the first real evidence of early civilization in the area besides the temple.

Traversing due east, the soldiers soon discovered a deep gorge, a long and treacherous chasm partially concealed by a lot of lush vegetation and there was no question about giving it a wide berth.

How far down the rift dropped into the earth, they did not know? Beneath those tangles of vines and masses of ground shrubs, there was a chance that traps lay waiting, camouflaged holes through which they could fall to an uncertain death. The risks of getting any closer did not make sense; their mission was not about discovery. Rescue lay further up the valley.

To anyone's knowledge, this area had never been explored and these scientists were apparently the only people mad enough to come this far from civilization.

According to so-called intelligent sources, no indigenous Natives are known to be living inside this entire region. The men were now within the grave embraces of the Vale of Iblis.

****

Major Trentino silently signalled for the men to gather around him. Phoenix Unit sat hunched and waiting for orders. Joining them, he hunkered between adjusting his Sig Sauer SSG 30000 rifle. The major's specialized weapon was fitted with a Laser Optronix DME 30000 for pinpoint accuracy over great distances. His favourite weapon of choice; although a bit over the top for a rescue mission, when a Crossbow would simply do.

"Well signores, it's time to tell you what our mission objectives really are." He commanded instant authority. The men looked expectantly at him, "Your orders are *simple* enough, simple just like you bunch of pussies!" he teased laughing. They laughed too and listened. *"So this should be easy, eh boys?"* The men laughed again, nothing could be further from the truth. "We are headed into MalisIblis where some scientists have been working. Excavating there since May this year." He paused, "they uncovered an ancient structure, a lost temple, Si, way out here in this bloody God forsaken place. Uncharted jungle until now and some imprinted manuscripts were also discovered by the boffins. So here we are. We hope to find them not too far away."

There seemed to be general mooting between the men as the major continued, "The manuscripts have been interpreted and the information included, as far as I understand, are images that were sent back to a company called

ONCOL. ONCOL in turn passes this information to Vatican officials, as Rome funds the mission. Rome's politics and economics do not concern us. *What does is the absolute safety of our people.*"

"Signore, signore, if the scientists are meant to be *lost*, then why are we here?"

"Soldier, what are you implying?"

"If they are really lost, then why do we know that they are still at the temple?'

"We don't know that for sure. The Vatican also reported to us that there are no indigenous tribes. I personally do not believe that. The expedition is here for several reasons. One is to record and extract as much about ancient civilization as possible, another is to collect as many artefacts and treasures already discovered in the name of our holy father. Oh, and biotechnological discoveries found here will pay plenty for other missions. So, part of this expedition is to collect flora and fauna, herbs and as many unknown zoological specimens. There are potential medical benefits for all mankind and in your simple language guardsman, it means, megabucks!"

"Sounds like exploitation to me signore. Have you even seen any of this money? Ah, eh, I mean any of these images signore?" Sergeant Moretti smiled, returning casual banter as the men chuckled with him.

"Negative. I am paid by Peter's Pence, just like you Moretti. And as far as any images, they are deemed too classified," he replied with a frown and tightened lips.

"Not very trusting, are they signore," the sergeant sensed a cover-up.

"That may be."

It did seem very risky not to keep him fully informed especially in such a hazardous rescue mission. *Why indeed, it must be something they have not told us.* Trentino held his own personal reservations very private.

"Boring farts as well signore!" Corporal Bianchi spoke in an accelerated tone, he could not help himself while letting off wind.

"The fathers have lost contact with this group and have had no further communication from them for more than a week." Trentino ignored the man's flatulence, "What they have found appears to be something priceless. What exactly it is, I don't know; classified." His throat tightened, "Our own unit's objective is to scout and secure this area and establish a safe perimeter and watch and wait for the rest of our command to arrive." Gauging his men's mixed reactions, he asked, "Any comments signores?"

"It still doesn't add up signore, now does it?" Private Hernán Narváez stated bluntly. A ruthless and cold-blooded killer, and also a man with a complete lack of humour. The men were not fools, they smelled a rat. In a monotone voice, the private continued, "Signore, we all know that there must be more to it. There is no way we are here and not going to see some serious aggro. Fact is I do not trust the Vat. If everyone wants to stay alive don't trust them, that's my advice." He cocked his automatic weapon indignantly. "Am I right maggiore?" Narváez seemed almost at ease with the idea, and showed no more emotion than a rock.

The other guardsmen did not know whether to laugh or cry at Narváez, with his normally unmoving long face. Trentino knew his men intimately and silently measured the private; *I will have to keep an eye on him.*

Narváez was always two are three steps ahead of the others. Narváez, shorter than the others and the most aggressive in his command, was always handy in a tight spot, provided he was controlled.

At this moment, the man was a complete wildcard. Narváez loved the Pope but not the cardinals. *He could go any way* thought the major, as he studied the private and watched him pan around the jungle with his sub-machine gun.

"As I said signore, if the Vat expects us to do this then, we should sort things out quick and quiet like—" A clinical kill would suit him best.

"Stick to my orders Narváez. Remember these are civvies," he explained. "I do not know any more than that. My orders are clear and simple, yours are too. First, reconnoitre and secure a safe perimeter. Stay undercover and observe. The target name is coded *Nest.*

"Signore," called Bianchi, "*Who* the merda makes these bloody names?"

"That's just the way it is son. Ok listen up, the scientists' safety is of paramount importance, come across anybody or anything else, do not engage." The major emphasised, "We will only move into secure the temple once the other units arrive and support us."

"*Nest,* signore."

"Eh?"

"You said, code name Nest" Bianchi corrected the major, his voice fading and wishing he had kept his mouth shut.

"Mmm, you can take the point corporal," frowning at him, "See anything then report immediately son." Nodding directly his way to go. The peeved off guardsman tightened his lips and sped off, *smart-ass,* he thought.

****

The light was quickly dimming, and it would be completely dark in ten or fifteen minutes, being so close to the equator. Visibility was made even harder after a recent hot downpour, when soft mists began rising from the lush floor. Steadily the misty moisture hovered to their thighs. The heavy rain clouds had departed unveiling in the short twilight an early moon rising. Grey-white luminosity began to wash eerily over the forest expanse.

Up ahead, the men could hear at first a chuckle of noises, but moving in that direction it became clear and powerful. Unmistakably they recognised the turmoil crash and cataclysm as large volumes of water being driven through the forest. Without transition, like pulling back a thick curtain, the soldiers emerged out of the trees and into a clearing. The darkening night sky was married to a silvery lunar light translating mystery into melancholy.

Squatting down, their torsos stuck up out of the low ground mists. Having endured many hardships, the men should have been poised ready, but instead waited in silence against the enormous resonance of a gigantic waterfall. Safely concealed behind the edge of a tree perimeter, from this insignificant place everyone appeared mesmerized, and captured by the magic. Their minds went neutral. Standing before them the temple soared up and it established immediate domination. Timeless within stone, it captured a story of the past and held the present for future subjugation.

They had made it.

Resting for a moment, impressed by the loneliness and formidable nature of this place, it seemed completely unthinkable that anyone could ever be here. An awesome superstructure stood right before them. The temple, wrapped by immense trees growing alongside these steep valley slopes with impossible rock-faces, encased it all securely.

All around and beyond the vale, hills shrouded an expanse of infinite rainforest, and no wonder it made this place impossible to detect from the sky. The guardsmen adjusted their eyes to the darkness so they could just about discern trees and shrubs growing on some of its massive terraced rock-structures thus completing its natural camouflage.

A thin clearing, roughly twenty metres wide, formed a large perimeter base around the temple. The soldiers scanned the area and saw an encampment white washed in bright moonlight. They could see large tents, camping equipment and light machinery. Several large, wooden boxes were stacked up like a wall, which contained botanical or zoological specimens and artefacts. The whole place was in darkness and appeared abandoned.

Taking a deep breath, the men waited. To them, everything appeared awe-inspiring. They stared at the eastern side of the vale and parts of the temple structure, all silhouetted like a ghostly sketch against the blackness and dark shadows. They had not expected to see such an intimidating spectacle, feebly trying to suppress their exposed trepidation. The men wisely moved back into the safety of the forest cover once again.

Their attention fixated outwards beholding a high place of worship, to the distant temple top. A place of ancient stones and sacrifice. Beyond this and towering above the temple existed an imposing sight, it was a magical lunar-lit waterfall.

Silvery moonlit liquid cascaded over the mountain-top, seen hammering downwards and in this enchanted light, its shiny reflections appeared like infinite light reflecting ropes, held in an X-ray stasis.

With the sudden drop of hundreds of feet, the intense water force quickly met the valley floor and immediately atomised. Luminous clouds gathered from a deep pool sending copious volumes of water vapour up through the magic of the moonlight. The men's minds seemed trapped in this ethereal atmosphere watching this spiritual moisture rise with ghostly luminosity. Rising, its spirit evaporated into the waiting darkness.

Major Trentino's electronic night-sight edged out from the forest edge. He gauged the dimensions of the pyramid to be over eight-hundred feet high, with a square base each side all measured digitally to be the same in length. It did not form an apex like the Egyptian pyramids, instead, as expected, it resembled more Inca or Mayan in design.

Observation of the ancient building showed it to be divided into levels; the facing side seen with large stone steps leading up and tapering to a flat-topped platform. An altar stood peaking up in the distance, close to a very tall pole, a monolithic stone of some kind. It sat next to a large angular building. This mega-structure's shear height and scale was much grander than the design of the Chichen Itza Observatory.

The superstructure stuck down inside here, a hidden valley. It made no sense at all. Who build it and why? And, where were the scientists?

At the base of the temple a small encampment lay abandoned. It sat alone and insignificant, any welcome chased away by the ghosts of the forest. Something was wrong, seriously wrong. No fires nor lights, no sound of any activity anywhere, it was completely deserted. An unnatural danger lurked everywhere inside the sultry air. They all felt it. The only sound came from the lonely lament of that eerie waterfall. Before them it stood.

The "Temple of MalisIblis"

Place of the dead.

The daylight had gone. Lunar shadows began moving around intermingling with silvery grey patches, as magical silver shimmer appeared around tree-lined edges and surrounding forest. The moon was quickly on the rise bringing with it silvery shadows which white-washed everything. The temple's numerous tall stone steps ascended high to the top. Silvery cut-outs of focal lines in many sections of the stone structure stamped its presence, outlining its wet surfaces.

Peaking at first over the tall tree tops, the full moon was on the rise with its widening halo floating around it like a ghost. The soldiers sat squatting and watching its heavenly ascent into the starry night, its silvery light dousing over them. The men hid from its bright reflection as the surrounding opaque mists sucked them down like quicksand.

****

God must be watching over us, thought Trentino, pressing his fingers gently onto his breast pocket. Holding his Bible, calm settling his nerves, he whispered, "And then God touched the earth reminding man that he still cared, still loved his own creation." He sighed softly, for this was such a moment.

Everyone drowsed in this moonlit fantasy. Aghast and motionless, for the first time the major looked unsure. Countless droplets of silvery white water kept falling off from forest leaves.

A history of recent rainfall glistened for a moment like the many dancing fairies descending from heaven to earth. Fearful eyes from camouflaged spectral faces beamed up from the illuminated mists, and yet how the soldiers still marvelled at the temple, beholding it like a new miracle.

"Snap out of it Sergente!" A brisk order came from the major. Only minutes had passed but it seemed like hours before their numbed senses were at last torn away from this lunatic hypnosis.

"Take three men, check and secure the outer perimeter and report back in twenty minutes. Be quick about it." The spell broken by the major, he commanded authority. Trentino stared in disbelief shaking his stopped watch, the time ticked again. God's moment had ended.

The sergeant acknowledged it with a firm nod, gathered his men and silently set forth around the perimeter encampment keeping out of sight. The company needed speed.

The atmosphere changing by the second, new turmoil began moving, turning tranquillity upside down in an uncanny mood shift. A deep breath seemed to tug the air as the forest sucked gently inwards. Invisible forces inexorably began pulling everything inwards towards the temple.

The soldiers traversing around the temple stopped, gauged this strange phenomenon, and knew it could not be good. The shifting air pressure became increasingly heavier, pressing the hot atmosphere onto them. Was there another deluge on the way? Impossible because the evening sky was crystal clear.

The soldiers saw the stars sparkle above them, universal beacons held there twinkling with indifference in the heavens to the strange happenings on earth. There was something intangible at work where the temple stood, and in this moment an indescribable dread cast over all things and saturated the air.

The major's orders were crisp and clear, his goal to reach here was completed. That was his job. Make it safe and secure. No rescue and to report any unusual activity for the main forces arrival next day. He knew nothing else, the rest of the mission was classified with the highest security. It would then be up to Colonel Rossi, the Commander of Operation Aequinoxium, to arrive and take over his watch. Until then they had to wait.

The oddest rescue mission I've been on. Merda. Rossi will fill me in when he arrives tomorrow. As self-doubt seeped into even his resolute mind, he thought, *get the scientists and get the hell out of here!* Acknowledging thoughtfully with himself, *Narváez might be right.* It was a strange and unusual feeling as he had always been so sure of himself.

Once again, evening fell over the rainforest, and the night birds that should have started their calls, had not. Tonight, there were no sounds at all. No distant noises of secretive ocelots or screeching monkeys or hissing snakes. Silence, screamed of night survival, while the frightened forest waited.

It all seemed so impossible, almost as if life had stopped. What was wrong with the forest? What was wrong with nature? With one massive deep breath like gigantic lungs the air sucked in deeply towards the temple and held still. Motionless, the jungle too had stopped breathing.

"Signore, signore, what is going on!", the soldiers' mental stability clearly in question. He wanted an explanation from the officer, "Do you feel the air?" He was looking for some reassurance. "Signore, do you feel… *it?*" the soldier kept on repeating as trepidation grew.

Uneasy, the soldiers began instinctively re-positioning themselves in a secure formation around their officer, implying peril. The men were squatting on the ground with their weapons pointed towards the apparent threat, the temple.

What is wrong here, there is something… more? The major thought and felt the same way, except there was something else, something he could not quite define, a primal fear inside him. There it was again, doubt. *Something is not right.* A great menace harboured in his mind that he had felt before. It was earlier in the morning, just before the ant attack! He instinctively knew it in his bones and thought, *this place is evil, it's the Devil's work.*

"Get ready men!" His voice was as compulsory as a commandment. The men began loading their guns, nerves on edge. Even the noise of the waterfalls forgotten, it could not penetrate the lasting silence.

Unexpectedly a strong night call broke from the direction of the deserted encampment. Everyone heard it. A lone predatory animal roaring loudly, and in defiance at an oncoming menace. It had followed them and like the humans, was waiting for something unstoppable. King of the rainforest, top of the food chain, the large jaguar protested at this freak of nature.

The air heaved out.

The air inhaled once again.

Feline and human alike took a deep breath in rhythm, as did the tall trees. Their strong bows pulling slightly inwards towards the temple, and then stopped. All things were spectators to this display of raw power. The air waited, and held some more, then pushed forcibly back out, and quickly filled up again with another lung full of forest. This breath-taking moment lasted a lifetime.

The jungle braced…

The major had touched his pocket bible for divine guidance. His eyes had dilated fully in the darkness, when suddenly all hell broke loose. *This is it!* Trentino's sixth sense screamed. It had always kept him alive and right now was no exception.

"Hold on men!" he called out. "Hold on men, here it comes!" And no sooner than his words came out, an immense fury, immediate and cataclysmic, hit them when the earth began shuddering.

Instant and violent, the rippling ground trembled in unstoppable waves. Its effects shook the trees and grounds around them, bursting adrenaline through their shaking bodies. Everything undulating, its tectonic grind created huge rumblings louder than thunder. Destructive effects abrupt, every grain of dirt vibrated energetically inside the unearthly vale.

Exploding like a detonated Atomic bomb, the source resonated from inside a hidden fault line, unleashing forces with great clatter and clamour. Its immense power breached the earth, forcing the deep fissure to pull apart. A gateway into hell, the chasm next to ancient mine-works suddenly cracked open as easy as eggshells, and all the way across the Iblis vale. Cut off, there was no way in, or out.

Boom! Boom! Boom!

The noises triggered excruciating pain, and sharply pierced their ears the instant the cataclysmic clamour began. Great air pressure started squeezing them with unending determination, lasting several excruciating minutes. There seemed to be no end to the torture, and it felt like an enormous hammer was thumping heavily and causing constant pounding inside their heads that it numbed all senses except for pain.

Tree branch to twig shivered against these mighty percussions. The men tried to keep their balance and were quickly repositioning themselves by lowering their centre of gravities while the forest floor continued to undulate violently. The major dropped down to the ground for extra stability.

"Are we being attacked signore!" Yelled one of the bewildered men who was confused that there were no blasts or explosions.

"Earthquake!" the major shouted. Whatever its source, it seemed more akin to devilish thunder. Minutes passed with no abatement to this hostility, every muscle and organ was shaking.

Mystified, the major began trying to understand; *no clouds, no storm, only clear night sky.* The stars shifted above his distant gaze as a new pattern in the heavens appeared to be born.

Merda! My eyes are deceiving me, playing tricks, how else? My men expect me to know things, explain things, have answers and tell them what to do! I know nothing. My God, the stars look the same and yet, I think they have moved across the Sky. But, that's impossible.

His head hurt thinking about it; he sought clarity and tried to make sense of the madness surrounding them by watching trees falling and whipping branches. The man sensing the source, the epicentre, seemed to be emanating from the immediate vicinity.

This is the epicentre! And that's no ordinary quake! The major recognised enormity, that this wide-reaching phenomenon was not a natural event.

The seismic activity going on and on, with body and bow quaking and all were helpless against this supremacy. A force not in harmony was taking control. Everything was shaking, blurring their eyes watching this in and out of focus forest floor rippling in waves below them and everywhere around. No one could see or guess these far-reaching consequences.

****

Uncannily at this same moment in time in another place, a location over five and a half thousand miles from the Iblis vale, the same disturbance struck with sudden might and aggression. Instant violence shook the South West of Scotland in late afternoon, in and around the quaint village of Mauchline. The petrified people could not have predicted anything like this could ever take place here.

The atmosphere instantly pressed down on the village and surrounding countryside, catching two boys holding their ears in agony. The sky flashed a warning of an impending peril, when the earth's crust started undulating like sea waves.

Scott and Cameron began screaming in agony when the freak earthquake hit. The boys were visiting Prophet Monument, and were exposed on top of the tower when they were thrown around helplessly. Feeling dizzy, they watched everything around them rebel. The Monument was the highest point of the village where a large area of the Shire could be seen.

These unearthly convulsions continued, and with greater magnitude for several minutes more. Deep rumbling noises travelled up from a place much deeper and darker below, a place worse than anyone could ever have imagined permeated into the air above and across the land.

It passed, and the countryside sighed in a strange silence in the aftermath. Soon sirens could be heard in the distance, and the barking of dogs finding their courage again, while others remained frightened, howling non-stop into the darkening evening. One thing was for certain though, the world would never be the same again.

The boys not to be put-off of their fun, had already paid to get into the tower, the older boy Scott put a pound coin into a visitor's telescope to look for any damage. His excitement raised when he saw something peculiar. Scott looked twice to be sure. He was right, confirming a darker shadow against the dim late autumn afternoon. He could see it, a black mist drifting along the *muir* or moor, and it seemed to be coming out of the old quarry. *Strange,* Scott thought. *Never seen that before.*

These earth-changing events were inextricably linked to a source coming from a place called *Nowhere.*

Cold, is the land.

It was the prophecy.

****

Back at the temple, the Swiss guardsmen stared out and into a weird forest light. The trees moving with unseen hands as the earth continued to shake. In horror and disbelief, unspoken fear etched across their faces when the trees began to buckle and break around them.

Fresh supple vines were stretching like bowstrings between trees, snapping in bits with great velocity. They were propelled in every direction and suddenly, living had become a lottery.

The horror ramping up a gear; all around trees kept toppling and were releasing lethal vines, whip-lashing what looked like silvery lines into the air recklessly around them. Some passed close by, slashing lethal pathways through the nearby foliage like cheese-wire. Without warning, the quake stopped.

The destruction ended, leaving trees creaking and cracking while others that were unable to stand anymore finally came crashing to the forest floor. Larger manmade structures would have fallen by lesser forces but the super-structure in front of them amazingly appeared, undamaged.

The tents within the encampment were now all leaning in a semi-state of collapse. Still rolling were some large wooden boxes of supplies or equipment of some sort, strewing its contents with complete disregard. In a few minutes of its beginning, all havoc had halted and became strangely silent once more. The jungle waited. Was the devastation finished?

Seemed like it, thought Trentino. The silence in its aftermath remained unsettled, and more akin to a morgue. Gradually they became aware of only one sound again. The lonely waterfall. There it was! Higher than the temple, with its crisp, clear crashes.

The flowing water came from the nearby high mountain, displaying a spectacle of unspeakable beauty in the moonlight, so surreal. A torrent of water hammering to the earth, it too catching the moonlit magic and conjured copious white mists at the bottom pool, flowing from it and away in a fast-moving river like metallic quicksilver leading through the vale.

At the temple, the same unearthly light cast its enchanted luminosity over the huge stone terraces, portraying this holy place in a supernatural frosty silhouette. The moon's shadow drifted higher throwing its ethereal illumination over all the land.

Sensing that the mayhem had ended, the men thankful for being alive looked about nervously. Not a murmur of life, as quiet chaos settled into the forest. The eye-catching landscape wholly hypnotic. It was no dream and more of a marvel while they emerged tentatively standing up from the gaseous ground mists, every man wondering, *what was this place?*

"That was too close for comfort," said Major Trentino's calming tone. The officer bringing everyone back to reality, "What that Merda was, God only knows."

"This place, it is unnatural maggiore." A soldier gasped looking at the wrecked campsite.

Major Trentino rubbed his eyes while surveying the colossal stone building before him. He thought, *Such breath-taking beauty and yet, unbelievable. It is intact! What building could stand such power.*

Studying the large structure for weakness, he found none. He waited a moment more, then quite unexpectedly saw something move on the temple wall.

Something moved up there on the wall, I know it! Narrowing his eyes to focus more, the major was convinced.

He had seen a chance movement up on the mid-plane terrace of the temple, more than just a silvery shadow catching his trained eye. Something else had moved up there, in a miniscule shift in motion, and that was enough. His keen vision had spotted it. Alerted he quickly brought his night vision scope from his crossbow into that direction. The major swiftly zoomed up and onto the third tier, focusing between light washed stones and dark stepped shadows. His mind shouted to him, *no movement,* which implied a hidden danger, his eyes glued to the scope.

"Check your weapons," he whispered with menace, they looked at him, then at the temple. "Two, no, three men up on one of the platforms, about two hundred feet above us, and —" he paused confirming, "They are all fully armed, AK47's"

"What the inferno, do scientists need machine-guns for maggiore?" Apparently pleased at this new and welcome development. To Bellucci, this meant only one thing, killing. At least this was something he could handle.

"Either the scientists are going out for a spot of hunting or we have some unwanted company, signores." said the major firmly. The officer lowered his crossbow telescopic, whispering under his breath, "Get ready."

****

CHAPTER III

THE LINK OF OSLEIOTECT

The seasons change very little near the equator, staying much the same from one month to the next, everyday like an equinox. However, this was much different from any other, a unique year with a different solstice, one where the sun's rays were slightly misaligned on the temple. A peculiar seismic activity had already occurred earlier in June of this year, which crucially shifted the temple's position. A negligible shift, when the expedition had arrived, yet could not have known about this misalignment and its crucial importance.

A miniscule change, never the less one that would affect everything. Small enough to throw off the sun's profile causing it to not fit perfectly within the stone orifice of the tall obelisk. The obelisk stood on the high temple top.

The sun's energy did not pass through the purposely-carved obelisk anymore. The obelisk of cosmic origin and underlying godly design was purposely built to focus the sun's warm power and push its way through a perfectly cut hole. Transforming its solar energy and binding it to the standing stone which glued its cosmic energy into the temple structure's interior rim.

And on this special year, the "Rays of Life" had missed the inner curvature within its stone circumference. Something in the cosmos had changed. The world would never be the same again.

Earlier in the year, the expedition's archaeologists had already witnessed their first seismic quake upon arrival. It would not be the last and worse was yet to come. Given their inadequate and superficial knowledge, based on ignorance and innocent greed for power, none of them could have known the true significance of these events, that somewhere in the universe, "God's Chain" was broken...

The last epoch had occurred five hundred years before the expedition's arrival, an event that had always occurred at regular intervals. At each epoch, the strong and well-defined rays from the sun would channel their spiritual energy through the thick stone orifice and direct them onto the south plane of the tall temple observatory, the viewpoint located in the middle of the temple top.

This year, as predicted by the Shamans, and despite this prophecy being an occasion unlike any other, it was a new type of epoch, one that would profoundly affect all weather patterns throughout the world. The seasons across the globe are the result of a 23.5° tilt of the Earth's axis, any shift or deviation from this angle, however minuscule, would cause a chain reaction affecting all ecosystems; climate change would be inevitable.

The sunlight was so strong, radiating its energy from the heavens onto the temple, and though powerful as it was, it could not chase away a sinister black shadow. This shadow had come and would neither fade nor disappear. It remained there on the temple top with menacing affliction; *the prophecy will come first and Smite.*

The sun's rays could not travel through the stone orifice anymore. No, this unglued light could not pass through its black space; the way was no longer open. In its stead was a dreadful dark shadow. This place was once where light bound to God and now bound to the power of darkness. The cosmos had changed. It was the prophecy. *All will shake in terror.*

This morbid black menace had no ending. *The prophecy, cold is the land* and a dark surrogate of wholesome malice as a cold substitution for a lost golden face, for a shadow with moody malcontent, a blackness stood silent and menacing, there it remained. Again, the prophecy, *nowhere to hide.*

On this special epoch, when it finally arrived as day turned into night, a lonely luminance cast several gossamer *lines of silvery light* onto an ominous stone altar. The powers of light were still able to resist darkness and held the cosmos in delicate balance. The close position of the altar to the tall obelisk enabled another ethereal line to form, one that could only be seen in this first full moonlit evening, when it fell across the altar and froze inert. On the following evening, and by the candescence light of a blue moon, another diaphanous sliver of moonlight quietly appeared, this time created along the vertical plane of the altar. This brief instant past with an additional silver line of moonlight conjured in godly design.

In the air and all around the stone altar, by now many ethereal lines had formed, each line designed and determined by the carved-out symbols in all stone spires around the temple, one spire standing at each corner of this great and mighty pyramid.

A spiritual light power, for this moment unperturbed by the shadows of darkness, these complex symbolic geometrical formations of presence, and ones that could only be seen by those who had *the vision*. The expedition camped below had no such foresight, they could not see or be aware of this quiet battle of *wills* going on between good and evil. This vision was invisible to the human eye. Depending on whether it was a *full* or *blue* moon then some of these magical lines of presence existed, in fact they were more of a feeling. Human eyes were very limited, and this vision here, was a *vision for the soul*. Indeed, up on top of the temple was a hallowed place.

The civilian expedition arrived in late May and started excavating around the structure in June. Working hard day in, day out, time passed quickly and by now time was nearing the end of October. The scientists had endured many hardships and eventually and had managed to clear a lot of the temple of overgrowth. Light and darkness had been in a state of equilibrium in complete balance in this universe, up until this day.

Nature had changed. The scientists and archaeologists through their own ignorance and secrecy were unaware about the *scripture's lost teachings* and oblivious to their own and imminent peril by being here.

The *link* of *Osleiotect* was dreadfully weak, and on this evening, following that last sunrise, it marked a new epoch as prophesised by those who are long dead. They had left ancient codices and scriptures and esoteric details of the past, and told their stories of the future in multiple knotted strings called Quipu's. It would tell those who were able to read them of these grim changes to come, in a warning. All these things were about to happen, but this night was different. Unknown to the people of the expedition, they were chosen as forces of humanity and gathered together there against the *power of darkness*. This too was written, in the scriptures of the prophecies and a final warning of man's apocalypse.

Things now in motion, as predicted by dead prophets, the Shaman of the Rainforest. Now, it was time of the first prophecy, and in this time of gathering darkness the shadow remained, blacker than ever, deeper than the night and cruel like its creator. Next morning, a new æon dawned and the shadow, it was here to stay.

****

CHAPTER VI

MY JOURNAL

The scientists had adapted their forest skills to purpose-built furniture by binding and strapping bamboo together using flexible vine. Learning many things about living and surviving in the jungle; to their satisfaction the seats were surprisingly well made of skin from animals that they had hunted for food. Nothing was wasted and in evidence many animal skins stretched between the sturdy wooden frames to make more tables and any other types of furniture. Copper, silver and ceramic dishes and ancient pottery sat on top of numerous stone shelves left behind by previous occupants. What was left of the expedition was stuck inside these hot confinements within these temple walls.

Feeling a little dreamy, in the sullen subdued light coming from a few Oil filled lamps. Everyone imprisoned inside this ancient and spacious stone confine, listening to their constant hiss, the sounds from the lamps oddly relaxing. In muted solitude away from the others, sighing softly Christopher slowly opened his journal, and began writing.

Déjà vu…

My Journal, 30th October Year 5,125. Mayan Time.

I wish to God that we had never come to this awful place…

For those who may read my Journal after I have gone, this is a final record. Why I write maybe of little or no consequence because there is no way out. If you are reading my words, do not waste precious time looking for our bodies. I only pray that we are all, delivered from evil. Leave before it is too late!

Christopher swallowed hard before considering his final words…

Our expedition had been moving through the rainforest for about six months. We should have listened to the grim forewarnings of the tribes Shaman not to seek the lost temple because this is truly an evil place. All interest and high ideals that we once had for helping humanity has since disappeared. I have failed.

Held against our will in one of the few rooms charted. Every room explored so far is named and collated by the senior Archaeologist Professor Fabio Mancini. As such each identified by location, categorized, given a logical classification and referenced. This room, our Cell is labelled E1L1RM2. All this seems so unimportant now.

Tonight, is our first evening sleeping inside the Temple of MalisIblis. It is a depressing stone dwelling. We are prisoners. This room is one of the many found throughout this colossal labyrinth. A place full of dark tunnels and hideous chambers that drives men insane because... everything I have witnessed here is wholly frightening. The only truthful way that I might attempt to explain these past events inside my own mind is to say, I must be mad!

We puzzled for a long time outside the temple walls on how to gain entry. It remained this way until only a few weeks ago when we finally got in! I can barely recall what occurred then on that fatal morning at the entrance, everything is blurred and happened so fast that I am not sure anymore. I try to recall, and it pains me so much I fear for my own sanity. The others feel the same as I do, that is, those of us who are still alive...

Our precautions for personal safety doubled before entering the temple. Once inside we quickly realized that this place was unique and would become a study of a lifetime. A goldmine, and one that The Washington Post or National Geographic Society would pay a king's ransom to have its contents published first! Well, they may have to wait just a little bit longer. I only hope that we live long enough to see tomorrow and yet a quick ending with a bullet would be better than what lies inside these thick impenetrable walls. It is a God forsaken place...

Like the night before an execution, there is no escape and no hope. As I look around this make-shift containment, *the others are sitting quietly, and I think, everyone is wondering the same thing, will it be our last supper?*

I have witnessed with my own eyes hideous monsters, devilish creatures inside here, waiting... waiting to kill and waiting to eat. Our captors do not believe us, although even they are gradually becoming aware that things are not normal inside this wicked place. They too are frightened. I see it in their eyes, the same. MADNESS! There are much worse things than dying. Heed my warnings and leave while you can, for there are some things inside this place that are not of this world and are wholly evil. I pray to God that we may still get out, we must...

Brows furrowed, *has it really come to this?* Christopher like the others dared not go to sleep because of the bad dreams. His journal would keep him awake; yawning hard while rubbing his sore eyes, hoping that his record might serve as an obituary and warning to those who might follow in their footsteps.

****

In this semi-darkness, an unexplained primal fear was taking hold of them all. Self-doubt and uncertainty of what was going to happen festered, everyone was looking around in fear while trying to occupy their worried minds with anything else. It was short-lived as their wandering thoughts returned like a fly mesmerised towards the beacons of light from the oil filled tillies that lit up their frightened faces with a makeup of patched shadows. In this diffused light, it doused their shocked and sallow complexions.

Though this ghoulish group made light of their dark and hopeless situation, trust had turned into mistrust with each other. No one believed in friendship anymore. Deeper in, somewhere within a disturbed psyche dwelt more private thoughts, horrible ones, ones that festered and fed in this disharmony and ones that could not be spoken. The temple bred malcontent.

****

Llamas had been used as beasts of burden for transporting supplies of food, coffee, medical equipment and were mainly self-sufficient in all areas while utilising their own newly found survival skills. This dirty looking group were a mixed bag of people, a collection of scientists, archaeologists and historians accompanied with their professional guides then able to navigate through these dense jungles.

Tarot had played a hand at the very onset of the expedition. Their numbers had once been sixteen strong; fate dealt them a *thirteenth trump* and the *chariot card* was turned next; now only seven people remained alive. To win this game of cards then *a union of opposites* could only do it, like the *black and white steeds* between the *chariot, everyone must pull together* in the same direction. It was the only way to survive.

To harness emotions, wants and needs of the survivors together would give them a single unified direction. Not only that, great control and will power would be required by everyone to win this fatal game of tarot. Over half of them were already dead. Their luck had run out, all killed in horrible and cruel ways and for what? These unanswered questions exasperated Christopher. Everything remained shrouded in complete mystery, even now. The expedition had been a complete disaster. Christopher felt a strange tightness in his throat as he swallowed anger.

For what? This was supposed to be a bloody legitimate civilian expedition! Endorsed by the Brazilian government, so why are we captives? If we stay here we are all dead, everyone! Why? What is this place, and why is it so important? Why have we been forgotten, does ONCOL not care about us? What about the Vatican, are we not important? Surely, someone will come to save us? God, they must come and rescue us. God hear my prayer, send someone to help!

****

Betrayed and misguided they found this prison to be a terrible place, a chilling place, a soul-destroying place. Some of the group ate their meagre rations for comfort while others tried to quietly forget their own disturbing thoughts by reading old yellow stained manuscripts or ponder over this strange construction, their prison called *the Temple of MalisIblis.*

Its very existence defied all reason, so fantastic it all was, better to be christened *Devil's temple* and yet, Christ had little or nothing to do with it. In this extreme environment flora grows exceptionally fast and where once the temple had already been cleared of the forest by the scientists, the jungle was already reclaiming the giant stone structure back for its own.

The survivors placed under so called *safety* for several days; at first guarded inside their own encampment and then later moved behind those windowless walls and more secure premises. Each person was always accompanied by a protector even to the latrines. A make shift lavatory had been constructed within an anti-chamber next door and it seemed like blasphemy inside these ancient walls, not to mention a personal degree of humiliation. They had no choice with an AK47 machinegun pointed at them!

Waxy candle light and oily paraffin lamps sculpted bizarre caricatures around, each person becoming a mixture of light and dark shadows magnifying their frightened emotions and extenuated vagrant shabbiness. Everyone appeared unkempt, not allowed to wash or access bath facilities since yesterday morning. The place stank, and things could only get worse.

Surprisingly these hot and unpleasant conditions were not as bad as it might have been, were it not for the rudimentary ventilation system built by a civilization long ago. Stale air moved through vents and ducts. Relived for this airflow and yet everyone was amazed it ever existed in here at all.

If the illumination had been better, bright green and golden yellow painted bands, easier to see painted over the top and bottom of the walls and the frame of the doorway, forming an apex shaped arch above. A large thick stone door was locked shut. Stucco designed patterns embellishing the front and back surfaces of the hard-stone door, the skilful design continued across the walled interior, giving it a rich aesthetic appearance. Stucco by design was one of the most characteristic features of art and architecture seen in Islamic and other countries. This lost culture apparently saw a similar beauty.

A complex of gold symbols engraved deeply into one of the interior walls where there were heavenly bodies painted of the solar system, and obvious to all they represented the sun, moon, planets and constellations of the zodiac. All shapes drawn with deep yellow tones against a background of red-stone blocks that protruded into this room giving the surface a three-dimensional model. The profiled wall provided for a natural shelf, where a few large candles already sat lighting up the multifaceted wall, with serene shadows and buttery patches over the dry floor. It all demonstrated the high importance that the heavens played by its former inhabitants, whoever they had been. This cosmological chamber linked by the same theme to an earlier discovery on the top of the temple.

The ceiling inside this temporary accommodation displayed other drawings of engraved figures and sad faces of people and one could imagine them speaking to them, calling out like some classical tragedy, a struggle of fate. Maybe this was a final holding place for enemies before execution, a sacrifice to appease their gods. Outside their prison was one of the many other narrow and claustrophobic corridors that led deep into the centre of this mysterious super-structure.

ONCOL Scientific Corporation directed commissioned them to find knew cures through scientific discovery and exploration, part funded by the Vatican and other important and interested commercial business concerns. It all helped spread religious education and doctrine. Finding of the temple seemed at first to have been a lucky bonus, a chance discovery and secondary to their main bio-technological directive. They were wrong about that. Such a find was suited for other subsequent expeditions with more time to chart and collate artefacts with many stone scriptures; intuitively this told Christopher that this discovery had been his inevitable fate.

The archaeologists meticulously logged every artefact and described in detail each one piece by piece. This always proved to be a very time-consuming activity and at times extremely dangerous work. Their zeal for discovering new things and taking time not to disturb any item they found was essential to preserve its lasting chronicle. From floor to ceiling, everything photographed and recorded. Mystery of mysteries, the temple provided more questions than answers, why and who built it? How old might it be? What riches could still be inside here? Where did the civilization go and what was the real reason for being here in a lost and far forgotten place eight thousand feet up above sea level? Lost inside the misty green interior Christopher, like the others, all awaited judgment day.

Christopher Hrycuik sat down and thought back to when they had first met the *Zaplithowatres*. Unlike the professor of the expedition, he had not listened closely enough to the chief or heeded his grim fore-warnings. Nobody would ever believe what had happened inside the temple. Some discoveries had been gruesome, some terrifying and others completely unbelievable.

Hours passed inside the semi-darkness and the young man with sore and blood shot eyes kept holding sleep at bay. He needed to record his thoughts with consciousness slipping from his grasp, his writing becoming more laboured.

"My God… this is the end of the World!"

****

CHAPTER V

HEADHUNTERS RUN!

Months before…

Everyone had set out on this epic journey in early February, knowingly to endure an uncharted wilderness. Each step proving a challenge for body, mind and spirit and they all needed to dig deep to survive this primordial world. It was going to be an exploration of a lifetime!

The expedition were mostly volunteers, enthusiasts and adventurers, everyone coming to explore the rainforest with the hope of discovering something new, something wonderful and something ancient.

Travelling much than anyone had done in recent times, boats had been used in parts of the journey, then leaving these and all further major waterways behind, the group picking up animals on route from friendly tribes. This an essential part of their plan for packing their supplies into the interior.

Their route was becoming much more onerous than first expected, except for the expedition leader and forest rangers who were expert guides and more than ready for another tour of duty into Amazonia.

The rainforest seemed endless, hacking an unchanging path for weeks on end. The trees in this part were well spread apart and grew to astounding heights. Without abatement restless warm winds kept pushing acres of long green grasses in carefree ways, making hissing sounds more akin to the pleasing noises of the sea. The determined expedition stopped now and again but their way was always ahead, trudging on through the mud marshes to their continual consternation and boredom maximised. Thick grasses looked impenetrable, growing higher than the tallest man in an environment created to be a navigational nightmare, even for the rangers.

However, spirits were generally high, hacking and talking as they slowly moved on their way and in parts, laughing with good-hearted banter at whatever might possess them. Some could not believe why they ever came on this, so called holiday!

It was not all fun. On many occasions feeling utterly spent, others would be cursing continuously while cutting their arduous way through. The grasses formed thick mesh-works of basket weaves. A natural phenomenon like this slowing them right down at times to a sweaty standstill and forcing them to traverse into alternative routes in many places.

At the head of the column of explorers, *Carmello de Matiz,* their South American guide, stopped. Looking curiously around while holding his hand upwards to signal to the others. A small man standing no more than five foot four, his clear and brown skin tone had light scarring on his left cheek, black hair with a natural middle parting divided his short mushroom style. Knowing that the jungle was always ready to present at any moment new dangers for the unwary and expert alike.

For this stretch, Carmello was feeling extremely uneasy, and unlike his usual self, the man normally with an infectious sense of humour keeping people's spirits high. That was a bonus in a place like this! The guide had been uncomfortable for hours. The expedition paused, everyone watching the small man. His keen dark brown eyes were alert and were scanning the long rushes for something. Sniffing a few times, he caught a scent. Turning his head to point his ear this way and that, while listening closely next to the wall of grasses. Their sounds almost relaxing swaying in waves in the warm winds, the man waited.

Mathieson Stuart, the expedition's senior guide sensed Carmello's apprehension up ahead of the column. He lowered himself and the senior ranger was suspicious while thinking, *something is wrong*. Mathieson lowered his centre of gravity in unison with his friend ahead. Even from this position far back in the column the tension cloaking anything hidden inside the thick grasses, there could easily be a black caiman, a python or even a jaguar to name a few dangers. Carmello stiffened just like a creature ready to pounce.

The senior ranger knew that Carmello to be always in tune with nature. *What is wrong with him?* He asked himself with growing impatience. Mathieson was also an excellent guide but not as good as his natural subordinate, the senior guide, holding his breath.

Suddenly Carmello's eyes opened wide in horror when several bamboo tubes silently came pushing out towards him from the tall grass. At the same time, other tubes began randomly appearing around the whole expedition.

Then came an explosion of urgent rustling and deafening noises of threatening voices. The horrified expedition froze, listening to the angry yelling and calls of rage and war. All screaming and all shouting.

The enclosing grasses suddenly burst wide open, stunning the explorers into incapacity. All they could do was stare at the wild natives. They had only one thought in their minds, *headhunters.*

Mortified, the panic-stricken explorers watched the dark-skinned natives standing fully upwards. It did not look good being completely encircled like this.

The natives appeared taller than anyone could have imagined, an imposing and furious fighting people who began moving rapidly forward feigning an attack, then stepping quickly back while testing their defences. The warriors continued goading less than twenty feet from the bewildered scientists.

Menacing battle calls cowed the terrified expedition. The tribes' insane aggression shouting abuse at an increasing frenetic rate. Ready to kill!

"Headhunters! Run!" A scientist shouted from the back of the column.

Suddenly birds winged away all around them in a chaotic scramble of flight and confusion. Their pack of llamas bolted off carrying away the expedition's supplies in fright. Hoofing it, the animals were out of sight in seconds.

These hostile warlike gestures continued with frantic waves of their bows and spears in the air. A gauntlet that challenged the expedition all the time with blowpipes aimed at them with deadly certainty.

What were they waiting for? Are they taunting us, goading us to make a first and fatal move? Mathieson gauged some game in the fraught air, *maybe not poison darts, maybe tranquilisers! Headhunters!* The senior ranger felt fear for the first time and his instincts were to run!

Some of the scientists were visibly shaking with fear and the noise was head-numbing them into shocked submission by the fearsome headhunters ranting their obscenities.

"No, stand still, wait!" Fabio the expedition leader perceived their feelings and steadied them.

****

A few of the natives had big stomachs although most were muscular and supple in appearance. They all wore necklaces with many pointed teeth extracted from wild animals they killed; or maybe even worse.

They wore green headbands just like the bands around their biceps, all men except a younger boy. The warriors all had repulsive large hoops driven through their noses. They had bare painted chests and posteriors, and were nearly naked except for their manhood; that area was completely protected by a wooden sheath, positioned in an upwards and tapered direction.

With no more time to lose, Fabio overcame his initial shock. The man in charge of the expedition turned to face an enraged warrior with a smile. Smiling brightly and widely he began speaking in an even and calm tone to the native. He advised the men next to him in a clear voice.

"Do not panic. Pass this message on quickly down the line." The professor instructed the man closest to him. The man was shocked and tried to grasp Fabio's steady words, *Come on.* Fabio demanded, "Snap out of it man and listen to me, do not look alarmed, and smile," he said while looking at the scientist. *Smile for God's sake, keep smiling at them.* He prayed, turning his head and grinning widely at the irate warriors around him.

Some of the men understood and quickly began copying the expedition leader, all smiling even though they did not feel happy. Fabio started speaking through his clenched bright white teeth like a ventriloquist and said, "Keep smiling boys."

Appearing quite relaxed, the professor's authority was not in question, Fabio quietly continued his guidance to the others, with their lives hanging in the balance. If they were going to survive the next few moments, he needed their help, *right now.*

"I know this is difficult men, *smile* at them, *as wide as possible* and wave slowly. Come on, copy me." He used slow open gestures and the others watched then followed his lead. Staying completely calm, the older man demonstrated why Fabio was chosen to be the expedition leader. "Look, I'll show you." Fabio began waving to the hostile natives, his eyes fixed and steady onto the nearest one, knowing that at any second this eye contact might signal his own last moments, and that of his besieged expedition.

Jesus let's all just smile! The leader's brain cells igniting like new spark plugs, each nerve on knife's edge and in these combusting moments of life self-preservation there it was, self-doubt.

Unfortunately, ambiguity began creeping into his mind, *this is taking too long! Christ, I do not think this is working. Damn them, are they going to kill us all! I must… keep…grinning… I must...* his confidence was stalling. Fabio's face began extenuating even more with a wonderful smile.

Gesture was everything to these people and at last to Fabio's obvious relief the rest of the expedition members were also doing the same.

Everyone could see that Fabio's appearance was completely one of fellowship and friendship like a practiced missionary.

Taking his wooden staff out of the water the leader took a deep breath through his smiling teeth and began walking slowly towards the nearby warrior. No threat was made by his staff, who were only used as support, slowly sunk into the water below his ankles while he began strolling leisurely forward. Greeting them loudly to be heard over their din, the deadly distance closing.

Fabio's hands opening in a friendly gesture of good fortune although inside him it felt much different. His confidence faltering by the second. From somewhere deep inside him he defied failure and tried to ignore this lethal firing squad of blowpipes tracking him as he moved inch by inch towards them.

"We come as friends!" Fabio shouted loudly. "We come as friends! We are friends. We come in friendship. Hello, we come in peace, can you help us?" Fabio kept repeating the same simple message over and over again.

Counting the numbers of aggravated warriors, Fabio counted six in front; some he knew were out of sight, maybe twenty or more on either side. Some were also at the rear of the column. The expedition's last stand would be pitiful.

The nervous scientists mimicked Fabio, watching him anxiously while he approached the indigenous natives. The bedlam just got noisier, and it looked like these men could not be reasoned with. His tactics were not working.

Fabio, Mathieson and Carmello knew that this encounter was not going well, a last-ditch effort of bravery, each man nodding to each other and began moving together in slow synchronization to face the natives. Fabio closed the gap with a light brown warrior holding a large blade with strange bright blue razor-sharp edges that caught Fabio's attention.

Fabio wondered, *strange luminous blade he's got, but is he calming down?* Continuing with slow friendly gestures he began speaking in a gentler low voice. *Is it my imagination or are they shouting less?*

"Hello, hello, hello, we come in peace, I am Fabio. My name is Fabio."

Leaving his staff stuck in the marsh, they continued with both hands open and then widened his arms to demonstrate that he had no weapons. Fabio spoke in a broken South American Indian accent, praying that this linguistic mishmash had better work.

The closest warrior appeared to be the leader of the tribe, an older warrior; his chest marked with large tattoos, an angry face painted red and blue with waved streaks. The other natives were much younger, their faces yellow and red in colour. Some had short beards and short hair, and all had a tribal hoop through their noses.

Mathieson, anxious not to offend him, seemed to be floundering somewhat with one of the warriors, the native becoming increasingly more frustrated and unable to understand the black American's broken accent, a mixture of Spanish and English.

Carmello on the other hand spoke best with one of the young warriors close to him, the only native who had a red band on his forehead with amulets to match. Then as suddenly as the tribe appeared and began shouting, their angry voices unexpectedly stopped. Everything became calm, settled.

The young warrior extended his hand and shook Carmello's firmly. The boy became instantly at ease with the guide, as if they were equal and united in a brotherhood.

Phew! Thought Fabio looking around, *that was too damn close,* relief instantly seen on everyone's faces, native and explorer alike!

Loud laughter suddenly overtook everything, instantly ensuing new friendships, echoing a lighter more jovial atmosphere throughout the jungle. The young man with the red band on his forehead shouted and articulated his authority to the older native, both speaking quickly in an accent that only Carmello could guess.

Carmello was born in Brazil, part Indian and part Portuguese. The forty-three-year-old guide was fluent in many languages and appeared to be able to comprehend enough to communicate in their unique language. *Break through!* Fabio's relieved face brightened and began really laughing this time with the natives.

The youngest man appeared to be around fifteen or sixteen years of age and more important than Fabio first thought, the boy gripped both him and Mathieson at the same time. His exceptionally strong large hands shaking each man in complete friendship almost as if were long lost friends but neither of them connected or bonded best as he did with their Indian guide.

The atmosphere between both cultures had suddenly changed, and the relieved scientists became noticeably surprised, their body language becoming visibly more relaxed, helping ease any worry for whatever was going to happen next.

The natives began gesturing for them to follow, the boy leading the way. More rustling and other warriors began appearing out of the long grass behind them, their long blowpipes lowered. It seemed best to go along with it. Soon everyone was quickly walking together. The natives seemed to skip happily along beside the stressed-out expedition.

Some of the natives insisted taking their packs and heavy loads and soon others appeared pulling their llamas that had scattered. The young leader hiked up ahead so pleased with himself. He moved nimbly like a gazelle and began running and dancing with delight. Fabio gripped Carmello's shoulder in comradeship.

"Thank you Carmello," said Fabio, recognizing his guide's true importance in saving all their lives. "I think we have just survived our first encounter with these forgotten people, believe it or not, they are friendlier than I could have hoped for."

Not often did it happen, and with the great Fabio, his face expressing his utmost gratitude and relief. The guide acknowledged this complement and could not help himself grinning mutually with Fabio.

"Friendlier than you had hoped for? Did you expect to come across these people in your plan then professor?" suspicious, Mathieson probed Fabio.

"Friendly, for headhunters. That's what I meant," Fabio said while changing his tune and becoming aloof once more.

The natives began singing, their melodic notes, happy, tuneful and truly the ice between them was broken. Both parties moved quickly through the rainforest. Two days later from the marshes the forest opened onto higher ground, it was a large clearing. There it was right in front, the native village!

Constructed using wood and bamboo, the huts standing high above the ground using thick wooden pillars would protect the people from roaming wild animals and rising floodwater. The rooves were green with jungle coverage through which campfire smoke rose.

More excited than ever the young leader ran on ahead to what looked like the biggest tree house near the centre. Seeing them arrive, younger children and women came out to greet the warriors and at first displayed a vague curiosity at the strange visitors, before surrounding them for a better look. The expedition was then quickly hustled away towards a large bushy tree house.

Numerous animals were kept in pens such as pigs and other small animals. Strange looking big chicken-like fowls were running madly around in and out of the pens. They had small yellow heads with long thin beaks and large bulging eyes; the bird groomed with short shiny red and blue-purple plumage. It could easily be a species they had never seen before. There was no telling what type of bird this was.

The fowl gave out odd sniffling noises from their beaks and clearly, these birds could not fly. All they could do was run about crazily, hovering with their beaks, digging left and right quicker than the eye could see, a hazy but effective movement continually over the ground.

Christopher thought, *daft looking little creatures, and so much like a jungle vacuum cleaner lifting those bloody insects.* Interested, the keen biotechnologist watched them sucking up multitudes of nefarious-looking arthropods in seconds!

The natives laughed and made friendly gestures to the visitors and encouraged them to climb up the wooden ladders into a tall tree house above their heads. Once up at the top, they were asked to sit down around by a fire burning on top of a large flat stone. Soon each person received food and water.

Inside the hut, a large fine woven wooden chair sat with its carved tall backrest. A few of those odd-looking chickens were company inside this abode, pecking and hovering as they did, all around this long-woven room. It seemed obvious that the tribe's people used these birds as a kind of fly spray to kill all insects. These peculiar- looking birds were very quick and surprisingly nimble and the chances of any insect bites were considerably reduced with these things about!

A large bamboo door opened at the end of the long room and a small dog appeared about the size of a Dalmatian, barking eagerly seeing the group, it dashed fast towards them slipping wildly on the floor, tail wagging excitedly. A tall man then appeared along with the young boy warrior close behind him.

It was difficult to guess the age of the man. His copper toned face looked much like the boys' and old enough to be the father of the boy. He wore a headdress of large colourful feathers, a large cloak with multi-coloured feathers and similar styled underwear.

Ouch, they thought. The distinguished man sat down on the raised wooden throne and commanded his dog to come to heel in a loud voice and they were all surprised that his dialect was pleasing to the ear.

The Chief looked interested and welcomed his odd-looking guests in quick speaking tongue;

his vernacular moved up and down in pitch fluidly and although no one could really understand him, he seemed to be openly friendly and hospitable, gesturing everyone to come closer and meet him.

Everyone shook hands firmly, a sign of trust, all except for the only female visitor of the expedition. The Chief looked past Harjit and did not acknowledge her presence. The girl not offended by the man's ways guessed that this was his custom. The young woman could not help herself smiling pleasantly at the older man, although her thoughts of a mischievous school girl made her imagine what the men in the expedition might look like, if they all had to wear those same strange looking woody sheaths the Chief and others were wearing on top of their groins.

Suppressing her deep desire to laugh, the urge came out with a nervous chuckle as the older man brushed past with his rustling stylish attire.

What a camera shot for National Geographic that would make, if only. Harjit grinning from ear to ear while staring at the other men who cast eyes of disapproval at her. Nobody could understand what the medical student was finding so funny.

The Chief introduced his young son and spoke his son's name as *Zoujaxtoni,* who they had already met. The boy immediately began to articulate his father's words, taking over as an official interpreter. Sitting down with a grin the Chief was apparently also amused at the sight of his oddly over-dressed guests.

The boy gestured and named his father as *Lizerif*. Conversation ensued lasting over an hour with Carmello talking the most, in useful dialog between the boy, Fabio and the tribal leader. The others sat at the back listening from the other end of the room.

In a pleasant tone, the tribal leader spoke to his son throughout and with much laughter. Other tribesmen had since climbed into the house after the visitors, stood at the back of the large room and were laughing with the Chief.

The Chief got on very well with Carmello who seemed to be naturally more at ease with these friendly people who were known as the *Zaplithowatres*.

After this meeting the explorers were taken to another similar large treetop hut for rest, it was not far away from that of the Chief's house. Their new abode was given in honour and respect as newcomers.

"When do you think we will get something else to eat, we finished that lot off earlier, I'm bloody starving?" Dr. Christopher Hrycuik asked.

"Mmm, smells like they are cooking something good right now," Fabio concurred.

"Great! Listen, what's that? It sounds like they are shouting up to us!" Christopher's tone ready to go.

"Si, they are shouting at us alright, to join them for dinner. Someone is coming!" Carmello advised, "Food." They got up gingerly, all their faces eager to join the tribe.

****

In the lively darkness, the tribesmen sat eating around several large campfires at the centre of the village. Women wore orange grass skirts with no tunics on top, exposing their bare flat chests. They were busy providing meals for the men. The women called the visitors to come down from the house and attend dinner then went to collect them. Everyone by this time was completely ravenous, having not eaten properly since the morning. There was laughter and merriment as the scientists appeared. Whatever they were cooking smelled delicious! A feast fit for a king, they were delighted to be special guests and sat expectantly on the ground in a large mixed group and received the main delicacy *in their honour*.

There was a type of meaty broth in a large pot bubbling nicely, a variety of vegetables and copious amounts of tubers boiling in tasty juices. Staring a little closer to a large bowl next to the pot, an odd expression came over the expedition members' faces. Each person's eyes widened. Presented before them was the tribe's main delicacy, cooked, colossal maggots!

These grubs had been freshly killed and cooked after being harvested from the decaying trees outside the village, and each good for eating. Best ones were those about three or four inches long and full of a nourishing juicy fluid. It would take them some time to empty the bowl. Tonight, well they had nothing better to do, except eat!

The explorer's stony faces painted a peculiar picture to the amused tribe's people, trying to understand the foreigners' apparent hesitation, especially since they had looked so hungry. Their eagerness dampened after climbing down from the treetop while eyeing their meals with repugnance. The newcomers stared at each other with half-hearted smiles. *Who would go first?* In the firelight, the tribes' people were not sure - did the newcomers' skin tone change colour?

"What's this? Yuck." Christopher sighed a moan, his eyebrow raised a little with a nervous twitch, then raised a little more alarmed as large maggots of sizable portions were put on the largest leaf and given to him. Christopher whispered to the expedition leader for guidance, "Fabio, er, its slop."

If ever the young man needed some leadership, it was right now. The women managed to scoop out the wood pulp from the same trees while harvesting the grubs. This was used to produce thick slurry resembling a bowl of porridge, minus the flavour. Everyone accepted the hospitality.

"Grubs up, Chris." Carmello chuckling a little at their awkward dinner.

"Fine food, young man, fine food." Fabio smiled with satisfaction, being much more at ease learning the *Zaplithowatres'* ways and customs. Christopher and the others were not as overly enthusiastic or impressed by this culinary vision as Fabio was.

"Eat hearty Chris; eat hearty." The banter bursting from Carmello who began laughing loudly at him and the others, "Eat and enjoy!" And then he laughed with the excited natives even more, who were simply overjoyed at being hosts.

Carmello joked again and was back to his old self, the sounds of their laughter were genuine. The women on the other hand were curious as to why these newcomers showed an apparent lack of appetite? They could not understand the tentative, fingering of their meals when, only moments before they had all looked so hungry.

Hoping not to offend their gracious hosts, the group tried their best to ease over the maggots, some deciding it best to chew them quickly and then wash the remains away. While others decided to hold their breath and swallow rapidly as possible, no messing about, but it did not help. The bread pulp was a starchy food with no taste. It gave little incentive between chewing and sucking the thick fluid out from these giant maggots. The stew even though it did smell good, their appetites had lost all sharpness because they could not shake off the distinctive strong taste from those grubs!

The men all drank a distinctive brew, akin to a warm beer that made things a little more palatable and light-headed, thank God. What really began to bother them was something else, and as they ate their nutritious protein meals, staring over at the bubbling pot, there was plenty left. *Oh no, tomorrow's breakfast!*

****

In the coming weeks and months living with these friendly people, they became good friends, the Zaplithowatres happily taught Fabio's party how to survive and learn their indigenous ways of hunting by using dogs to catch rats and other such rodents.

Finding out about their history and culture proved one thing, and there appeared to be no evidence of human sacrifice or grim shrunken heads. It was the women who took members of the expedition into the forest with their stone axes and foraged for food.

On one such hunting trip, the women took Christopher, Carmello and another companion named Kees Acampilchtl, a Brazilian government official, who was on the trip to oversee the expedition.

New laws had insisted that he be with them. His job was to ensure that the expedition did not exploit his country, in terms of bio-piracy and exploit the country's own culture's historical wealth. The government's new policy would help keep companies and individuals in check, with heavy financial penalties and even imprisonment if anyone was found guilty trying to steal what were natural resources and historical importance. Yet without him, there would be no expedition, his attendance was mandatory.

Kees, an amateur archaeologist and lay scientist in his own right, could shut down the expedition if there was any sign of exploitation or impropriety.

During the trip, all three men overheard women talking although it was only Carmello and Kees who could grasp this in parts, speaking their unusual language about an old tale. A tale of a mysterious temple was found somewhere much further into the forest. Fabio appeared surprised watching Carmello's growing uneasiness.

"We heard them speaking of a temple that only appears after six to eight or more generations, called the *Temple of MalisIblis, or Nombre of the Dead.*" Carmello swallowed a hidden thought and continued, "To others it is called the Devil's temple." He added in a faded whisper, the man was afraid to mention its last name.

"What?" Fabio's face lifted with keen curiosity at this news.

"Si, this is what we heard," Carmello acknowledged.

"That would mean that if there were eight generations, and the life span of an average native might be sixty years, then that would make each sighting of the temple to be every five hundred years!" Fabio concluded looking inspired.

"Crazy, every five hundred years!" Kees gobsmacked, could not believe what was being suggested. "What kind of temple does that? How old do you think this native civilization has existed? I mean, if they know this structure appears periodically," Kees paused a little considering the wild consequences, "and even if I believed this extraordinary story, that would suggest many generations have already passed."

"How many?" Fabio pressed.

"If the temple had been observed only twice then that would make this tribe's roots more than a thousand years old! The whole thing is quite absurd, impossible. Nothing disappears to reappear every five hundred years, it must only be a fable!' Kees dismissed it, disappointedly knowing the unreality of the legend.

"Not so stupid, comets come and go periodically." Carmello added, "Regular as clockwork."

"Maybe more than twice and that would make them ancient descendants indeed. If this temple really exists, then its disappearance can be more rationally explained." Fabio's tone was clear, "It's simply become lost in the undergrowth and dense vegetation. In my mind it's the only logical assumption." Fabio stated, "I would expect that some of the generations of this tribe might even forget where it is located. Inevitably lost again for another five hundred years." Fabio's tone was certain, without question. Christopher nodded in agreement with Fabio because it was the only rational explanation. Carmello was not so sure.

"They are very good hunters and partially nomadic." Carmello volunteered with less certainty, but he already knew these peoples' best traits, "They are not the forgetful type."

"Once the women realized we were listening in on them, they all fell quiet. I assume that they should not have spoken about it." said Christopher.

"Very interesting, where is the temple?' Fabio turned and asked the men quizzically, watching their dumbfounded faces. "Mmm, thought so," he said with a lacerated sigh that hurt their inadequate report.

"We do not know. What we *do know* is this. The temple has been seen again. *And, this is such a year*." Carmello solemnly volunteered.

"It is only a legend." Christopher put the story into perspective batting ill rebuke back to the expedition leader.

"Quite." Kees corroborating the foolishness of getting worked up over here-say and gossip. He had never heard of this legend.

"I'll talk to the Chief tonight and ask him what he knows." said Fabio. What he did not mention to the others was that he already knew of this fabled story.

Professor Mancini decided to ask Lizerif what he knew of this mysterious place, to try and persuade the Chief of the tribe to help him find the temple for its historical and cultural importance. In fact, if he approached the subject the right way then maybe his people would guide the expedition to the temple. It would bring him and his people immediate prosperity. The importance of such a discovery like this, would make not only this country know of the existence of a new civilization but the whole world! Kees was easily won over with this idea; even if the story was unfounded, he could see the economic benefits straight away. Tourism alone would bring much wealth to his country remembering that Machu Picchu was built by the Incas.

****

Later that evening inside the Chief's home, after dinner Fabio, Kees and Carmello all sat together with Lizerif and the son Zoujaxtoni.

"Why have you come?" The Chief sat proudly up an arched back an asked politely using his son as a go between, linking the language and culture barrier between them with surprising ease.

"We have come to ask about the lost temple, the Temple of MalisIblis, also known as *Nombre of the Dead*. I—Fabio was unable to finish his sentence.

The Chief immediately shook his head in swift retribution, raising his hand to mute the intrusive newcomer. Fabio took a deep breath. The bewildered old man cast a look that press-ganged the professor into an uncertain silence. Taboo would be an understatement! Obviously, this subject was something he did not want to speak about and for an awkward moment, a deathly silence threatened the peace.

Fabio showed acute anxiety and apology in his awkward posture as he knew that he had overstepped his welcome. They may be deemed to have become troublemakers. Fabio felt rising nausea in the pit-of-his stomach, gauging the Chief's instant transformation. The severe backhanded expression for crossing an unseen boundary told it all, washing away any new friendships which left the Chief with a stony suspicion as he measured the professor for his real intent.

Is this why my new children have come to me? Thought the Chief. *Have they come from the forest to win my favour and take advantage of my family, my people and my friendship?*

His son appeared shocked rather than suspicious, he did not know which way his father would react; there was much more to tell because the boy was scared and astonished that these newcomers had heard of the temple.

A long sigh eventually came from the leader of the Zaplithowatres tribe; the embers in his eyes cooled to freezing towards Fabio.

Fabio held the older man's icy eyes. The Chief gestured with his open hands showing great concern for this bad news and foolhardy adventure. He began speaking gravely to his *new sons* while the boy interpreted his father's gravid fears.

"A legend," Zoujaxtoni lowered his voice to no more than a whisper, his tone implied great danger. Suspicious in case he might be overheard by someone or something in the dark forest, something not human. "It is a bad prophecy. My father has never seen it. He has heard of its existence from old stories. My new sons," the boy narrated while the Chief began speaking in short sentences choosing his words carefully. "My father says this: "I cannot say its evil name. I am your father and I have taken you all as my *new sons*. I plead with you never look for this place. My people have not seen it and yet we all know that *it has returned*. This is such a year as told by our *Quipu*. The forest moans at its appearance in the Iblis vale. Legend it is." Looking at them with gravid eyes, "Yet some things are certain. If you find this place and if God favours you, then *death will come as comfort*." The boy swallowed finishing his interpretation, "There are things inside that place, much worse than death," he finished watching his father's fearful eyes.

The Chief bent towards the group from his chair gesturing for only Fabio to come closer. In a low tone, he spoke into one ear. The boy listened to relay his father's grim warning.

"*Some things should remain undisturbed and unfound, there are things that must never be awakened.*" He gave the professor one final warning. The boy mimicked the Chief word for word, "Only evil will be your friend in that lonely place, *my sons*."

The Chief arose slowly as if weary and with a solemn heart, and the conversation was over. The great man read Fabio's eyes, leader to leader. Lizerif's face twisted in pain as he looked in Fabio's eyes. Before him, he saw his new son's *death.*

With stooped shoulders the older man bid them a sound sleep and retired. Once his father had left, the young boy pleaded and warned his special brother Carmello, not to go, never to look for that terrible place. It was a fearful quest. Zoujaxtoni was deeply troubled for his new brother's safety. He knew that they would find it.

The boy waved farewell and climbed down to the ground, they watched him go quickly into the tall majestic rain forest. Faraway they could hear an ominous rumble of thunder, getting much closer with each passing minute.

Disappointed they had not found anything more positive from the older man, the group left the Chief's home and retired back to their house, accompanied by a flash of lightening shooting unrestrained energy across the sky. More thunder followed, rumbling the beginning of a storm.

****

After a few more weeks living with the natives, it was nearing their time to depart from the village. Another beautiful day dawned in the rainforest, the smells of lush greenery and fresh flowers looked up towards the early morning sunlight with bright anticipation. The air perfumed mixtures better than anything man could ever hope to make. The Zaplithowatres planned something special for them.

Walking together they all headed happily to a secluded place hidden far away in the forest. Without warning, a clearing opened to a large and spectacular pond. Everything was large; large in colour and life, from water lilies to jumping fish.

Everyone stood astounded staring in all directions. Up above skywards they all looked in wonder and heard many colourful birds flying around this exclusive habitat, living their lives with an eagerness for the wing and an electrified excitement.

Massive cobwebs trapped the lively sunlight warming its silvery dew on silk. The warm energies created a light gossamer haze that expanded like a shy phantom through rainbow lit patches with webs acting like flawless filters, masks of silkiness that produced a multitude of colours spreading out like a godly gate. Around the pond, the webs hung from tree to tree vibrating like a nervous fence shaking in the soft breeze.

This divine and wondrous place was more beautiful than words could say. Walking on through a large web it appeared to dissolve on touch. They had stepped into the Garden of Eden!

Soon they all gathered around this magical clear pond, fresh water so pure that it must have godly qualities. Here they waited, listening first to the natural sounds before a grand ceremony began in their honour. They were leaving.

Much music and merriment were made of this day with old tribal songs and lively traditional dance. The native women and tribesmen all bidding them farewell for their new *adopted sons,* from the *outer forests!*

These people had produced a surprisingly pleasant type of wine and seemed red as any bottle of Garnet, but much nicer to the palate. A lively free taste with a lovely full-bodied bouquet fermented from small red water lily, with a luminous purple and translucent white rim border that they could see floating freely in the nearby ponds.

The tribal ale seemed to taste of honey nectar! Zoujaxtoni came up to Christopher as he turned smiling at this wonder, noticing he was being honoured once more and given an extra helping of tribal delicacy to eat! Carmello chuckled.

The group stirred, their hearts felt a tinge of regret listening to a newly composed song, one made especially for them, sad and melodic, a symphony of sounds amid the birds and buzzes, all magically harmonizing in the striking flora. The music was a mixture of magical flutes, panpipes, maracas, musical bows and charangos. The sound was stirring to the spirit, Harjit and Christopher unexpectedly sobbing together. Unknown to them they played this sadness for their continuing quest.

Next day everyone assembled in the Chief's hut. Remembering that this was where they all had first met, here again and for the last time the young boy, the Chief's son appeared to say farewell.

Zoujaxtoni greeted and bid them to follow him into a larger room, which they had not been permitted to enter until now. Cautiously they wondered what was inside.

There stood Zoujaxtoni's father, Chief Lizerif, standing and wearing all his ceremonial attire and smiling proudly at them. He gestured everyone forward with his powerful arms to view what looked like a complex of knotted strings.

An arrangement of strings thick and thin of many rich colours; tones of deep red, sharp blues and a long and thick main one, made of shiny metallic gold. From it, two were silver, a third deep red with a thin silver thread within it and the forth a very short white one. Numerous subsidiary strings came off curved strings knotted onto the main cord. Fabio instantly recognised it as a *quipu*.

The Chief sighed quietly knowing that this was a special moment.

"Si, it is a three-dimensional system of knots." advised Kees, "Many colours and varying lengths of string. All representing a numbering system; a numeric code describing their history." Kees was familiar with things such as this that are displayed in national museums. *Encryption*, thought Christopher.

"Might be, but I think in this case, it is more accurately a family record, a family tree." Fabio guessed, staring at no less than thirty-thousand knotted strings.

"Come and stand by my father and I will tell you his words," the boy encouraged as the whole team of sixteen entered.

The group assembled together, and stood looking a bit uncertain, not knowing quite what to expect as the Chief began pointing at the main golden cord. His tone conveyed sincerity, as his son narrated for him once more. The boy watched his father's thick fingers point and flow through his ancestry, gliding slightly above the main golden cord of the quipu,

"My father is showing you a complex of predictions and a legend all wrapped into the history of our people. The golden line is the oldest, *most noble of noble bloodlines*. My father does not know how old it is, but it is ancient. It is a different bloodline from ours and yet is part of our history. This quipu was passed down to him by his father's father and in turn given to him by the Khipukamayuq, known as the *Knot Keeper*. It goes back many thousands of years".

The boy stopped talking and looked up at the people who were by now dumbfounded, everyone staring at the large table where the quipu sat. The golden line was very long, starting at the left as a shorter string at right angles to the main. The Chief demonstrated by moving his finger down vertically and then along the extensive horizontal piece to finish at right angles and downwards vertically again.

"*My goodness, this is a real privilege.*" whispered Harjit.

"This bloodline is as ancient as earth itself, and as old as the temple you seek. The knots, they tell the tale of when the temple appears. Each knot represents every, as you would understand it to be, æon. Many of these as you can see with your own eyes have come and gone. The golden line has ended this year, with the final knot at the end," said the boy.

"My God it's older than the Pharaohs!" Fabio gasped.

"My father says," the boy watched his father's finger go down a long red string with hundreds of knots, "this is my bloodline." The room went silent as the Chief's brown finger moved to the silver. "And of the people who came out from the temple, one line has ended, and one *continues*."

They were astonished at what was said about a people from the temple, and seeing their knotted line end, and another one trailing long and open.

How long is a length of string, Fabio wondered? Everyone carefully watched the Chief go to the only white string, it appeared different, with no colour. Whiter than white and newer. Fabio counted fifteen, which raised his eyebrow. *Its end is knotted... Merda!*

"There are fifteen knots, one for each of his new sons." The boy swallowed.

The air was still as a held breath. The room fell silent. Measuring his new family, the Chief nodded with approval, and in his eyes, they saw *sadness*.

"It is an honour, oh great Chief," said Fabio. Even the professor felt humble in this man's eminence. The Chief's son conveyed to his father the professor's honest sentiment and he smiled kindly towards Fabio. Lizerif stood, Chief of Zaplithowatres! The Chief extended his strong hand, shaking each person in a strange albeit, special and fraternal way, including Harjit! It was a friendship and bond of everlasting brotherhood.

Fabio's mind was disturbed yet calm, *what has the old man seen?* Hints of hesitation settled into his nerves due to the Chief's grim prediction that did not favour their return. It was time to go.

****

The hard-working group of archaeologists and scientists had already discovered ancient buildings in other parts of South America, so they knew what signs to look for. Fabio never spoke of his surreptitious holy orders to anyone in the group, the less they knew the better. After spending about six or seven weeks with the mysterious Zaplithowatres, they managed to learn some of their ways living with nature.

A people who were nomads in the forest for part of the year and the rest of the time lived back at their village. They were the last of their kind, a once noble people coming from great ancestral stock. Their gene pool diluted over time eventually had become headhunters long ago, although this practice had been stopped in the last centuries after the days of the Portuguese and Spanish Conquistadores. The legend that was told, was only to the children and by the Chief of the village. It was then that those Conquistadores had heard of the fearful legend and would torture the natives to tell them more. Their greed for gold too strong and any warnings given to them were not heeded. The legend, spoken about only once, was not to be spoken about outside of their own people. The Chief would make children fearful to ensure they swear an oath of silence, and never to speak of this to anyone. This way, the legend would not be forgotten but because of the Conquistadores years before, rumours about it had moved out of the forest.

Weeks later they set up camp again for the night, by now much further inside the rainforest and far away from the Zaplithowatres. Another hard day over, everyone was exhausted. Wearily inside the privacy of his tent, Christopher sighed and began writing in his journal.

My Journal. June Year 5.125 Mayan time.

This year seems most fitting and fun for such a mysterious and worthwhile journey, and yes of course I am using the Mayan calendar! We are all very thrilled. It has been six weeks since marching from our temporary tree-top home and that the tale was told. It seemed to be much more distressing to the indigenous people, and yet strangely enough, it is tied in with some of the scribes already known to my holy order. We have been told nothing of these by Fabio. He has something to hide, and that, I'm sure of!

The temple is a place of mystery amid mysteries and I feel there is much more to find out. Why are the Zaplithowatres so frightened? I do not understand, maybe they do not know themselves or have simply forgotten what the legend really means. Myths are born from forgotten legends and this is a dark myth that should never have been, forgotten.

There were stories of a lost temple holding great wealth of ancient secret knowledge. The Chief did not want us to find this place. The legend says, that only on every, One Thousand Equinoxes would then the temple be found. My guess is, if the legend is to be believed, then the last time the temple was seen would be about five hundred years ago, back at the time of the Spanish and Portuguese Conquests. There is much more, there must be. How exciting! A myth becomes legend once again. We will find the truth, and of that I am certain!"

This myth was much older than even the Zaplithowatres knew! The truth lay ahead.

****

CHAPTER VI

END OF THE WORLD

Having climbed increasing numbers of steep ascents, broken through numerous barriers and fought vicious vines with blood poisoning thorns, the expedition was still remarkably on route. They had not yet discovered the entrance-way into the secret valley of MalisIblis, or so they thought. Christopher took over the lead to head up the expedition.

"God, this place is a complete mind fuck!" Swore Christopher, the young brilliant scientist and unconventional Catholic priest, Dr. Hrycuik. He found no problem inventing ungodly anger with *no mincing of words*, and what could be described as a not so different, plain talking Presbyterian minister! Even Christopher would admit that his own untamed fury came from his mixed upbringing. Especially here, his choice words helped him carve an almost straight path through the Amazonian rainforest.

After hours of torture, all his earlier enthusiasm for finding new species of flora and fauna was for the moment furthest from his mind. He was normally able to tune into his environment but today everything seemed mundane. In front of him were just masses upon masses of more tedium, thick and unending vegetation and he was incessantly engulfed by abundant amounts of foliage. His tired sweaty body screamed for rest. Mind-numbed and bored he kept on going like a machine, cutting a narrow channel for the others. Fabio and Mathieson followed him with the pack animals helping to widen their route. They would take over lead soon.

Slashing left, hacking right, the boy priest trampled down everything he could. Uneasily lifting his leg one way then positioning it awkwardly down on the next, and any moment his ankle was gripped by unmovable vines throwing him off balance and again tripping him into another curse.

Frustration knew no bounds. To his right, a large cheese plant leaf unexpectedly swept across his path, smacking him on the face.

Slap!

"Shit!" he shouted, enraged again at the large heavy leaf stubbornly blocking his way. It blinded him but he was past caring and continued regardless. Not sure of his footing, he stumbled once again, "Shit!" He shouted.

"Shit!" He whacked away more of the insult with his machete.

Slash! Slash! Moving on, slash, slash, slash! Not to be beaten, he was determined not to stop.

It must be someone else's turn soon...
Christopher could not go on much longer. He was right, the men behind him were about to take over

when suddenly he lost his footing and begun slipping.

"Shit!" Christopher slipped again stumbling a little, losing his balance and heard a sickening noise from under his feet. His heart sank when something else broke.

Crunch… he dropped out of site! With no chance to even react, Chris was now gone; disappearing like a magician's illusion

Christopher suddenly disappeared right in front of the two men's astonished eyes when a hole suddenly opened and swallowed him whole, just like a giant mouth. Vanishing from the expedition, he began a ride to hell shooting down below, falling and sliding through a fast chute of lavish vegetation. Only the two stunned men saw what had really happened.

In seconds Christopher travelled fast, dropping hundreds of feet, hitting an incredible speed like a bobsleigh as he tumbled far from the rest of the expedition.

Belated realisation and in partial shock, the men began shouting after him. The group looked down the chute and could only hear his fading calls, a lonely voice getting further and further away, below far into the green depths and out of sight.

"Wait! Wait, watch out!" Fabio shouted a warning to the others, "Take your time, not too close!" The professor called to the others attempting to hold off his worried colleagues. As he did so, precariously he was also being pushed by the gathering group behind him, knocking his body involuntarily towards the hole.

Fabio scrambled out of their way to prevent ending up like the unfortunate young man and re-positioned himself behind the fraught people while the group jumbled forward in a crazy haste, to listen to Chris's fading calls. The young man was already a great distance away.

****

Christopher's scary slide unstoppable, the young man desperately attempted to keep balanced and face up the best he could. But ill luck made his slide even faster.

"Shit! Shit!" Christopher Hrycuik held nothing back, cursing in blind panic as he had no idea where he was going. "What the, aah!" He shouted in his helplessness. He looked left and right and around at the fast passing blurry vegetation.

It was hard to see and he was caught in a nightmare that crashed him downwards through grass and mud, large leaves and small branches slapped at his reddening face. He stuck his hands out for protection. The acceleration dizzied his mind, it could only end one way, badly.

Knowing that the worst would hit him any second, his mind mentored him, *I must keep my balance. Keep my knees bent and dig my boots into the surface. Slow down. Watch out for boulders.* He kept telling himself all of this while at the same time thought, where *the fuck am I going?*

"*Oh!*" he shouted out his dread knowing survival may depend on a split-second choice. *What is this, bloody hell! Keep calm and keep your head up, I am going to make it!* Christopher tried but he couldn't push away his own self-doubt.

Twenty seconds had passed and by now he was free falling out of control, sliding helplessly further away. He tried to think more clearly, concentrating hard while ignoring the pain. Instinctively he knew that at the end of this slippery railroad, it would be a one-way ticket to certain death.

Trepidation grew in his mind knowing the channel could easily lead to a vertical drop off a cliff. *Shit this is it… God help me!*

"*Ahh!*" He knew his ride was over. His feet shot downwards into the empty air. He dropped with a sudden bump, mud and foliage continued his roller-coaster ride again and in a different direction.

"Oh no!" He shouted more, his body passed over loose mossy surfaces that greased him, helping to reduce his friction burns. His hands were not quite so lucky, all cut up as he tried desperately grabbing onto whatever plants he could, anything to *slow down.*

Still moving, covered in broken plants and dirt, his eyes blazed wide while he watched like a spectator in full horror, with his journey about to end. Up ahead he could see his ultimate demise coming fast and straight at him. With grim realization, he hurdled towards the grey light which led him towards the end of the track.

He exploded unceremoniously out of the breaking foliage and flew in free flight like a rocket. He travelled through grey mists with an airy weightless feeling, dropping through a light cloud and fell tumbling towards the inevitable. Chris screamed.
Death awaited.

Plunging straight into a pool of thick mud, with a sudden jolt that winded his yell, mud blasted in every direction. Christopher was stunned into a daze and slowly lifted his head. He was astonished that his railroad to hell was finally over. The drop short, he had landed on top of a dipped plateau waste deep in thick mud.

Confused but alive, he gathered strands of thoughts together and looked around at his brown surroundings while checking himself for any serious injuries. He sunk a little further into this stinking mud.

Knowing that his danger was not over in this mess, and surrounded by shrubs and buzzing insects, he got up, grabbed onto a long branch and eventually got out. Bruised and cut he lay flat exhausted on top of dry ground. Miraculously he managed to somehow smile, resting heavily and shaking his head in disbelief.

"Thank you, God." Christopher laughed at his good fortune as a light mist swirled around him, evaporating quickly in the sultry heat.

The dissipating cloud soon exposed more of the surrounding foliage. Yet everything in front of him remained opaque and unseen. He did not trust what he could not see. With no greenery in front of him, his smile vanished like receding water vapour as the blanket of grey ahead shifted with an eeriness of empty space beyond.

The grey cloud started rolling back and moving further away, when it magically vaporised from his view. Gone. He was left mud-caked and his jaw dropped while staring at the unveiled landscape. With mixed fears and relief sweeping over him, he observed his new environment and realised that he might have fallen more.

"Fuck, me." His mind quickly sharpened with a smile at the realisation of his narrow escape. *I am alive.* Christopher's natural white teeth stood out brilliantly in contrast to his dirty exterior. Half-groaning and half-laughing, he felt a sudden euphoric surge of happiness go through him. Ten minutes later he heard his companions getting closer.

****

Mashir, his companion, was first to appear to the rescue. The others were much further behind and he was so relieved to see his friend in one piece, alive and in such a mess. Seeing that he was fine he began laughing, enjoying this moment of his unkempt friend.

Christopher's pride was the thing that was bruised the most. He moaned while rubbing his sore posterior with some degree of embarrassment.

Blushing in a deep red colour disguised by his muddy short-cropped beard. Christopher scratched his black marine-like haircut that was styled with distinctive tram lines cut near his mud-splattered scalp. His handsome fine-featured face, albeit completely filthy, remained unscathed with only a few minor cuts. They needed to be looked at as soon as possible.

"Nice face pack, trying to improve our complexion, are we?" Mashir's smile and laughter taunted him.

"Mmm, what kept you mate?" He ignored the jibe while raising up his hand to meet Mashir, both men pulling up together.

They looked deep into each other's eyes, knowing the outcome could have been much different. Both young men burst into fits of laughter! Looking around studying their new environment, Christopher could not believe where he was.

Wearing long muddy green shorts and a camouflaged short-sleeve shirt to match, Christopher Hrycuik walked to where he had emerged. He had lost something; he stretched down to pick up his brimmed hat. Quickly re-aligning it with a smile, he turned around and began staring past Mashir and at the fast receding mists. At this moment, he saw something quite enormous, unveiled to him like a disparate curtain revealing something extraordinary in the distance.

Christopher questioned his own sanity because out of the murkiness he saw something big. His vision was still unclear, and he stared in the distance in disbelief. *A large hill?*

Where they were standing had become more permanent, perched on a semi open space; a natural break in the jungle which allowed Christopher to observe the rising foliage in front of him. His eye line moved upwards and to what looked like the highest hill and judged it to be between five and seven miles away. The finer details became clearer by the second as the mist vanished.

Perception took substance and Christopher then realised that the foliage on the hill was only a disguise. He mentally defoliated it cutting away its green outer skin. His mind profiled a steep shape.

He was right! Covered under a blanket of trees and shrubs there lay something unnatural, something made with structure and not a hill.

"My God, there it is!" Christopher said. "I have found it! Mashir, look behind you man!" Christopher's eyes crystallised solidly in full amazement at his discovery. The mist vanished and both men stood staring at a far-off colossal structure. The temple!

These were life-changing consequences!

Able to at last observe in every direction, it appeared to be a narrow and steep valley covered with high and almost un-scalable rock-faces. Except for the natural adhesive ability of certain vegetation, those had partially taken root on its shear surfaces, remaining like undaunted green fingers gripping into the stone. Some climbed in parts to great heights, the masses of vines with their uncanny tentacles smothered onto perpendicular rock-faces. Vertical at the highest parts that even with their creeping tenacity, eventually failed with their woody phalanges falling short half way up.

"Behind you!" Warned Christopher.

"*Sorry Christopher?*" Mashir's face morphed, eyes instantly fixed on Christopher's cautionary tone, "Are you alright?" The hazel eyed surveyor was concerned that his friend may have banged his head too hard.

"Yes, I am fine *Mr. Mashir Abdul-Mutaal,*" giving the sharp featured Iranian his full title, "And no thanks to you pal." He said with a facetious and cheeky smile as he pointed to an emerging structure. "Look, turn around. And *what* do you make of that!" Facing each other, Christopher saw it and Mashir felt it.

"I do not see what you do." The sharp featured surveyor's eyes opened wider, a step behind Christopher in mental recognition.

"Playing catch up are we...?" Christopher was so pleased with himself. "This far out, I think it can only be one place. It is the lost Temple of MalisIblis!"

"Praise to Allah!" Replied Mashir. He was a long thin sallow skinned man, always conversing in a polite manner with a proper English accent, which was the most common language spoken between both men and the expedition. Everyone also understood a mix of Italian, Portuguese and Spanish.

Entering the vale, it seemed to be the only way in. Far out of their scrutiny through the vale lay more impenetrable rainforest. Standing here both men felt insignificant and dwarfed by the imposing valley ahead. Thankfully the way further down into the vale did not look quite so steep, as a fast-tracked entry point. Christopher looked curiously at such a discovery; *it's not Mayan, so what civilization constructed it?* There it stood separate and all alone, a mysterious mega-structure, sitting in the middle of *nowhere*.

****

"Is it the ruins that we have been told of?" asked Mashir, "The Nombre of the Dead?" His voice drifted in a dream, then his frustration awakened curiosity, "I cannot make it out as good as you my friend, a hill yes, but a temple I do not see." Mashir's sober eyes scanned the whole area as his concern intensified.

"Lighten up man!" said Christopher. *What's with him...*

"Oh, it's nothing." With fresh new enthusiasm Mashir continued searching the distance for the same sharp image Christopher could apparently see.

The surveyor had a keener eye than most but could not quite pick out the detail of the structure. Straining for more evidence, any evidence! Then suddenly there it was.

"Chris, you *are* right! I see it now, a rough outline yes, you are right! Thank Allah, it is found. It is your discovery Christopher, congratulations!"

"I am happy enough but *it's really not my bag*, it's not that big a deal to me. My work is why I am here. I have *more important reasons than a lost temple*."

"Yes, indeed my friend. I understand you completely, the bugs and drugs. Sorry Chris, my own interest as you know lies in ancient structural design." Mashir recognised that saving millions of lives was a worthier cause than to his own selfish reasons for being here, and in casual words stated simply, "All is as God will's my friend, even unto death."

About twenty minutes later Professor Mancini arrived to join them, him and his team heavily out of breath. Everyone appeared bedraggled because it had not been an easy descent for the group. The animals found it less arduous as they were more adapted for this terrain than their owners.

The temple was mostly camouflaged foliage growing on long stretches of terraces, the actual definition of the structure pyramid. Despite being disguised in thick spongy mosses and low shrubs growing over the higher levels, the professor's expert eye picked the profile of the temple out right away.

"Christopher, said Mashir enthusiastically, "I will climb that tree over there." Mashir volunteered, "I will see from a higher vantage point above. From here, it is definitely a man-made structure."

"Oh, really Mashir! Who else could have built it. Aliens?" Christopher chuckled, "Be careful though," agreed Christopher knowing that the trees grew very high into the canopy.

"Si, we don't want any further mishaps, now do we, Christopher?" The professor could not help ticking the young scientist off for his earlier disappearance.
"With disregard to personal safety Mashir began climbing the nearest tree and was soon lost from view. Fabio was pleased to see that Christopher was in good shape despite being amusingly dirty. Later, Mashir's accelerated voice echoed ground-breaking news.

"On the life of Allah!" his voice echoed, "I think you might be right about this place Chris!" His voice resonated off the trees, "Chris, Fabio it is big, *real big!* It's as high as a thirty-storey building and there's something else. I can make out a sizable geometrical building on top!" The others waited for more information. "Built in stepped edges all the way up," he held their attention,

"Gauging from what I see, maybe six hundred to eight hundred feet high. Can you hear me professor?"

"Yes, go on what else can you distinguish?" Professor Fabio Mancini called with schoolboy excitement; he could not get enough of this wonder.

"There is… *Wow!*" Mashir exclaimed as he almost slipped from his perch in eagerness. The precarious mishap forced him to briefly lower his binoculars as he readjusted his hold on the thick swaying branches. The trees in the woods creaked together in rhythm.

"Well come on!" Impatient for more, Fabio could not contain himself.

"And…" Mashir considered what he was observing.

"Go on!"

"Professor I see a strange tall monolith…covered in vines and…" The surveyor pondered at its intended purpose lifting his binoculars once more, "It has a stone building on top and an altar!"

The rest of the expedition had by now caught up, elated to make such a fantastic find especially after such a demanding and dangerous journey. They would all be well rewarded.

"What else could it be other than the temple? Out here so far away in this wild place?" Doctor Hrycuik stared stonily at Professor Mancini, expecting some sort of recognition or at least a thanks for discovering the lost temple, but the professor's thoughts were miles away.

Lord, if my expedition had been heading further north in this unexplored wilderness, we might have passed this place. Christopher's sudden disappearance was indeed very fortunate. This discovery will make me famous! It is my expedition and I will get full recognition, which is what I have always wanted and deserve.

Giving Christopher no acknowledgment, the professor was too busy secretly planning his own fate and fortune when suddenly his mind jolted back to reality, as Christopher's stupid question sunk in. He ignored it.

"Come down Mashir, well done!" He called upwards. Turning to the group he said, "We proceed down to the valley floor and close in on the temple while daylight is with us. The journey I estimate will take two, three days at most. We can make our base camp next to the temple." The professor pointed in a general direction to a lower flatter green area below them. An unexpected rustle of branches broke his parade when Mashir dropped down and joined the group quicker than expected.

"Do drop in." Said Fabio drolly. The others giggled as the surveyor got up rubbing his sore posterior. The drizzle had moved away from the distance, exposing a high waterfall where it cascaded from over the high rock-faces.

"There is a river or large stream in the distance," Mashir said while waving his hand towards it. 'The source, as you all can now see, is coming from that high waterfall," advised Mashir.

"You can see Signores *and* Signorina; drinking and washing should not be a problem anymore." He smiled pleasantly towards Harjit, who was the only woman on the trip.

"Thank you, Fabio. I expect that the stream passes not far away from it *over there*." The girl drew an imaginary line through the far-off tree line next to the temple.

"Thank the Lord, we have found this place and it looks as though we are going to be here for quite some time to come." The professor began shaking hands with all his elated colleagues in whole-hearted delight as he basked in his crowning glory! At last he now could get on with God's work.

Christopher had made sense of something unnatural about the shape of the temple that led to its discovery, and there was no taking that away from him. Displeased, Christopher frowned at Fabio's mislaid confidence.

****

The journey to the temple took longer than Fabio had planned, the expedition eventually arrived five days later. At last they stood below the enormous building staring at it in complete astonishment, the structure more enormous than first imagined.

Awestruck for a few minutes, Fabio broke the spell by assigning duties to everyone as he realised that it was imperative to establish a base camp as soon as possible. They were all soon pitching tents and were clearing away the immediate area of jungle.

Nearly impossible to make out from afar, the temple was completely camouflaged as it lay beneath a blanket of cloud forest. Anyone could be forgiven for mistaking it for a hill from a distance. The incessant background noise of the waterfalls could be heard crisp and clear, its irrepressible racket resonating everywhere. They would soon get used to it.

Soon after erecting the rudiments of his campsite, Fabio chose Christopher and Mashir to join him in an initial reconnoitre of the temple. The others continued with their unending camp duties, so the small group set off with only one backpack of provisions. Ascending through low shrubs and weaving between treacherous thin long vines, they made headway. The men rested only for brief moments to look around. Their energetic eagerness showed no bounds, what would they discover? Out of breath and elated, they all stood on top and on the very edge of an ancient world, they reached the summit!

Now they stood on top of God's World!

Surveying his new kingdom, Professor Fabio Mancini looked out in triumph. An academic thinker and great genius, he postulated inwardly with smug assurance and certainty of obtaining great recognition. Of that he was sure, as he exhaled a loud sigh of exultation.

I have discovered the Eighth wonder of the World! Fabio was feeling one with God.

From this very high vantage point, four tall stone spires at each corner of the temple were observed. Impressive stone obelisks were standing with purpose and built firm and secure, and demonstrated an unending struggle for supremacy against nature; the clinging vines adhered up the stone columns to strangle them and yet, the forest had not claimed everything.

What seemed like a gigantic mound in the centre of the structure lay hidden, underneath the layers of foliage of fresh greenery was an impenetrable stone pentagonal structure. A structure seamless on each side and of equal length, each wall stretching thirty-three feet wide and rising vertically; exactly sixty-six feet straight up from the height of the main temple roof construction. Unseen from where the men stood on top, was a flat surface that could easily resemble a helipad.

"That large structure next to us is an observatory." Fabio said. He was clearly honoured to be there looking at the overall temple.

And not a stone out of place, I would have expected erosion.

"I'm going over to have a closer look at that mound." Christopher considered the sizable building at the centre of the temple top, but the professor was too captivated. Fabio did not speak immediately; the professor's mind was preoccupied.

"Oh, and that, over there!" He looked towards the different stone obelisk where Christopher was heading for, "It is some sort of massive… *Intiwatana," the Professor burst eagerly.*

"Eh?" Mashir was impressed by his superior's archaeological knowledge, "What's it for?"

"It is a hitching post of the sun," replied Fabio. "This monolith is in a central location and those other larger columns on each corner of the temple are strategically positioned. They are all parts to make a whole system. I am certain they would be used by this civilization's astronomers to observe the heavens.'

"Amazing hypothesis professor, how exactly?" Mashir asked.

"The angles from these four pillars are used to predict the solstices. They are orientated towards the four cardinal points, north, south, east and west. They come to a focal point where Christopher has just about reached." Fabio pointed towards Christopher.

Fascinated, Mashir and Fabio further examined the immediate area while Christopher by this time had jogged over and began climbing up numerous stone rectangles or large steps, like platforms all stacked on top of each other. On top of it all sat a large stone table covered by rich green algae and royal rusty red mosses. Christopher could clearly see below the temple and the forest beyond.

In a perfectly high elevated position like this and directly above Christopher was the *Intiwatana*; a narrow stone monolith rising between twenty and thirty feet high. The stone column was strangled with twisting creepers adhering hard to its surface and nowhere seemed safe from these tenacious growths and coverage of thick mottled green-yellow algae. Christopher knew that this was the same tall structure first observed by Mashir after he climbed the tall trees a few days earlier. Christopher looked around where he stood.

"A sacrificial altar," he whispered to himself. The scientist studied the ancient place. The monolith joined seamlessly onto the bottom slab at the foot of the stone table. Hunching down, he began clearing away the foliage and after about ten minutes stopped to take a breath when something caught his attention. "Christopher, what is it?" Ever-observant Fabio called over to him. He had been watching and listening at his scraping activities. So, when he stopped, naturally the professor wanted to know what Christopher had found.

Ignoring Fabio, and Christopher, who was completely engrossed, began blowing away the powdered yellow-green algae from the nearest wall. Like a bloodhound, the probing professor quickly closed in on him.

"How fantastic!" Christopher exclaimed. The man paused briefly and kept on rubbing feverishly away at the strange structure with a red toothbrush. *There is something.*

Strange carvings became visible on the wall surface. Also engraved into the stone base were ancient complex codex symbols or scriptures. The keen professor arrived to see what was going on.

"Jackpot, I think. Look at this professor!" Feeling his superiors zeroing in on him. The older man immediately gluing his eyes onto the strange codex. Fabio quickly squatted down and sighed with scholarly interest.

"Let me see," he said eagerly.

"Ancient symbols telling a story," said Christopher, "I will take some snap shots for our album while there is still good light." Christopher began searching for his digital camera inside his rucksack. "Bloody hell, I've not got it!"

"Not to worry," said Fabio, grinning with his irregular teeth. He had that eventually covered too. The professor pulled out his personal camera and captured the immediate area. Next, he handed it to Christopher to take several character shots of the professor next to the codex.

"Si, these seem to be codex hieroglyphics of some ancient kind," said the professor. "How old?" Fabio was momentarily lost in thought. "It is too early to say." He was not really expecting an answer from any of his colleagues. "We will be taking pictures of these full narratives back with us for further analyses."

The place suddenly became more like a photo shoot than an excavation site, with bold Fabio standing alone and smiling next to the find. It was important to him that *he* be given full credit for this unique discovery.

"I lost my bloody own camera, shit, and it cost a fortune too!" Christopher was clearly angry with himself as he began scratching his head furiously in self-annoyance at the thought of Fabio stealing his thunder.

"I would say this is one of those times when *you* would prefer to have specialized in my field, archaeology, rather than studying all about those silly herbal secrets lurking somewhere under the canopy? Is this not the case my energetic pioneer?" His tone was condescending.

I saw the writings first thought Christopher. He said nothing, but his feelings festered longer than he would have liked; quite unlike a normal priest, Christopher felt badly that his anger was brimming over. *I will show that arrogant asshole,* and without thinking he decided to challenge Fabio's knowledge. And that, is the last thing he should have done.

"Professor! It is really old, pre-1000 B.C," he decided to confront the professor's last rhetorical question with a fact, understanding that his impertinence would serve to *really annoy him.* "I am sure, here look professor. This would be during the time of the first Mayan ceremonial centres." Christopher pointed at the codex, he had dared to hypothesize and lecture against the great Fabio. The professor moved in closer.

"Before you correct me — Fabio began but was suddenly interrupted.

"It is likely to be much older than *that* professor." Christopher cut him off. Talking over from the professor's much softer voice, he said, "And from these basic inscriptions, *that I uncovered," yes, yes - a conclusion that will annoy him* he thought, "They are one of the very earliest of civilizations. We still know nothing about them yet." Christopher was going for the jugular.

Smiling confidently, Christopher had done his homework beforehand, but homework was all it was. The Great Fabio would have his say. Christopher's throat tightened watching the unperturbed Fabio smile wider at him.

"Don't leap to any hasty conclusions, young man." Fabio was just warming up. "The earliest recorded Mesoamerican empires were the *Olmec* about 1200BC to 300AD, and for your edification it was they who were the ancestors of later cultures. Our assumptions might change in the coming months."

"But it was I tha—" Christopher tried to say something but swallowed awkwardly.

"Eh?" Fabio repositioned his round glasses onto the bridge of his straight pointed nose. With an air of self-recognition and self-centred achievement, he finished the scientist off. "Oh, and the Mayans were never discovered in this part of the continent, ever." The professor had successfully wiped away Christopher's attempt at any recognition.

For an older man, Fabio's medium athletic build, about five-foot-nine, silently stood straight up and turned away leaving Christopher sagging. *Lesson learned* thought Fabio smiling more.

In his early thirties, the professor was a very fit man with long black hair tied back in an unkempt ponytail trailing down his back. Caressing his small, black, sculptured beard around his mouth and chin, he was a *very young* professor.

He graduated from the *Universita Degli Studi di Messina,* which took him ten years to complete both his PhD *and gain* his professorship in archaeology, reading Lost and Ancient Civilizations. His mind was diverse, he had a pompous attitude and was very experienced and had exceptional organizational abilities. These traits made him the perfect candidate to lead this and many other large expeditions.

The professor quickly attempted to piece the symbols or glyphs together, but his initial effort proved harder than he thought; yet not impossible for the flawless professor. Assembling and disassembling made no difference in deciphering the cryptic details. Right now, it seemed to be just a jumble of shapes. Pushing out his bottom lip a little like a baby, the man resigned himself to try again later. He would break it. Fabio thwarted for the moment, his eyes burning like lava as he attempted to melt its stone secrets. He could not. Instead, he walked off in a sulk.

****

Mashir saw Fabio leave. The surveyor, in his sweat-soaked baggy shirt and shorts, lifted his hat and wiped the running sweat off his brow while observing the structure. The young, twenty-four-year-old Mashir, was in his prime. Although his frame was thin and wiry, he was very strong. His long limbs gave him great reach with natural-leverage, which was the reason he could climb trees so easily. A styled, black tapered beard was fitted neatly on his perplexed face. Could anybody make sense of this place?

"Looks amazing Chris!" Mashir said excitedly. Christopher worked feverishly with his trusty toothbrush. "This is what the professor has been looking for. It will make this expedition even more worthwhile," said Mashir realising the temple's hidden potential. Mashir's main studies at University were in Architectural History and not solely building surveying.

"To be fair," Christopher reaffirmed his own conviction for being on the quest, "I have found some new specimens already that may help us in the syntheses of new drugs. In addition, ensuring the religious education of these indigenous tribes is towards Christianity and *not Islam like you, eh pal?*" Christopher teased his friend with a semi-stern face.

"Allah, protect me from this infidel's misplaced teachings!" Mashir smiled back warmly at Christopher as they began laughing at both religions.

To Christopher, the temple was one of discovery and doctrine. His Vatican sponsors expected the former, and the Vatican Curia the latter. *It was important* to make a distinction and a timely reminder that this expedition was not all about charting, history or making money for the company; to him it was more about saving lives and saving souls.

The company, ONCOL had other ideas. Faceless people making decisions from afar; ONCOL *did* expect high financial rewards to come from this expedition. They expected results and the bare facts were that their business was making money. It did not seem to matter how or where its fortune came from.

The tapping of undiscovered wealth of others did not bother them. Curing people was a nice thing, a good thing, and very commendable. But all the finer virtues were only a smoke screen. Inside the machineries of ONCOL, there sat an inner circle of hidden people that did not care about helping others, and the only thing they wanted was to increase their own wealth by whatever means.

****

Sometime later Fabio came back out of his strop, and then everyone walked back to where they first appeared on the temple top. Standing together on the edge of the temple gave them a fantastic and panoramic view of the secluded vale!

Beautiful and primordial, they watched the light fading fast. Everyone was a witness to the forest transformation before their eyes. The definitive forestry began melting away along with its rugged rock face enclosures. In the distance, gloomy mists could be seen rolling inwards and sweeping with it a colossal blanket, extinguishing the last shreds of daylight.

"Mashir, you've dropped a memo from your pocket. Here, take it." Christopher bent down to pick up the piece of paper for Mashir.

"No, I've got it! Thanks Chris." The surveyor moved like light speed and swept it up before Christopher got half way to touch it. "I was drawing these earlier, only some sketches, nothing important." The Iranian shrugged loosely.

"Come on man don't be littering around! The tourists will be doing that soon enough." Christopher joked.

"Sorry Chris, I'll take better care." He scrunched the paper up and put it in his trouser pocket and zipped it up tight. "Rubbish right enough," he agreed. "Over there, what a view!" Mashir gazed out changing the focus and everyone concurred at the sheer scale of the place. "Breath taking."

"It's all about to disappear." Fabio pointed out the dimness and felt that he had spent enough time on the temple. "I think we should get back to base camp."

Christopher felt uneasy. The atmosphere inside the vale was amiss, something intangible was not quite right. As evening approached, he did not want to be exposed up here. Christopher felt spooked and he was not sure why. It might have been the dark red, rustic algae observed on the altar that reminded him of human blood and sacrifice; or simply, impending doom. *A feeling only…* "Let's go." Christopher's hard tone implied a warning.

In the dying daylight, campfire smoke drifted up to meet them. From far below, the smell of food teased their aching stomachs. Fabio sniffed the air loudly.

"This place has made me ravenous! It smells like a hot meal coming from base-camp! Come on, it will be ready for us by the time we get back."

One question burned; *what had they discovered?* Full of ideas for another day, the men quickly descended the large steps.

Threats were everywhere in the forest and somewhere not too far off they could hear the alarm of a family of orangutans going berserk, disturbed by a prowling cat as nightlife began once more in the forest.

Mad buzzing noises came from crazy mosquitoes and seemed never ending. Continual clicking of the crickets beginning their nightly serenades, all timed to perfection.

In the distance, a fateful scream echoed from the forest depths as an animal died. Night survival and death; the circle of life was all part in parcel of living and dying in the rainforest. One thing was constant at the temple; the sounds of the waterfall. Darkness came swiftly.

****

The next day, the mist had vaporised and with it the magic of the night. The sun was high and blazing above their encampment, the view breath-taking with a myriad of colours abounding everywhere. A sudden flurry of wings clattered above the tents. Looking up, they saw multi-coloured flocks of excitable birds flying off.

Mind numbing and endless, the waterfall's constant noise produced an acoustic pattern that gave a distinctive arrhythmic impression of one minute being closer, then softer and lighter further off. Today things were different. New sounds came resonating through the forest; the workings of man. A human presence shifted away a green mass that created a safer boundary.

This defoliation was their priority before proper archaeology could begin. Five days into the excavation the team had already levelled a perimeter by clearing a small area of jungle, at the front south facing side of the superstructure. On the temple, ten huge blocks had been cleared, each massive block of equal height and length measuring twenty feet and stretched to form rows, creating giant terraces. Vines still clung on in most places, and were able to spread outwardly from the forest floor making any clearing work extremely arduous.

Unexpectedly, everything dimmed and turned black. Bewildered, they all stopped what they were doing and looked around nervously. Day suddenly transformed into night.

Unknown to the unsuspecting researchers and archaeologists, this was a year of geo-positional misalignment of the sun, which caused a unique event when a total eclipse of the sun took place, right now.

The observatory, which was built near an altar, had been part of an ancient people's worship, where a high stone monolith stood with a perfectly round circle cut through its pinnacle. It should have channelled the sun at this crucial moment. *Not now, not anymore.*

If the legend is to be believed, then the temple could be seen in this place for one full earth year, and like clockwork, recurred every five hundred years thereafter and forever more. If this time chunk, a mythical measurement known as an aeon, was as predicted, the temple would appear once again.

This aeon was different from any others that had gone before. On any other day, during such a special year, the sun's passage would travel straight and directly through a stone hole inside the tall monolith above the altar. This had been a regular occurrence for each aeon. It demonstrated for those who knew, this to be a balanced power of God.

A low rumble echoed through the forest when another earth tremor struck in the darkness. Short and sharp, it shook everything. It was the second one this morning. The sun's bright orbital focus that had already burst inside the stone orifice had suddenly vanished the same second this uncanny eclipse occurred. Natural daylight was substituted by supernatural darkness. After the tremor, the forest became silent.

Everyone stood quietly outside their tents and watched warily together. With mixed emotions of fear and bewilderment, the morning brightness disappeared. They stood in shadows and sallow silhouettes. Panic started to grow in the forest. No man or animal understood what was going on. Feeling naked and vulnerable, they stood as if they had turned to granite, and everyone held their breath when another tremor rippled through the ground, even stronger this time. It passed when sunlight suddenly exploded the darkness away, and nature regained its foothold again.

A change had occurred, and the sun's rays could not realign properly because the temple had shifted. Almost immeasurable but enough, gauged by the misalignment of sunlight in the centre hole of the stone monolith. The orifice where the sun's face should be viewed in the stone no longer cut through. In its place an evil shadow had formed. A slender shadow filled a blurry space where myths end, and legends begin. An imbalance had occurred. It was the prophecy!

The people of the expedition all felt an instantaneous fear, everyone praying in their own fashion until the sunlight had reappeared and in those glorious first few minutes the forest sighed relief and as daylight tentatively awoke once more.

It began with a lone jaguar's defiance towards heaven and then came a single bird whistling into life, followed by more encouragement by others that suddenly sparkled with a heightened sense of beauty and new hope in its music. The animals heard them and awoke again, pumping more life through the veins of the rainforest with increasing light.

Yet something was wrong, an alteration had taken place in the form of a disturbing shadow. In the sultry heat and the dawn's morning light, the temple had appeared once again out from the darkness.

Things were much different after that solar eclipse, and unknown to the expedition, something above on the temple top was not right, something unnatural lingered. An evil black presence in the form of a black hole held in stasis by the power of darkness and stone. It would not leave.

****

A safe border had been created around the temple. Masses of dense foliage cut in all directions to about twenty metres and all thrashed right back from the walls and to a new tree line. This would keep the ever-creeping jungle at bay and help show any prowling animals. Fabio estimated that his work would take about a year to complete before considering a return to civilization.

The professor's expedition consisted of men with different nationalities and religions, all who were specialized in their own fields of work. Some skills did cross each other's expertise creating a competitive tension in the teams. That, plus being together for such a long time would inevitably lead to bitchiness and rivalry. Luckily, there was one person that brought some sensibility for the men in those awkward situations. A young Indian woman, a medical student named Harjit Singh. With her young age, she could instinctively smooth arguments and cool disputes with her natural mediation abilities.

Down to hard work, time passed quickly with the first month yielding numerous samples obtained using specialised equipment called tubular perforators. Geological markers were taken from the temple's outer stonework and were all collated and stored in marked crates.

Some evidence of old stone works had been discovered at a nearby quarry where a dangerous concealed fissure existed, a place to work bordering the entrance to the valley. Fabio hoped that the detailed analysis of this find might show a relationship between these different areas. Maybe this indication would give a time when the temple was constructed by using modern dating techniques. Superficially, the temple seemed to be a type of sedimentary rock of deep red hardened sandstone, but what they could not know was that it was much older than anyone could ever have imagined.

Hot and very sticky, the weather could be so changeable making it difficult, but the excavation site so far had exposed many more rows of massive stone terraces right up to the first tier of the temple. In the forest, nothing had ever been easy and after another day's toil the nearby stream was a cold and welcome respite for washing the grime off.

Equipment and limited fuel supplies had been carried in by llama power, specifically for this job. Most people used muscle and machete to cut away the awkward parts when the power tools broke down. Christopher's specialised knowledge of biology and the rainforest allowed him to locate certain trees and to provide additional stockpiles of natural fuel oil. Keeping them in wooden drums made of vines and wood. It worked just as well as kerosene. His time with the natives had been very useful.

New supplies would not be arriving for a long time since the expedition was to be kept under wraps at this early stage. Fabio made sure of this, reminding everyone of the importance of secrecy. The professor insisted that there would be no airdrops for quite some time to come. All this had already been accepted by everyone. The Brazilian government and Vatican seemed to be in bed together with this expedition, and neither of them wanted to attract the wrong kind of attention from treasure hunters and unwanted media.

****

Endrissi Berganaschi, the Structural Engineer, and Fabio's second in charge, was on top of the temple clearing all the vegetation off. He was steadily working his way downwards with his own team. Each tier was three feet in height and stretching across in parallel rows about a quarter of the length of the superstructure, they knew the temple must have been an engineering nightmare to build. The huge steps were built from the base to the first tier, separated by a short partition on either side of the steps.

Fabio stared up through the green tangle above him, listening to the din. He could hear the other team in the distance. Speaking to his top student Alessandro Marchesi, they conversed about the technicalities and defoliating strategy.

"At this rate professor," said Alessandro, "Clearing this area alone will take another five to six weeks." The younger assistant gauged. Both men wore similar wide brimmed hats protecting them from the elements and pests. Alessandro worked on a stone level directly above the first tier with the professor immediately below him.

"Si, Alessandro," said Fabio. "We should move faster as we move further up the pyramid. Less stone to cover so the lengths of the walls get much shorter. I saw some small trees above that might present a temporary obstruction." He paused. "We will meet Endrissi's men eventually, they are already getting closer to us. The other guys are also fast shifting the stuff from the base, and we will all gradually come together."

"Professor?" Alessandro Marchesi said, looking at his mentor. "Endrissi's team are concentrating on cutting away the whole of the top plane. The observatory is also cleared. We were speaking at breakfast about his team's advancement. Endrissi said he has split his team, some working their way down through each block and row and the rest on top. He has remarkably uncovered the altar completely."

"He'll take longer to reach us." The professor said while scratching his beard in consternation. He thought, *it's not exactly what we agreed.*

Envious, Fabio wanted to be everywhere and discover everything. It was his glory, his fame and it belonged to him and him alone. Obsessive Fabio harboured his dream with more than just a small degree of envy and felt the urge to take control.

I must get up and have a closer look at this altar. This is my triumph and no one else's.

The student narrowed his brown eyes, refocusing his attention to foraging a little, then became ultra-careful again. Studying each section meticulously, he made several notes and took additional pictures as he repeated this regular pattern.

Being trained by the great Fabio himself was a privilege. Alessandro continued cutting away around his feet and quite close to the ledge of the wall when he suddenly stopped. Looking down he saw something very unusual. *My God, what is that?* Observing odd-looking scratch marks, he let out a nervous scream!

"For the love of Jesus Christ professor, inscriptions are in the rock surface!" He hollered. He was so thrilled as this was his first ever discovery as a real archaeologist! Alessandro wanted to clear any excesses of algae from the wall straight away, but his training suppressed this immediate urge.

Holding back a tide of excitement, his young eagerness was dampened. He swallowed a groan, knuckling down once more with his fine brush. Fabio smiled at his good choice of a student, one who was extra careful; revealing more intricate red arched stonework.

"Ah my boy! I think we have found an entrance." Fabio was elated at the find and took over the immediate dig. It appeared to be the apex or archway!

"An entrance to what?" The boy moved back unconsciously and was happy that the older and more experienced man took over. A strange feeling of apprehension came over the young student.

"We shall see my boy, we shall see." Fabio stared ahead and surmised what this place might reveal. It did resemble the top of an entrance, although he was not entirely sure of this initial observation. Immediately below them it was still engulfed by copious amounts of vegetation, which obscured a large wall façade.

The archway's curvature continued leading upwards into a point that appeared then to be its apex, before curving wider and back down symmetrically on both sides. Fabio realised that it would take quite some time, blood, sweat and tears to clear its lattice of vines and vegetation that had adhered to the surface. Strong as limpets, they knew that once the vegetation was gone, the results would be worth every effort.

Enthralled with boyish excitement, both continued working non-stop into the night. The lamp casted eerily over their dig. Both men were seen from the distance and cast in the illuminating light. Student and master could have easily been mistaken for possessed grave robbers, like Burke and Hare, by all the tired onlookers in the base camp below.

Fabio knew that every now and again there are deeper mysteries to life; he had known for some time that some things demand questions and some things demand answers. This place, is such a thing.

From the campfire, the others wondered when or if they would ever come down. Alessandro seemed like a son to the professor. Now it was time for sleep, the campsite became quiet.

****

"Phew! Finished." Fabio exclaimed. Shattered, both men stood up stiff as boards and completely filthy.

The hiss coming from their lamps waning, fuel almost spent, Fabio slowly turned them both off. They stood back triumphantly and smiled as they finished by sunrise.

It was on the south-facing wall, early morning of the June solstice, in which a proud and intimate moment found them both; student and mentor alike. Side by side, each shared a sense of great achievement. They had uncovered the complete entrance to the Temple of MalisIblis!

Standing overawed, and proudly on the first tier of this colossal stone arched doorway, it dwarfed both men. The entrance was twenty feet high. The size of the block structure on the second tier was higher than this one. Its locus was a third of the way up the temple structure and its construct was midway along the wall length where they stood. Below them, there were many steps to the forest floor.

The men had not completed any analyses or fine measurements. Most of the surrounding vegetation still needed to be uncovered and cleared. They had meticulously exposed the important part.

The foliage above the entrance was relatively untouched and unseen underneath the woody tangle of vines. A stone walkway lay camouflaged below the thin and twisted creepers like elongated worms, crawling slower than the eye could perceive, stretching on their long journey upwards to the heavens.

"Well done Alessandro my boy! This part is cleared, good work," at last Fabio was very pleased with his student's apprenticeship!

"Thank you, professor." The boy was overjoyed at his complement.

"Without a doubt, this is the way in." Fabio paused, "Si, interesting times my boy, very interesting times." The great man pulled thoughtfully at his beard.

A large stone doorway was partially encrusted with mottled brown yellow and rustic red algae. This was matted thickly onto its hard surface. Fabio soon realized that other steps were adjoined and widened outwards from the entrance base and continued going upwards to the top of the temple.

The huge doorway was indented inwards from the surface with a marked stone border around it. It had finely engraved smaller stone blocks. All were designed to hold together by the great skill and craftsmanship of ancient stonemasons or some lost guild.

There would be no cement found in this temple. Everything was built with seamless joints and with peculiar architecture with engraved designs that included drawings of *lidless eyes* all carved into each of the smaller stones.

"God, professor, this place – I do not like it. It looks evil." Alessandro stared fearfully at the stony eyes bordering around the doorway.

Swallowing his nervous horror, the young student felt at any moment they would follow him.

"My boy, my boy, come on!" Professor Mancini smiled sympathetically at the young man's naivety, raising a tone octave of encouragement in his voice, "They are probably there to ward off evil spirits that might approach the temple."

Onto each eyelid was inscribed the same small codex patterns -

Watching unemotional, cold stone eyes stared at each of the men, lifeless and lidless. It was as if they were observing them with an odd kind of certainty.

Fabio smiled at his student. *Wet behind the ears* he thought, but then realised that they both were worn-out, tired and dirty. Yet, each man demonstrated an obsession with an essential prerequisite in their trade. The extra time they took to scrape carefully at the surface of the door and trying to remove the thick encrusted algae was unexpectedly paying off. Suddenly, it broke away with a crack revealing something even more surprising.

"Oh!" Alessandro jumped. "Professor, look!" He shouted.

"Hmm, quite a prize." Fabio's attention was fully focused on the find. "Observe those extraordinary inscriptions in the door my boy. It is a story." Fabio fumbled in a riff of excitement, "I'll take a few pictures and send them off via satellite for immediate recognition analyses."

The professor pointed to what looked like an ancient language that had suddenly become clear under what was only a thin algal layer.

"What language is it Professor Mancini?" The hesitant junior assistant asked, "The symbols or glyphs may be a warning of some kind like the tombs of Egypt. Do you think there might be mantraps inside, signore?"

The student was right to be curious and cautious because there could easily be any number of murder holes inside those ancient walls. The professor ignored him for a moment then spoke.

"It looks like the stone has been painted or stained with red and yellow and assembled into types of iconographic patterns." He returned to the student's unanswered question, "Si, there may be *some – obstacles* within the structure. So be extra careful when you go inside." Fabio lifted his right eyebrow showing academic interest, "Always be on our guard in such places, we will need to take the required precautions."

"Signore...?" Alessandro did not like the sound of it.

"Then this is all part of the excitement of any original find. A little danger never hurt anyone, now did it my boy?" Fabio grinned ear to ear at his student's uneasiness.

Fabio a seasoned campaigner knew that he would confidently guide his star pupil through the danger. The professor did not expect an answer. He turned again to view the ever-watchful stony eyes…then felt a pang of doubt in his own bravado.

"Si professor."

"When we get inside, be careful my boy, be very careful." The professor continued trying to read the unintelligible inscriptions. Both men took out their notepads, because their new study had begun. It was like learning to read and write all over again, staring at the complex Stucco designs which surrounded the door surface.

Carved into the middle upper area of the door were puzzling inscriptions that may well be a description. Some of the surfaces were so eroded it made reading difficult. In some parts, the flattened text had vanished, gone. This was a missing link to the story in an ancient message.

"I think this is going to take more time than I realised my dear boy." Fabio said.

Alessandro Marchesi was his top student, who despised arrogance and came from a poor country farm.

This expedition was a once in a lifetime opportunity and to work under a great professor was an offer he could not refuse. The professor's vast knowledge was respected in many circles and after spending years at the University as his star pupil, Alessandro wanted to lose his shadow and make a name for himself.

It was strange that he felt resentment towards his master and quite unlike his true nature, Alessandro could not explain his new feelings towards his mentor. It was this place... *it had to be.* The jungle did strange things out here.

Fabio continued scrutinizing each phrase and soon realised that this unusual language might-be-read in any direction. Who would know?

Where will I start? Perplexed, the professor's mind began to pick at the codices.

They read...

⊓⊔ ⊔⊐⊓⊔⊔ ⊓⊓⎡⊏ ⌐<⌐⌐⊔ ⎡⊏ ⊓⊔ ⊓⊔⊓⌐
⊓ ⊓⊓⊔ ⌐⌐⊏⊓

⊓⊓⊔⊏⊔ ⊓⊓⊔⊓ ⌐⊔⊓ ⌐⊔⊓ ⌐⊓⊔⊔ ∨⎡<<
⊏⊓⊔⌐<< ⌐⊔⊔⎡⊏⊓
⊔⊔ ∨⌐⊔⊔⊔⊐ ⊏⊔⌐⊏ ⊔⊏ ⊓⊔⊐ ⊓⊓⊔ ⊏⌐⌐⌐
⊔⊐ ∨⊔⊔⊐⊏ ∧⊓⊏⊓ ⊔⊔ ⊏⌐⊔>⊔⊔
⊔⌐⊔⊔ ⎡⊏ ⊓⊓⎡⊏ ∨⌐< ⌐⊔∨ ⊓⊔ ⊓⊓⎡⌐⊓⊏
⊓⊓⊔⊓ ⌐⊔⊔ ⊔⎡⎡<
⊔⊔ ∨⌐⊔⊔⊔⊐ ⊓⊓⊔⊔⊔ ⎡⊏ ⌐⊔∨⊓⊔⊔⊔ ⊓⊔
⊓⎡⊐⊔ ⌐⌐⊐ ⊓⊓⊔< ∨⎡<< ⌐⊔∧⊔ ⊓⊔⊔⊔
⊓⊔ ⌐<⌐⎡∧ ⎡⊓

"It is difficult to identify any particular South American codices here." Fabio said to

Alessandro, "Hmm, and no decipherable pictures of real objects that I would expect to observe." The Mayan writing system is a classic example. Mayan inscriptions as you know Alessandro, is largely religious with each glyph representing an entire word."

The older man continued lecturing his student, quite oblivious to Alessandro's increasing annoyance and fuelling the young man's petulance towards him.

Not any more for Christ's sake Fabio! The student's head was beginning to burst, and his beetroot face became redder with resentment.

"From your basic studies my boy, you will recall." Fabio arrogantly seemed resigned to be always teaching his student. "Hmm, Knorozov! Remember now?" Fabio exclaimed, "That in their system, it consists of both logograms and phonetic signs, representing symbols etcetera. Do tell me please that you remember?" Fabio was surprised when Alessandro stood up.

"Si, of course you are right professor," Alessandro feigning. "These are totally different, not like the *Professoresden* or *Paris* codex at all and probably much older than those." Alessandro countered his mentor with his sarcastic tone.

Regretfully his short-lived revolt had the opposite affect with the professor, who found the student's opinion contrary, if not impertinent, point of view, to be mildly amusing. *Very good Alessandro* thought Fabio, pleased with the student's idea, although surmised that he may soon have to swat this impudent young student.

Fabio's student *did* have a lot of potential; Alessandro had a keen analytical mind and had great attention to detail, which was exactly why he chose him.

Forgetting his impudent student for the moment, the expedition leader trailed his fingers over the stony surface and felt the smooth indented lines of symbols.

Professor Fabio Mancini, already well known in archaeological circles in his own right, published accredited books - The Ways of the Toltec's and Mayan Dynasty.

"My boy, I think this one will take just a little more time to figure out."

"What about the others professor?"

"We will see if any of our colleagues make some sense of it, but I do doubt it."

"Why not involve them?"

"I suppose it might make them feel more engaged with the subject." Fabio said. He began taking more digital photographs of the red stone codex and glyph patterns.

Suddenly there came a mad rustling din above them on terraced steps, when unexpectedly Christopher appeared out from the foliage, rudely jumping down to meet the two uncertain men.

"Ah, there you are! What are you looking at?" Christopher asked.

Fabio looked at the twenty-three-year-old scientist.

"You should leave this kind of thing to *our* profession Christopher." The leader of the expedition chuckled while poking unscholarly humour at the bright young bio-technologist. Christopher was having none of it and was quite ready to make an immediate hypothesis on their archaeological find.

"You both look terrible!" Christopher saw their dirty bedraggled bodies.

"Thanks for that." Fabio sighed at the man's uninvited entrance.

"Both your eyes are red with exhaustion." He was right. Chris looked at both fatigued men.

"Oh Really? This is an expedition and not a beauty competition."

"Sorry professor." Christopher paused, "I watched last night and both of you were still at it into the wee hours. You should definitely get some shut eye."

"I would have asked you to come up knowing that. Then again, maybe not. You would only get in the way." Fabio was annoyed at Christopher's forward approach.

"Cheers," replied Christopher ignoring the professor's bad manners, "That looks interesting. A cipher." Christopher postulated with growing self-confidence.

Both archaeologists resumed their work discounting this new arrival. *Maybe he will go away* thought Fabio rudely. Christopher decided not to leave, shocked at the professor's annoyance with him. Fabio continued brushing at the stone.

"Look Fab," said Christopher, who knew that the professor hated this nickname, "Professor, hear me out, I have seen inscriptions like these back home in Scotland."

Both mentor and student chuckled at Christopher, both heads shaking in disbelief, unable to contain the absurd fantasy. Fabio got up and began laughing openly and even Alessandro could not help himself.

"Completely absurd," Fabio replied, creating immediate tension. This compounded with a long time spent in close proximity with each other was taking its toll on everyone's patience. Oddly, this feeling of open conflict and disharmony was on the rise since the expedition entered the vale.

"Nonsense, what kind of fool do you take me for! *Come on* Christopher, this place is ancient, these symbols are ancient too." Fabio was laughing even louder. "You are grievously mistaken, what age were you when you saw these childish symbols, eight or nine years old?" Fabio's eyes were blazing amber red.

The professor resented that a country bumpkin like Christopher, born in a reformed country like Scotland, with a few qualifications in science could attempt to upstage him, the idea was unthinkable.

This is my own specialised field of research, not a bloody doctor of plants, he thought. Fabio had secretly dreamt of this place many times. *This lost temple is my discovery and will surpass even Hiram Bingham's who discovered the lost city in the sun, Machu Pincchu, July 1911 in the Andes of Peru or further back than this, in 1867 by a German adventurer Augusto Berns, who looted the tombs with the Peruvian government's blessing!*

Not as well known or prestigious, the professor was also aware of Herman Gohring who in 1875 was tasked by the Peruvian government to map a route through from the interior to the Pacific.

The professor's egocentric mental rant continued, *this is my Amazonian expedition, my discovery. Mine alone! It is I, Professor Fabio Mancini who will have world recognition that I justly deserve!* Fabio thought posthumously of himself, and while he reinforced his own right, these internal deliberations were cut short by Christopher. He decided to interrupt the professor's self-given award ceremony.

"Professor, you are not *listening*?"

"What?" *How dare he interrupt me.* The professor nursed a wounded wrath when Christopher penetrated Fabio's wave-off dismissals.

Anger hid below the brim of Fabio's hat. He looked up slowly, listening deliberately to Christopher. The Scot was bravely getting through the archaeologist's self-eminence.

"No really," Christopher insisted, showing a surprised look at his successful intrusion, Chris gulped, in a breath of embarrassment. "I remember at my home in Scotland, Scott, my younger brother, spent countless hours with his pals looking at this stuff. Yes, as impossible as it seems, ancient codices like these were cut in similar fashion into a red-stone monolith. The monolith was set into a larger wall, making up an integral part of a long stone bike shed in the local school, for all to read."

Christopher visualised the old slate roofed shed in his mind again, the building an open shelter for the student's bikes and a place to hang out during breaks.

"Seriously?" The professor said.

"Hear me out professor. To make a long story short, I know how strange this might seem. The professor stared at him on a short fuse, but was still listening.

"And?"

"And, these shapes you see on this surface are the same type of coding that my brother showed me. I find it all hard to believe myself!"

"Impossible." The professor's soft voice cut through Christopher's keenness to wear away at the young man's confidence.

"I'm sure of it! I wish I still had the photograph he sent me. I left them back in Rome. It would prove that these ancient writings are the same. It was Scott and his group of friends Cameron, Cole and Ross."

"Oh, I really don't care who they are. What you say is in fact nothing but trivia," the professor sighed. His dwindling patience moving on.

For a brief second Christopher reflected on the years gone past and the last time he visited his mother's home in the west of Scotland.

His face gazed over the forest, his imagination conjuring up a far distant scene and another life. He saw himself standing above the boys like a dream watching his younger brother touch the monolith's stone surface.

Christopher's timeless daydream continued in a twisted reality as his brother's slim fingers rubbed the textured stone with mysterious excitement. Scott wanted answers. Looking at the codices here, so did Christopher.

Christopher unconsciously began rubbing the stone in unison with his brother's image, lightly brushing over the missing codices, *what do they mean?* Only a second had passed and although it appeared that Fabio's patience waned, against all odds the professor looked vaguely intrigued.

"Professor, I think the monolith in the village was—"

"In what village?" Alessandro interrupted. The young student who had been listening, was very interested about anything that might give a clue to how this temple came into being. Alessandro's mind was more open to change.

"Its name is Mauchline, and the monolith is about four to five hundred years old, according to the local library."

The older archaeologist yawned widely when without any warning Fabio's patience cracked.

"Complete and utter nonsense!" Fabio exploded. The man was unable to contain himself and threw his leather grip Rock-Pick down, "Spec... speculation," the professor stammered. "This is all from a small boy and of all people, your brother!" Shouting irately, "You expect me to believe this! Really, if this is all you have to offer doctor. It will not do. Not do at all." Professor Mancini yelled in an accelerated tone pausing a little out of breath. "Too much of a coincidence don't you think!"

Startled, both younger men standing back from the professor's tirade, each was a bit shaken by the sudden and volatile outburst. The stunned doctor waited to see what would happen next.

Dwarfed by the stone structure in front of them, the professor looked up frustrated. Then the storm cleared.

"Just trying to help professor, surely you can see that." Christopher swallowed.

"This structure," Fabio's shaky finger pointed a warning at the temple. It is *thousands* of years old and these inscriptions were first written thousands of years ago." Fabio said in a shade of anger, "And not five hundred years ago Christopher, I am sure that early analyses will confirm my judgment to be true." Once again, he intimated at Christopher's lack of knowledge and experience.

"But…" Christopher's protest saw only futility.

"Enough of this. I am hungry. Let's go and get something to eat," dismissing any further debate from the men.

Fabio stared coldly at Christopher's naivety and shook his head at Christopher's blasé attitude. An uneasy silence came between the trios. The professor seethed inside. *I might have expected this from someone of his education and… simple background.*

"Professor, I'll wait here for a while. I had breakfast earlier." Not surprisingly, he did not want to accompany the professor. Christopher said nothing more but had his own thoughts; *he is losing it man. That was uncalled for and I need to get away from him for a while. Whether he likes it or not I have seen these types of symbols before.*

"Fine." Fabio stated bluntly, "Just do not touch anything," he ordered.

Christopher watched them go and was glad to see him heading up to the top of the temple. He would work there for the rest of the day.

****

After a while, Christopher stood up awe-inspired and gazing out from his high perch, studying the fast approaching evening. The man observed a breath-taking sight. A once clear blue-sky, accelerated into shades of wonderful luminous tones of orange, red and green before quickly melting away. And like clockwork, the forest began transforming right before his eyes. Watching its lively tones smoothly running off into a moody blackness that defined the treetops in all directions and against a deep rich orange line of amber. The rainforest silhouetted like this, reminded him of the warm embers of a coal fire in a fond distant past.

Night had come...

In the evening light, Christopher reflected on heart-felt nostalgia when he was a young lad at home with mum and dad. In the warmth and semi-darkness of his living room, he had shared precious moments sitting around the coal fire one cold winter evening, and remembered as a family talking about when Scott would be born. It would be that year.

Christopher reminisced about his deep love for his family, at that time he was a lone child. He felt content and thought more about when he was a boy in the winter, listening to the soft sounds of the snow landing and settling on the frozen windowsill.

"God, it all looks so beautiful!" Christopher sighed and looked out from the temple. He hoped that the great architect in the sky heard him, as his face bathed in a luminous orange yellow ambience going fast.

Its firelight effect expanded quickly across the sky, widening from its deep defined line and softening in tone. Just then, an all-engulfing blue blackness with pinpoints of white light came to spirit his senses. He called it heaven!

Yet this transformation, from day to night, had taken less than ten minutes. In the tropical heat it felt like a million miles from his family and childhood.

Oh, how different it is. He stood and wondered on the temple where many before him had once stood, and in that last fleeting moment at the stone altar, Christopher felt so small, and so alone.

Standing there, something intangible broke his dreamy state. Confused, he questioned what he had heard. Did he hear something else? Was it the sound of a soft memory of snowfall melting into water?

No, it had been real and not a memory, stretching out more with his feelings into the night. In the wilderness and always present was the continual and almost therapeutic rush of a waterfall. *It's not that either.*

"There it is again!" Christopher quietly recognised a female voice.

"Christopher! "A lone voice shouted from below. "Christopher! Where are you?" It repeated louder this time. "Are you all right? It's time to come down!" A moment of spellbound silence followed. "Christopher!" This time he sensed more urgency in her voice. A clear sharp voice broke his trance.

"Harjit, I'm fine!" He called back. "On my way!" Chris quickly found her and were soon both heading back to base. Once again, the nocturnal Amazon reigned supreme.

****

Next day began fine and fresh and so different to what would happen later, when a complete shift would occur. Then the rainforest would be hit by torrential rain and gales dampening even the most resolute of spirits.

Doctor Christopher Hrycuik decided to leave. He was categorically peeved-off and chose this moment to organise an excursion away from the camp and Fabio.

Christopher unquestionably had to leave and get away from Fabio. After all, biological research was why he had come on the expedition. His team departed early, keen to get away. They were going back to the vale entrance where there was an extensive gouge in the forest floor. It would hold many secrets.

His small exploratory escapade would take them five to seven miles Southeast from base and this exploration might take between three to four weeks to complete.

Christopher's primary objective, his job, was back on course. He was going to gather samples of insect and herbal specimens and the gulley was as good a place to begin this important work. Endrissi Bergamaschi, a keen geologist, and Fabio's second in command, would be taking the lead on the geological part of the survey. He would be gathering copious amounts of rock samples and measurements at the fissure. Between both branches of science, they hoped they might help unlock the mysteries to this part of the rainforest.

Their journey took the best part of four days to hack a trail. Progress seemed tougher this time due to fresh growth and bad weather; it covered over their previous route and by now it was barely distinguishable from the rest of the wild forest. Carmello, the South American Indian guide, and with his partner, an American named Mathieson, both were excellent at getting their people to any destination quickly. Eventually, they had made good headway. After a difficult climb, they reached the mouth of the vale and stood not too far away from a precarious looking crevasse.

A green mass of furious vegetation voraciously ate downwards into the pit, and well beyond their visibility. Established shrubs rooted all around the top ledges although nothing quite gripped as well as the Cat's Claw, which distinguished itself by its large woody vines and hook-like thorns that resembled a cat's claw.

Steadfast and growing well on the inside walls, the direction of growth was hard to tell, plants like these could easily grow to thirty metres or more. Beautiful reddish-orange flowers bloomed everywhere making the entire area jump at them with abundant diversity.

Not too far away, along the northeast side of this fissure found Christopher standing on a high vantage point observing below to the elongated crack. The treacherous gap also extended far beyond his view burrowing further away into the dense jungle. A mist had not long lifted to expose far outwards and away from the vale towards where the open vastness of the green world beyond, appeared. Watching out, he saw the endless rainforest expanding below and away as far as the eye could see. It was hard to believe that any civilization had ever existed out here. At the end of the world.

****

CHAPTER VII

GATEWAY TO
THE UNDERWORLD

Foliage gripped thick around the fissure, taking two days for the group to partially clear, a necessary chore that had to be completed due to the many hidden places. Small cracks and deadly holes underneath were all disguised by greenery. Large mounds of stone blocks were covered by a blanket of copious amounts of vegetation. It too would have to be cut away to examine them properly. During the clear up operation surprisingly, an old pulley system had been uncovered near the precarious breach in the earth's surface. Remarkably, the system was still in good condition and was possibly evidence of old mine-works.

"We are standing at the entrance to hell," said Carmello gritting his teeth. The small man did not care for what he saw and sensed danger within.

"Come here and have a look at this place," called Endrissi. He was suddenly astounded by a new find he made behind tonnes of vegetation. He spotted something unusual and began pulling at it like a madman.

Each shrub, twig and turf no quarter given and soon Endrissi had exposed a large concealed entrance. The surrounding rock appeared to be made of red sandstone. It seemed to be a large cave.

"It's a mine entrance made long ago," stated Carmello bluntly, with no more enthusiasm than tramping on an insect. He had got them here, job done and wanted nothing more to do with this place. The ranger guide began walking off to help the others with their makeshift campsite.

Mathieson and Endrissi were more determined than ever, putting in extra energy to clear the immediate locale. Meanwhile, Christopher and Harjit set up their camp by the fast-flowing stream joined by Carmello.

The water passed quickly towards the crevice, dropping out of site. The sounds of turmoil came from the bottomless fissure and inside the guts of the earth, there the stream would find another route out to the rainforest and to places far below the cloud forest. On it would go as it continued its mega-journey towards the sea. The daylight began dipping fast, and they knew that in ten to twenty minutes everything would be in complete darkness.

Harjit and Christopher moved a little away from camp to be in a more private secluded place, emerging soon on a high vantage point standing close together. They could see for miles. To the east, the temple's mega-structure was partially covered. Over to the west, lay a green expanse, the rainforest, and freedom out of the vale. Their spirits high, they both knew that they would see this adventure through to the end.

Normally Harjit would have had her hair tied up and tucked under her hat to keep the bugs away, but this time she let her hair fly around in the warm breeze, moving wildly. Chris remembered an intimate memory at that moment; the first time he made love to her when Harjit's sallow skin began to arouse him. It always did.

Her soft body and warm fresh face enticed his fertile imagination. Dusk closed in, and Harjit stood there for a long moment staring towards the route the expedition had taken. Harjit spoke softly.

"The wind has got a voice here, Chris. It is, talking to us," she said gently. The girl sensed that the forest winds had changed as her faraway muse turned darker.

Born in India twenty-four years ago, Harjit Singh was part of a large Hindu family. Her young face sculptured to perfection, her fresh natural ambiance hiding her circumspection. Never the less, Harjit's warm and natural personality glowed from her smooth copper toned skin.

She is so beautiful... thought Christopher.

Wearing her ex-army combat outfit, Harjit seemed more like a soldier than a fledgling doctor in an accident & emergency department. She blended in so easily with the surrounding environment.

This was at odds and in stark contrast to her head attire, a scarlet cloth headband holding her black shiny hair in place. Underneath her camouflage hid a curvaceous body, one that Christopher knew so well. Harjit's face was nothing short of stunning, a girl with a flawless face and sculptured to perfection. Her skin tone was of copper and she was the envy of any man.

Christopher seemed entranced with her unblemished beauty, taking a deep breath in this private place, before turning to each other holding hands and drawing closer. Out here in the wilderness it made them feel quite small, while wondering what future lay before them. The magnitude of the Amazonian scenery stretched before them, feasting their eyes on the last moments of daylight together.

"It is God's garden," said Christopher sighing softly.

Harjit looked out and felt something else, something quite different, something unspoken. It lurked around the vale like an unchallenged dread. Squeezing his hand, she remained quiet.

****

A few days later, their investigation started in earnest collecting as many new specimens for

Christopher's on-going analysis and data bank of undiscovered species. This was his dream! A quest to find that wonder drug. The ancient pulley system had by now been completely uncovered, a manual machine still in very good condition.

"Strangely, the pulley is made of a black hard heavy metal which would suggest that this civilization was very advanced, anywhere else in South America. It could only hope for Bronze." This fact intrigued him while examining its traits.

"Why different here?" She asked, "If the mine workings are as ancient as the temple well, this tool has not even rusted?" Her question needed some rationality.

"Incredible." Christopher raised an eyebrow at Harjit.

"Unless…" Harjit deliberated for a moment, "These tools are *more recent* than the original mine workings. That's it!" She exclaimed, "Someone else has been excavating in more recent times."

"Interesting, I wonder why? We will find the answers to this and many other questions soon," replied Christopher.

Surrounding their campsite were numerous *Castanheiro Do Para*, Brazil nut trees, all swaying with their fruit pods growing at the ends of thick branches. It was a common species growing throughout the Amazon rainforest, reaching as high as forty-nine metres.

One late evening, both tired, Christopher and Harjit gazed sleepily into the campfire's lively flames. The moon shone its lunar light-beams down onto the forest floor. Large moths and other odd-looking insects were fluttering around in a mad spectral dance, dodging with the multitude of fairy embers rising from their campfire.

Harjit turned to Chris while slowly taking off her red headband and began shaking her head. Her black shiny hair falling loosely around her shoulders, staring longingly towards him, with her large eyes.

Feeling her natural attraction pulling at him, Christopher tried to control his own desires and spoke softly to her.

"There is something about this place that both unnerves me and yet, intrigues me," he questioned the forest. "What do you think Harj? What fate befell these people who worked here? *Where* did they go?"

Harjit turned her face up towards to the moon in reverence and said, "The mysteries of life Chris, the mysteries of life." Melancholy mixed with mystery was in her tone. Harjit looked so wonderful, she bedazzled him. Across one half of her sallow skin, her face was shimmering in beams of moonlight, the other in fire lit amber tones, warming her skin.

The young girl opened her mouth seductively, her full lips arousing his inner senses. Spellbound, Chris studied her deep hazel brown eyes.

Harjit perceived him watching her and hinted a smile when Christopher stammered awkwardly.

"There, there," Christopher fought with his emotions. *God, my heart is racing*. He cleared his nervous throat and managed to speak again.

"Yes, Chris?" She smiled warmly.

"There… is so much to learn here and too many discoveries to make. Natural resources are in abundance that may help cure cancers, diseases and disorders, all here, just below our feet." The young man re-focused.

"That's fine Chris." Her words crumbled his mental blockade, dissolving his defences like sugar in water. Harjit needed his touch and his comfort. She moved closer. Christopher's willpower was vaporising before her.

"This place does not feel right," Harjit whispered fearfully. "It scares me, Chris. I am sorry. I cannot explain my feelings." The girl paused, her chest moving quicker, "Oh Chris, you must think I am so stupid." Her voice yielded. "Call it what you like, call it woman's intuition or just, call it crazy." Harjit froze.

"Harj what is it? What is wrong?" He touched her gently.

"We should all leave this place and get out of here." She felt a primal fear inside. Her demeanour was clearly distressed.

"Harjy, come on." Christopher although anxious, was trying to encourage her. "I'll protect you." He looked out at the darkness in the surrounding forest. "I don't blame your instincts. This place would scare anyone. Listen, try not to worry Harj," he said in a soft tone. He quickly glanced around to see if they were alone.

Harjit eased closer to him squeezing his hand. She needed reassurance. Christopher felt uneasy about his true feelings towards this girl, *this is wrong.* He knew it in his religious teachings. Yet, he had been wrong before. Harjit closed in, taking charge.

Hidden premonitions crept into his faltering thoughts and he felt an unexplained fear as well. Too long he had held this unnatural feeling in check; it was the *Zaplithowatres* ill forewarnings. It haunted him. *They said never to enter this place.*

Subconsciously he knew the mood of the expedition had changed and they all felt it. It changed much more than they all realized. Their perception of this place was altered ever since entering the capricious vale. It was the same intangible fear. His male instincts moved to protect Harjit.

"Don't be scared Harjit." He tried to reassure her. Christopher's body shifted to touch her as he began caressing Harjit's bronzed cheek. A soft tear rolled down her face. Christopher followed the teardrop with his finger along its curved path towards her open mouth, holding her face and kissing her tenderly.

Christopher smiled, a man no longer in control, completely entranced by her natural allure. *How beautiful she is.* His kiss netted a sparkle in her large eyes

"My feelings are different from yours Harj," he lied. It was a last defence to stop his urge, "I believe things will be just fine, you'll see." *She looks so vulnerable,* he thought.

Christopher needed her and embraced Harjit's body tightly, his lips kissing hard on hers. Harjit answered without speaking. She knew what to do.

Eagerly she held his face between her cupped hands moving her lips around and around, each kiss longer, stronger and more passionate than before. Both bodies were on fire. Each kiss was deep and primal. Nobody was around; only the night kept them company.

Far away in the back of her mind, Harjit heard her brother speak within her conscience, it was *Vivek.* He had heard about their friendship but was unaware of their intimacy. They had become so close before the expedition began. Her brother could see the obvious clash of religions, anything deeper was unthinkable.

When he found out, Vivek instructed that she end it with him. "This man is not a Hindu," he would say. "Harjit, he is a Catholic priest!" She remembered his strong words and angered feelings.

Her family had migrated to Scotland and that was how she had met Christopher. Harjit knew there would be more trouble to come at home and it would be difficult for her family to accept their relationship.

There was at one time no relationship, because of Christopher's religious position. This happened before the expedition. Maybe it was wrong in others' eyes. Now, she lived for today, for this moment. It felt so right.

Harjit was born in the beautiful City of *Varanasi*, the City of Light, a city that was five-thousand-years-old. Harjit spoke fluent *Sanskrit*, India's oldest language, although she was more *westernized* than the rest of her family. Harjit spoke fluently in a Scottish accent. A dedicated daughter, she never forgot her roots, her family and religion. They were all very high in her mind and spirit.

Christopher liked Harjit a lot but felt instinctively protective towards her. He did not really want Harjit to come on this trip; the expedition was likely to be perilous. If he were honest to himself, his attraction for her was growing stronger, daily.

His faith would hold him back most of the time; his work, the rest of the time. How could he shake his guilt, and in a quieter moment like this? He prayed for forgiveness. *For my sin Lord, am I really cut out for Priesthood?* He had asked himself many times.

Strong willed, she insisted on coming, forcing her way onto the trip and tenaciously passing others, on her own merits. She left many male competitors in the dust. Her qualifications were impeccable, she spoke Italian, Spanish and English, which sealed her position on the trip.

He could not stop her. To do so might suggest some impropriety and draw attention to his guilt; his sin. It was these qualifications and the fact that no other final year medical students wanted to take part in such a dangerous expedition. It made her an ideal volunteer. The ONCOL Corporation did not refuse her application.

Harjit had only one year left to complete her PhD, taking this year out as medical research for her Doctorate. Two years earlier she had met Christopher at the University Student Union in Glasgow. She was immediately attracted to him, especially when he talked with other students about his specialised research. Years before, Christopher had misspent many happy-hours propping up the bar, while studying as a poor student, drinking many beers and playing uncountable games of pool with his mates.

Never forgetting these early student days at the university, Christopher was always keen to come back at any opportunity to lecture. It was here that their intimate friendship began.

To her surprise and initial disappointment, Christopher moved away to work for a private business called ONCOL, based in Italy. They had seen his brilliant potential and being a devout Catholic, he had already been recruited spiritually by the Vatican, to serve God. To sign up for this unusual mission into the rainforest was an honour.

He was going through the priesthood at the same time, and they both knew that their secret affair was completely wrong. The stakes were never so high because he risked being excommunicated if their private lives came to light. One night, their human weakness prevailed after one of his lectures. Since then, both formed a much closer friendship.

Christopher had impressed her at first as a unique scientist. His work was never stuffy to listen too, as he explained his work with youthful energetic vigour. Discovering herbal cures had caught her initial academic attention on his work and was intrigued by how Chris refined an oncomutagenic range of anti-stemic Cancer drugs that was at the heart of her own studies.

His lectures were very popular and Harjit attended all of them, listening attentively to his abstract thoughts, and then the practicalities he discussed back at the Union Bar. The more she got to know him, the stronger her attraction became. Won over by his boyish charm, he never acted anything like a conventional priest.

He would protect her, and in this far-flung moment in Amazonia, Christopher held her hand, felt her human fallibility and sorrow. An inevitable and unshakable bond between them existed. Some would call it, fate. He wondered why she was so sad.

"I'll take you back to base camp tomorrow," said Christopher firmly. "And I'll arrange a pickup for you. Stuff Fabio's radio silence! It is crazy of him to have complete radio silence deep in like this! Does he think we are at war or something? If anyone else wants to go with you, they'll keep you company."

"Come with me Chris? Please leave with me." She feared for his safety too.

'No, I am sorry Harj, I cannot. My place is here."

"Then, I will not leave without you." Harjit pleaded.

"You must."

"No Chris, if you do not come with me, I am staying too." She re-assembled her naked wits, rebuilding normal composure.

I am Harjit and I am strong. Harjit tried her best to bolster herself, lifting her natural barriers against him to protect her herself while hiding her greatest fear; that he will not go with her. *Does he not love me enough? For the Goddess Parvati. We will never leave this place alive. I feel it.* Her face became paler, losing its liveliness. Harjit's confidence hit rock bottom. Christopher saw her demeanour quickly diminishing.

"*Harj,*" he whispered tenderly. "*Come closer.*" He kissed her again. Christopher smiled and squeezed her hand sympathetically.

Suddenly a mad rustling came out of the darkness, brash sounds drew closer from nearby bushes, forcing both to stare surprisingly in that direction. Discreetly moving apart from each other, they waited. They had company.

Endrissi Bergamaschi appeared and joined them. Endrissi was a big man and an eager geologist who had been all around the world working with ONCOL Corporation.

He had a PhD and studied in geology, building technology and architecture at the University of Rome. He was recently promoted for the expedition and was placed second in command to Fabio. Endrissi was more a *company man* than even his boss.

Endrissi, unaware of their intimacy, sat down dropping his heavy rucksack on the ground between them. He didn't notice anything. Endrissi appeared to be thrilled about something more important. His eyes blinked rapidly, they always did when he got very excited. He began talking to them.

"At a guess and without making any firm commitment, as you know," Endrissi began, "I would say that this fissure has been kicking around here for no less than a few billion years! A crack like this one is likely to be a fault-line. Are you ok, with this?"

The man committed his overly wordy technical view, and always looked for acknowledgement and understanding from his listeners. That was his way, and in most cases, he was usually right.

"Hey, Endrissi! What's in the bag?" Christopher asked casually.

"A lot of rock and stones located in this area, look at these!" He opened the full bag like a kid in a candy shop, "Typical sandstone, these occur in strata of all geological ages. North Africa formed in the Mesozoic Age, probably from blankets of desert sands. However, the typical limestone that I would expect to be here is from the shallow marine seas. It is a surviving record that the continent was repeatedly covered from time to time." Endrissi looked up very excited at this and said, "Do you go with this?"

Christopher began to wish he had never asked. *I have done it this time.*

"Si, sure." Christopher replied matter-of-factly; no question as Endrissi went on.

"Mainly the Precambrian, Palaeozoic and Mesozoic eras; there is a broadband straddling of these equatorial regions and as we know very important oil reservoirs are found in this type of sedimentary carbonate rock. Unfortunately, this is *not* the case at this location. We will not be discovering crude oil on this trip and that means no bonuses, signores. You'll not be ok with that I am sure." Endrissi frowned with a causal smile bemused at his unappreciated dry joke. Harjit and Chris turned browbeaten to each other.

Endrissi held his hammer in one hand and began poking about in his bag of boulders. The rucksack must have weighed a ton to any other man, but he transported it like a camel.

"Signores, did I here you say, signores?" Harjit giggled a little at Endrissi. "And thanks for the outstanding lecture." She mimicked a large yawn of absolute boredom. "And for your info

Endrissi, you are paid by the company, not us." She reminded him that she was only a volunteer entitled to no bonuses, nor was Christopher.

The men surprised at the girl's response, jostled her a little for some fun, and made Harjit giggle louder. She instantly prodded both men back. It only made them even worse, jostling her even more. Their fun ended in fits of laughter.

"Maybe no crude oil is to be found under these rocks Endrissi, but there is plenty of oil inside these trees." Christopher pointed upwards. "Those are Brazil nut oil trees, from which you can obtain a clear yellow oil. It has a pleasant sweet smell and is used to make candles. Interestingly, it is also an antioxidant and is well documented for having anti-cancer properties. The liquid can also be found in soaps and shampoos."

The scientist imitated Endrissi with a long-winded analysis, making flippant fun from an herbal perspective, along with the same rapid eye mannerisms of the geologist.

"Are you ok with this signore?" Chris added.

"Well," Endrissi smiled as he scratched his head while recognising that he had met his match tonight. But Christopher was not finished, and smiled more.

"In fact," he went on, "Its seed pods are good for monkey pots. Monkey pots are small smoky fires carried around to discourage black flies. I'll show you later."

No sooner had he finished speaking when a rude American voice broke and spoiled his fun with the geologist. Mathieson unexpectedly appeared from out of the darkness.

"What the fuck are you two guys on about now?" Said a no-nonsense American voice, "Both of you mothers are speaking a pile of shit, man." He challenged both men's childlike tit-for-tat conversation.

In his usual very direct manner, he demanded to make some sense of Endrissi and Christopher's crazy talk. He felt that if a person were talking boloney or just anything that did not include him, he would immediately switch off. On many occasions, the Americans they knew got openly aggressive. It was his way.

The American's elongated accent spoke slowly in a soft Texan dialect, and despite his faults, Mathieson was an excellent guide. Everyone in the expedition had got used to his abruptness, typically cursing, swearing and generally winding people up for his own peculiar amusement.

In response, Christopher and Endrissi simply smiled at each other, quite resigned to his pushy brash candour. After all they thought, *he was an American.*

"Well Mathieson, since you asked me so nicely, the Precambrian rocks are the oldest in this continent; plutonic, meta-volcanic and meta-sedimentary and around three point eight billion years old."

His lecture continued making special emphasis on the numbers, which would incite the ranger's brashness even more.

Don't fucking bother, man, thought Mathieson.

"There are three different developmental stages and as I said, the last being about 570 to 245 million years ago." Endrissi's thought, *this will sort him out.* He continued, "Extensive sedimentary rock cover is indicative of acrid conditions here at that time, which formed these sandstones. I think in the Triassic period around two hundred and eight million years ago. So, with any luck we might find a couple of fossilized monsters stuck in stone." The geologist fed Mathieson more extrapolated verbal fodder. Turning up the gas on the ranger's pressurised frustration, he said, "Getting me so far?" Endrissi bluntly rammed boredom home.

Endrissi's face dropped in shock as he realised all too late, Mathieson's anger brimming over. *Oh sugar, I've gone too far this time.* Goaded beyond even the patience of a saint, Mathieson predictably exploded.

"Well thank you *fuck* for that Triassic crap! Look man, the only relic to find down that big hole in the forest is you! You're full of bullshit man!" He had a furious outburst at the gobsmacked geologist. The ranger was disgusted at being made a fool of, between the geologist's *superior* education and his arrogant rhetoric towards him.

Mathieson was a man known for being direct; he would not suffer fools gladly and would be very quick to put anyone in their place, like now.

Everyone knew that this was just one facet of the ranger's colourful personality, that could cause easy offence to the unwary. Mathieson did not like smart asses either.

This *chip* stemmed from a deprived upbringing, and right now his wrath would nail both Endrissi and Christopher to the Crucifix. But the geologist could not help himself by stubbornly countering the man's fuming irrationality, because for some reason he always did this in his usual bemused manner, so Endrissi began laughing.

He knew how to rub Mathieson the wrong way. Endrissi, with a Kamikaze mentality, continued to anger Mathieson; *I will make him wish he were never born*. He began to blink rapidly, undaunted and continuing with his verbose explanation.

"Maybe, this is not such a good idea Endrissi?" Harjit cautioned the geologist. She anticipated more trouble to come but Endrissi chose to ignore her.

Christopher and Harjit were also at their wits end and were becoming wearisome at the perpetual joke. The American's eyes tore a defined hatred at his tormentor, glaring deeply at him with clenched teeth.

"I will speak above your head, it's technical." said Endrissi confidently. "In South

Patagonia, a number of tablelands rose from the humble Atlantic to the Andes not far away and these were covered by rounded pebbles and crumbling sandstone. Eruptions spread sheets of basaltic lava over. Are you ok with this?'

Everyone had enough when Harjit and Christopher chorused loudly together.

"*Shut, the, fuck, up, Endrissi!*" They were joined by Carmello who arrived a few seconds ago. Meanwhile, Mathieson simply glared down at Endrissi, simply shaking his head having no more wish to further take part in such a foolish conversation and stomped off muttering obscenities.

"*Job done. And you fuck off too Mathieson.*" Endrissi shouted after him. The Catcall echoed into the darkness.

For some reason even Endrissi knew that this time he had gone too far. Illogically he thought that the black man was really getting to him, shaking his head not quite knowing what had suddenly come over him. Feeling guilty, he picked up a sizable boulder tossing it over and into the fissure's hungry dark mouth. The nearby black crevice held a deep secret. While Endrissi waited for a clatter of noises., there was no impact; no sound, nothing.

Endrissi questioned his own judgement with a glum stare. The rock dropped straight down for thousands of metres far into the bowels of the earth. Eventually it struck the bottom. The impact awakened something bad. A life form, that moved with purpose, a thing not of this world, in fact it lay dormant below for a very long time. It had come from *nowhere* and was nothing short of hellish!

Endrissi's forehead furrowed, resembling layers of the rock surfaces he loved so much, his eroded skin bearing evidence to the full force and exposure to the elements over many harsh years and wild environments.

"I would say that is one bloody deep hole." The thirty-five-year-old geologist whistled long and loud.

"Yeah, that's a real scientific test you did Endrissi." Christopher added dryly.

The geologist was about five-nine in height, built of powerhouse proportions and was made of solid muscle. A real goliath of a man, with heavy-set bones and a solid frame, was not one to be messed with.

God had played the man a trick on his scalp because Endrissi had been completely bald from a young age yet had a large bushy beard. The rest of his body was as hairy as an ape. Not a stone left unturned when Endrissi was around, he always found boulders of all descriptions anywhere in the surrounding environment.

****

The following week found the team working under arduous conditions and were subjected to vicious thunder storms. Battered by torrential rain, they cleared the area and explored the immediate vicinity bearing no pleasure at all. It just became an existence. There was moaning and blasphemy from everyone. During the clearance, sizeable shaped mounds were being continually uncovered around the site which turned out to be massive blocks of cut-stone. The group slashed more of the green masses away and soon exposed another mystery, ten tall stone statues.

After the storms passed everyone's spirits lifted for a while, but all was not well. Something was wrong with Carmello. Normally, Carmello would have a witty comment to keep people in good humour, and like Endrissi, was always up for a laugh. Today was different because Carmello was not himself. The small man seemed to be struck by a dark depression. It felt to him that an unseen force was eating away and burning out his soul. Everyone watched with unease.

With all mounds cleared, the team stepped back and stared with great curiosity and academic intrigue because before them stood ten tall stone effigies. Grim stone figures standing as if on guard, each one fanning out from what appeared to be the entrance to some mine-works. Defoliating these statues completely revealed their sculptured and determined faces. *Who were they?*

Solid rock warriors displayed their strong physique, gripping stone spears and held stone shields with unwavering hard stone faces. Each warrior stared inwardly towards large engraved symbols on the double doorway. Were they really reading those ancient inscriptions on the surface of the stone doors or were they standing in unison in a ready stance with stone muscles poised to move against something?

"What do you think these sentinels are trying to tell us? What do they represent?" Christopher pondered at their Medusa masquerades.

"Or are they trying to keep something inside?" Harjit replied solemnly. "They are looking into the cave, not out." She tensed the pit of her stomach while displaying a fraught look of apprehension.

"What's inside that we should fear, Harj? *Do not worry so much.* From a layman's point of view, this outward looking stonemasonry resembles a similar type found in 16th or 17th century northern Europe." Said Christopher who then began demonstrating more about the stonework.

"Remarkable." Endrissi was at a loss for words.

"Above this, it is built onto the original structure of that Inca type architecture which suggests that this structure may have been added at a later stage. A different time to enhance, finish or rebuild the main part of this ancient structure."

The scientist postulated while marvelling at their latest find. Christopher was about to speak again when the excited geologist began blinking with thought. He could not help himself rudely intercepting the conversation, curtailing

Christopher's extrapolation of building events in the South American continent.

"On or around AD300 to 1100, like the Twannku culture," on went Endrissi, "They too had developed a greater skill in stonework which was copied by the Inca, and afterwards seen in the city of Cuzco in the fourteenth and fifteenth centuries. Jump in any time Chris." But it was Harjit who was off the mark first; she needed better account and more specifics.

"What really happened here Endrissi?" Harjit was vexed at his rhetoric. "My initial observations of this building lead me to agree with Christopher on this one. This stonework is a hybrid. I disagree however with him on everything else." Self-assured Endrissi smiled down at her like a teacher.

"Eh?" Christopher waited for Endrissi's reply.

"Si, I too find it unbelievable that this construction style could be seen outside America," said Endrissi. "And it is without a shred of doubt, to be found anywhere in Europe," his accelerated tone unshakable.

"No." Christopher stated bluntly standing his ground. "I don't and maybe this place was not finished or had collapsed. Sooner-or-later like us other Europeans discover this place and repaired it. Simply put, they took over mining operations. Gold is such a motivator don't you think?"

"More like fool's gold," said Harjit, disgusted at man's greed.

"Who knows, even Endrissi is guessing, sorry Harj." Christopher sounded increasingly frustrated.

"We should find some evidence of this. It is more likely either the Spanish or Portuguese who have visited the mines before us." Carmello wisely said.

"Yeah man, I like that idea, about the gold that is! Makes this shit expedition worth it." Mathieson appeared almost as if he had been secretly listening as he jumped out from the dense woods behind the structure.

"I have not heard of any explorations of this area or seen it in any literature. Then again, maybe none ever returned." Christopher generalized. "Surely they must have seen the temple?" He too sensed something was misplaced and felt uncertainty in his bones. Maybe Harjit's feelings were right all along and added, "The stonework is definitely a mixture of indigenous and European influence." Not to be put off, "I think they are trying to mimic these original people's ancient ways. These statues are something else! "It is a real mystery, and a salute to the stone-crafters of old. Sculptured, who knows how long ago before the arrival of any Conquistadors." He lifted his shoulders in a confused shrug.

"Why are they all looking inwards?" asked Harjit, "Are they trying to keep something inside? I keep thinking this, I cannot help it." Harjit lowered her voice into a caustic whisper; she could not shift her dread at some unseen threat gnawing inside. An awkward silence came over them.

Suddenly God sent the sun gloriously to burst out through the trees and instantly vaporised their dispirited sullenness. When the forest lit up in a show of wondrous energy, it was spreading quickly into a mixture of thin rays and wide shafts between tree and branch. The shafts filled the forest in misty droplets of crystal green water vapour. This orchestra of light beams ended in that sombre instant beholding the birth of a moment.

"I presume mining has been going on here for centuries." Endrissi rolled on ignoring the girl. In his chauvinistic opinion, Harjit had nothing to offer than woman's intuition. Fabio and Endrissi had something in common here, the man droning on with his own geological analyses.

"Really..." Harjit seemed more distant.

"The bedrock would be mined using the pulley system we have already seen. They would be able to lift those massive stone boulders up and out from the fissure, and slap those onto the surface right here. In my studies these raw boulders are likely to be part of a four-stage process, before producing the end-result, these massive rectangular blocks."

"Really," she yawned.

"What I can't work out is..." Endrissi speculated eagerly.

"Oh, you can't! Well that's a surprise!" Harjit turned off.

"Listen, this is important," as he frowned at the girl's impertinence. "The stone at this site is not as hard or as dense to that found at the temple. Here it's more porous and a lighter red-colour."

Endrissi had already compared the naturally mined rocks at this location to the precision-modelled larger stone blocks that built the temple.

"That's interesting," Harjit's face suddenly lit up in the warmth of new-born sunlight. "You know, the Incas did not know anything about the wheel. Yet here we have discovered *rollers!* This civilization is obviously far more advanced." Harjit returned Endrissi's postulation. "It might take as many as two thousand men to move 110,000Kg blocks."

"Yes, it does." Endrissi stared at Harjit, taken aback at the girl's instant knowledge, and not quite knowing what else to say.

"Odd though," she continued. "At the temple the blocks are much larger and all cut using stone tools. So, what is going on here? A large piece of this jigsaw is missing don't you think Endrissi?" Harjit directed her question straight at the geologist trying to put him on the spot.

"Yes, a piece is missing." Endrissi was perplexed and wanted to say something smart but the slim American suddenly appeared cutting into the conversation. He had something else to add.

"Yeah Endrissi!" He challenged. "You're the fucking missing piece man, you're it!"

Mathieson laughed. "You really are a stupid fuck." The American repeated his taunt.

Red-faced, outsmarted and insulted, the geologist decided that he had no option and said nothing else.

****

At the entrance, thick yellow-green algae appeared cemented onto the large stone double doors. The seams were encrusted and shut solid. They stood together for a moment when Endrissi went forward. The geologist with detailed interest immediately began chipping the crust off with his trusty hammer, while Christopher began searching around the extremities of the entrance.

Christopher's foraging soon exposed two stone levers hidden behind vegetation. One was on the left and the other to the right of each door. The levers were inset into stone arches. Excited at his unexpected discovery, he put his full body weight onto one of the levers, pulling down while trying to move it. Using extra force, it still would not budge. He needed help.

"Aaahgrrrr!" Christopher called out. "Endrissi, come over here a minute." Looking across to the busy geologist, he said, "Endrissi!" He shouted at him. "Get over here and help me push this lever, it might open the entrance!" Endrissi turned expectantly. "Come on man, hurry up!" Christopher straightened his stiff back and rubbed his sore hands. He was ready for action. The geologist got ready beside him.

"Ok let's do it!" Endrissi said. Both men combined their full weights, attacked the left lever with maximum effort and Endrissi's solid frame made all the difference. It moved a little. Sweat pouring off their foreheads in intense effort, muscles bulging over the lever... Yes! It moved some more.

"It's going Endrissi! It's going!" Chris started panting harder.

"Aaaagrh!" Bear like Endrissi growled. One last effort and the lever went crunching downwards in a wide arc, as timeless bits of crust broke away.

Delighted, they grinned at each other. Heavy stone doors ground inwards and crumbled seals of encrusted algae. They could hear hollow sounds echoing from inside as it opened.

A slice of daylight streamed inwards, lighting up the dark interior. It sent a mystery of reflexive shivers up all their spines. The rest of the team waited to watch the two men. Endrissi over-excited, quickly got out his torch from his rucksack. Nothing could hold him back from going inside!

"Not so fast man." Christopher warned. "You should at least use a little caution." Christopher waited outside holding the door while looking inside.

The others seemed amused at his nervous hesitation while valuable seconds ticked past, nodding their heads resignedly while peering warily around inside, giving it a quick examination.

The starter's whistle gone, the others chose this moment to get going, rushing passed and following the intrepid Endrissi.

Once inside, the team immediately stopped, as a sudden shock hit them as they were confronted by the stark darkness. Taking a deep breath in, everyone panicking, they scanned their torches in every direction. All except the pioneering geologist, each person had second thoughts of what to do but it was only Christopher who saw their danger.

That is odd, there are no handles inside of these doors. If anyone is inside and the doors shut, then this place is a tomb!

"Wedge that door Carmello, and be quick!" Christopher shouted to the guide, "Wedge it shut right now! This place is not what it seems." Carmello was the only person who had not marched straight passed Christopher in some crazy gold rush! The ranger hated the place and had been reluctant to come inside.

Endrissi realised their danger, and recognised his own ill-judged pearl. Alarm suddenly written on his face, he ran quickly back, passing the bewildered others to the entrance. Endrissi set immediately to work and helped Carmello place heavy boulders in front of the open door, mumbling his embarrassment. He knew that he should have been more of a leader than an impetuous schoolboy.

****

The place secure, Endrissi returned inside and stood by Harjit as the others spread out a little taking care where they walked.

"Were these people slaves and held inside here by their captors?" Harjit asked Endrissi about her grim idea. Spooked, she needed to know answers.

"Makes sense, and once their job at the temple or here was complete, which would probably take a lifetime, they would most likely then be sacrificed to the Sun Gods. All good South American civilizations back then did." Endrissi smiled sardonically. He tried to lift his voice, but it fell dead in the darkness. "Ok people, let's scan this immediate area before we go back to camp. But right now, touch nothing, just observe. I mean it. Everything has to be collated first." Endrissi knew the importance of this historical find.

Carmello found some old wooden torches lying on the dusty floor, made of bound cloth material with a slime-like feel to them - an oil coating that would help keep them in good condition. He also found several oil vats that still contained nut oil! Saturating the cloth and igniting them, they burned brightly, showing a large hallway to Endrissi's consternation.

"Oh, what are you doing Carmello!" Endrissi shouted.

"Just checking."

"Touch nothing!" The geologist insisted.

"This place keeps giving more and more, doesn't it?" said Christopher humorously.

The place was nothing he had ever imagined. Flamed light shone on bewildered eyes and opened to see brightly coloured walls and drawings. Pictures of what appeared to be of great times of wealth and wonder. And there was another displayed painting of many people caught in some sort of catastrophe, like a famine and another, a scene of sacrifice and subjugation. *What did it all mean?*

The wall where they entered, on each side of the open doorway, were detailed pictures of people running and trying to flee from some enemy, perhaps the Spaniards or Portuguese? One dreadful drawing was of entrapment or imprisonment with numerous flowing squiggly or curved lines; and from the expressions and small faces they appeared to be strangled or drowned.

Everything represented something, one that only this dead culture would understand. Had it been a great flood like in the Bible? Whatever happened, it would take many years, if not forever, to understand their story.

****

Time passed at the camp and Mathieson had been gone for days surveying with Carmello, both guides arriving back unannounced one evening, and both exhausted. Soaked to the skin, Mathieson looked annoyed. With machetes and electric torches in hands, sitting down heavily with an insane look on his face.

"Hi boys! Good to see you in one piece." Endrissi said tentatively while standing up. He welcomed both guides to their campfire. The others had been relaxing outside their tents laughing and drinking coffee when the men came out from the darkness.

"Now that we are all seated and taking it easy, me and my friend Carmello here have been out working our mother asses off." He paused while they waited to hear his news.

Both men's faces were naturally dark skinned and glowing in the fire light, which accentuated their profiles. Christopher probed the fire a little with a stick moving the burning logs and creating myriads of embers to flare quickly upwards into the evening sky.

"Give us a break Mathieson, we've been hard at it too you know." Christopher rebuffed and knew that the guides were tired; but there was no need for insults.

"How did you get on?" Harjit brightened the conversation.

"Well, we traversed the complete fissure and it spans five miles north-east of here and about the same to the south-west. It takes an all-round trip of twenty miles to get back to this location, it is one big fucking hole and it's ragged next to the edges. One thing is for sure man. This is one black hole you would not want to fall into."

"It was fluky in the first place for the expedition to even find this entrance to the valley, right here is like a natural bridge." Said Carmello.

"This crack is a natural barrier to just about anything that comes its way, the sides to the valley are straight up and sheer as we already know. Where you fell down the slope Chris, it was not too far away from here. Lucky shit man, you could have as easily found a one-way ticket down the other way to the bottom of that hole!" Mathieson pulled a face but his intimation clear, not having a care if that had happened.

"More than just luck guided us here. Passing through into the vale unscathed was more than luck and good scouting, to miss the fissure like we did," stated Carmello. The guide paused as if deep in thought. "Chances of having had an accident was high, it happened to you Chris but luckily you were unhurt."

After speaking, the guide began pouring out a mug of coffee. Carmello had always felt that a veiled force had guided them towards this superstitious valley. The others were beginning to think that the smaller man was too exhausted, and good rest might help him.

"I need a drink." Mathieson took out his hip flask.

"How wide do you think the pass is then Mat?" Using his nickname, Harjit asked inquisitively.

"No more than a half mile wide man, we were lucky that the fissure cut off the vale completely. Then there would be no other way than jumping over or climbing up the valley rock face." Mathieson replied smiling at the girl.

"What were the odds of finding it then?"

"Not good. It is almost like we *were* meant to find this place then and maybe Carmello's feelings are not so far from the truth." Endrissi speculated in a low voice. Everyone stared at the small guide staring hypnotically at the rising flames of their campfire.

"It's nothing short of good fortune," added Mathieson. "We could so easily have walked straight by it. Good work from us scouts, that is what I say. Getting your *mother fuckin asses* passed here. I won't mention you falling on your sweet ass, boy." Mathieson looked at Christopher and smiled.

Endrissi, as everyone now began picturing Christopher, covered in mud again and skidding down on his backside finding a quick way in.

"There is something not right here, this place is evil my friends." Carmello cut into their hilarity. His tone morbid, "See those warriors? They are looking inwards at the cave, not away. Harjit knows it too, she knows something is wrong." Carmello watched hesitantly at the stone statues in the darkness. Their stone silhouettes appeared more life-like from here, unnerving. Harjit watched the mysterious figures too.

"So, what are you driving at Carmello?" Insensitive and unimpressed, asked Endrissi who wanted to bring him out of his shell.

"Too me, they are not guarding anyone from entering the mine, it's more like they are guarding someone or something from coming… *out*." Carmello's solemn voice dropped to a quick whisper. "*As if on watch.*"

The stillness became infectious as everyone stared towards the isolated stone sentinels. Harjit said nothing, harbouring a quiet fear.

"Relax man, *cool it.*" Mathieson was becoming concerned as he observed his companions' dilemma. He changed the subject by continuing his update of their latest exploits and eating their late meal. Fearing the unknown, Carmello exhausted, said nothing more. An hour later, everyone began turning in for the night. A strange sinister atmosphere descended over the camp…

Mathieson was soon snoring loudly next to Carmello inside their two-man tent, but it was not the noise that stopped him from sleeping. Carmello knew that the mine doors were wedged open, it was what was inside that terrified him.

The sound of animals seemed closer tonight, a hiss or a screech magnified through the forest while orchestras of insects played their nightly overtures to the sounds of continued survival. Not far off from where they slept behind their thin tarpaulins; hidden in the trees, a large cat saw their campfire. The tents were highlighted by the large fires.

The predator snarled, sensing the unnatural human presence, moving cautiously towards their camp, its soft feline paws silently passed, heading on towards the cave. Staring inside from behind the statues, its cat eyes calculating what the darkness held. Curiosity dared it to enter. Instinctively, the jaguar snarled even louder, but it dared not proceed. Slipping swiftly back into the deep forest, it moved on down into the hidden vale. It had seen enough.

In the coming days and weeks that followed, work continued in the immediate locality. During this time many artefacts and stone tools were being discovered below topsoil, showing more evidence of civilization. Endrissi insisted that all work be done before going back into the mine.

Centuries inside the rainforest would cover most things, so it took a lot of painstaking toil and effort to clear. Something had happened to the people that once lived here, making them leave. Maybe it was the knowledge of the approaching Europeans was enough for them to leave. It was unlikely that any attack took place here because there was no evidence of dead remains, only numerous pots and relics of tools that had been found scattered. There was no proof of physical skeletons, graves or any genocide. Where the previous inhabitants went too was still a complete enigma. It was as if the people had simply disappeared!

The scientists concentrated working in their own fields of expertise and with luck on their side, because they were able to discover several new species of plants in that time. Further analyses of this would be completed *invitro* when he got back to the university in Italy. In the meantime, Christopher would be busy studying, collating and categorizing the specimen's obvious properties that might yield important results.

All his new specimens were packed away into the *Oncol Smart Safe Pods*, provided; these passed the Brazilian Government scrutiny. The last thing Christopher wanted was to be accused of bio-piracy!

Kees Acampilchtl, their Brazilian government official, would make sure that there would be no repeat of Edward Thompson in 1870 with gross pillaging – an American explorer who exploited Mayan culture artefacts. However, in this case, Kees being the official agent, would make sure that all specimens or artefacts were not hidden and taken out of the country without his say.

Christopher and Harjit placed the specimens into their respective Smart Pods, safe environmental crates that allowed them to *still to grow in transit* and keep the same relative humidity, pH, light and temperature. This pod, a marvellous invention he designed while still a student at the university, sealing his Doctorate.

Christopher was quickly commissioned by the ONCOL Corporation for work in the field using his revolutionary invention.

The pod's external hexagonal shaped walls, made of a light, hard polycarbonate material, was once constructed from their flat pack into robust micro-climatic chambers. Information was converted into digital signals streamed data in continual fine-tuning, and kept the climatic chamber exactly right for any specific programmable habitat linked into a synthetic bio-network. The ingenious design also accounted for scalable convection, and wind currents on the surface barometer probes that simulated first with analog and then digitally converted inside this sealed crate.

Looking on the ground, Christopher studied small green brown plants with their small speckled white blotches that spread all over the surface and around the base of the trees. Where these plants grew, he saw no thick brown vines with those strange poisonous flowers. The plants apparently fended off the indigenous vines found in this region.

"What is that plant Chris?" Harjit asked.

"Hmm…I really do not know. A new one I suspect. It seems to inhibit the growth of that parasitic flower and its vines. Interesting. I will name it, *Harjit's Palms*. It has obvious healing and loving properties." The young man smiled tenderly at her.

"Oh, you're so sweet!" she smiled affectionately.

"I have already found a new variety of Cat's Claw growing here and this has been used for over two thousand years in one form or another." Christopher was beginning to show off his knowledge to the girl. "The *Ashaninke* people used this to treat asthma, gastric ulcers and cancers."

"You are a very, very bright star Chris." She took his arm and squeezed it.

"I hope this new species exhibits similar anti-inflammatory properties, diuretic or spasmolytic properties too, and if so, I have no doubt it was already used by the ancients as a tribal remedy," he conjectured.

"Your Scottish accent is sometimes hard to follow Chris, and I love it." Harjit leaned towards and kissed him making Chris blush.

Christopher heard those alarm bells chime again in his head. *A weakness!* It was wrong and they both knew it. *She was his weakness, his sin;* Harjit Singh was becoming more than just a physical attraction to him; hiding his internal struggles they were all becoming unbearable. He knew that soon God would test him.

The enormous Brazilian nut trees above them were swaying slowly, creaking all around as an unexpected gale suddenly began blowing. Both became aware that the foliage around them suddenly became violent in the increasing turbulence.

"Looks like there's a storm coming." advised Christopher.

"Yes, let's get back to camp. I feel like an early night."

"You'll be lucky."

****

It was another rough evening, and the next day was not much better. Harjit decided to do something different and give Endrissi a hand while Christopher continued his survey most of the day. Later, Christopher joined the two guides under the shelter of their large communal tent to eat their meals. Time passed, and the sultry wind began picking up pace.

Endrissi and Harjit were working in the mines until night, by which time the gales were sweeping through the forest. Thunder could be heard not too far off. Through the space in the trees directly above the fissure, darker clouds could be seen; clouds moving in disorder all embroiling there. At the campsite, the men looked up and became more unnerved at the crazy sight. Suddenly, a huge crack split the heavens!

Everything lit up so brightly it shocked their souls, then came immediate darkness. Guttural thunder rumbled again moving the air when thunder came clapping harder this time. A force released, jolting his body into a past dread, shoulders sagging in defence, with a weight pushing down on him. FLASH! Their faces lit up in shock of the night.

"Shit, that was right above us!" Christopher trembled in alarm.

"The rip in the earth is forty metres wide and is *very, very deep*," said Carmello. "Even God does not know where it leads!" The small man held onto his hat.

"Get real, you sad fuck," said Mathieson. The American had no time for Carmello's prophetic nonsense.

"There used to be a bridge which straddled the fissures mouth at one time. We found some evidence of this on the opposite side. It could have been connected to the wreckage over at this side. These people must have been, *great miners!*"

Carmello's ragged brimmed straw hat matched his muddy and tattered brown shirt. He got in such a state from fighting his way through the unexplored rim in the earths breach.

"I'll give you that man. Great indeed!" Mathieson nodded.

"They probably discovered some precious stone minerals while digging out these massive blocks." Endrissi added, "these blocks must have been moved up the valley to their final resting place at the temple."

"There are too many of these blocks kicking around here," replied Christopher.

"Maybe they were going to build above and around the current temple, a bit like an outer shell, making the temple look even bigger for their Gods," postulated Endrissi.

"Maybe they finished. There is no further evidence of any other additional buildings over at the temple. I would have expected to see many more," pondered Christopher. "I reckon they stopped digging because something major happened! What that might have been I have no idea."

"The crack in the earth... *is dangerous*." Carmello squeezed his tone. "Something evil has been released. I feel it." His voice competed against the weather's din.

Another crack of lightening came, brightening the sky, animating the forest in a mega FLASH! Thunder too, and crackling all becoming part of an amazing electric storm, lightning flashing more. The scene became more like a warring barrage than a storm, as if cataclysmic events were unfolding. Christopher stared fearfully into the smaller man's scared face, somehow suppressing his own fearful instincts; he wanted to help Carmello.

"Shit, come on *Carm*, loosen up a bit. You have not smiled since we entered this valley." Christopher's trance was broken. "*Where is that wee funny guy I used to know*, the one that always laughed and joked?" He was reminded of better days. "Look, I really wouldn't listen to that tribal leader on this one." Christopher attempted to defuse disillusionment; "There is no seismic activity in this location. It's not a fault line, you can ask Endrissi when he comes back."

Christopher understood and respected the small man's superstition but needed to feel better within himself.

"Superstitious mumbo-jumbo man." Mathieson said abruptly. "Stop being an idiot." Mathieson as ever unsympathetic, finding it all quite amusing and was always one for *ridiculing* any person, and yet making it sound funny to onlookers. It was just another annoying trait of the American. He didn't realise that Carmello wasn't himself.

Hurt, Carmello winced a bit at the man's mockery towards him; Mathieson's jibe having the opposite effect. Turning his gaze away from Mathieson, he pulled his waterproof poncho over his head. Carmello fixed it into place on top of his shoulders.

The rain began pelting down heavy outside forming a sizable muddy pool near the large open tent.

"You make a fool of me." The small man sounded disappointed.

"Shut the fuck up, Mathieson. *You, asshole,*" swore Christopher, the man livid with the American's big-headed sarcasm. He had gone too far this time.

"Say what!" Grinning, things had been far too quiet for him, loving conflict especially with the Scotsman. *Yes! The Scot's gone for the bait.*

Predictable son of a mother. Mathieson began staring and smirking more at Christopher's annoyance.

"I mean it. This place feels wrong. It is *evil*," Carmello ignored the black man; the sallow skinned South American continued speaking over and over like a recording, as if no one was listening to him, "I feel it in my bones, and I can smell it in the air. *Something* is rotten, and it is coming from down there." He swallowed while nodding his head with eyes fixed onto the blackness of the fissure.

Harjit came running and joined them under the tent, the girl completely soaked; although this did not seem to dampen her enthusiasm. Her eyes quickly narrowed seeing the men like this, she felt their tension. An instant apprehension came over her; *what was going on?*

Taking a deep breath, she stood with her mouth open. *Something has happened, another argument? These are becoming too regular, what is happening to us? It's here... this place.* Harjit knew the place had bad karma. Standing behind Christopher, she turned him while unclenching his tightened fist.

"Hi, Harjit!" Christopher appeared surprised and said, "You're wet."

"Hello, Chris," she paused a little out of breath. "I have been in the mine with Endrissi!" Excitement and great self-achievement was running through her voice. "Come on everyone, let's get back to the mines. Bring your kit!" *My God,* she thought, *I came in just in time.* Harjit took charge, encouraging the men to help her and Endrissi.

Christopher and Mathieson automatically picked up their rucksacks and went with her. Carmello did not. Carmello instead chose to ignore her, the man walking slowly towards the fissure, as if to face an internal battle. He looked miserable and disheartened, *almost suicidal.*

"What about the plans! Harjit, please stop!" Christopher concerned, trying to catch up with her fast pace towards the cave. This is not what they had already agreed too and certainly not a structured approach for exploring mines. He kept asking, "What about Endrissi's plans, has he changed his mind? We have to be very careful!"

"Yeah right, *Pussy.*" Mathieson spoke out and away from ears reach of Harjit. The girl stopped, as the rain smashed heavily off their oilskins!

"Ok, brain box, now what do you make of this piece of stone in my hand?" Opening her hand, Harjit held a stone shaped like a crescent moon about three inches by seven, "I picked it up inside the mine works."

"Bloody stupid going it alone Harj." In the balance, Chris could not understand the stupidity of her and Endrissi's impromptu tomfoolery, both people exploring the mine without warning or firm planning. This was the second time that the so-called, second in command of the expedition, Endrissi, had made a wrong decision.

Resigned to this discovery, Christopher suppressed his anger at Endrissi's irresponsible determination, and unscientific practice. Yet he continued to stare at her strange artefact. Christopher tried to judge whether it was a waxing or waning moon.

"What do you make off it Chris?" She asked.

"I have no idea. We may find out more during our quest." Christopher knew at this point that all planning was out of the window, and against his better judgement would go along. "Ok Harj, show me where you found it."

"Quick then, out of this rain Chris, follow me." Oddly, her initial fears were forgotten for the moment. With something tangible to work on, it pasted her sanity together and with no hesitation, they entered the mine. Ahead, they could see a bright light, it was the geologist. Endrissi turned and greeted them with a smile.

"Glad you could make it!" He said in an elated voice. "This place is ancient. It could be as old as 500 to 900 A.D. However, the mega-structure further up the park a bit, I'm not so sure off." Endrissi's brow furrowed, once again in lecture mode. "We will probably take a series of laser scans here as well as at the temple. To do this we have in our scanner kit; an Optec ILRIS-ID portable scanner, to help us reveal the internal structures. It beats any normal camera although I would need a vantage point for it to be effective. Are you both following this?" jerking his head annoyingly to one side and backwards expecting to see their combined Pavlovian agreements with him.

"We see what you mean." Chris agreed, *shit here we go again.*

"Yes," answered Harjit robotically.

It took several minutes of Endrissi's verbal battering before they could really see what was going on inside the large shadowy stone room.

Inside it appeared to be a pentagonal shaped hall with a complex of engraved codices seen everywhere! They recalled from their previous visit, parts displayed murals of food, agriculture and war; it was a great story. Ancient debris lay scattered on the hard red-stone floor.

Harjit guided Christopher to behind a stone table at the far wall and to where she had found her stone artefact. Looking behind the table and into a darker corner recess, her investigatory eyes explored a little more. She could see something else... *What is that?* Harjit wondered.

Peeling away the layers of dark shadows, Harjit made out an old wooden rack that held what she perceived to be rows of tall speared battle-axes all about five metres in length. The rack obscured her unsure site, *there's something else.* Something she had not seen before behind the wooden pole handles when a gradual awareness made her skin creep.

In darkness, sitting all alone was a skeleton in armour! She shuddered unexpectedly as it appeared to be watching her. Alarmed, Harjit's eyes widened while her jaw slowly dropped.

Its skull matted opaque and grey, she guessed it was more likely to be Portuguese in this part of the continent. The soldier's armour and metal helmet all covered in dirty cobwebs. His head was slightly bowed down towards his chest plate and tilted slightly upwards looking in her direction.

Normally, skeletons did not bother her being a medical student, but here in a god-forsaken place like this, it did. She was off guard, when the dead soldier it seemed had materialised out from the darkness. This new find brought the others quickly over to stand courageously behind her.

"Thanks a lot, guys." *Typical.* She hinted sarcasm in her soft tone.

The skeleton's hand gripped an empty bottle, at one time might have contained water or wine. On top of the small table, there was a leather pouch open and spilled of its contents.

Their torchlight reflected on a poor man's dream. Precious gems! It was an invitation and no mistake! Like Pied Piper, their shaky light saw crystals sparkle of every colour. They drew closer to the gems. A rusty metal spear lay across the table next to the rich soldier.

"Conquistadores," Christopher stated. "I knew it. This guy must be on some kind of last sentry duty. Maybe this place was a guard house and this bag of gems his final payment." He contemplated picking up the small tattered leather bag. "Fabio will be pleased."

The group moved in behind the rack of weapons to get a better look at the dead soldier and his gems. Christopher decided that he would collate this evidence and take it back to the base camp while Mathieson's greedy eyes began counting his bonus.

"Best to leave the stones where they are and untouched for the moment Chris." The geologist said firmly. "What was the soldier guarding?" Endrissi wondered, "Maybe more of these little beauties."

"More gems?" Mathieson smiled.

"Look," Endrissi followed the dead man's invisible guideline stuck out pointing the direction with a white bony finger. No mistake, he was directing them towards a rough wall and another shadowy corner on his left side.

What was that, another stone lever? Endrissi wondered. "Look over there!" His tone mixed, nervous.

Everyone turned and sure enough, another lever waited for them. It was set into the large rock face where the stoneworkers had designed walls to join seamlessly with the natural rock face.

They decided to follow this important discovery, everyone that is; except Harjit, her interest and mind remained firm and fixated onto the dead soldier.

What is that, what could it be... she saw something around his neck that hugged him like a warm scarf.

Underneath those cobwebs, something is there. A type of rope was wrapped around his bony vertebrae, my God... he was strangled!

Harjit started breathing quickly, her heart thumping and hyperventilating out of control, while something unconscious numbed her mind, the girl's voice was paralysed. Her fingers trembled while travelling easily through the soldier's sticky webbed scarf. Underneath she bravely touched his death cords.

Disturbed by her intrusion, the skeleton's head turned questioningly around at her, as the thick cobwebs drew stretching more, pulling while its neck vertebrae ticked like the sounds of cogs in a grandfather clock.

Tick... Click.

Tick... Click, click.

Tick... Click, click, click. Time held her horror. One after the other the ratchet sequence revealed a bleached white face!

It's grinning at me. "Ahh!" The girl screamed at its webbed sockets.

The soldier's head twisted its bony neck around to look at her little more, and finally stopped with a last solid "click." Its death vines could not hold its weight any longer when it's neck snapped. The skull severed from its backbone and dropped off, striking the table hard and heavy. It began a warped roll along the table.

Finally ending its macabre journey by bouncing onto the solid stone floor, hitting it with a sickening crack. The conquistador's grinning jaw finally wiped away into pieces of shattered dentistry over the floor.

"Oh my God!" She called out.

"Hell, Harjit… *can't you leave things alone?*" Said Endrissi unhinged by the unexpected surprise.

Her legs began visibly shaking as she felt her dry voice coming nervously back to her throat.

"He was strangled with these *vines.*" Gritting her white teeth.

"Are you ok Harj?" Christopher was concerned and held her hand. "Not very nice is it kid. What the hell… it happened a long time ago. It is all a bit of a puzzle. That's why we came here," he nodded to the geologist. "So, who killed him and why? Not for money and that's a fact because the gems are still here."

Christopher guided the girl away from the mixture of metal and bone to where the others were standing.

Mathieson's mind on the money, he and Endrissi pushed the lever and a trapdoor suddenly opened in the floor!

"Well lookee here." Mathieson's wide eyes greedily studied the new entrance. The man was overly excited with this new find. "Shit I'm rich." Mathieson whispered under his breath.

"A hidden passage!" Harjit exclaimed.

"Torch." Endrissi ordered clinically. He wanted to see inside right away. The light shone in and it appeared to expose a steep stone stairway.

Inside, red walls stood out, and steps worn smooth going downwards, amazed that they could see crystals within the stone type glinting in their naked flame and torchlight held by the explorers.

The group quickly pushed on, descending further to about forty metres below ground level where the steps led into a dark cavern system. Determined to get rich quick, nothing could stop Endrissi and Mathieson's bloodhound instincts.

The group kept on moving inside, further and deeper, continuing through a labyrinth of caverns. Creepy shadows seemed endless as naked flames waved blindly around in the damp air. Sometime later, they came to another part of the system leading down slippery stone steps. These steps wider and more precarious, they observed this to be a new construction, with each step inserted by design into a cylindrical shaped outer wall going around and downwards like a vertical shaft. This dangerous stairway had presented itself to them with no room for error. Down they went...

At its centre, it appeared to be like a mineshaft, and a fatal accident waiting to happen. Swallowed groans told of their wariness exposed to a dangerous black hole and what looked like a gateway to the underworld.

"Wow! Careful everyone and keep your hands touching the wall to guide you, that will keep you steady. Step here," the geologist lifted his flaming torch over the dark centre looking downwards. "And you are dead." Endrissi stared into the deep shaft dropping a small stone.

"Come back," Harjit insisted.

"Shit it's a fucking deep black hole alright!" Mathieson joined Endrissi and agreed, "There must be many levels. Look, over there." Mathieson saw the start of another level below them, "Light is coming in from somewhere else. Its filtering from outside, *I guess.* So, there must be an opening from the fissure."

"Si and that would account for the ventilation this far down. The fissure must be a way of transporting the stone masses upwards." The geologist hypothesized.

****

The sounds of water falling could be heard most strongly coming from where the diffuse light entered, filtering in from one side of the stair column; it was an opening up to another area. The noise they guessed was likely to be the stream crashing down into the crevice as it plunged on its way past a gap on the far side of this emerging cavern.

"Let's ask our masonic friend. How far down does this journey go then Chris?" Once more Mathieson's tone hinted sarcasm, again testing the priest's patience.

"I am not a freemason and for your info pal, and down all the way to Hell in your case!" Christopher finished, Mathieson smiled smugly.

"Whoever built this place was busy." said Harjit, "I cannot see the bottom of this pit. I think that this part," pointing to the hole, "was *only* used for transporting slaves. Up and down they went in a wooden shuttle. This empty centre would account for it gentlemen. It is a medieval lift system and purpose built for people to go mining." Harjit had unintentionally solved the mode of people transportation, *"It's a place of fear."*

Unexpectedly, Endrissi decided to drop his oil-soaked torch into the shaft. Its burning flames rotated endlessly downwards until its life began to flicker, becoming more distant and a tiny dot to be extinguished in some bottomless pit.

"Now, *that is* one bloody deep crater!" Endrissi gasped and said, "This must be older than time itself. If people dug this out, *what the…F… for?"* He screwed his eyes up in dismay. They all knew that the answer to that riddle lay below.

"Do you think dropping that was such a good idea?" Very annoyed, Christopher shouted up. Once again, he could not believe the geologist's thoughtless actions. *How on earth, and he's second in charge, my god! What a fucking idiot…* Chris knew that by dropping one of their few torches might prove critical for their return journey.

"I would say it drops down many miles." Endrissi said while ignoring any sign of concern.

Mathieson began nudging him irresponsibly towards the centre of the shaft, while still holding him securely by his shirt bottom.

"What's down there E?" The ranger's horse-playing around, attitude too much to resist capitalising at the geologist's expense.

"Fuck off Mathieson! Let go!" Endrissi screamed.

"Come on E have another look man!" Mathieson hustled him a little more.

"Don't fool around guys!" Harjit shouted immediate rebuke; she could not believe the American's craziness.

"These people must have dug to the ends of the Earth." Chris whispered to himself. "This exploration of ours is going to take years." He concluded under his breath with an inkling of the enormity of the task.

Looking up at the group above him, Christopher watched their distorted faces with flamed torches in hand and wondered about their real commitment. What they all could see was quite unbelievable as their light expanded far into a massive cavern, dug out to allow people to move up and down quickly to various locations in the mine.

The hole in the floor had to have been a medieval elevator that no longer existed. Ropes made of natural Vines had long since disintegrated. Surmising that the Vines would be, looped over a stone wheel and the wheel fixed into the Cave's roof. A wheel, suggested an influence of a more advanced culture, like the Portuguese! Assumptions they made were that animals or humans would provide the raw pulling power.

The group continued walking down to the next level below. Once again, the walls were full of numerous carvings and paintings depicting inhabitants who worked the mines. In full colour, their stories unfolded.

"This place is breath-taking, quite breath-taking." Endrissi's expression of wonder told it all. "Look at this amazing chronicle, it is everywhere to see, it tells of many people who fell from the top of the fissure to their deaths." The geologist felt the hard wall with his hand. Trailing his fingers along a Sea of Blood leading to the bottom of the mines were depicted in black.

"No Endrissi, more accurately this is a blood sacrifice." Murmured Christopher grimly. "Look here... some warriors with axes and spears forced those poor people over the edge, falling to their doom... it's a brutal society."

Everyone knew that with most civilizations in this part of the world, ritual blood sacrifice was often the end for captured enemies. Mutilation was common practice, not killing an enemy but instead capturing them at all costs, and then later sacrificing them to their Gods. Extraordinarily this ritual is meant to be an honour to die in such a way. In some macabre cultures, they would skin the prisoners and then wear their skins!

"It did them no good, now did it?" Harjit stated. "Nothing else exists of their way of life other than these horrible stories depicting their end." Lowering her tone, "Only sadness remains…" The girl looked around hesitantly and whispered to the others, "Ghosts walk here, *I feel them*…." Harjit's sadness measured their demise.

"I think they were murdered." said Mathieson finding himself embroiled in the guesswork. "Look over here, these are European soldiers, conquistadores; *we know this already*. The men have armour and helmets. It is an obvious subjugation of a people who were pressed into slavery. It was their search for gold and other treasures that brought the soldiers here."

"Like those little gems in your pockets, eh Mathieson?" Endrissi had spotted the guide take some treasure earlier without his permission. This was as good a time as any to say so, after his larking about. "You will be handing them over once we get back."

"Sure," said Mathieson showing no embarrassment, but the man had no such intentions. "Anyway, after these slaves had completed their tasks for their overlords, sure looks like they were dropped into the pit. No evidence. A good Christian burial I would say. God damn killing mother fucks."

Mathieson was a Jew, and because of his aggressive nature, this caused disharmony between him and Christopher. It was in his makeup to have yet another reason to dig at the young priest's religion.

Harjit began piecing the story together, "So that explains why the mines look as if they have been renovated, likely to be back in the 16th or 17th centuries. Probably built by European stonemasons who repaired parts of the structure, as opposed to imaginary forgotten skills of the stone crafters thousands of years before them." She paused then added, "These guys were like mercenaries, butchers, *European pirates.*" She could not think of the right word. "*Bastards!*" She shouted, not normally one for swearing.

"Well-said Harj." Christopher nodded in agreement while they continued staring at the sickening wall paintings.

Tools made of hardened iron and steel lay in evidence over parts of the cavern system, and the type used by the Europeans.

"While you lot mess uselessly around here, I'm going down those steps to the next level." Mathieson pointed to another wide opening in the stone floor. The man headed for it shouting back, "Don't be late ladies!" Mathieson on the chase again, moving like a bloodhound and quickly disappearing hunting for his fortune.

"He is so full of his own *shi…*" Harjit's patience at its limit, *he should have waited.*

"So full of *shit.*" Endrissi completed her sentence smiling boyishly at her. She returned a quizzical understanding while shaking her head when the geologist true to form... with no further thought went after him. The race for wealth was on.

"Come on!" He urged, "We can't let a *yank* beat us to whatever treasure is down there!"

Harjit's face became a picture of disbelief and wondered if Endrissi had lost his sense of reality.

"Look out for any markers," called Christopher. "Keep a mental note of any features everywhere you go and keep looking behind you in case we need to retrace our steps!" Christopher's voice echoed despondently after the mad men. "Harj, bloody hell just look at them go! What are we mixed up in?"

"They are both crazy." The girl responded grimly, "completely mad, Endrissi's lost his marbles too?" *We need an escape plan* she thought.

The priest's mind wondered what might happen next, remembering his scriptures that might help him. *"Be sure of this, I will be with you always, even unto the end of the Earth."*

Matthew 28:20, why this one came to his thoughts Christopher was unsure. He sensed they were all on the brink of something life changing.

****

Mathieson Stuart, a forty-one-year-old hard-hitting Detroit boy, brash to be polite and very, very determined. The man's strength of mind sometimes confused with bloody mindedness, the difference was often hard to distinguish. It had to be in his upbringing and had been tough to say the least, growing up in the backstreets of Detroit where blades and bullets are commonplace.

His mother was an alcoholic and his father worked as best he could to make ends meet as a Taylor, a hard working-man trying to keep his family together. Mathieson was the younger of two brothers; frightened of nothing much, not even the law.

Being Jewish and black-skinned made it harder for him to survive in Detroit with the Jewish community and anti-Jewish backlash. The earliest Jewish settlers came at the very beginning. High Holy Day Services held at the Masonic Temple of Beth-El and their teachings helped provide some hope in their lives. It was not enough.

Streetwise he knew how to navigate past immediate dangers, slip through the net of the law and into a more profitable position. Adaptive and able to take advantage of any opportunity that arose, his survival depended on them.

He was born to survive. Survival of the fittest, he and his brother were always one-step from prison. The Sheriff officers knew them well. Knowing his background might have helped Christopher understand the antagonism towards him but Mathieson never spoke of his murky past or deadly encounters.

Back then, Mathieson's better instincts prevailed and recognised that he needed to get out of the States to evolve or die, so he joined the Texas Rangers, not fitting in there and then becoming a Navy SEAL for five years. He served in Afghanistan, the Middle East and South America. He left the forces after and ended back on the streets again. Mathieson recognised that he could not go back to that old lifestyle and being stopped by police for no apparent reason at gun point with his brother, Matt knew that he needed to get away. Pulling on his training once again, it made him ideal material to become a guide or ranger, swapping his concrete jungle for a green one. So, he headed for South America.

Mathieson had always thought Christopher was a real pain in the ass, a know-it-all, and a smart, *nice boy*, pleasantly polite and very soft. He took an instant dislike to Chris ever since the first time they met.

At any opportunity, Mathieson would talk about the priest, getting a great deal of fun out it at Christopher's expense. Their churches were different. The Old Testament told of *God's chosen people*; the Jews and not the Christians. The American loathed their differences, yet they had a lot in common, both coming from lowly beginnings.

Adaptive in his career the American had become a seasoned jungle guide and he did not think that Christopher had enough stamina or experience to be here too. He judged him to be only a kid and very wet behind his ears.

From the outset of the expedition, the forest ranger had objected about the Scotsman's presence, exhibiting open hostility towards him. It had nothing to do with *class;* maybe it was religion. What made him such a bitter person, not even Mathieson knew that answer or why he detested the Scotsman so much. It just seemed so right.

Christopher learned to be on his guard around the American, and the strange thing was, *even he* found Mathieson quite likeable at times. His brashness could be quite hilarious. One thing was a fact; the dark-skinned man was always dependable. He was determined and ready to carry out his mission keeping them safe, *until now.* Mathieson disappeared as he did and looked like a man possessed...

****

The team quickly caught up behind the slim figured American. The deeper they went, the clammier it became, following down the cracked stone stairs soon reaching the next level below. Flames from their torches waved around endlessly, chasing the darkness back into the deeper caverns beyond their sight, and into places where the darkness waited. It seemed to sulk there.

Regrouped once more, they waited impatiently while Christopher ignited another oil-soaked torch they had been carrying in plastic bags inside a rucksack; keeping some spares for the way back. Dazzling luminosity burst from the roof rock structure! Light jumped around the multi-facetted surfaces and seams of self-perpetuating energies, igniting within its crystalline microstructure and appeared like crystal fairy lights.

Looking around at irregular boulders, lying everywhere inside this shadowy area. These could easily cause them to stumble or break an ankle. It was difficult to measure exactly how wide or how high the ceiling was but their presence echoed a deep hollow reverberation, indicating just how large and expansive a subterranean place this was. It was big...Really BIG!

In this new light, a wondrous site befell them as it showed off the cave roof structure, changing without transition from a sandstone disguise. Becoming a glassy mixture of dark blue and black crystalline rocks, with long twisting zigzags of speckled white dots, resembling long strands of frozen forked lightening. These bizarre lengths expanded through the full length of the gigantic cave. Its integral rock crystals above glinted like distant stars.

"Breath-taking," said Endrissi.

"I don't think we should go any further, this place is immense. Just look at it! We really need to plot out a map," said Christopher. "It would be too easy to get lost."

Chris pressed Endrissi more and wanted to curtail the man's haphazard approach to this stupid exploration. Endrissi ignored him again because he had spotted something more interesting.

"Look over there!" He called, "Catch a view of that!" Endrissi pointed to what looked like a goliath of a hole in the cave floor.

This new feature captivated the man's delirious attention running and stumbling immediately towards the colossal hole. They all could observe that indeed, it was an enormous cavity and one as deep as the roof was high!

Deep, so very deep, that the bottom could easily be two hundred to three hundred metres straight down into an unfathomable void. They all felt intimidated, all except Endrissi. Soon the scale made them feel quite giddy.

"My God." Endrissi said and stopped. He was short of breath. Once more in his life, Endrissi was speechless. His eyes baring down into a massive crater below his feet, it was a geologist's dream! Endrissi began analysing the weird and distant rock formations underneath. He saw that the bright crater appeared similar if not identical to the ceiling above them, giving an impression of being inside a gigantic bowl. "How can this be?" Endrissi's voice whispered into a distant fade.

"Don't look down!" Calling out, Christopher's instinctive fears grew. Being higher up than Endrissi, he was able to reposition his torch to spread light, giving them better visibility.

"You *are* a pussy man," said Mathieson speaking into his ear. The American pushed brusquely past him. "By the time we plot and mark out this area, we will be fucking alongside those *tourist guide's* bunch of mother's." Mathieson mumbled in his usual sarcastic way. The ranger moved fast towards the sloped rock-edge, and in seconds was very close to Endrissi, passing him too.

Smaller rocks bordered the great hole, marking life from death. Harjit and Christopher were both shocked at Mathieson's rude departure towards the precipice.

"Steady on Mathieson!" Christopher shouted angrily at the man's foolish haste. Then that was Mathieson's style. Endrissi instantly followed right behind the American, both on their way like an unbroken enchantment. Neither had torches. It seemed like certain suicide.

"Mathieson!" shouted Christopher, "Do watch out over there, watch that bloody ledge *you fool!*" Christopher's red-face knew that nobody could be complacent, especially here.

"Mathieson don't run, Endrissi you stop right now!" Harjit called after them. Nobody wanted any stupid mistakes yet both watched incapable of any intervention.

"Look out you guys!" Christopher went into an all-out panic. *Crazy, crazy fools, where are they going… right down by those rocky slopes, my God right to the edge?*

The pig-headed ranger kept going and thought, *this is my job; I do the exploring.* The American was in no mood to reply to the young upstart. Harjit looked at Christopher in utter dismay, shaking her head.

"Chris, they are not listening to us," whispered Harjit. It all seemed like a bad dream of impending disaster. Her eyes could not look away!

The American's zombie mentality was stuck in a trance like a waking dream, his greed entrapped by the crystals glinting all around him. Rich gems were everywhere! His intention was to get digging right away.

I'm rich, I'm rich! "I'm fucking rich man!" He called out in blind euphoria. Marching ahead, he reached the ragged periphery and saw the sheer drop expanding out before him. Eyes full of more rocks, more gems, more everything.

Mother f… these rocks must be gemstones! I am going to be mega-rich! Staring excitedly, he could see massive forked seams abundant with glinting gemstones, in some parts individual clusters kept blinking and glinting like a precious universe. The American continued to ignore Christopher's wary words of warning. It could as well have been in another language as they echoed off the distant walls.

Mathieson and Endrissi heedlessly disregarded his distress flares, and like the fate of the Titanic both men went full steam ahead racing between a large rock and the edge. Their iceberg waited. Disaster inevitable!

Endrissi quickened his pace to keep up with the American when Mathieson suddenly stopped in front to re-position his foot between the rocks, to get a better foothold. The geologist touched the other man's left arm and pushed in delicately next to him. Endrissi squeezed more, between a big rock and the ranger.

Harjit's face instantly paler, watching them squeeze between a massive boulder and the crater. Petrified, she shrieked loudly.

"Oi! Stand still!" Harjit already ran precariously after the men with her arms held outwards, the girl powerless; yet she still tried to stop them from FALLING!

"Shit, steady… Oh! Steady!" Endrissi's tense voice snapped at the American, "Mathieson, what are you doing!" Endrissi's voice truncated. The man signalled an overdue fear. This moment of awareness was too late. The warning was too close, his body tipped into Mathieson's!

The geologist nudged Mathieson. The American unexpectedly twisted around facing Endrissi in a look of disbelief when Mat found his back automatically exposed to the bottomless Pit…

Let it not be real he thought, Mathieson was ill fated and found himself unbalanced. *This is not happening man!* Illogical, but it was. He was dead and he knew it. His mind shouted out. *Hold onto him, he's my only hope!* Mathieson felt weightless for a second, selfishly stretching out his long arms to try and hold on to the geologist.

He arched his back awkwardly on the edge, as the white in his eyes started bulging red. For a split moment he felt his heart stop, and nausea move in the bottom of his stomach. Disaster was done, and all in a stupid second. All too easy and all so sudden, finally he knew death.

Mathieson battled for balance and realised in the race for life that they were both losers. Endrissi tried to pull away from him, but his own forward momentum pushed him into Mathieson's arms.

Looking on, Christopher felt sick.

Endrissi squealed.

Harjit screamed!

Mathieson said nothing as he gulped for air and for life.

Endrissi's eyes riveted into the other man's soul and he recognised the terror in him. His own anguish too much, trying to pull back but could not, both men toppled more. Mathieson held onto the geologist like glue gaining partial stability in his last-ditch effort to stay alive! But, he was already past the point of weightlessness and inescapably, gravity did the rest.

Grasping crazily at each other, madness bound them. Falling inwards, nothing else mattered. Dropping like stones into the richest place on earth, both men would be wealthier than they had ever been, ending their lives inside a sparkling black void.

"Ahhhh!" Mathieson screamed.

"Myyy… Goddd! Nooo!" yelled Endrissi.

From where Harjit and Christopher stood, it looked like an awkward lover's hug and certain death.

****

CHAPTER VIII

THE KEY OF THE GODS OF THE SEVEN RAYS

Harjit and Christopher froze in stroboscopic thinking, each fearful thought held their frames of life millisecond by millisecond, while watching the men free fall into the huge crater. Nothing could stop it. The men had been fooling around and then next second... gone. Looking on like sick spectators to an execution, they were full witness to the men's bodies dropping to certain death.

It was over in seconds. Inside the colossal cavern system, the echoing screams had come from both men's frenetic and final cries. Horrifying. Then everything stopped. The men struck the bottom and disappeared out of sight. How? The suddenness and shock simply nerve numbing. Instantly, a gigantic splash came to them, just like the noise made by jumping into a swimming pool. Harjit and Christopher watched with crazed gasps when everything became incomprehensible.

The volume of sparking space changed instantly into an eruption of water, exploding upwards, rippling in waves across a gigantic pool.

Waves of fluid expanded outwards below them, wider and wider in circles the shock surf moved out in every direction. Were Endrissi and Mathieson submerged below in water!?

Both men instinctively held their breath, baffled and unable to understand the cold tsunami of confusion washing over their bodies. Water! What was going on?

Survival kicked in. Each man flapped their arms around like propellers trying to regain their balance. The pool was not deep, both men instantly feeling the sharp pain of jagged hard rock sticking into their backs and buttocks, legs and arms before their bodies came up bobbing buoyantly in between the rock floor. Gasping to breathe, their lungs burst in spasms coughing out water. It was incredulity seen on their fraught faces.

Running over immediately, Harjit and Christopher appeared on top of the rock edge and stared down fearing the worst. Instantly, their mixed emotions were held in limbo as they saw the two bewildered men bobbing in the water. Flamed torchlight shone over their drenched caricatures from above. There they were, soaked in no more than two to three feet of water. The men quickly gained control of their watery environment and finally sat up together, watching the waves rippling around them.

The water surface had once been perfectly smooth and like an unblemished mirror, was now gone in chaos. The water disturbed like this meant that everyone could see what this disguised crater really was, a massive pool! More akin to an underground lake in size, and by this time the first ripples were reaching its far-off banks.

Watery flames reflected lively off the wet surface around the men's awkward demise, a minute passed allowing time for bewildered Endrissi and Mathieson to stop coughing. Then a perfect silence prevailed.

No one spoke.

Harjit looked at Christopher.

Christopher looked at Harjit.

They all looked at each other.

Harjit and Christopher were like a pressure cooker that burst into uncontrollable fits of laughter with involuntary pent up frustration. It was pure relief and everything emotional suddenly exploding.

Without warning, both men ruptured into laughter as well, joining the delirious pair above. What a site.

Relieved, both Mathieson and Endrissi shouted out who sat there soaked, looking at each other like Laurel and Hardy.

"You're a complete fool Mathieson!" Endrissi shouted while already smiling between sporadic coughs. The man was not prone to cursing but this time he had too. "I told you about not going too close to that bloody edge. *You're a complete fucker Mathieson!*"

"Listen *mother*," Mathieson said. "You shouldn't have pushed me, *son of a bitch, hahaha!*"

He shoved Endrissi further in the water, grinning widely while drowning out the tension.

They both continued to ridicule each other like adolescents as they started to cool off and shiver. The water was freezing.

"Here let's give you guys a hand, shall we?" Harjit interrupted the uncontrollable merriment as she and Christopher assisted both men out. Dripping wet and shaking with cold, at least they were alive. Everyone joined in fits of hysterical laughter blurring their eyes.

Harjit never caught short and was always well prepared. Once they were out of the water, the girl gave each man a silver copper foiled cover; a *space blanket,* to wear for warmth. She took them out from her small rucksack.

"Here put these on guys." The soaked men welcomed her quick thinking.

"Look at that!" said Christopher staring with his torch high once more, "See there it is again, the surface. That's marvellous! It's a complete optical illusion!" Everyone turned to see that the water surface had once again become smoothed over like a mirror image of the sparkling gems above.

"Wonderful to see, if it were not for these two idiots, er… mishap!" She joked.

The whole water surface, from near to far of the bank had again become polished to perfection. The formation of a deep bowl effect contained its curved lightening appearance within.

Everything glittered once again. Still like the air, nothing moved.

"Yeah, fucking wonderful Harj." Mathieson's mood sufficiently dampened, he just wanted to leave and forget his embarrassment.

The lake had become deathly still, no wave, no movement not even a ripple. It was a complete mirror image of that lustrous night sky above. Nothing was said to each other, they all knew instinctively to leave and head back the way they came. On their way back to ground level, Endrissi and Mathieson were again talking excitedly, planning their next visit and how to become rich.

****

Back at the temple, weeks had since passed from when Endrissi's team had gone to the mines. At the base of the temple, tonnes of dense foliage had been chopped down to clear a path all around the massive structure, making a safe perimeter.

Small three-man tents were pitched in a semicircle and positioned next to the campfires that were kept lit at night. That should be enough to keep inquisitive predators at bay. A wooden fence constructed for containment boxes was placed in a well-organised assembly point within the encampment. These were used for any newly discovered artefacts. All securely placed for transit, and some of Christopher's *Smart Safe Pods* were already much in evidence. Some crates made of natural resources were bound by vines and placed on top of one another. They sat behind the tents and at a safe distance, provided some protection from the tropical elements.

This section of camp was about twenty metres away from the larger ex-army mess tent, where the teams would relax and eat meals together, plan their detailed research and debate on their latest findings. Inside, also acting like a make shift laboratory; was a large table, gas burners, microbes growing on agar plates, bottles of chemicals and jars of gelatine.

A larger fire kept continually burning in camp, which was used for making meals. The fire was protected from the rain by wide canvas tarpaulins suspended overhead for those sudden downpours. In the grand scale of things, their encampment was completely dwarfed by the megalithic structure next to them, the temple soaring up into the sky.

The south-facing stone terraces of the temple were by this time bare of most large plant-life that had been growing on it, the team used old dead vines and bushes from it to make fuel. It appeared that the stone surfaces once defoliated looked almost new. A facelift of centuries of growth were taken away and remarkably made it look like it did when it was first built.

The stone's appearance was deep rich red like sandstone that had an internal glint sparkling from it depending on how the daylight struck the crystal. Originally, its crystalline structure had been formed eons ago, and what exactly this integral crystal was, no one knew, not even Endrissi.

Unlike other pyramids and temples in South America, which were typically built out of limestone and a common stone type formed here, the *temple stone,* was not made of limestone or anything like the true density of sandstone. It was totally different and harder than diamond.

Staccato complex designs had been unbelievably etched into its surfaces that continued all around the four sides of the first-tier terrace. More was exposed on each subsequent tiered block work above.

Next to camp, wide stone steps began their ascent from the bottom of the structure, leading upwards, becoming shorter and tapering inwards as it went higher; reaching what they believed to be a massive solid stone entrance. This level was located at the top of the first tier. It had been completely uncovered and cleaned meticulously, with the ancient engraved writing already mused over for many hours.

A message, thought Fabio. The apparent entrance in front of him measured twenty feet across where multifaceted codices encircled around the immediate huge doorway. Identifying this as a possible way inside was far from certain.

A patterned border with different markings and shapes, traversed up and around its curved contour doorway, and then shaped into a pointed arc like those found in Arabic buildings. No handles, and no obvious way to gain entry, the stone-faced door appeared to be seamless and a puzzle that reflected Fabio's erudite consternation.

Is this really an ancient access point? Fabio weighed its possibilities; *it could easily be another stone, monolith set into a wall recess. Incredible. The temple is in first class order. Only parts appear eroded, rubbed away, bloody unfortunate some of these ancient codices are missing here. There is more to tell in these writings...* Fabio desperately wanted to get inside.

Fabio left his enigma climbing upwards and headed for the top. The professor passed each subsequent tier in turn to where sat a brutal looking sacrificial altar, and behind this death stone, a tall stone monolith stood with engraved ancient writing. Behind this, a large stone observatory stood in the centre of the temple top.

Codex seen on the monolith could just be observed, and for the moment undecipherable, the symbols being far above head height. Illegible stone scribes were arranged around a perfect circular hole near the highest part. The hole held a black void, anybody who looked at it from below assumed that it had been painted this way or made of black stone. They would not be able to distinguish the difference. The blackness had not always been there. A hole built for sunlight to travel and shine through, yes! After all, this structure was a sun monolith and now, only blackness remained. Something had changed it, something bad.

This freak was told in a tale on the stone totem, a monolith built to worship a god in the sky, its surface full of macabre drawings, and the gods were not appeased. Fabio interpreted that the drawings were of people all fleeing towards the sun, running into a temple to escape some enemy from outside its boundary. A prediction of the future or relic from the past, and against the known laws of nature, here existed a hole, one that light would not pass through, not anymore.

Fabio had deduced that this was a depiction of deity worship, whatever or whoever these people once were, their enemy in Fabio's highbrow opinion were *not the Spanish or Portuguese*, and could *never* have been them.

No European culture inscribed, not out here, because such a vile depiction and worship such as these were of a non-Christian God, and nothing short of blasphemy. If their enemy had been Spanish, then this keeping of another belief was not in their style. The Spanish priests of the day would passionately smash any pagan effigies to dust. Yet, here the evidence remained. Their enemies were therefore not Spanish, and if not European then who? Fabio gave up.

The archaeologist, Fabio, was still unaware of this direct contradiction with the latest discovery over at the mines with Endrissi's team, and if he knew the Europeans had been there, then he would wonder... how could the Spanish be at the mine-works and not have seen such a colossal structure? Ignorance is bliss. A hidden danger awaited them all.

The following fearful inscriptions were arranged around the sun circle at the top of the monolith. Fabio knew the implications but lacked the key to break the code.

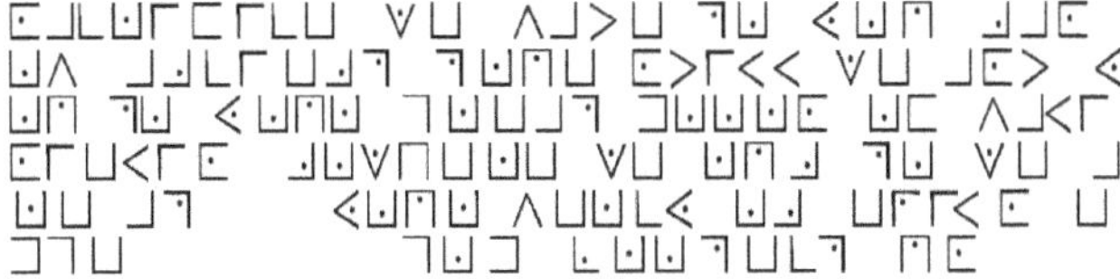

These inscriptions, if deciphered would read…

SACRIFICE WE MAKE TO YOU NASOM ANCIENT TRUE SKILL - WE ASK YOU TO YOUR GREAT DOORS OF MALISIBLIS - NOWHERE WE RUN - WE ARE AT YOUR MERCY ON EVIL'S EDGE - GOD PROTECT US

The mortal message teased him.

The altar soaked by the latest downpour, saw the underlying red-stone still showed years of mottled green-brown and red algae adhering to its surfaces, which provided natural camouflage from above. Like a large table, the altar was carefully cut and measured exactly, eleven-feet-long by seven feet wide and three feet thick. It lay on top of four squat stone legs rising to about waste height. With solid legs built on top of a larger rectangular slab. Precisely thirteen feet long, nine feet wide, three inches thick and placed here by its sun-worshiping architects onto a larger base slab below it measuring, twenty-four feet by thirteen.

This solid stone table was not flat but bevelled higher in the middle area, which would effectively elevate a victim's chest to curve upwards for easier extraction of a victim's heart. Stone pegs at either corner of the table bound the prisoner into a fixed and fatal position.

Indeed, it is a place of sacrifice thought Fabio, the professor imagined the brutal terror inflicted. From ground level to the top, Fabio was overawed by it all. He had found the lost temple, and for now it remained a complete enigma.

This place should not even exist he thought, taking a breath of deep satisfaction. *What wonder! What mystery!*

****

His broad head furrowed with great consternation. Fabio pulled tightly at his greying beard, his growth with a distinguished thin white line inside the darker bushy mass. His fingers scratched into his unkempt mess.

Still no word from his Italian masters, and there was no question of breaking into the temple or blasting away like those early explorers did in Egypt last century. The professor could not stoop to this methodology. To Fabio, this uncontrolled violence would be utter blasphemy and intellectually defeating. Even if it took him a year to understand the riddle, he was determined to break it.

Time was not on his side, *Fabio knew this* only too well; he was expected by his masters to find *a lost relic* and quickly bring this back for his Holiness, a *Godly gift.*

If not… then he knew that his funding would certainly finish on this project, his expedition and fame over. Fabio never contemplated failure, never contemplated his replacement *and never* felt his blood boil so much as now. Nobody would steal his thunder. *Never!* With an anger welling within, his knuckles turned white with rage unconsciously clenching his archaeologist's hammer. The man, even *the Great Fabio,* could be forgiven because *this place, the vale,* it did that to people. There was no rational explanation, but it seemed to make everyone antagonistic and angry inside. It was said to be cursed.

The expedition had exclusive permission to explore this vast area. No one else knew what they were doing here, that is, no one except the mission directors. The Brazilian government was totally ignorant to why the professor's team was truly here. Searching for new species, flora and fauna would do for now, an excuse for one, archaeology for another.

The priest knows nothing, Fabio smiled wryly, but there was absolutely nothing to prevent *others* from coming here. More expeditions, mercenaries, or tomb raiders could pitch their tents next to theirs and take what they wanted. Another reason for secrecy.

Their location was not known by anyone, even the mission directors, with a vague understanding of where they were, because unexpectedly the whole area was being subjected to some strange and new intermittent interference. It affected all electronics, this and a combination of shifting weather patterns, seismic activities and the phenomenon known as the *South Atlantic Anomaly*.

The anomaly caused an increase in electromagnetic activity; a natural phenomenon affecting the vale and far beyond. Amazonia being so expansive, and this location so minuscule, it had always been easily overlooked.

Fabio himself had not been given all the information either. It was not necessary for him to know everything, and the professor was completely unaware of where all the funding had come from. The man assumed that his Holinesses, Peters Pence collections and the company were behind all his monitory resources. This was only partially true.

There was another resource, a secret observer and an unscrupulous business sponsor waiting for profitable news inside Italy. Don Luzio Ilario had a large stake in this adventure. He owned many casinos and financial businesses inside Italy and wanted, more than anything else, total power. There was something hidden inside the vale, something powerful or so legend told, and he wanted it. He was filthy rich, influential, diplomatic and deadly. He knew no moral bounds. Fabio and his team had no idea just how dangerous this mission was about to become.

****

There must be a way in, there must… perplexed Fabio did not know that these ancient stone-fitters were much more skilled than he would give them credit for or could ever imagine. This megalithic construction was second-to-none for functionality, austerity and precision; a skill set out of this world. Fabio's archaeological practicality and scholarly cognition played hard with these enigmatic riddles, his mind on overdrive trying to work out how to get inside.

This door will not open easily, it is a construct built to stop a forced entry. A barrier for protection. This Relic that I search for must be very valuable indeed and a treasure of unimaginable proportions. They want it. And whatever it really is, I will have it first!

The professor smiled thoughtfully while pulling at his beard again. Arrogant and chauvinistic he had always been, but this new feeling he kept getting was one of deep conceit. A disappointed guilt stared back at him while he suppressed a panic that percolated from inside his temperamental mind. An irrational state, he was losing self-control.

"I must get inside first, *I must.*" Exasperated, Fabio spoke openly. Suddenly he froze, hearing someone else approach from behind him. He turned and saw his young student getting closer, breaking his quiet time. *What does he want?*

"Sorry to interrupt your private deliberation professor." The boy studied the massive doorway as he stood. Fabio's blank and remote face changed colour when the boy said, "If this had been a normal trapezoidal doorway, then it would be much easier to gain entry." The young man joined the cerebral company. "This one is beautifully fitted don't you think professor?" He waited for a response, prompting the professor again. "What are you going to do then?" His eyes were met by Fabio's instant rebuke.

"I am going to kick you down those steps young man if you don't shut up! Don't you see I am very busy?" Fabio did not like the idea of smart arsed pups trying to outsmart him, and this was not a good time.

Startled into shock, the student defended, "My apologies professor." Alessandro was blown away by the man's uncalled-for wrath and decided to quickly depart and stay away until the expedition leader regained his normal composure.

The boy was obviously upset and embarrassed. Being his star student, Fabio would normally at least placate the lad, and take him under his wing. This outburst he could hardly ignore. His mentor was never openly hostile towards him before now, so the professor had changed. Let down, Alessandro was badly upset as he marched off.

"Sorry Alessandro!" He called after the student. "I am under so much pressure at the moment." However, the truth fell on deaf ears. "I really do apologize to you my boy!" Guilt washed over him. He had overstepped his mark as the student took to his heels ignoring the professor's raised concern. "My apologies Alessandro. Alessandro!" The boy was gone.

****

The young Architectural Technician, Cesaré Padovesi's Golden Crucifix caught the morning Sunlight while looking upwards at the hard temple wall. This was his challenge for today!

A serious man most of the time, he found relaxation by playing computer games. He was about 5ft 9 inches tall with short thick blonde hair and a middle part which made him particularly good looking, in a handsome-ugly sort of a way. His broken nose did not spoil his other attractive fine features or juvenile expressions, this seemed to give him that extra character for attracting the opposite sex. Oddly, he could not quite understand it himself but there it was, a fact. It did not matter whether it was a hidden scent, his personality or simply his fresh innocent smile, Cesaré loved himself. His eyes were undaunted measuring the temple's East-facing wall.

Ready! He thought confidently. Cesaré did not doubt it, self-assured and fit. He felt great. With such a beautiful morning like this, nothing would get in his way. Using his petrol-engine portable power saw with a 300mm diameter diamond tipped blade, his plan right now was to cut straight into the etched stone base.

The technician knew the equipment intimately, its power with a typical speed of 3,000 to 7,500 rpm, would easily do the trick. Laboriously he had ensured its carriage and fuel here, and now nothing would stop him. This was his moment.

I'll make my own markings here, payback. Chuckling while pulling down his goggles, *I might even make my own symbols on it!* Laughing to himself, *who would know?* Its engine was erupting into action.

The noise of combusted action smelled of petrol and was strangely addictive; this in stark contrast to the natural smells of the jungle. Sounds of animal screams and bird whistles dimmed while the unnatural revolving high-speed metal-on-stone dominated. Grim grinding sounds produced on touching the hard surface sent sparks in all directions. He loved his little power tool sparking like an out of control firework. Pressing harder, this was his dream come true.

Immediate and violent vibrations kept juddering through his arms while holding the machine in check. Pressing down more with his bunched shoulders increased the pace and flashes of white heat, all flying away at a frightening rate. Their curved embers fanned over his shaking body. Breathing harder, his effort short-lived, when unexpectedly the blade's life ended. It vanished when its hot metal shattered into dying sparks and bits of flying blade being thrown perilously away in all directions. His human intervention halted. The circular blade broke when its metal shards came spinning off, just missing his leg.

"Merda! That was close!" Cesaré cursed the sweat dripping off him while watching where the broken blade had landed with menace. The man not to be put-off, he tried again and again with several replacement blades on the stubborn stone, the temple proving more than a match for his equipment. Shaking his head, each time he got the same result. Standing up, he took off his protective goggles and gauntlets and inspected the stone. Disbelief was written all over his face while standing backwards. Cesaré thwarted.

"Incredible, what is this stuff made of?" Confused he had never come across such a hard stone, studying his handy work... *no damage, none!* If he didn't know better, it was as if some enchantment was protecting it. Then he got an even bigger surprise as his ears picked up hearing somebody approaching.

Cesaré heard him before he appeared; Fabio marched around from the far corner of the temple and came towards him faster than an express train. Cesaré gulped.

My God here comes Fabio, Merda! He is in a crap mood today! The Technician's bile sickened him. He turned his eyes away from the older man's blistering gaze.

"What are you doing Cesaré? I told you specifically that I don't want this place *damaged!*" Fabio strode like lord of the manor and instantly inspected the stone for damage; he was mad as hell.

"The only thing I have marked is my own confidence. This merda wall has broken the only power tool I have." The young architectural technician gauged the damage to his machine. "I don't understand how these people built a place like this. It was not with any technology we have, and we are meant to be smarter than them, *aren't we?*" He looked at the building with incredulity... *not a scratch.*

"Just as well for you there *is* no damage my young man," Fabio said pausing, "*Not a mark?*" He concurred making sure, "None at all?" Fabio scrutinized the area in complete disbelief.

Not a scrape, nothing, completely smooth except for the ancient etching done many years ago. It begged the question, how?

"That's fine then." The technician said too quickly in his own defence.

"It's not fine, not fine at all! You disobeyed my explicit and direct orders!" Inconsolable, Fabio continued his rant. "We have been here weeks and there are more questions than answers, now this. THIS!" The professor himself also could not believe that with hi-tech power tools, the stone appeared impenetrable.

"I was just trying to help." Cesaré dared to appease his displeasure. "Scusi, sorry. How could these people that use only stone tools, be able to build something like this? At best bronze or copper tools, maybe? I tried some of my hardest carbide tipped chisels earlier to no avail and it showed nothing, not a dent." Said the technician trying to rationalize with the unreasonable man.

"Conosci cosa c'è - You what!?" the professor almost choked.

"*Come on Fabio,* there is not a scratch, look anywhere!"

"That is not the point."

"Lighten up professor." He protested. "No damage means, NO DAMAGE!" The young man was at the risk of further retribution. "Clearly our tools are quite capable of cutting a variety of igneous rock. This civilization we presume did not have such advanced technology as our own and yet, they cut this rock to fit. It's incredible." Cesaré had much respect for an ancient culture that must have been nothing short of a miracle to build.

"And *ours,* cannot do what theirs can?" Fabio questioned. It did not matter to the professor, the man holding back further retribution for now, but of this disrespectful misdemeanour. It would not be forgotten, and he would make sure that Cesaré got the first ticket home, at the first opportunity.

Cesaré showed no emotion, his pride would not give the professor that satisfaction.

That arrogant son of a bitch. He is becoming bloody worse, ever since we have entered this vale. Fabio must be losing his marbles. The technician said nothing more.

****

Fabio battled to understand the expedition findings so far. His current thinking was of little use because there was not enough to go on with no answers and no big picture. Using his practical experience, he pulled on his vast knowledge over many years, yet the stone language and codex cypher made no sense to him.

Making copious notes he estimated that each of the massive stone blocks were maybe two hundred tonnes or more. Their sheer weight probably would seal them on top of each other. More inscriptions were found at the top of the pyramid added to the mystery. *It all has a meaning* he thought. Inside the structure, the professor believed he would find all the answers.

Today he hoped to get an upshot of a secure satellite view containing laser readings and images that might break his impasse. Detailed pictures of the site sent to ONCOL laboratories and resulting analysis of the samples of ancient writings seen on the temple walls, might help him gain entry. Later, when the analysis came through the results were very disappointing. The professor shook his head at the futility of his efforts, and another failure. ONCOL could do nothing with his local laser readings. They could not penetrate through the dense structure. That simple. The temple rock seemed completely impenetrable.

****

Weeks past and Fabio's demoralised team had not managed to come any closer to solving the stone riddles. Fabio expected that Endrissi's group would be due back from the mines any day. This morning felt different, Fabio sensed a strange elation unlike the way he had been feeling lately, recognizing that this environment was affecting his judgment. He felt it. He knew it.

****

Running days behind time and unfortunately for Endrissi, today this would be his last attempt going back inside the mines before reporting back to the impatient professor. The professor had already expected them and to have returned by now. The geologist badly needed a result too, insisting to the others that this time they would be more careful. It did not take them too long to see again the magnificent *reflecting pool* and there it was waiting; perfect, and breath taking. Carmello decided not to join them inside this time, the man too busy in camp collating mountains of information to take back about places and landmarks to where he and Mathieson had already scouted out over a week and a half ago. Christopher felt unsure of Carmello today, with his normal good humour only lukewarm, *what spooked him?* The small guide superstitiously believed there was a malevolent presence deep inside the mines. The scout could not explain his feelings even though he had confessed his fears to the young priest *that he was frightened.*

Christopher knew that Carmello was scared and for his age, he was perceptive and mature. He remained silent as he would with any *confessional*. The ranger's fear seemed irrational, and yet strangely none would admit it but they all felt uneasy.

There the group stood once again, looking down at the pool mesmerised. Watching its perfect rest. This watery expanse was truly a miracle of nature. Carefully moving on, they passed into more unexplored areas. Photographs taken here would not do its reality justice. Continuing along a narrow rocky path that extended onto the far distance, its rough walls reflected wet surfaces in their flamed torchlight.

Hoping to find a way, everyone anxiously observed they were nearing the end of the mine, when unexpectedly a different route opened into another cave. This route declined further, so did the temperature, especially in the darker recesses. Moving below other levels, they continued their adventure while being careful to mark their route for their return passage.

At times they would build a small pile of stones or take a mental note of any prominent feature. Being the first people to visit these mines in so many centuries, everyone knew that they all had to be on their best behaviour, *even Endrissi.*

Walking through endless caverns, they wondered at the great artistic carvings displayed on dry walls. It felt a little eerie and claustrophobic down this far and to think that people had once worked under these dreadful conditions.

The mines seemed to extend infinitely downwards, they were deep, very deep. The ancient miners and stone-workers at that time had delved far too far. Eons had since past, and this forgotten people had searched not for diamonds nor gold but something else; something much more precious than anything on the earth. They did not find what they sought there, and instead dug deeper down into the deepest part of the mine where they found something not of this world, something, evil.

Endrissi and the others surprisingly found partially melted candles on each level, putting them to good use. Once lit, their ghostly shapes and shadows became grim reminders of those people who had once walked the dingy paths. Mines abandoned more than once, but today, a new breed of miner had entered. A miner of knowledge. And yet not everyone here was as honest as Christopher or Harjit, both of whom had no desires of greed or power.

The group were getting too deep for any natural light to be able to penetrate this far down and yet, some stubborn illumination still managed to somehow peek through a choked-up orifice not far away. Almost indistinguishable, there was a hole in the wall of thick vines. Behind its thick twists of camouflage, the fissure lay just beyond. Down the fissured rock face, the tangled mass gripped like death from its black void. A mishmash of madness disappeared into the gorges fetid depths.

"Listen, it's the sound of water behind that shit man." Mathieson looked at the trellis of browns and greens while lowering his tone, speaking louder and looking around. "This place is really fucked-up man."

Christopher thought curiously, *that's unlike him.* In the cavern system they saw more evidence of construction with wooden support structures overhead. All bewildered, they studied it with amazement and awe. They wondered how on earth they were still able to move those massive stone blocks up levels from underneath. It was still a complete mystery.

"How far down do you think this place goes Endrissi?" Asked Harjit, her quiet voice sounded smaller than an intimidated squeak.

"Deep, very deep." Endrissi's tone solemn. He felt it too, the brooding malcontent. "Remember I dropped the torch?" The demonstration had been enough.

Endrissi started walking carefully to the strangled opening with nothing else to say on the matter, heading towards thick vines. The meshwork acted like a sort of safety net between them and the fissure. Walking closer, with his flamed candle nearing the web of vegetation, its intrusion scaling around the inside walls, its living infestation growing in all directions then stopping before him.

Putting down his candle, the bulldog of a man suddenly began hacking wildly at the woody barrier with his machete, arching it around and around like a circular saw. Soon the limbs of the plant were breaking and crashing all around him, some of it dropping into the sinister abyss. Only after a few minutes of intense destruction, Endrissi looked satisfied watching into the empty space, and the fissure.

The bigger the hole he made, the more natural light got through. So Endrissi started up again, cutting away until it was large enough to stand on. A sudden rush of fresh air and noises instantly flowed through from the surface. They all felt it, breathing its cleanness. An interruption, as torrents of water plummeted downwards in front of him, the sounds deafening, Endrissi felt giddy watching it. The geologist began holding onto its organic sides for support and with a degree of stupidity began balancing himself on the very edge. All he wanted to do was get a better view!

"I'm out! I'm OUT!" He yelled like an escaped prisoner. Endrissi's eyes stared down into blackness below, the man baffled at the void, gauging that there was still a long way to go! *Christ, how much further* he wondered?

****

In the sizeable area around them lay many discarded large blocks of rock, all left standing in their virgin state. Stone blocks were two or three times the height of a grown man or maybe higher. While Endrissi stood watching his own handy-work, the others were busy photographing more illustrations on the inside walls. Some sketches demonstrated the first stage process of block production, diagrams of the raw materials that were to be used to produce them. These were depicted using hundreds of slaves, all put-to-work digging at the rock faces. The drawings demonstrated boulders being lifted to the surface using the complex pulley system. Their guesswork had been correct! Pictures here and in other parts of the caverns also displayed grand and magnificent buildings, a people, a temple and a strange city.

"What? Where *is this city?*" Whispered Harjit. The girl's copper coloured skin appeared radiant as her blended natural tones in the floating candle light. Christopher stole her warm glance as she smiled at him. The sounds of water echoed more into the massive cavern as their candle began wafting quicker with the new fresher air from the opened fissure.

"Who knows Harj? Maybe it is just a concept, maybe it never existed, or maybe the city is buried somewhere under the jungle, who knows?"

"Christopher, they were trying to build it, these were their plans before something awful happened, something terrible."

"Maybe, but don't you think that this isn't terrible enough? Those poor sods. We will never find out but what we do know is this. There *is* a temple, and someone did build it!" He tried to seal some rigidity into their existence when an American voice broke his speculation.

"Yo!" Mathieson's voice caught their attention. "Yo, you two, it's lovely and dark over here mothers!" The American jibed while calling over to the candle-lit couple.

His sweep of the area had now provided several opportunities to find another way further on, the down side being that each exit looked just dim as the other.

"What is it Mat?" Harjit called back.

"Endrissi man!" Mathieson's eyes looking away from the girl, his attention trying to get the geologist's too. "Come on Endrissi, come on!"

"There seems to be a whole civilization in this city, look here Harj." Christopher pointed to more drawings "A whole storyline is here. Blessing or sacrifice, I think."

Meanwhile, Mathieson forgot Endrissi and came up closer to Harjit and Christopher to see what was going on, and to get them to move along with him. His eyes roved over macabre scenes, seeing a whole people thrown down a hole! Angry Gods observed feeble attempts to appease them by a so-called civilization in decline.

"Come with me you two, Endrissi will catch up." So, they walked further on and perceived the pictures' changing to more colourful; made up of blues, yellows, greens, whites and reds. The red described the people digging deeper and deeper into the mines back in their glory years of discovery. "Endrissi you mother!"

Endrissi was distracted and turned to see Mathieson. He looked inside momentarily towards the other ranger and then towards where his beleaguered followers were walking away. The next moment he could hear raised voices; they were coming from the men. The geologist watched passively, seeing Mathieson quickly squaring up to fight Christopher!

Disbelief registered in Endrissi, standing confused and alarmed at the men's antics when unexpectedly he heard a strange noise. Something else was coming from behind him from the fissure.

Above him there was an unexplainable blood curdling sound that seemed to compress inside his ears. Endrissi's neck quickly span around as he stared upwards in fear.

Louder and louder, closer, FASTER. Above him, the light blackened and blotted out, when he could see something travelling down the fissure at high speed. Frozen in chilled blood.

****

A minute before the fight, the three other explorers heard the main noises of the torrents of water dropping down the fissure. Walking carefully away with their torches and enflamed candles, all mysteriously casted wavering shadows onto a painted engraved wall, they were engrossed at the unfolding sad tales of stone. Inside, none could hear what Endrissi was shouting and what he was about to do, not yet.

"Lookee here." Mathieson's interest picking up, "What's that, they have dug up? It's something else." The American's eyes fired into action.

The colours were fading by simple aging. The pictures were antique and much older than the ones they had seen further back up the cave system, to where conquistadores had first appeared in this chronicle as this ancient story unfolded.

Unlike the dead guard earlier, and various artefacts lying scattered around in the mines, at a guess these were probably mid-16th century, this new find here was different. What Mathieson observed in the stone drawings that these people had dug out was of special significance, priceless and as such was the stuff of legends.

"What do you think?" Asked Harjit.

"Harj, we are all going to be very, very rich indeed!" Mathieson laughed gleefully, while rubbing his hands. The man was unable to contain himself any more, his intense exhilaration demonstrated once again, his own self-motivated purpose.

Christopher quickly reminded the ranger and said, "Look Mathieson, any finds we all make, *any*, belong to the mission and not inside your own pocket."

"Who tha F do ya think ya're speaking to *mother fucker*." Mathieson snapped back. "First come first served. Have you not read the script pal, in the contract, finders-keepers." He laughed loudly just to cream the Scotsman off. "You don't know much, and you are a fuckin' lazy shit anyhow Christopher!"

Christopher's self-control tested to the full, bristling in rage, blistering into eruption. His face brimmed redder and redder, after all this time, Christopher had enough, his furious thoughts controlling him. *I am not taking much more of this shit and BAM!* In his mind thinking, *that's all it'll take, BAM! The American asshole would deserve it.*

Christopher mimicked a hand strike in his mind, a rehearsal sitting on the edge, he felt himself slipping closer and closer towards violence. The insults and continual goading would have to stop, or he would end it.

"Shut the fuck up Mathieson!" Christopher retaliated.

"I'll kick the shit out of ya, if ya don't stop!" Yelling at Chris, the American sneered with open satisfaction, *this is fun,* thought Mathieson. The man prompted the Scotsman more, making the scientist's life complete misery.

More than banter, this was personal now. Mathieson knew what he was doing, mentally glowing inside with malice.

Where is this coming from? Christopher's logic tried to penetrate his reflexive instincts. His self-control frayed some more. *This whole thing is OTT! What has got into Mathieson? He is worse than usual. My God, and what has got into me too? What's wrong with us both? It must be gold fever or something crazy! Ok focus on him. Watch it he's getting closer… he is going to attack me!*

Christopher began breathing quicker and quicker staring at Mathieson's fast paces coming towards him, the man sensing an imminent attack. Christopher's heart drumming harder. *I'm up for it!* Chris screamed into himself ready to defend. All of his thoughts of restraint and cognitive willpower disintegrating in a second, losing self-control into straight anger his mind ready to fight his attacker.

Tension and hatred were mixed up and compressed, suddenly all coming to this! Gauging the unhinged American, the man was now only feet away.

An all-out war. Both men squared up face to face, Christopher's fight responses sharpened to a point. He expected an instant strike from Mathieson.

Adrenaline loaded muscles in Christopher, he had never felt so aggressive, the flight or fight hormone surging through his body. *I'm up for it! Ready and BAM… now!*

When quietly, an unexpected voice disturbed their craziness, breaking their clash as Christopher moved to hit first. Her words lighting the darkness.

"Boys, boys." Came a soft sensitive female tone, soothing the storm, "From boys to babies, cool it boys." She said, her voice lofty, floating, "Come on, *don't be so silly*."

Christopher's body stopped before it got going hearing a voice of reason and diplomacy, Harjit held their war, both men checking each other angrily at arm's length, but it was not over yet. Eye to eye, red tempers simmered, peace only seconds from failing.

The girl's small frame sensed this and quickly stepped in between them, restraining their tensed arms with her tender touch. A delicate squeeze for a short moment was enough, allowing them breathing space to make them think again and reassess their own stupidity.

"Sorry Harj." Christopher said.

"Yeah me too." Mathieson agreed.

"Have we all lost our reason? *Have we?*" Harjit questioned their basic instincts with logic.

"Gentlemen, I think babies have more sense than the two of you put together." She balanced ridicule with humour. "You think, that to discover this treasure is the answer to everything. It's not." The girl stated bluntly, "Grow up for Pete's sake guys and put your handbags away, or I will knock some real sense into both of you." Harjit frowned, smacking both their heads gently together. Tight lipped, the men smiling at each other in semi-agreement. Harjit smiled too, standing apart.

The girl was not a tall person, wearing camouflaged attire disguising her womanly figure, everything about Harj was in correct proportions, and for her twenty-four years of age, female diplomacy and reason had worked. Harjit's attractive features and natural intelligence were not to be underestimated, and Ace card to play with these two. Her wide hazel brown eyes hypnotically attractive, Harjit breathed softly relieved that she had managed to stop the fight. Somehow, she knew it was not over between them, not yet, not by a long shot. *Shit that was close.* She was unable to believe what had just happened. Whether this type of female persuasion would work again, Harj doubted.

Chris thought *where the hell did all that come from? I was up for a fight just then.* He shook his head in disbelief because of his lack of self-control. Christopher disappointed himself; after all he was a priest. *It's the vale...*

Unknown to the group, it was that hidden enemy again, working on everyone's mind, continually chipping away at them and blackening their thoughts. In its solitude, something malignant festered, a real danger growing from within. Mathieson moved off and began studying the wall paintings once more. Not happy, but at least nobody had been hurt.

"Harjit, I agree with you," he whispered. "Something is not right here, I can't put my finger on it, but I think I might be cracking up." The girl nodded, recognizing the feeling, she harboured it too in some group insanity.

"Chris, we are all cracking up here." Harjit looked over at the American mumbling away by himself, a motherly eye keeping track on his deliberate movements. Mathieson's darting eyes moving quickly, his head catching up a second later. She knew he was losing it. *Something is wrong with him, what to do...* out of place and unhinged, Harjit knew that they would need to leave the vale soon. Their sanities depended on it.

Only seconds had really passed since their disagreement, when Christopher turned to study more of the walled pictures, following them along he stopped, and strangely raised an eyebrow.

A life-sized man stood etched against the red-stone wall, holding a large yellow disc high above his head. It was a depiction of a Shaman standing on top of a temple. Clothed in a fine coloured cloak and feathered headdress, he wore a golden medallion and gemmed armlets to match. The large golden disc displayed strange symbols and long forgotten writings on it and were moulded around its circular edges.

"So, life-like." Harjit said. "Maybe this is what the conquistadors were really looking for; *this object*." She whispered quietly to Chris.

"It must be worth millions if it's real and must be somewhere underneath." Christopher pointed down towards the three dark tunnels leading out of the area, "Maybe it's down there."

Harjit observed the American, and she could see Mathieson was alone and becoming quickly agitated again, so she decided to interrupt his dark thoughts.

"Mathieson! Come over here and see what Chris has found. Can you help us decipher its code?" Harjit knew he was a loose cannon and by bringing him in close, might make him feel useful again.

Acknowledging her inclusiveness, Mat knew himself that *this time* he had gone a step too far with the Scot. He approached the wall drawing and became quickly mesmerized by the golden disc. Harjit looked disappointed. The American ignored the girl and was immediately engrossed in all-consuming greed. Sighing gently, she conceded to herself that probably he was beyond her help, recognizing whatever was working on his mind was growing stronger and taking hold of all his bad traits.

She had felt it, they all felt it; an intangible evil. The trick was how to protect against it. Suddenly a man screamed, a yelling voice somewhere beyond where Endrissi was standing on the fissure's edge.

A horrific wail, the scream held on a crest of an octave, solidifying their blood into ice, it was *not* Endrissi. He was still there. But his eyes were fixed upwards in horror. Everyone stared in the geologist's direction.

The yelling was getting closer by the millisecond and in an instant, the sounds of death, passing quickly bye. Endrissi's head now looked down into the fissure trailing after somebody dropping past him.

Startled, all three looked at the geologist who was frozen in total shock. Endrissi did not move, stiff as a statue, his eyes wide-open. His mind tried to scream, and his lips moved but he was incapable of sound.

At the opening to the fissure, Endrissi's white knuckled hands gripped hard into the vegetation on both sides. His legs began shaking on the edge of the Abyss. His head followed the blood curdling screams when suddenly the shriek stopped.

"Endrissi! Endrissi!" Christopher shouted from behind. Christopher quickly ran and reached the stricken man. Chris stopped a short distance from the geologist. "What was it Endrissi? What has happened?" Endrissi had no response. "Man, talk to me why did you scream like that?" He watched the traumatised geologist. Harjit and Mathieson arrived together and waited. Endrissi tried again his wordless attempts to speak.

"Stop screwing around man," said the concerned American. "This is not funny." Mathieson was scared too.

The big geologist was precariously too close to the edge and gripping unconsciously onto the pliable vines. In this state of mind, he could easily fall.

Endrissi seemed passed the point of caring; swooning a little and with pupils fully dilated. Harjit's voice kick-started his consciousness and caused him to speak.

"I… it was not me…" He stammered on. "I, I did not scream, not me..." He mumbled slowly. "I, I did not scream." He repeated himself over and over again.

"Snap out of it man, we heard you clearly from across the other side! *So, come on*." Agitated, Mathieson did not mince his words. The ranger could not handle this situation either, and his response was predictably brutal. "Are you suddenly some kind of vegetable?" He held his hand up in the air impatiently.

"Give Endrissi a break asshole!" Christopher branding the American's way, Christopher's nerves still raw from their earlier argument, then switched off to him.

Concentrating, Christopher began inching closer to Endrissi. The last thing he wanted was to do spook the geologist even more. *He might jump…* He reached very close to the hole that Endrissi had created, exposing the fissure.

"Take care Chris." Harjit urged quietly.

"Endrissi, what happened?" He spoke in his best Italian. "Endrissi, you called out, *why did you do that?*" He prompted him again. "Endrissi come back from the edge." Chris pleading, "Come back to us we *need you back here!*" His voice competed against the watery onslaught dropping beyond.

The geologist lifted his shaking hand and pointed over to his left, where something lay stuck between vines. Christopher positioned himself closer. A dirty yellow object lay on the edge. He began balancing on the abyss, Chris more concerned for the man's safety rather than something made of straw.

Eyes glued onto the geologist only a few metres away; Chris readied himself to spring to help the dazed man. Reaching out while taking another step closer, when without warning he unexpectedly stumbled; falling ahead and landing on hard vines!

"Ouch, shit!" Christopher cursed a little while anxiously looking up at Endrissi's trembling fingers. Endrissi pointed down to where a straw object sat only inches away from Christopher's face.

"Oh Chris!" Screamed Harjit.

"I'm ok Harj, I'm ok." His breath back, carefully rising from the rim edge and in his hand, held a straw hat! *What's this... a straw hat, how... oh the fuck no?* Tragedy tightened around Christopher's throat.

"Chris what is it?" Harjit asked as grim reality washed across his face.

"Carmello's." His voice lost in unquestionable thoughts. Swallowing hard, calling out, "It's Carmello's hat! It was him, he must have fallen!"

Harjit who had just reached them, stared into Christopher's eyes to make sure he was ok. Composing herself, she continued walking quietly over to Endrissi. She firmly held his wrist. Drawing closer to the big man while listening to him speak.

"Si, Si that is right, he fell only moments… ago…" Endrissi, his frame sagging in great sadness, his head bowed, eyes towards the drop.

"My God." Harjit's moistening eyes felt grief for Carmello, thinking, *Endrissi saw him fall! How horrific.* Instinctively, she needed to save Endrissi from falling over the edge too. Harjit's patient voice floated softly in the air. "What is wrong dear Endrissi?"

The man remained silent. Christopher watched her rescue close in.

"You know, that gave us all a bit of a turn." Her maternal instincts felt for Endrissi appeared to be on the edge of extinction. "Can I help? Come back to me *Endrissi.*" The girl whispered to him, when unexpectedly his words suddenly came blurting out at her.

"Si, he fell, fell, passed me and, and I was looking up and wondering why the light had gone out. But it was not the light, it was him, blotting out the light falling down towards me. DOWN THERE!" He screamed while pointing into the fissure. Swaying unsteadily on top of a thick vine, he broke down crying, putting up his other hand to cover his tortured eyes.

Harjit stepped forward and held him and wrapped her arms safely around the man while bringing him away from the edge.

The hurt ran deeper, and the fear Endrissi saw in the dead man's eyes could never leave him. The horror, the screams, the certainty all etching like acid inside his mind. Carmello's death mask stuck inside his brain forever.

Reliving repeatedly that awful moment, he saw the ranger's arms and legs flailing helplessly trying to swim wildly in mid-air! Bizarrely his hat came flying off, sailing past Endrissi.

In that split second, life was so precious to both men. Each held the same terror when both eyes met. In that last moment of insanity and friendship, it left only screaming and death.

"Come with me Endrissi." Her tone gently soothed his burned mind. "Be careful, this way." Harjit slowly brought his hands from his face. Holding him firmly, she guided him back to safety against the spray from the rushing waters. Harjit seriously looking at him, she knew that he would never be able to speak about this again.

"Poor bastard." Mathieson said. Nobody could survive a fall like that, the personal tragedy for his friend and grotesque reality of what happened began to penetrate the American's hard thick skin. The ranger quickly helped Harjit by taking Endrissi from her. "Ok man I've got you."

"God save his soul," prayed Christopher.

"Amen." Mathieson nodded.

"We should try and find him." Harjit ventured.

"The drop is too deep Harj. We don't know just how far this chasm goes," said Christopher's pained face. "It might be totally unfathomable."

"What! So that is it! That's it for poor Endrissi! *I don't believe you Christopher!* I know you. *You never give up!*" She was blazing at him and sobbing with no hope.

"We could never find him, I'm sorry." Christopher spoke sympathetically, "If you did find the poor bugger, do you think there would be anything left to bury?" He plead in anguish with the girl. "*I am… so sorry. There is nothing any of us can do for him.*"

"Don't give up on him Christopher, don't!" Harjit resisted this grim reality.

Christopher re-considered for a moment more, *maybe we should try…* recognised it would be foolhardy and totally crazy, and began to doubt his better judgement. Was there an outside chance of recovering his body? Then Endrissi spoke.

"You all know, this must have been. How those so-called Christian bastards murdered all those people in the pictures." Everyone stared at the geologist. "If they did not convert to our ways, that is… *the Christian way,* then they would be executed. The natives were murdered. Totally ruthless and I think…." The man taking a deep breath said, "Genocide was practiced here. We see it in the drawings." Turning his face towards the fissure and with that lib tone of his said, "*Are you with me?*"

They stared at him...

He stared at *them*...

They stared at each other… at his emotional detachment.

It was the weirdest feeling felt by the other three, when Endrissi spoke again as if nothing had happened. "Find him and you'll find out what happened to these people."

Harjit suddenly began crying; she knew he had lost his mind. Christopher held her tightly, taking her grief as she was striking her fists helplessly onto his shoulders. Deep inside, she knew it was useless. *Poor Carmello* she thought. Christopher shielded her in his arms while oddly watching Endrissi's unsurprised blank face, repeating himself robotically.

"Do you go with this?" Endrissi asked.

"Ok let's go find him." Mathieson agreed. "Harj is right." Mathieson stared around challenging the darkness and this utter madness.

"It's not a game." Christopher countered, his cognitive powers back, knowing the impossibility and odds were stacked against them, especially now. "The risks are too great." He felt a deep fear stirring inside him because any moment he himself might change his mind.

"Let's get away from here. This place is jinxed." Endrissi urged them in a dull tone to go.

"I need to say a few words before we go. Sorry Endrissi, I cannot leave until I do this," stated Christopher. He had made his mind up.

Christopher could not compromise everyone's safety. Their lives depended on his decision. Kissing Harjit, he walked over to the gorge's edge. Looking down into the darkness below him, Christopher pulled out his Bible. Perfectly steady, closing his eyes, his faith against the dark pit. Lifting the Bible high into the air, and in defiance he spoke loudly against the water's din.

"Lord Jesus Christ! We commit the soul of Carmello. Jesus taught us." Christopher paused, emotionally upset and said, "As recorded in the gospels of Matthew and Luke, the Lord's Prayer." Chris bowed his head. The others did too.

Bible in one hand while holding out his small silver crucifix in the other, the cross attached to a chain around his neck, he began reciting the Lord's Prayer with full conviction in his voice, echoing its fine words into the darkness below him, reaching down to Carmello's corpse. Clearing his throat, Christopher resumed.

"Lord, please take care of the soul of our friend Carmello De Matis. He who has just departed from here awaits your judgement." Christopher made the sign of the cross and paused to say to everyone. "Let us pray. Our Father, who art in Heaven, hallowed be thy name." The priest went on, "Thy Kingdom come, thy will be done, on Earth as it is in Heaven…" A minute later, Chris finished his prayer, knowing Carmello's death dealt them a great blow. His untimely end, remaining a mystery.

Mathieson seemed determined to return to the mine-works, although he was for the moment quiet and moody about his own personal loss of his friend. He felt guilty.

In these sad times and through his hard exterior, the ranger had still a good part inside him. In the dead of the night, sometimes he and the others would hear Christopher *whispering* and *praying*.

Mathieson swallowed hard and as they all watched at the precipice to hell, everyone stood in a sober mood of reflection. Neither Harjit nor Mathieson made the sign of the cross. It was not their religions, listening to Christopher saying his prayer. Harjit prayed the following in her own way.

"Oh God, lead us from the unreal to the real.
 Oh God, lead us from darkness to light.
 Oh God, lead us from death to immortality.
 Oh God, lead us from darkness to light.
 Oh God, lead us from death to immortality.
 Shanti, Shanti, Shanti unto all.
 Oh Lord God almighty may there be peace in this Celestial region."

It was her own prayer for Carmello, and hope for them all. *They would need it!*

****

Further exploration was out of the question, and if they had continued further into the gloom, they would have found more evidence of human sacrifice; as the aggressors put men, women and children to the sword and threw them into the guts of the earth, where Carmello now lay. Soon, the group would be returning to the temple, bringing with them their terrible news.

Returning to the surface, knowing that long time ago the European soldiers had forgotten their religion, but then, they too had been in the grips of the vale's influences. It worked that way, the greed, all possessing appetites, all-turning to hatred and gluttony for gold and precious gems. It was their *devil* within, one that each man has in him and magnified by an evil that lay waiting for them inside the vale. Those were like now, indeed black days.

Something moved down in the depth, something was disturbed in the guts of the mines. In the darkness, amidst a pyramid of bones, it awoke once again.

Those ancient people had dug far too deep. Centuries ago, human flesh had arrived. Now like then, something began slobbering over Carmello's fresh remains. It remembered those old days of plenty and was anticipating a new feast this year.

This one, surpassing any that had gone before. It was the prophecy!

A dark mist began materialising around the monster, the thing was made not of this world, nor flesh, nor bone and in this binding blackness, soon, very soon, *Smite would emerge.*

"They will come first and Smite"
The Prophecy!

****

At last they were out! It took the best part of a day to get there. They took a deep breath of fresh air. The truth of the tragedy seemed surreal. Everyone looked frantically around for evidence of his last moments. How could this have happened? They were not surprised at all when he could not be found. Sadly, they half expected to see the small man's happy face that reminded Christopher that there had not been many smiles from him in these past weeks.

Everyone felt an unshakable guilt. Could more have been done for him? What made Carmello suicidal? Why did he fear this place? All unanswerable questions yet, each person felt an unshakable dread growing inside them. What was it? And now, everything seemed so pointless.

****

Meanwhile in Europe, back inside Vatican City, *Operation Aequinoxium*, the Cardinal Giovanni Dalla Gassa's meticulously engineered contingency plan was ready, this being a catch all, just in case the civilian expedition failed. The fabled Reliquae had always been his prize, and this plan was still to be put into action. The men of the Crossbow Regiment of Swiss guards were on manoeuvres at this moment in northern Italy. They would be deployed when required, to go to the Amazon rainforest and take over. At this moment the Ninth Degree *Paracadutista* (Parachutist) Assault Regiment had not arrived in the Amazon, not yet.

This Special Forces, *Black Op*, had already been sanctioned but it would not be there until a few months later. Their mission orders would come direct from a *four star of Comando Forze di Difesa One*, AKA COMFOD One, simply were to find and take the Reliquae. One question remained; would there be anybody alive to save?

Again, the Prophecy

"All will shake in Terror"

That evening Christopher sat up in his tent and sadly opened his journal and began writing.

My Journal August 31ˢᵗ

Today we lost Carmello. God rest his soul. It feels so unreal. I am personally responsible because Carmello told me how he felt. He said that something terrible was going to happen to him… and it did. I never listened to him. I did nothing. He believed the Zaplithowatre's forewarnings, and like the natives he understood nature. Everyone is greatly moved by his death.

Endrissi is not the same, but he is ill. Harjit has had to sedate him. We will be leaving the mineworks tomorrow at sunrise and return to the temple. Harjit is right, we should leave the Vale of MalisIblis, now I feel it too… the malcontent. This valley is wholly evil! Fabio and the others need to be warned… Something is not right. A great evil here working on our minds, something intangible gnawing bit by bit at our morale, sapping our souls.

A full moon is above us tonight and I fear to sleep. There is a festering inside the cortex of my brain, no it is more than this, much more… it is an assault on my very soul. I beg that God protect us!

Switching off his lamp, Chris found some comfort reciting a prayer, the Protection of St Joseph, for everyone. Inside their tents all could hear his lonely words drift across the lunar-lit forest. They could not sleep either.

The Prophecy.

"Cold is the Land, Nowhere to Hide"

Next morning, they were all up early and bedraggled. Eating a quick breakfast, they had a lot to do and more than anything else, they wanted to leave this place and not return. Nothing could keep them at the mines a moment longer.

"Look at this," said Harjit, prompting the others. "Carmello had packed maps in his rucksack of earlier surveys of the expedition and the recent exploration around this area, with you Mathieson. An old book, cameras, rations and some garments. I think he was getting ready to..."

"Leave us." stated Christopher coldly watching Harjit give over his belongings.

"Yeah, making a run for it." The American advised. "Taking what he could and getting out. Unlike him, sad son-of-a-bitch."

Mathieson deeply regretted that he personally had not taken his friend's *manic depression* more seriously. Their next worry, was the geologist. They all hoped Endrissi would feel better in a few days, *Harjit was not so sure.*

****

Arriving back at base camp four days later, Endrissi seemed fine and much more like his old self but Harjit knew the contrary. She knew that he had seen into a dead man's eyes and that would have screwed up anyone.

After initial handshakes, Endrissi quickly took Fabio to the side and told him quietly the terrible news. Bewildered, Fabio's eyes drilled into

Endrissi's as the Professor kept shaking his head at the thought of suicide. This behaviour could not be allowed to undermine his expedition, it was something he could not accept. *Now, an accident, Si!* That would seem more fitting and more likely to happen out here. His death would be much more acceptable for his masters to believe. *Si, that would do.*

Later that evening, Fabio had arranged a communal meeting inside their large green ex-army mess tent, The Marquee. Fabio had a duty. He needed to explain what had happened to Carmello to everyone. First, he would put a positive spin on what the expedition had achieved so far. Try to bolster their spirits first knowing that today the expedition had reached a watershed with this devastating news. It was critical for him to get everything back on track. No one would be leaving here and that he was certain off, and unquestionably not until the job here was done. His reputation was at stake and his world recognition too. Everything depended on the success of this expedition. Carmello was gone. He acknowledged it was terrible but there was nothing he could do about that. Looking at everyone sitting, he got their attention, when a hushed silence settled. Fabio began.

"I have looked at this." Fabio lifted the ancient book, "This is the one which sadly poor Carmello found at the mines." And I think it is a most fitting memory to him, because, it is a priceless discovery." Fabio generating interest, "I cannot yet interpret the ancient language but by observing these pictures on the back binding…"

The professor demonstrated an illustration to murmurs of muted curiosity, a drawing of a man standing in rich costume dress with a precious metal necklace and golden armlets to match, a headdress with golden feathers shaped around his head, a leader or chief. Fabio continued.

"This is a picture of a Shaman of a vanquished people. Look at him proudly holding up in two firm hands high above his head, an object about the size of a large plate. A golden yellow disc with coloured rays being projected outwards." Fabio's excited tone gathering speed while watching for a reaction from the captivated group.

"Yeah!" Mathieson interrupted. "We saw the same thing. A larger drawing of this same dude, inside the mines!"

"Thank you, Mathieson." He smiled at him arrogantly. "Christopher informed me of this already."

Mathieson's face changed into resentment as Fabio continued his lecture.

"There is a complex engraving on its surface." Fabio displayed the book to the others. Everyone looked more inquisitively at the picture.

"Well, what else did Christopher tell you?" Mathieson's tone livid.

"Well, he didn't but I can. So, listen." Fabio watched Mathieson's face turning instant purple with anger. "Does anyone know what we have here, or what it might represent?" The professor smiled at all the blank faces, *thought so, at least they are interested* and said more, "I believe these people dug this disc out of the mines!"

Only the Great Fabio had this knowledge, and only he knew what the picture meant, or so he thought. Professor Mancini handed the book around to mumbles of forgotten enthusiasm as he went on.

"Professor, is it the Seven Rays?" His prized student Alessandro Marchesi dared to suggest.

"Yes, well done my boy! It's called *The Key of the Gods of the Seven Rays*, bloody amazing!" Fabio tried to steady his thrilled voice. "This illustration proves how a Shaman travelled from here, and all the way to Peru where it resided for many years. However, that trip was very bad timing *for him*."

"Say what!" Dollar signs flashed in front of Mathieson.

"Bad timing for him because this was when the conquistadores decided to drop into Peru for a visit." Fabio snorted humorously, "And decided to set up camp there." Lifting his voice, "Permanently!" The group began laughing.

"Come on Professor tell us more!" Shouting out eagerly, the student was fascinated, and Fabio happily did so. "Once the Key of the Gods rumour became known, they relentlessly hunted for its gold. The story tells of an older

Shaman who fled from Peru and travelled back here with The Key of the Gods. It had returned.

"It's a bit far-fetched professor," said Cesare Padovesi, the architectural technician.

"No, and if I interpret this correctly and because I don't often get things wrong." They laughed again, "This Shaman transgressed from *our world* into another, through an open portal." Fabio paused watching their mute faces when...

"That's *bull professor!*" Mathieson had enough, rudely interrupting him.

"If you would be so kind not to barge in like that again Mathieson." The Professor articulating his authority, "I have read that legend, this disc is a *catalyst* to an escape route from here, into the world of gods! It was supposed to have been achieved, according to these people's beliefs, so it symbolized their ancient religion."

Everyone fell quiet except Mathieson who kept mumbling in angry denial under his breath.

Fabio's fascinating fabrication sounded plausible. The professor winged it. *They have all taken the bait!* The professor was relieved and cruised on.

"The Spanish pursued the Shaman though they never found him or the disc, but they must have been close, too damn close! Now, it has come back to its place of origin. It must have been dug out from the bottom of the mines, centuries before the Spanish and Portuguese conquests!"

"That is a fantastic story Fabio." Endrissi gulped, "It's not so romantic inside. We will *never* find it." His voice slowing at the very thought of returning to the mines. "I can't go back. *It's a terrible place.*" Endrissi sagged, gritting his teeth.

Awkward thought Fabio, unsure of what was coming next as everyone focused on the geologist.

Everyone felt anxious and embarrassed because they could see his pain. It was obvious; Endrissi was still suffering from acute stress. Christopher with no hesitation swiftly walked over to the distraught man's aid.

"The mines extend for miles and go down forever," backed Christopher. "It would take years if not tens of years to explore it properly." Christopher brought everyone back to this cold reality. "Listen to me," he said.

Mother of God, who does he think he is, thought Fabio. The professor took a deep breath because Christopher had not finished.

"I think that we should contact ONCOL and instruct them to come here and pick us up," said Christopher, turning towards the gob-smacked professor. "Fabio, we should call it a day, for pities sake!" Pleading more, "We cannot go on, not after Carmello has been killed!"

Mathieson interrupted the debate. "Come on Endrissi man, I'll go back inside with you to look." He volunteered. Ignoring Christopher's unthinkable idea of going home, the ranger already witnessed the mega riches inside and wanted more. This was a get rich quick and his big chance, backing the Professor all the way!

"Professor don't listen to him. This is your Expedition man, just go for it!"

"Indeed." The professor curtly replied and was about to proceed when Harjit said, "No. Christopher is right Fabio." Her clinical tone exact, "Professor, to go inside is irresponsible." The girl displayed no emotion. In her medical opinion she knew it would be the biggest mistake for everyone, and especially Endrissi.

Fabio countered, "I am most upset about Carmello, a good friend and experienced colleague. His untimely accident is tragic, but you know that *he* would be the first person to say, *keep going* and laugh about it. So, laugh about it too, I say. His spirit was strong, and he would not turn back." The professor bolstered for expedition votes.

"Under normal circumstances, maybe, but this is not normal." Harjit said.

"Si, *keep going* he would say, keep going and get out of here! This is more like him latterly, *Carmello, he knew things about this place.*" Said the exasperated geologist, Endrissi warned Fabio while the professor frowned at him.

"I am not insensitive to what has happened and before we all go running away like cowards, everyone should know about this Shaman. It has been told in other stories of *Arama Maru*, who according to the legend passed through blue light, which emanated from the disc. Then a doorway opened. He was God, *along* with the disc." Fabio continued with his circus act, as Mathieson and others were nodding in agreement. "May I also add, that this disc might not be found inside the mine-works, it might be elsewhere, maybe taken and hidden inside the temple? We will be the first people ever to discover it!"

The bait complete, Fabio waited for more nods of mooted affirmation and was not disappointed, when they came after a short pause. Fabio had painted a mysterious and romantic atmosphere, so most people voted to stay. The mission back on track! Professor Mancini enthralled with himself, gave them more to think about.

"The Spanish conquistadores that pursued the Shaman, brutally and systematically persecuted and executed his people. One thing that always seems to be consistent about the story is, as much as they tried, the Shaman and his precious disc had vanished. Neither was ever found."

"How do you know prof?" Mathieson asked.

"Mat, I can't know for certain, but what I do know is this; *even* if they had taken the disc, the Christians would have melted it down to destroy any remnants of any other religion. Those days were barbaric back in the early 16th Century, in the days of Hernando Pizarro."

"Really." Mathieson wished that he had never asked.

"This legendary disc is much older than this time period. It goes much further back, and that's why we're here."

Harjit looked seriously at Christopher, both knew that the Mission had taken a new direction, when unexpectedly another voice made its own opinion felt.

"I would have done that too," commented Mashir. "And, when we find it, let's melt it down and be done, that's what I say!" Mashir burst into laughter at his open jibe towards the professor, while watching Fabio's face turning livid.

"That will never happen," stated Kees. "Because such an artefact is not the professor's, the Vatican's or yours to take. It is the rightful property of Brazil." The no nonsense Brazilian government official stated, putting them all right.

His task on the expedition was as *guardian*; his responsibility included all finds of any natural or archaeological resources. It was he, and not Fabio who had ultimate authority here. His voice wiped any thoughts of riches from their faces.

"*You are* a complete mercenary, Mashir," said Fabio, ignoring the bureaucrat Brazilian official's bullying tactics too. His dry tone focused straight at the Iranian, when unexpectedly everyone broke out laughing. Such an impasse seemed ludicrous.

It all seemed so silly, but for this moment, their recent loss of Carmello was apparently forgotten. Fabio breathed a sigh of relief laughing along with them, his smokescreen complete. But, Mashir had more to say.

"We are looking at the true *Gate of the Gods* in Amazonia and not in Peru. If he Key of the Gods of the Seven Rays, is here well…" Mashir recognised the artefact's true potential. "Then I agree with Fabio, maybe it is inside the temple. and just within our grasp." It appeared that the excited surveyor was also caught in the professor's trap. Fabio smiled and nodded his agreement.

Most people at last in high spirits decided to get their local fermentation brew out. Passing it around seemed the best thing to do, so Christopher had a few beers while sitting down next to his friend Mashir.

"Pity you do not like this stuff," Chris began smiling.

"It's against my religion Chris."

"You are well informed Mashir." Christopher staring quite astounded, because once again his friend's knowledge seemed endless. "Always full of surprises you are pal. I am impressed, but then, I gather you already knew about the key eh? "The Key of the Gods of the Seven Rays?" "Man, and I thought you were just a surveyor, *not a Historian!*" Chris raised an eyebrow a little; "You and I have been friends for years." Christopher chuckled, "So, what else are you not telling me about yourself Mashir, eh?" Mashir gave a little awkward smile.

"I have many interests Chris, the history, well that is a sign of a misspent youth my friend, nothing more than that." Mashir smiled and giggled in a boyish snigger. *"All is as God will's it my friend even unto death."* Christopher lifted his beer mug considering his friend's words.

****

CHAPTER IX

SACRIFICE AT SUNRISE

Rare as they were, later that evening a few transmissions arrived from the ONCOL Corporation. It was the result of his satellite scans, the ones Fabio desperately wanted. Inside the privacy of his tent, his desperate eyes kept searching vainly for more information.

There must be some mistake? These results are wrong, all wrong! There are only pictures of the bloody jungle, forest images and fuzzy patches. The coordinates must be way out! Satellites can pick up the smallest of images, so this place should have been easy! The area has been security-cleared to show this structure, so why all this rubbish? Why all this interference? Is there something wrong with our navigational instruments?

"Hell, and blood!" Fabio called out, realising his worthless results. Against his better judgement if events got worse, he would send Harjit, Christopher, Endrissi and the undisciplined technician along with Mathieson to guide them back home. They would take with them his detailed maps, pictures and small artefacts.

Instinctively, Fabio would ensure that part of his story would get out and would give him worldwide recognition in case something overcame him. Fabio knew he would receive the final accolade that he deserved for discovering the temple.

Harjit and Endrissi were risks he could no longer afford; *Endrissi had lost it,* Mathieson was a Jew and the girl a Hindu. The professor shook his head thinking,

My expedition should have been a pure Catholic one, the interfering company insisted on the others. Suddenly, Fabio realised his deep prejudice. *God what am I thinking, they have been very useful!*

The professor had been more open-minded at the onset of the expedition, taking on his staff for their abilities. He was not normally a bigot; pompous yes and arrogant too but without question not a bigot. Something unexplainable inside him had changed.

He knew it. Badness like an infection had impaired his better judgment, affecting tolerance towards others. These strong feelings of resentment were growing in him. He knew that too.

Explicit instructions stated by ONCOL, that all communications be kept at a minimum. To reinforce complete secrecy, only the mission leader is sanctioned by protocol to do this. Fabio was therefore the only person with a cell phone or communication device. As bad luck would have it for him in this climate, his few devices did not work reliably. The only way of communication for the expedition was through his neat but limited Ventessi solar powered computer, with built in satellite antennae. The transmissions were not easy at the best of times because of an unexplainable interference inside the vale, and this suited ONCOL.

Fabio trusted the Vatican implicitly but not ONCOL, disliking the company intensely. The Vatican needed their expertise, analytical tools and ONCOL's financial investment for the expedition. Unfortunately, he needed their technical expertise.

Without warning all data transmissions signals suddenly failed.

Fabio's tent flap unexpectedly opened, unzipped and abruptly pulled back, when Endrissi's head suddenly thrusted inside, catching him unceremoniously in the Mosquito net.

"Bloody net!" Endrissi growled.

"Don't bother knocking," said Fabio sarcastically while looking up from inside his small chaotic tent, all so different from the professor's well-ordered mind.

Books and boots lay in disorganized harmony. The professor's clothes were thrown to the bottom corner like a barricade. Looking up in surprise, Fabio was on top of his sleeping bag, with his fingers tapping desperately onto the frozen keyboard.

"Ciao Fabio, what are you doing?" He asked the bearded professor.

"Endrissi, how are you feeling?" He looked concerned at the geologist.

"*Bene - fine*. Anything interesting?" Endrissi enquired.

"Not good. The magnetic interference moved and scrambled my connection."

"Si?"

"Gaining entry into the temple is still problematic." Fabio said with resignation written on his face, "I never thought it would be easy, but getting inside still proves to be quite elusive. I sent off digital photographs to ONCOL and received back info and to be honest, its utter garbage. The results are very disappointing. Anyone would think that they are messing me around!" Fabio's troubled forehead blushed.

"Oh?" Like a magician's trick, Christopher's face suddenly appeared behind Endrissi's. The scientist's head stuck in through the open tent flap.

"Surely not professor?" Endrissi stated critically.

"Ah please, *do* come inside and *join me!* We might as well have a meeting here."

The men were having second thoughts, and maybe this surprise entry was not such a good idea, both looking questioningly at each other.

"We're just passing," said Christopher warily and was about to go again when Fabio wanted them to know his results.

"No stay. I have downloaded the results and the analysis is very disappointing. It is bizarre and almost as if ONCOL cannot find us! Their report informs me that our photographs show nothing of note, which is total nonsense. The company has got them wrong, seriously wrong." The men waited with bated breath and blank faces, both feeling trapped inside with Fabio and a time bomb.

"What's up Professor Mancini?" Endrissi asked tentatively.

"Professor what's on your mind?" It was a loaded question, but Christopher wanted to reduce any ill rebuke and get it over with.

"I have been thinking, it would be wise to send some people back home."

"Oh?" Endrissi gasped, blinking involuntarily.

"Really, why? Who do you have in mind professor?" Christopher knew the impact on his own work at such a decision. He had critical work still to do.

"It will take months to get back to civilization. Those chosen will be expected to pack all evidence and specimens gathered so far. On your arrival back," Fabio continued, Christopher looking stupefied, "I want you both to call for additional aid for me." That answered Christopher's question. He had already been chosen to go home.

"What about a Helicopter? Surely that makes more sense than another long trip back through the jungle?" Christopher parried.

"You are not listening to the professor, Chris. ONCOL cannot find us. They don't know where we really are!" Endrissi was tense. "What do you think that Fabio's been doing all this time, Panto?" The geologist began blinking faster.

"Si, I know, it's far from desirable to be stuck out here in the middle of nowhere, but Carmello has been killed. Try to contact them again Fabio." Christopher insisted.

Blanking him Fabio said, "We will speak of this again in another few days. Time is not on our side and my top priority is the temple. I need a breakthrough and to gain access now, not next year! Unfortunately, the temple has proved to be impregnable with any of the tools we have brought with us, and frankly I am at a loss. So much depended on those bloody scan results." It was a hard pill for Fabio to swallow; he had quite literally hit a brick wall.

"Impregnable how?" Christopher levered more.

"There's no satellite laser imaging to help us and our own images show nothing internal. The whole area is an electronic nightmare," added Fabio.

Christopher remembered Fabio had made him feel rotten just before going off on his mini-expedition, remembering that the professor had disregarded him then. Even so, his-own natural enthusiasm and scientific spark pushed forward again.

"Look Fabio," he paused, "Give me another shot at deciphering those inscriptions, there is nothing to lose and I might even surprise you." Christopher waited and urged him again,

"Come on professor what do you say?" Christopher pressed the stubborn intellectual more, "Come on you have nothing to lose," he smiled softer.

Fabio logged out of his dirty electronic gear and sat upright staring seriously towards Christopher.

"Si, yes go ahead, just do it," ordered the professor. He resigned himself to accept the young upstart. "Get us in and I'll order another plate of those lovely maggots for you as a reward!" Fabio added with a wry smile.

Christopher's face lit up, *what is this; he has a sense of humour after all, that's the old Fabio!* Chris was amazed at his U-turn.

"I hope you have a stomach for good food too then professor and *please do* order a plateful for yourself; double helpings and eh, don't forget Endrissi!" Endrissi's eyes stopped moving when they all began laughing. Their impromptu meeting was over.

****

Hours passed, and daylight would soon be gone. Stumped, the team studied the enigmatic inscriptions at the entrance. Its secrets kept.

"I need a bit more time. I said it before and I'll say it again. These symbols *are* strangely familiar." Christopher reminded the professor once more, scepticism washing over Fabio' s face. Chris recognised that look. "Fab, look here. These symbols represent letters, and most are similar to symbols used by the late 17th century secret societies, as far back as the 1680's," advised Christopher.

"Nonsense." Fabio's face nipped back.

"I know it is improbable and even sounds far-fetched, yet here they are right in front of me. I know it! Give me a bit more time that is all I am asking for. *I will crack it.*"

The scientist watched Fabio hoping for a reprieve, and not an order to send him back to civilization with the others, *not yet.*

"Christopher, these markings are much, much older than you can know, they really are ancient." Fabio disagreed. "There is nothing back at that time, in building technology in the 17th century to be able to create such a structure as this one here. And for your own edification, what you suggest is a century after Hernando Pizarro. Understand this, the Europeans had absolutely nothing that could build such a magnificent structure as this one. They did not have the tools or the technology. Quite how this has been done by an ancient civilization, well that too is a complete enigma. Even with our modern equipment today, we cannot model this kind of marvel." Fabio began rudely tapping the solid stone constitution, "So unless we get inside and very soon, the funding from the Vatican will dry up and the expedition will be over." The expedition leader's disgruntled tone evident.

"Then give me more time Fabio! I have observed some of the building processes at the mines. That is only part of the story, because the rocks pulled out from there were massive and cut with a great accuracy. These were then moved here to the temple, their final destination, and I guess around the 16th to 17th Century."

"Hmm," Fabio considered it. "You did mention images of the Portuguese had been drawn, but they are more likely to have arrived on the scene long after the temple was completed. I would say they were only digging for more treasure and gems like what you found." Fabio bounced his ideas off the younger man trying to piece together bits of the jigsaw. "What happened to the conquistadores, where did they go? There are many old stories in post Cortez days of searching for lost treasure in Peru and Amazonia. Tales of Spanish and Portuguese expeditions that went much further into the interior. Most vanished."

"Some additional processes that were not described in the mine drawings must be at work on these final cut stone blocks," added Endrissi, pulling on his geological knowledge. "We know that this temple stone has a different structure, because careful examination of it shows a crystalline glint within." Endrissi spoke facts." As a geologist, this is bizarre and would make the construction at the temple of a different stone than those from the mine blocks. "Compared to the mine blocks they are without question *not the same type!* The type mined and pulled up by manual elevator then deposited onto the surface is not the same stone. Why they needed the blocks I don't know. *Do you go with this?"*

"Yes and no," Fabio squinted curiously. "What you are saying is that it's *not the same stone?"* Fabio asked.

"Which puts a complete damper on my relocation theory," said Christopher. His tone of disappointment was all too obvious.

Endrissi's blue eyes began blinking faster again. He was keen to help both men string things together. Geology was his department.

"I know, I am speaking above your head, come on, don't make me do all the work here, *think,"* said Endrissi confidently.

"You are not." Fabio gestured his displeasure at Endrissi's superior knowledge. "Go on."

"The stone was subjected to some earth-shattering change to its structure, after getting here, and one that would normally take millions of years or more. I would therefore postulate, that this temple stone has come from somewhere else; possibly an entirely different area or continent. Strangely, I don't recognize it at all." Endrissi guessing too, "And that is unfortunately my problem."

Christopher shook his head in disbelief. He didn't agree with Endrissi's theory.

"Where else could they have come from?" Like a scalpel, Fabio's words sliced at Endrissi's deductive powers. Yet he knew that Christopher had seen both stone types too and respected the geologist's keen eye for rock.

Meanwhile, Harjit had been sitting quietly listening to the developing conversation and could no longer be a spectator. She had enough of their conjectures.

"The temple was built long before the Spanish or Portuguese ever came to these parts," said Harjit. "The stone dug out hundreds of years ago and left in the mines were going to be used to build *over the temple,* not make the temple itself. Making it bigger." Harjit cemented the conundrum, "This temple stone does come from another region and was here long before anyone knew that the mines ever existed!" Harjit paused building her case to a confused audience.

"Eh?" Even Christopher contorted his face.

"That's basically what I just said," stated Endrissi.

"Nonsense." Fabio dismissing her idea and Endrissi with his stony face, "No Harj, have a look around you. It would be impossible to move stone lumps like these from a different region then over this terrain. Think again."

But Harjit would not be silenced, "I have listened to you all and I have seen inside the mines. I have viewed the murals drawn on the mine walls too, those horrible stories. Those people are of a wholly different civilization to the ones that built this temple!" Her tone was convincing.

"Unbelievable." Unimpressed Fabio watched the confident girl with distaste.

"Yes, it was done long before even the Egyptian pyramids and those buildings were constructed with massive blocks and moved over great distances." Harjit speculated but she knew there was still a very big jigsaw piece missing.

"Nice try Harj. It does not explain these European symbols. I recognize them as late, pre, or post 17th Century." Christopher threw a spanner at her theory.

"They are not European symbols Christopher!" Fabio kept on insisting.

"Look, I don't have the answers to everything. I agree there are a few missing links in my theory and I also believe Endrissi *is correct* about the stone blocks. They come from somewhere else; but *not the mines*." Harjit took a breath in, fixing her gaze on each man in turn, narrowing onto the professor's, "And professor, you too are also correct."

"Well I knew that," said Fabio brimming while the rest of them stood speechless.

"The temple is ancient and who knows how old." Harjit's cognitive candour not finished, she kept on going, "Four hundred, maybe four thousand years or even more! This is a temple built by another Civilization. Not by the indigenous tribe who were slaughtered at the mines later by Europeans. Oh no, it was not them. The people who built this temple are *very different*." The girl reasoned with the puzzle,

"Remember, what the *Zaplithowatres* believed in?" *Another World* holding this thought to herself.

"You see Christopher, *even Harjit* denies your misconception." The professor smiled smugly at the scientist, although Fabio believed the girl's understanding was also flawed. Only a tale, and a myth he had used. However, his team had more to say.

"These symbols, I tell you Fabio, I've seen them before." He raised his voice, Christopher challenging him again.

"You are mistaken Chris." Endrissi backed the professor and Harjit.

"In time I will prove it. I will get in." Christopher's face livid.

"Be my Guest," Fabio countered.

"That's all I wanted to hear you say!" Christopher called out and marched off.

****

Everyone knew what was expected of them as work on the temple increased. Any notions of imminent departure were put aside. The days quickly turned into weeks. There never seemed to be enough hours in the day to dent into a lifetime of work. Re-measuring, collating, illustrations and photographs taken, it all would be invaluable for future Historians. The building was about the size of a small hill even with natural foliage removed. No crack or blemish could be found. Signs of weathering on the stone appeared negligible apart from some of the eaten codex. Topsoil lay in many parts where algae clung by a wing and a prayer on its surfaces; this easily wiped off to expose a rich and shiny glazed red stone surface below. Temple work was difficult and laborious and could take a good thirty minutes or more for even a fit person to climb from base to the top.

Tired and overworked, between his scientific-research for cures, Christopher would continue to try and crack the strange codex attempting to bind myth and legend into one his expectations. Christopher remembered what some of the old symbols might represent filling in the blanks in a tedious and time-consuming effort.

Mashir occasionally helped supply additional and more enigmatic inscriptions from on top of the temple, as if Chris needed more, but that was the easy part. At this moment, the Doctor's dogmatic perseverance was working and eventually the jigsaw was taking shape.

Christopher had a bad night, waking up early just a bit before sunrise. He was sitting alone in the large marque tent, formulating his next substitution sequence.

This is like a test, thinking clearly, *a degree is a test, and if I remember back to my esoteric studies, degrees are also ceremonies or rituals that Freemasons go through. How strange to think that these symbols are the same and that they are a test too. I know it, I really do. But why here, and what for?*

Christopher had speculated at this incredible discovery, and to think there might be a real link between this dead civilization and his own. *Bizarre, how can this be,* he wondered.

As part of his own religious education, he had studied past doctrine and esoteric fellowships and knew that Freemasonry was not a religion, but *brothers* that believed in a master geometrician, God!

Staring transfixed, his eyes and mind were fixated on the written symbols that he had copied onto paper, when suddenly, he simply began breaking the code.

Oh my God! Chris mentally popped the positions of the vowels into what looked like common patterns, quite unaware his mind mixed seamlessly with his soft silent words speaking out to himself.

"Everything hinges on this language and is not too alien from my own English. I think this is where the link comes from. How 16th or 17th century English had anything remotely to do with this structure, God only knows. Did the Spanish or maybe the Portuguese commission some stonemasons of the past? That might explain the existence of these symbols. If this were true, then these symbols would be Freemasonic in origin; *a secret society.* I know they used symbols like these to disguise and hide secret messages. So, what exactly is hidden inside these words, what secrets do they contain?" His open dialogue with himself continued, silently.

I remember similar symbols. Scott showed me them back home. They were found in many places in the villages of Scotland. These symbols are of the same type. It might be possible to find some evidence of a person, an initial or a name that would identify someone. But why would they build a place out here and for the Spanish or Portuguese? How could it even be possible? Maybe these secret messages were passed onto those Freemason brothers. That idea is so fantastic, no wonder Fabio is laughing at me!" He paused for a moment at that incredibility… Christopher's tone of self-bafflement receded into a whisper.

"God this place is impossible, it shouldn't even exist." Christopher was gripped completely by his self-quandary, and totally unaware that Mashir had silently slipped inside the mess tent beside him, and waited listening. The quiet man watched from behind, silently and almost amusingly at Christopher's self-deliberations.

"Fabio and Harjit must have got the time and age of the temple completely wrong. This place cannot be any older than four or five hundred years old when many of the South American civilizations were building such magnificent creations. It is plausible and might explain a direct relationship with Europe. The answer must be in the Codex. I must break it all, I really must." Mashir then decided to introduce himself.

"Ah, Christopher my friend tenacious as always," said Mashir causing Christopher to unconsciously stop talking to himself. Christopher turned in surprise. His friend was standing right next him, "My apologies for disturbing you so early," said Mashir in a tip toeing tone. Mashir looked down while the scientist kept on scribbling onto a writing pad, while the Iranian man's eyes kept tracking alongside Christopher's cryptic hand.

"Do you always creep about like this?" Christopher asked with a furrowed brow.

"I did not wish to disturb you, sorry. I was restless and thought I heard your voice, and, ah yes! I can see that you have been very, very busy."

"I couldn't sleep either, this was troubling me. Anyway, how are you this morning Mashir?" Christopher's deep thoughts broken, and composure regained greeting the sallow skinned man. Closer in now, Mashir began examining Christopher's scribbles.

"I think you are definitely on to something here Chris." The surveyor also a knowledgeable man on languages.

"Yes, it's been interesting," smiling with some satisfaction.

"Can I assist a little?" Mashir quickly scrutinized Christopher's newly revised document. "If you don't mind me saying so Chris, please replace that symbol with an "L" and this glyph with the letter "R"

"Sure." While observing its new transcription, "Something seems to be formulating." Christopher was satisfied with Mashir's help and mildly amused because true enough, there was a common link with his theory. Chris paused to consider thoughtfully of his friend, and just how articulate he had been on the expedition.

****

God works in mysterious ways. Unknown to everyone it would be here inside Amazonia, that the powers of darkness and light would first gather against humanity.

Again, it was the Prophecy!

"They will come first and Smite"
"All will shake in terror"
"Cold is the land"
"Nowhere to hide"

Fate brought them together as darkness and light, and Christopher's goal posts had moved. He had changed from being a simple scientist and now become a tenacious tomb breaker.

****

Home sick, Christopher's mind moved back to Scotland, back to five years ago just after his father had passed away. Christopher remembered going to live in Italy to study religion. Chris already accomplished and a fully qualified bio-technologist, periodically travelled back to Scotland to lecture at the university in Glasgow and to visit his family. It was at the University that he first met Harjit. From then on, their paths were fixed by fate. Christopher reminisced his life experiences.

Italy, where I now live, is beautiful, the history, the architecture and my Catholic religion, but Scotland is where my heart truly lies, and now unfortunately for my sins, bloody Hell here I am stuck in this God forsaken place. I have only myself to blame and yet God's will, will be done, I really hope I am worthy of this challenge. Reality broke his thoughts again when Mashir prompted him.

"You seemed faraway just then Chris. So, what do you think?" Mashir asked while Christopher's keen eye looked again at the detailed symbols on the transcript paper. Stunned, his head pulled back in surprise, the answer leaped out at him!

"Well, well, well! What have we here?" His heart raced in excitement. Christopher copiously wrote the symbols on another paper. It mostly resembled gobbledegook, or an incomplete crossword puzzle but by adding some new consonants and slotting them into position, the results delighted him. His face lit up. "*I have it!* A little more time and I'll have the full scripture interpretation solved. I will have it all by the end of the day!"

"Excellent Chris! All is as God wills it my friend."

"Oh, I can see something! It's the first paragraph of the ancient text! Thank God."

TO ⊔⅃⅂⅂⊔⊔ ⅂⊓⌐Ε⅃⅃ΑⅬΕℾS TO TOⅆⅬ⊓
T⊓E ⅃AST
THOSE ⅂⊓OU ART ⅃O⅂ ⅃URE ⅤILL SUREⅬ< ⅃ERIS⊓

⊔E Ⅴ⅃⅃⅂⅃⊔⊐ ⅂⊓E S AⅬRE⊐ ⅤORⅣ MUS⅂
⊔E SⅬO>E⅃

OⅬE⅃ IS ⅂⊓IS ⅤA< ⅃OⅤ TO ⅂⊓⅃⅃⅂S ⅂⊓A⅂
ARE E⌐IL

⊔E ⅤAR⅃E⊐ ⅂⊓ERE IS ⅃OⅤ⊓ERE TO ⊓I⊐E
⅂⊓E< ⅤILL ⅬOΛE ⅃ROM ⌐ERE TO ⅃⅃AIM I⅂

"What does it mean?" Mashir encouraged him.

"Well there are a few obvious words that I can see, *and, it is in English!*" Said a relieved Christopher sighing hard. "And that makes it easy!"

"Incredible Chris." Mashir watched Christopher, and his mishmash text.

TO ENTER THIS PLAⅬE IS TO TOⅆⅬ⊓ ⅂⊓E ⅃RESE⅃⅂
⅃OⅤER⅃UL ⅂⊓OU AR⅂ I⅃ ⅃RA<ER I⅃ ⅃O⅂ ⅃
URE ⅂⊓EE ⅤILL SUREⅬ< ⅃ERIS⊓
⊔E ⅤAR⅃E⊐ ⅂⊓OSE ⊔E⅃ORE SAⅬRI⅃ IⅬE⊐ ⅂⊓⅃⅂⅃
SOULS TO ⊓IM AND ⅤERE
O⌐ER⅃OME AND ⅂⊓E< ⅤERE ALL
⊐ES⅂RO<E⊐
I⅂ IS ⅃UREⅬ< E⌐IL SO ⊐O ⅃O⅂ ⅃AⅬ⅂ER I⅃
⌐AI⅃ ⅃URSUI⅂S

TO ENTER THIS PLACE IS TO TOUCH THE CULTURE
THE THREE SHILS VILL SIND ALONE
COMRADESHIL MEMBERSHIL AND CRIENDSHIL
CLIE AS IS THE MITTH OC ARMS BUT VILL N
OT BE BOUTH
ALONE A TALLST HIS HOARDS
REMEMBER THE LRESENCE AND HUMBLE <
OURSELC TO UNIT< TO ONE TON VITH
LA TIENT LERSERTERANLE CAITH AND
LRA<ER
ALL VILL BE TESTED AND SO LOO> EAST NOR T
H EAST CROM MALISINI LIS
COR HELL AS ILLIS SMITE SURROUNDS <OU VIT
H NISLAIR

TO ENTER THIS PLACE IS TO THN THN
NOVHERE AND IS ALSO TO THIS LAND
VHERE TIME IS NOTHINI AND TIME IS ETER<
THNT
THTC VN< TC CUUKUN
THE LOST IS COUND SO MUST BE
TA>EN AS UNILIED IT MUST NETER
BE OR ALL IS LOST COR ALL TIME AND LURIC
ILATION ILLUMINATION AND
TLORICILATION VILL BE NETER MORE

SA< THE VORN NASOM AND ENTER TO MEET <
OUR SOUL OR BE LOST AND
COREHER IN NOVHERE

The Iranian surveyor pointed to a fraction of quickly interpreted text.

"I think it is a story my friend, please observe." Mashir narrowed in closer to the text, "It is telling you something."

"No Mashir. It's not a story, it's a riddle." Christopher countered.

"It is both." Came a voice from behind them. A silence followed Fabio's voice.

Twisting around, Christopher secretly groaned at this unexpected interruption. Professor

Fabio Mancini had appeared but did not look very well, and Christopher could see the professor was under considerable stress.

"Morning Fabio." Christopher greeted him with a smile but Mashir couldn't care less, instead giving the professor a disinterested grunt, pressing on Christopher more for his thoughts.

"Chris! Chris! How will *this* gain us entry?" Mashir intensified. The Iranian tried to grasp a mental leap, a jump of cognition that Christopher had already achieved. Fabio would not be ignored and spoke this time with more authority.

"If your interpretation *is correct,* and that, I am very dubious about." Fabio continued, "Then some words and sayings might be completely new and never even be heard of in our own language. For example, like a *name* or a *title* that is unique to it alone. Those sorts would never make sense to us ever because we do not know what they are! We could never make any obvious connection and therefore no direct interpretation or comparison. In English you say, and if your theory was right then it would really be in Portuguese and not, in English!"

"Maybe, but Freemasonry crosses all religions and language barriers." Christopher blunted his point, knowing that Fabio could still be right. The professor had cast more uncertainty on Christopher's theory.

"We have to be honest young man." The professor spoke with a great degree of scepticism and disappointment at his own failures yet twisted this *lack* into a focused jealousy towards Christopher.

"Oh, give me a break Fabio, damn it man. *You* can't do any better!" Christopher's voice accelerating, "Si, I am unclear about its full interpretation, *and yes, I do know this*. Look here my work *is* making sense!" Christopher's anger quickly lashing out at the professor.

"Chris, apologies," Mashir interjected, "I have some more text for you. I think it is another riddle. See what you make of it." Mashir delicately handed him his own scribbled piece of paper. Christopher looked at the arranged symbols while taking a step back.

"Oh, thanks and where did you get this one?" Christopher asked, the professor unimportant to him in the light of this new evidence, "Is this not the same piece of brown paper you dropped before?"

"A different sheet," Mashir replied. "This one is not the same one you saw me with. Those were some early sketches. This is—" The surveyor stammered a little awkwardly, "from up, up, t… the top of the temple." His cheeks blushed.

"Ok man, I'm not prying, just don't drop any more litter, ok," poked Christopher, while opening the dried-up piece of cracked paper for inspection. Not surprisingly, the symbols were immediately recognizable to him, the same symbols and a *different message indeed.*

"What do you think?"

"This paper is well worn and crumpled. Bloody hell how old is it? The paper resembles old cracked skin and the ink, or the pencil used is not fresh. Are you sure, *you wrote it?*" He studied the writing and looked at Mashir's face in disbelief.

"Old stock. Stuff I have had for some time and brought it with me from back home. Chris, it's all I had. The pencil I know it is rubbish." Mashir felt more embarrassed. "Hey, just work it out C!" He pressed Christopher on with flippancy, but Fabio was not idle, moving quickly to take it.

"I'll have it!" Fabio demanded.

"Ah! Wait your turn," Christopher parried moving the paper just enough out of his reach, leaving Fabio grasping at air.

"What! How dare you! I, am in charge, not you!" Fabio blustered.

"Yeah, as I said, wait your turn pal." He resisted thinking. *Christ, it's not even light yet and Fabio's off ranting again, what a morning.* Mashir was astounded into shock at the instant tension between both men. Christopher stood straight upright, his temper flaring, and all composure gone. Fabio exposed a tinderbox of rage against him. Christopher's eyes livid, the professor's own well-being under immense strain, his temper was raw and about to ignite. Saying nothing more, moved quickly passed Fabio. Chris annoyed knocking him a little, codex firmly in Chris's hand. Conversation, over!

****

Sunset not far off, Christopher was determined to gain entry and for all the heated words between him and the professor, still, he had promised Fabio. Chris like a solitary animal, kept at it, deciphering Mashir's symbols as daylight quickly began disappearing. Around five-thirty was when everywhere would plunge into darkness and in the dimming evening he wondered, what this night would bring?

The young man stood alone staring upwards at the mysterious stone codices. Gripping his resolve, Christopher's eyes were drawn fixed and focused. The Temple taunted him, teased him, while he waited for fate.

It had already exerted its *will* against Fabio weeks before. Now it was his turn to feel puny, weak and intimidated. It was much more than just the stone's impregnability. What could a mere mortal do against it? And yet, he was impossibly making headway!

Nightlife approached and with those familiar dins inside the forest, irate screeching monkeys moved rapidly among the trees, jumping from the branches. Noises of insistent bugs warning of their presence in a multitude of symphonies, in sounds and all growing excitably against isolation, noises as old as the forest itself. Solitude seemed to be all around, for it too could not be ignored. Christopher took a deep lungful of loneliness and sighed out long and hard his breath of life, when he sensed something different.

It was the coming change, and while the forest blared out its wonder in the hours of darkness, nocturnal survival announced itself once again. Listening to all the life and all the loneliness, Christopher felt small. Gently, a sultry breeze whipped up around him. Swallowing hard against tears he could only ask himself;

Is this only a stone monolith, inert with nothing more to tell?

The sceptics below at base camp. Christopher wanted to be here and to be alone in private with time to think. For a brief moment, resting his heavy head onto the hard stone. Tuning in his mind... Christopher needed more, he needed to *feel it...* On these stony steps so many miles from where he was born, Christopher asked himself.

God why bring me here to this lost and forsaken place!

Standing back, he focused onto the stone words, Christopher started to narrate them out aloud. His tone was as hard as the stone itself and in command. No sooner had he started his reading, he stopped abruptly turning swiftly around.

Gulping hard, Chris knew something did not feel right. Was it a chance smell or a change in the air? Unsure, Christopher sensed somebody else was here with him. Looking out from the entrance, something unknown threatened him, watching apprehensively, when out of the stone's shady terraces a figure shifted with a shadowed tone. A movement, hard to see in the blackness where it blended, but there was just enough alteration of space and darkness for him to perceive it. His dark skin was unable to hide him anymore in this dimming light, so this was the moment Mashir chose to stand out.

Christopher gasping in relief, it was only him! He had not heard the surveyor's approach and thought his friend had just arrived but, this was not the case. Mashir had been watching Chris for quite some time.

"Mashir, it is you!" Chris said, as the man stepped closer, his feet light and quiet.

"I thought you could do with some company my friend," said Mashir while swatting insects away. "Allah! These horrific pests are normally found next to water where the air is calm, *not up here.* These ones are different, stronger than all the others!"

Mashir began pulling down his hat trying to protect himself as more opportunists dive-bombed him.

"Good to see you again Mashir. It's lonesome up here." The scientist smiled, glad for the companionship.

"I have been waiting for this moment," said Mashir. "You have cracked the codex my friend?" A rhetorical question. Mashir had always had faith that Christopher could do what *he* could not! Both men stared respectfully into each other's eyes.

"It seems right." Christopher said as the sun began setting.

"I'm glad to be here with you in this moment," said Mashir taking a deep breath.

****

Christopher said he would do it by the end of the day and he did. Mashir listened to Christopher respectfully, while contemplating the Scotsman's natural genius for reading the codices directly from symbol to text, off from the original stone surface. Chris effortlessly substituted words from symbols, with no uncertainty or hesitation. Speaking in a steady and solemn tone, he gave an end to end perfect narration and said,

"TO ENTER THIS PLACE IS TO TOUCH THE PAST.
THOSE THOU ART NOT PURE WILL SURELY PERISH.
BE WARNED THE SACRED WORDS MUST BE SPOKEN.
OPEN IS THIS WAY NOW TO THINGS THAT ARE EVIL.
BE WARNED THERE IS NOWHERE TO HIDE.
THEY WILL COME FROM HERE TO CLAIM IT."

Taking a deep breath while balancing himself, he continued.

"TO ENTER THIS PLACE IS TO TOUCH THE PRESENT.
POWERFUL THOU ART IN PRAYER IF NOT PURE THEE WILL SURELY PERISH.
BE WARNED THOSE BEFORE SACRIFICED THEIR SOULS TO HIM AND WERE OVERCOME AND THEY WERE ALL DESTROYED.

IT IS PURELY EVIL SO DO NOT FALTER IN VAIN PURSUITS."

The wind strengthening by the second as Christopher's voice was becoming deeper, more guttural and almost as if it was not his own. Then without warning, Christopher became a priest again, raising his voice to above the now tumultuous wind that was suddenly making its presence felt and shouting out as if in a sermon.

"TO ENTER THIS PLACE IS TO TOUCH THE FUTURE!
THE THREE SHIPS WILL SINK ALONE COMRADESHIP, MEMBERSHIP AND FRIENDSHIP FINE AS IS THE MIGHT OF ARMS BUT WILL NOT BE ENOUGH ALONE AGAINST HIS HORDES!
REMEMBER THE PRESENCE AND HUMBLE YOURSELF TO UNITY TO ONE GOD WITH PATIENT PERSERVERANCE, FAITH AND PRAYER.
ALL WILL BE TESTED AND SO LOOK EAST NORTH EAST FROM MALISIBLIS FOR HELP AS IBLIS SMITE SURROUNDS YOU WITH DESPAIR!"

There were no fancy punctuation marks, only words, words of warning, words of instruction and words of wisdom. Chris called out against nature, his body seemed to be growing in stature and glowing in presence as he said them! Mashir watched the spectacle in awe. Any careful thinking gone, Mashir did not know if this vision was an illusion or real. The daylight fast fading when the final passage came stronger and louder. Christopher blared these Godly words.

"TO ENTER THIS PLACE IS TO GO TO NOWHERE AND IS ALSO TO THIS LAND. WHERE TIME IS NOTHING AND TIME IS EVERYTHING!
THE LOST IS FOUND SO MUST BE TAKEN AS UNIFIED IT MUST NEVER BE BY THEM OR ALL IS LOST FOR ALL TIME AND PURIFICATION, ILLUMINATION AND GLORIFICATION WILL BE NEVER MORE.

Suddenly the forest stopped, and the wind cut away. It died, leaving only an unnatural silence and stony words. One last thing in that last ray of light was needed, the catalysts, Christopher's words and daylight into night.

"SAY THE WORD NASOM AND ENTER TO MEET YOUR SOUL OR BE LOST AND FOREVER IN NOWHERE."

The sun had gone.

The night blacker and deeper than normal as everything plunged into darkness with Christopher's high-pitched recital finished. A deathly silence waited after his words in the surrounding forest. It waited in fear for something, nothing happened. Mashir was afraid to speak but this quiet moment prompted Mashir to whisper.

"*Allah forgive us,* we know not what we have done." His sharp faced features pained. In the darkness, Mashir extenuated his hand in mental agony towards his friend, to where the Scotsman stood shaking, *what is wrong with him,* wondered Mashir?

****

Harjit and Fabio saw everything. They too had climbed the steps arriving minutes later, standing with an oil lamp in hand, lighting up the area right behind them. They had been close enough to hear the recital of those ill-omened verses.

Wiry framed Mashir jumped into action to help his friend, holding onto Christopher tightly while trying to calm his rehab like body. The poor scientist had started a chain reaction of events and begun something supernatural. Trembling uncontrollably, Christopher's whole persona appeared mortified in the light of Fabio's lamp, exposing both men wrapped in a weird kind of brotherly embrace.

"My friend, my friend, *please... enough of this.*" The sallow skinned man pleaded. Mashir became more aware of this extra company, while speaking gently to the distraught bio-technologist. Mashir staring into Chris's eyes and fuzzy mind, Mashir tried to penetrate his friend's cognition. *"Listen, listen to me... my friend, you are scaring me."* Witnessing Christopher's stupefaction, his mental stability was under question.

Dropping heavily onto his knees, Christopher's transformed body crumpled in a heap, his head instantly rested limply on his chest, but his hands had involuntarily pulled onto Mashir as if holding onto a life raft.

The Iranian was suddenly caught off-balance struggling with him as Harjit burst into action. She was a well-oiled medic, quickly helping Mashir with Chris and lowering the exhausted man down safely. Christopher lay on the stone step, body at rest, his rigour silenced. Fabio looked at the temple and the temple remained, shut.

****

"What happened?" Christopher slurred as his eyes opened slowly in a daze, attempting to kick-start his lost memory. He struggled to remember anything but only his blank gaze remained.

"Augh!" Christopher called out in distress.

"Christopher, *Chris...*" Harjit's soft voice attempted to aid him.

"What has happened?" Christopher asked, hope coming back to him but then, he saw something in her troubled brown eyes. Chris was still unaware that his stressed hands kept gripping onto Mashir.

"You have been overdoing it young man." Professor Mancini smiling and drawing closer and answering for the girl. No warmth was held in that smile, "Well done, you made a sterling effort in the scripture narration." Fabio, a little nonchalant for his welfare, "You have *loosely* pieced at least a few things together. Let's get you fixed up and you'll be right as rain in no time." His uncaring tone was a touch too flippant.

Harjit elbowed the professor in the ribs, making him wince. Suddenly without warning a huge shock of flash lightning caught them off guard. The air suddenly changed, transforming the atmosphere surrounding them when a mighty explosion ignited in the skies!

Cataclysmic and powerful, terrible shock waves came at them, its invisible pressure waves rippling down through the air and bodies from above! Hunching for safety, all caught like stone caricatures, the flash brought their dark profiles to life. Heavy rain began.

In rapid succession of split seconds, numerous cracks and flashes of lightening came, splashing light and wetness across the temple, and lighting up their panic-soaked faces. Everyone was drenched and needed to move and move fast.

Christopher's mind witnessed the energized storm clouds directly above him, a heavy brew broiling above and rolling around like a witch's caldron. Its deep blackness rotated in a madness only few thousand feet above the temple.

Watching it with growing trepidation and dangerous curiosity, when the mass of turmoil and mixed madness, seamlessly melted inside Christopher's disordered mind. At this moment, uncontrolled electricity sent rippling energies through the chaos in the heavens above them. Chris was feeling light headed as if he were losing consciousness with the repetitious flashbulb patterns of light, when another explosive ignition blasted open the sky! It was time to get the hell off the steps!

"Chris! Chris!" Harjit screamed, the girl just managing to catch Christopher. Christopher slumped further, dropping his arms away from Mashir, Harjit taking the load and taking command. "Mashir come on let's get him out of here! Mashir hold him" she grunted. "Fabio you give a hand too and get him up!"

****

Why are they holding me, thought Christopher, looking around staring at them all astounded in their panic? He felt quite capable of getting up on his own! Totally determined Chris quickly avoided their floundering hands and broke free.

Harj and Fabio tried grasping him again, but Christopher was still unable to comprehend their ridiculous concern over him and shouted at them!

"I have to go back! Let me *go!*" Christopher yelled.

"Chris! Calm down. What are you doing?" Harjit's tone firm but her words lost while Christopher squeezed out from her wet handhold. Heavy rain kept pounding down adding to the panic when Christopher unexpectedly slipped between them, beginning his escape, the starter pistol fired, he was off!

He headed upwards, running as fast as he could, feet pounding through newly formed puddles, sending exploding water like depth charges around him. Ignoring the yells calling after him, like a man possessed he got as far away as possible!

Nothing could stop him. In minutes, he was already on the first-tier level, and without regard of the consequences charging through the great stone doorway, it was at last, OPEN!

"It is open, YES! YES! I have done it!" He yelled triumphantly through the entrance, sprinting like an athlete crossing the finish line. He did not stop. Unbelievably he kept on going! He could hear Harjit's distant calls following after him.

"Christopher! *Stop. Stop!*" Harjit's screaming voice could be heard while watching him run out of her view and into a ruinous path.

Inside, Chris kept recklessly running further into a labyrinth of connecting corridors. He could not know what was ahead. Mysterious wall drawn codices meaning nothing to him, their blurry images quickly passing him by, but their foreign words seemed to be whispering quietly into his deranged mind.

Running inside, Christopher was becoming conscious of his laboured breathing, it hurt more as the effort began taking its toll. Unstoppable like a tornado, he still whirled through the complex maze of corridors of stone going on and on when his consciousness saw only darkness ahead. Slowing, he stopped and turned, breathing heavily. Looking back, only blackness lay there too. Something else disturbed him.

How is it that I can see where I am going? Yet, blackness surrounds me? His conscious thoughts could not understand what was happening when sudden panic set him off again. Fear the motivator, Chris moving faster again when he abruptly turned left, and with bat like instincts shimmied right. He would not stop, not now! In this moment of darkness inside his mind, without warning, flaming torches suddenly ignited ahead.

"Ah light! I can see!" Chris yelled crazily when each cone of light along the walls uncannily lit his way while passing them. The *whys* did not matter anymore because his path, his goal lay set in stone and dead ahead. The problem was the large gaps in the floors, deep trenches hidden in the dimness. Each time he passed a torch it would instantly extinguish, leaving it to smoulder quietly in darkness behind him.

He could not think. He could not stop! Unconsciously, Christopher went hurdling over numerous wide gaps in the stone floor, subconsciously sensing hidden terrors below while jumping the gaps! Leaping over the last gap, he felt a presence below him, a vile consciousness inquisitively looking up at him.

What's down there? Terror chased his growing cognition. Out of control and for an unknown reason, Christopher felt terrorised inside. Running harder, his heavy breathing now of no interest to him, he was unable to hold back his screaming anymore and knew he would run until he dropped.

"AAAAaaaaaghh! AAAAaaaaaach!" His power of reason tried to penetrate this horror knowing that his survival depended on rationality that hinted that this escape was simply foolhardy. His mind cleared. All this running and blind panic was a mistake, a big mistake!

My God, where am I? Shit where am I running to? New confused feelings seemed to be affecting Christopher, sensing a change in his flight, his run slowing quickly into a laborious walk, like treading through treacle. *I'm slowing down, Christ why is this happening to me?*

Finally, he stopped exhausted, his marathon over and not a second too soon, when a larger gap appeared about four metres right in front of him. He could just make out a slim ledge left and right inline against the wall. Gasping at its size, eyes wide in panic, cranking his neck apprehensively around in fear, his gaze transfixed into the surrounding darkness and hidden dangers.

A great evil lurked inside this structure and like a torpedo sent from the dark oceans of the temple, it was coming for him and closing in fast. Chris sensed a bad feeling, instinctively dreading that whatever was behind him was horrible. That was when the last flame lit torch flickered in the slightest of air movement, something approaching disturbed the peacefulness of the darkness. He had been found! *It's close by,* thought Christopher, *I must get away!* Unfortunately for him, looking at the large gap, there was no way out from here or, no choice except to jump!

****

Heart bursting with a sudden adrenaline surge, Christopher sprinted instantly with the versatility of an American football player. He had no option, jumping and launching himself high over the gap, his full momentum just making it! Landing hard onto the adjacent ledge, his lungs screaming in agony but that feeling of dread remained with him, perceiving that he would not have long to wait.

Looking ahead, Chris could not believe it. What he discovered in the hidden darkness directly in front of him, was a rock-solid wall.

"A dead end!" He shouted in frustration as his voice reverberated throughout the corridor. With no option, he pirouetted on the spot hearing a loud growl coming from behind. In desperation, he watched where he had come from, when somewhere in the darkness beyond his sight a louder and more monstrous guttural growling noise, closer this time, made itself known.

Christopher gulped, he had been right all along. He was petrified and was peering into the darkness when he had heard it clearly and knew that something bad was about to happen.

God no! Let me live! Stopped in his tracks, dizzy and breathless, the full horror was displayed in his frantic eyes. He had trembling legs and fearful eyes. There was something in the gloom, peering further into the darkness. Yet, he saw nothing. *God help me. It must be in there! He faced* his doom when the growling came again.

Swallowing harder this time, it was at this moment Christopher saw large white fangs and the reflection of huge slanted emerald eyes. They stared viciously right back at him. Its huge fangs began teasing him in terror. Something big was inside that darkness. Then, there it was on the other side of the gap in all its full glory!

"No!" He yelled. Out of the coming blackness, fangs first and teeth next, ripping teeth then sharp claws extending. Appearing to be a huge cat; its slick body and powerful four legs all moving smoothly and with no hesitation came straight at him. It launched itself roaring through the air, its massive claws splaying wide for the kill.

Christopher had no time to think, lifting his arms for protection releasing a last almighty scream of death. On target, it had him. It roared triumphantly.

"God!" He gasped while his warm blood began pouring down his face. *Strange, there is no pain.* His mind reeling, knowing that his stupidity had cost him his life. Finally caught, his race for life was over.

****

The screaming would not stop, Christopher kept hearing himself yelling out. Springing upright like a catapult and into a sitting position, gasping for breath. Confused, Chris tried hard to come to terms with the fact that he was still alive!

What happened? His mind tried to understand. With sweat pouring down his face, he slowly opened his eyes, fearing what he might see, and anxiously gauging for some measure of sanity, *so real, an Omen.*

Feeling terrible, he wondered, *where am I?* In a mix of emotions, he racked his brain and looked hard at somebody; he floundered more for a memory of the person next to him.

Who is it? Harjit? Watching a girl who was preoccupied doing something, *what...* His conscious state wandered, his head banging in pain, Christopher moaned. His thoughts became more lucid, understanding that her plight seemed impossible while she attempted to hold him down flat! It was then that Christopher realised that he was the problem!

Harjit's soft hands pressed firmly onto his shoulders, gently moving him back down on a bed, the girl placed another clean damp cloth onto his boiling face. It felt good. A fatigue drained him as she restrained him more. Pills aside, Harjit knew how to reduce his high temperature. She looked desperately at him, her training working extra hard, but restraint be dammed because Christopher worked even harder to get up.

"Aaaaah!" Christopher let out more yells, he would not stop screaming, "Aaaaah!" Harjit took him and finally cradled him in her loving arms, rocking him gently like a baby.

"It's ok Christopher, it ok," she said kissing his shaking forehead. "It's going to be just fine, Chris." The girl was almost crying. Swallowing hard, repeating her whispers over and over again, *"It's going to be just fine."*

Shutting his eyes, the young man stopped screaming while her words floated inside his brain, melting the pounding inside his head. To him, they were rays of sunshine and her tenderness was a pill of passion.

"Harj," he connected, and Harjit answered.

"You've had another nightmare, that's all. Oh, thank the Gods Christopher, you have come back *to me*," she whispered, pressing her warm cheek on his.

"Ugh?" he listened.

Distraught, something closed inside her emotional throat; she was almost unable to speak. Her anxiety and happiness in overload but Harjit forced herself to stay calm focusing on his needs.

"You're going to be *just fine*." Harjit was relieved and sobbing a little. She had seen the effects of anxiety many times before in other people. Her mind struggled with an unfathomable hurt and unstoppable emotion. Yet she managed to cope and held her self-control. It was strong, very strong and most people would have capitulated into blubbering wrecks under the circumstances. Not Harjit, she had more to give, digging deeper to help Christopher. "Your temperature is coming down."

The stress was taking its toll, the girl bordering on the verge of uncontrollable tears, giving out a loud sigh and a deep breath.

"Harj," he repeated weakly.

"Phew!" The girl let go and instantly became professional once more. Her will power was back in full control. This instant of weakness chased away, rebuilding her clinical composure and response because, he still needed her.

Continuing her treatment, Harjit dabbed more sweat from his baby smooth brow as her patient relaxed. His pacing heart settling, Christopher closed his tired eyes. His chest began to ebb up and down in a gentle rhythm. He had pulled through. He was going to live.

****

"Hello, Harjit, what happened?" Christopher awoke groggily. Harjit was watching and studying him. Moaning softly, Christopher raised his head off his dry clean pillow. She smiled at him.

"You collapsed with infection and fever. We were all very worried about you. *Boni,* as you know is our resident medical doctor, it was he who gave you your life- saving injections to help you recover."

"Harj no, it was you. *You saved me*" The Indian girl's natural skin lustre radiated self-consciously. His words to her sounded like sunshine.

"Here he is now," she heard the doctor, when the tent flap opened and a small 5'4" man came shuffling into the medical tent, a cheery chap smiling at Christopher.

Dr Castiglion, the expedition doctor and Harjit's mentor, a man with piercing, metallic blue eyes, eyes that instantly seemed to measure up his next prognosis on whoever he stood next to.

Wearing small square glasses taped up on the right leg, its bridge sitting a little off the level on his straight nose. The Doctor's stethoscope was protruding partially out from his brown jacket pocket. A medium built man of forty, with receding short thick greying hair. Wearing a bright yellow short-sleeve shirt and long blue shorts underneath. It was obvious to everyone that he had no style at all.

"Ah, the patient awakes! Excellent!" The doctor said while quickly checking his temperature. "You have given us all a bit of a turn Christopher. And what you had, seems to have been like Malaria. Although Malaria has been largely eradicated from temperate countries, it is on the increase here in the tropics. You had a severe attack and your malarial-like symptoms particularly affected your central nervous system. This was likely to be the cause of your convulsions and sudden coma. *Very nasty.*" Nodding his clinical head in self-agreement.

The man was scurrying about busily; shoulders hunched a little, his head bobbing slightly in deep thought and observation. He seemed to give a squirrel like appearance foraging for food. The doctor took his pulse, with his clinical light checking inside Christopher's mouth and throat, then smartly moved a cold metal ring onto Christopher's chest, checking for anything rattling out of the ordinary.

"Oh, shit Boni, that's cold!"

"Means you are alive young man. I had administered a most rapid acting and most effective of all anti-malarial drugs called *Artemisinin* intravenously. And now, I have a few additional things for you to take from my trusty *tool box*." He joked. The doctor smiled while opening his medical case. "You need these Quinine Sulphate tablets, about 600mg every twelve hours and I also have these little beauties called Doxycycline and Malarone tablets, one daily if need be." Smiling again, his job done, "Now open."

"Do I really have to?" Christopher stuck out his tongue like a little boy.

"*Nasty* little *Plasmodium* buggers are they not? Get them first, or they will get you. Nasty. The Malaria parasite is a microscopic organism called a plasmodium, and it belongs to the group of tiny organisms known as protozoans but then Christopher, you will already know all about these things, eh?"

"Si, yes I do Doc," swallowing the sour pill and twisting his face in distaste, "Thanks for your help." He said when something else came to his mind, something important, "How long was I out?"

"Thanks to Harjit, *once again*," tipping his head a little, "It was *she*, who kept a very close eye on you, a most brilliant nurse, sorry Harjit, I was only joking." He laughed jovially and said, "A most excellent medical student and in her final year of course!"

"Doc, how long!" Christopher waited?

"Oh, and to answer your question young man, well this may come to you as a shock." Dr Castiglion paused working it out, "About a fortnight or so. You have been very lucky."

"What!" Christopher exclaimed.

"We were able to hydrate and feed you between different states of your illness. Still, you need to watch yourself and take it easy for a while. Don't worry young man, we will have you built up again in no time."

The doctor had saved his life, but his bedside manner was far from desirable, and comfort *was not his thing*. Christopher's shock instantly recognisable to the doctor, so he made his final inspection then took his leave. To him, Christopher would live, and that was the important bit.

"A fortnight, I cannot believe; it seemed just, just a moment ago!" No wonder Christopher felt drained by what had come over him, astonished at the suddenness of his illness. "Thank you Doc!" Christopher shouted as the man disappeared through the Mosquito net. Thinking, *A fortnight of my life gone,* then looking at the girl. "Thank you Harjit."

The tent canvas moved vigorously in the storm, pushing and pulling wildly, the heavy rain battering off the canvas. Christopher shook his head, not quite believing what had happened to him. And his nightmares, they seemed so real.

"The rain's not let up since you collapsed up at the temple entrance," said Harjit, bringing him up to date. "You know Chris."

"Yes? Tell me, what's troubling you."

"I wanted Fabio to call for help."

"And,"

She whispered, "*We* are on our own."

****

An hour later, Christopher knew they would not be leaving this place until Fabio had entered the temple. No question about it, the professor would not leave until the job was complete. Christopher had already sent an overly keen Mashir away to fetch for him a sketchpad and folder, and like a puppy dog the surveyor had retrieved it. Christopher was confident in his own abilities and would do it. The best way to be released from their commitments and sent back home from this God forsaken place, was to break the code and break it quickly!

He analysed the codex and partially broken code narratives on his pad, having done this from before his illness. After being idle for so long, his mind needed this mental stimulation. Code breaking would do it and something else, he felt an unexplained urgency; sub-consciously Chris knew he was working against time.

"You should leave it alone Chris." Harjit protested. "Rest more, let Fabio do it, he's the professor," urged Harj, but Christopher had rested long enough and got up putting on his clothes.

"Only I can do it," stated Christopher.

"That's what I'm afraid off." Harjit knew further protest to be futile and was not too pleased with Mashir, especially because it was he who had encouraged and insisted accompanying Chris to the temple before he was struck down with his illness.

Once again, Christopher found himself standing right in front of that great entrance; open only in his nightmare, now of course, it was completely shut. He feared, that this place would drive him mad, just like Carmello. Christopher's thoughts reflected his continual nightmares. There was something wrong about this place, feeling a deep-seated malice within its stone, a forewarning. Standing here, its wickedness felt stronger than ever. He needed to get inside.

****

The priest was not the only person who had *bad dreams,* somehow something spiritual was at work, because thousands of miles from here, and on another continent, in Rome, Cardinal Giovanni Dalla Gassa closed his heavy eyes, the pills had not worked. Cold sweat rolling down his creased brow, the godly man lost his battle to stay awake. Succumbing to his fate, Giovanni connected into darkness of Ether, and into a world of nightmares.

****

"This is not an inert structure," stated Christopher, his voice solemn, irreverent. "There is something about it, something spiritual, and look at these words. Come, look at them closely." The surveyor raised an eyebrow and was not quite able to understand his direction. "The word nasom." Christopher smiled, "It's not difficult, jumble it about a bit and well?" Nodding in affirmation, he asked again, "What do you see? *Come on, Mashir?*"

"*Allah*, Chris, what on earth is it you are on about my friend?" Mashir struggled to cognate some answer, any answer. The man mystified, staring harder at the symbols, wondering if Chris had really flipped.

Mashir began stressfully pulling at his small beard just below his thin lips, obviously irritated at *his own lacking*. Mashir's lazy right eye closed a little whenever he felt frustrated or beaten like this. There was something to tell, looking at the scientist expectantly for an answer.

"I will say it again, these symbols resemble, if not, they are identical to those found to this day in Europe."

"Some would disagree, Chris." Mashir reminding him of Fabio's intransigence.

"As I said, these are like the ones my younger brother Scott showed me when we moved too our new home in a small Scottish Village."

"That is nonsense. You cannot backup what you speak off." The Iranian looked doubtful.

What else had Chris to bring to the table, this is not new, surely, he has more information than this?

"I understand your disbelief Mashir. In the village of Mauchline where my family live, these can be seen if you know where to look. I have seen them. These symbols are the same, and they represent a *universal language* of coded words. A secret form of communication and *I'm convinced now*, that their origins begin *right here.*

"Oh." Both bewildered and amazed, Mashir's interest picked up.

"Yes, I have seen such symbols in my religious studies in Italy." Looking at the surveyor hoping Mashir would at least give him credit for his doubt, "Don't you see it yet?"

Christopher could not bottle up his excitement anymore, his voice picking up pace more rapid than a man could listen too, watching Mashir's brain trying to grasp understanding. The man falling short in a blank expression, Mashir threw up his arms in frustration and at his own dislocated thoughts.

"Not really Chris, see what? Tell me what! What have I to see?" His irate arms rested on his hips and was getting annoyed.

"Everything is *Masonic*. Look at those symbols. They interpret out to *nasom*, so move them about. It is a simple anagram, the letters become, m, a, s, o, n! You get *mason!* Yes, and it is spelled in English!"

"Allah, correct! You are a genius my friend! It's obvious as you say. I can't imagine why I never saw it before?" Mashir transfixed his gaze onto Christopher's, both men thrilled to bits. "I knew it! I knew *you were the one* to crack the code my friend, congratulations!" Mashir shook Christopher's shoulders in admiration then shook his hand excitably.

Even with his success, Christopher felt that at this moment, it was in Mashir's handgrip that he sensed the man's disappointment with him, as if they were only friends and not closer, like brothers. Something not spoken, Christopher remembered that same feeling once before and sensed it when shaking his hand while meeting with him many years ago at university. Then, like now, something was missing.

"Yes, *Mason* it is. All these symbols are Masonic. These people who built this place, some must have been Stone Masons. It is possible that the people themselves were of some other religion, not Christian and yet were still Freemasons." Christopher began filling in the gaps.

"Hmm," Mashir considered.

"Contrary to popular belief, Freemasonry is not a religion, it's more a way of life. A worldwide organisation, also known as *the Craft*, it accepts different religions as members, but each brother must stick to the rules and their own religious practices must remain outside the temple door. Those ancient stone-crafters toiled here centuries ago and in Europe, *yet something does not ring true*. Freemasons are good, seeking a pathway in search of God and finding it within."

"What do you mean Chris?" Mashir asked curiously.

"Freemasonry and all its principals are fundamentally *good*, yet, this place, is not. I feel its evil in my bones."

"What now?" Mashir did not want to dwell on this thought. It was too close to the truth.

"We should discover similar symbols inside the temple," said Chris looking up at the massive structure and wondering, *what else will we find inside?*

"Sorry, that's hard to swallow Chris," said Mashir. "How can this be even if the Portuguese or Spaniards came across in the 15th, 16th or even 17th century, then *surely* they could not have constructed a place such as this? A church or cathedral yes but not a pyramid. I believe as Fabio does... that this structure is much older. *It must be ancient!*" Mashir's earnest face conflicted with Christopher's theory.

"I understand what you are saying and respectfully disagree. It is a hard pill to swallow, yes but the truth is in this writing."

"And yet I agree with you my friend." Mashir stated bluntly. Christopher's face lit up gleefully. Mashir explained, "I am just as convinced as you are that these symbols are Freemasonic in nature or, so it would seem. Whether this place or the people within it were evil I do not know. I'm not so sure. With the wrong person in charge then even a Boy Scout group could be corrupted. It just takes one person at the top that has persuasive qualities, be articulate enough and totally ruthless. I must ask Endrissi what he thinks."

"I am not so sure that these people were evil either, it is this place…" Christopher replied.

"Hmm, there's plenty evidence of human sacrifice Chris," stated Mashir.

"I believe that different civilizations have been here at different times, each coming with its own practices, poles apart. Maybe, here long before the Christians and these poor indigenous tribes, and that would make my time frame longer than I can accept for my Freemasonry theory to be believed, because the Craft did not exist further back; and that, Mashir, is my dilemma." Their eyes met, both men stuck in a paradox and that paradox, was time.

****

A stream had swollen massively with the torrential rain, forming a river half a mile away from base camp, strong flowing winding its way down the Vale, its turbulent origins lay beyond the great drop called tower of *Seraph Falls*. Higher up to the north, sheer rock edges stretched down to the treeline, where fine mist particles expanded up and over the treetops like a ghostly opaque blanket. Away from the camp, Christopher stood on top of the walled terraces looking down, when he noticed Endrissi and Mashir talking privately together below him. It looked intense and obvious that neither wanted to be heard by anybody, the din from the river shielding their voices. Mashir did not look happy.

Fabio had since heard the latest revelation from Christopher. The professor had scoffed the younger man's theories and even now considered his new evidence, stubbornly resisting the Masonic connection.

What are those two up to this early in the morning wondered Christopher. *Thick as thieves,* watching Endrissi moving his cupped hand over his left breast and then suddenly saw him drawing it quickly across himself in some peculiar fashion, *and that's odd too.* Chris was perplexed. The next puzzle for Christopher was how to unlock the entrance. He had tried before and failed, badly. Was it really an inert monolith built into the terrace wall with meaningless symbols engraved on it?

Studying the structure above him, *it is much more than a premonition, God must have directed me here. Surely, why me… and why now? This is no chance discovery.* Christopher swallowed and feared an answer.

Like an old book or an old story, a legend had remained unread for millennia, and it was only now that these pages were about to be turned. It would be in these days, and much different to any that had gone before, that a huge event would occur. World changing! A pregnant anticipation held in the air as if something unnatural was about to give birth and yet, standing on the periphery of the temple. Feeling the stone on his palms, he took a deep breath. *It's an ill omen.*

****

Early next morning, in the darkness found Mashir, Christopher, Harjit and Mathieson all standing nervously together above the entrance looking downwards at the two men. Fabio Mancini and Beppi Genovesi assembled on the first tier, standing directly in front of the entrance and getting ready for a second recitation. It was windy. Beppi had been chosen to decipher the stone message exactly at the stroke of sunrise.

He was an experienced librarian and a fully qualified palaeontologist. Beppi's long black hair was stuck inside his wide brimmed hat, and he was a plump man of medium size. He was thirty-four years old and felt honoured to be chosen for this moment. He put on his round-framed glasses and readied himself.

Professor Genovesi, rather than an explorer, was mainly an academic and a father of two, married with a wife, sharing a home back in Rome. This would be his last field trip and very important to his own research. It would provide him with real practical experience that would give him invaluable status before settling into his new academic post at the university.

Small stone artefacts bulged heavily inside his shirt pockets, the professor found them earlier lying around the front of the excavation site. His face and arms were full of bright red splotches, evidence of bite marks from greedy mosquitoes. The pests had taken particularly well to the flavour of his haemoglobin.

Beppi would never have missed an invitation like this one to join a real expedition. Not just any, having heard of the great Professor Fabio Mancini. Then, *who hadn't!* The expedition had the Pope's blessings; two professors on the same trip into the jungle. This was a challenge he had to do.

Endrissi had gone to grab some breakfast before sunrise; this pivotal event was proving to be all too much for him. Fabio held his oil lamp up to his sober face and closely inspected the temple wall one last time. Meanwhile, Beppi prepared to begin his narration of the transcribed verses. Clearly, Professor Genovesi looked a bit nervous on this occasion, while holding the paper firmly by its edges, attempting to prevent it from blowing away in the wind. The sunrise teetered on the brink of earth's rotation.

"Well I don't really know what these words are meant to convey," said Beppi. "I certainly do not believe in any hidden mumbo jumbo nonsense." The man looked around a little awkwardly, then at Fabio who nodded his consent and understanding. Everyone knew that in less than a minute to go, he would start reading.

"Let's call it, *tradition*," said Fabio, but his tone seemed edgy. "Beppi, please begin," stated

Fabio. Beppi's pleasant-sounding Italian tone started, rhythmic and clear, as he read loudly to his audience, everyone completely gripped by the occasion.

"SACRIFICE WE MAKE TO YOU NASOM ANCIENT TRUE SKILL.
WE ASK YOU TO YOUR GREAT DOORS OF MALISIBLIS, NOWHERE WE RUN TO AND AS WE ARE AT MERCY ON EVIL'S EDGE. GOD PROTECT US."

Mashir listened and what he was observing was interesting but believed it to be a waste of time, because he knew that nothing would happen unless there was a blood sacrifice. He already knew, that the energy released by the taking a life was a spiritual force, an ethereal energy with cause and effect which was the greatest ingredient for sorcery. Yes, he believed in sorcery!

The group felt a bit imperceptive. Predictably, nothing happened except that the wind dropped to non-existent. Strange too, that an instant stillness settled over the forest and rather than turbulence, a quiet hush was heard washing through the leaves. Nature seemed to be waiting too.

Standing stupefied, the group was caught between an uneasy prank and a withheld nervous giggle. Watching the stone, then each other, and then back to the stone again, there was an unmistakably agitated fear here. Everyone stood silently, this stasis made no logical sense. A minute passed and their stress levels rose while the atmosphere was becoming more laborious and heavier, almost suffocating the MalisIblis Vale.

"Well, what did you really expect, the entrance to open?" Beppi smiled while watching everyone's faces. The fading lamplight also displayed his untold relief. Whatever Fabio had anticipated, simply had not materialised, yet an unnatural silence settled, and it did not feel residual.

"Hmm," Fabio's sullen face dropped disappointed. Beppi looked at him curiously wondering, *surely Fabio didn't think it too?*

"I didn't expect this," Mashir whispered cautiously to Christopher, both men puzzled at the peaceful tranquillity. No sound came from the forest, no breeze, no buzzing, nothing.

Beppi's face changed when a dreadful sensation of trepidation began growing inside him, deep within his body, a remote sensation of disturbance and discomfort when suddenly everyone heard screaming coming from the top of the temple.

Beppi's experience paled in comparison, when he, like everyone else looked up towards the screams of torture and agony. This was the last thing anybody expected.

Fabio held his lamp higher, staring up beyond Beppi, while consciously noting that Beppi was fine and nothing had happened. Disappointed just like last time. And yet, this was different. Something dreadful was happening above them.

The excruciating torture kept on going, a demented cruelty inflicted on someone that made everyone's blood run cold. Nobody moved to help as everyone was stuck in a mind dislocation. Each person cringed fearfully, tightening their shoulders automatically for self-preservation. No one had ever heard anything like it.

"It's coming from on top of the temple!" Christopher shouted.

Then something else happened.

Christopher smelled it first. Something acrid sensitized his nostrils, quickly turning around to where the odour seemed strongest. He stared at Fabio then chose to focus onto Beppi, when a high-pitched electric buzzing sound began to manifest itself all around them.

Zinging sounds of electrical zapping began sparking raw energy into the air, filling the dead vacuum. Its source reverberating inside their ears while the atmosphere surrounding them immediately energised pulling tightly at every hair follicle.

The screams from above were dying slowly away in the darkness and in their nerve-racked minds everyone stood, all completely unaware that new and dangerous events were beginning to take shape and unfold around them.

That smell is… thought Christopher, *distinct…yes; I remember it now, from my science labs years ago.* Linking his past, *it's getting stronger… an odour of, Ozone?*

The humid air thickened fast, and instantly threatened thunder as the inexplicable buzzing noises were becoming louder and more energized by the second. The defined sounds mighty, while electric short circuits started snapping and discharging its energies, when something strange began to form in mid-air in a crackling phenomenon. Strangely, whatever it was, it seemed to be forming into something resembling a transparent spherical energy field, and as it did this ball of light began dazzling them, hurting their eyes.

A swirling thing appeared like a genie holding itself about waste height, and hovering before the entrance, shimmering and rotating there, while humming louder and louder. Enthralled, the audience watched while the whole area became awash in a blue fluorescent glow, growing, gaining in fearful magnitude.

It was in this moment, that everyone could see they were all in imminent peril. Seeing its fast and frightening formation, everyone gawked questionably just what they had started, when everyone's hair began standing on end with static electricity.

Professor Genovesi stood transfixed in blueness and shaking in fear. Not smiling anymore, he was nearest. Petrified and still holding his sheet of paper when without warning its fateful verses ignited in his hand and the man gave out a short scream.

Flames engulfed his blistering hand. Complete mayhem erupted in the crowd witnessing the man's agony, this happening when more renewed calls of great misery started up again coming from the temple top!

Fabio's fearful eyes bulging, he stared around in horror, not knowing what to do other than holding up his redundant lamp in belated realisation of great harm seeing Beppi suffer. Recoiling backwards, Professor Mancini quickly jumped away from him and the nearby flames.

Everyone looked weird in this crazy blue air and witnessed the transparent revolving energy ball. Translucent and shimmering, it appeared with an external deep blue skin, all rippling, all energy. It enclosed an internal silvery white energy field. Both blue and white membranes, each made of pure electricity and both existing together only a few inches apart.

The orb's magnitude of energy kept increasing with the light intensity growing by the millisecond; its white transparent inner layer moved quickly outwards to meet its outer thin blue skin, both membranes bonded at the sub-atomic level. Fabio and Beppi could not see the stone codex; their views were blocked by a misty opaqueness as the sphere continued emitting an increasing high-pitched humming noise.

Nobody dared look away from the electric power station of spinning energy for fear of death. They watched on horrifically at Beppi's anguish. He kept screaming and screaming that his hand was burning.

The orb had fully formed in seconds, a fearful object about the size of a medicine ball. Its orbit was held in mid-air, mindlessly revolving and rippling with wild energy.

This was when it happened. The noise… zzzzzzzzzzzzzzzzzzzzzzzz! The sound intensified and produced a biting pain inside everyone's ears and minds.

Beppi could not move when suddenly a pure brilliant brightness of high-energy engulfed him. The professor was held firmly from escaping inside an illuminated straight jacket of light as he screamed and shook. The spectacle was horrific.

Protecting their eyes from the blinding light, their teeth gritted for Beppi's agony in unending torment. Everyone gasped at Beppi's horrendous ordeal, some of the men began dropping helplessly in revulsion onto their knees, but no matter what happened here; each person could not break that mortal contact with this dazzling globe.

Like opening an oven door, Fabio was too close to Beppi. Fabio felt the intense searing heat hitting his face and dropping onto one knee in awe, while still holding the oil lamp up, he couldn't let go.

A bright shining Nebula had instantly formed from nothing, bursting like a sparkler with a hue and illumination bleaching its blue florescence over the whole of the South side of the temple. Heat upon heat, focusing like a lightening conductor with an unearthly temperature, it pinpointed its pure matter onto its nearest victim, Beppi.

In the space of a few seconds from the energy ball's creation, it had swiftly struck the man's body, holding it and whiplashing him high up and backwards in mid-air with supernatural force. The poor man was suspended there in blue air. Beppi began shaking. He was powerless and began crying. It was horrible. Inside his roasting stomach and lungs, Beppi suddenly burst into flames, just like a container of kerosene.

"My God, My God, Oh my God!" Beppi screamed. The smell of his burning flesh nauseated everyone's senses. The man was consumed whole.

Everyone gasped loudly at his savage torture, while listening to his hissing blood and popping organs. In seconds, he had become a human inferno. He was suspended by invisible hands that could not hold him any longer. Bits of Beppi's body began falling to the ground.

What had been Beppi, stopped screaming. His disintegration turned into dust on stone, leaving a sprinkle of residual black carbon particles floating in the hot air. Finally, there was a strange sucking-in noise. Everyone heard it but could not guess at first then realised it was coming from the dying energy globe. Suddenly, the orb imploded, disappearing into nowhere. Nothing of its existence remained except one dead man. It was over for Beppi as bright daylight opened the sky at sunrise.

****

When all this mayhem was happening, down at base camp only moments before sunrise and before Beppi's cruel death, Aléssandro Marchesi stuck his head out the tent door flap, to find out what was happening above. His dark brown ponytailed hair dangled over his shoulder while Cesaré Padovesi pushed passed him on all fours, both men looked excitedly up at the ruckus on the temple. Cesaré's own thick ruffled short blonde hair and middle parting could not guess at this unusual commotion.

"What the Hell? Out my way and let me see!" Cesaré shouted. He always thought himself to be a fine catch for any of the girls, a magnet and *Adonis* or so he thought. He had cool short thin sideboards on his sculptured jaw and fine white teeth shining whenever he smiled, but right now Cesaré was not smiling. Staring up he took a deep breath in. *"Oh God."*

"Shit knows, it's up at the emple!" Aléssandro anxiously watched and instantly regretted being on the expedition. He asked himself, why he ever signed up for this deal.

Maybe it was because of his young friend Cesaré who he had grown up with. He had looked after him at school like a big brother but right now he wished to be a million miles from this place. Aléssandro felt responsible for him even now.

Cesaré's eyes were a shade of dark blue, straining in the poor light. His young face with brown freckles smattered a little around the bridge of his broken nose, appearing to look younger than his twenty-five years. The man had a natural cuteness.

"What are they getting up too? Fabio never leaves it alone does he?" Cesaré spoke in a quiet melodic Sicilian accent.

"Would you stop moving those fucking legs of yours Cesaré, they are so annoying. You do it all the bloody time. Why?" Aléssandro was irritated with his friend while Cesaré habitually kept moving or rubbing his legs together.

"What is going on up there Alé? Who is screaming!" Cesaré asked with growing worry. Macabre events were unfolding and their eyes were glued to the distance. They could see small silhouettes crouching and everyone seemed to be holding their ears.

Aléssandro and Cesaré began to see a small blue spherical energy ball appearing, and hovering in mid-air. The men guessed that everyone up there was in great danger, the orb splashed the darkness away from around it. The thing displayed raw power, swamping a deep luminous blanket of blue-violet colour over the temple stone.

Reeling backwards involuntarily, both men staggered when a sharp light flashed powerfully through everyone's bodies on the steps! In that split-second flash, Aléssandro and Cesaré could see the people's transparent bodies and skeletons, silhouetted briefly in a weird blue light. Both men gasped loudly, when a massive expansion of pure energy happened, so sudden and so quick. They witnessed Beppi become engulfed. The power, catapulted the helpless man into the air and held him up high like a blazing star, screaming.

"Oh God! Look!" Cesaré called out in grim abhorrence, nobody spared the grim details of the victim's flesh bubbling; Beppi's body wriggled and popped like a sausage on a barbeque. Paralysed, everyone watched helplessly, and nobody could save him.

"It's Beppi! It's got Beppi! It's roasting him alive!" Yelling like a maniac, Aléssandro's own sanity screamed out in disbelief.

"Christopher is shouting something, listen to him! *LISTEN!*" Cesaré yelled, hearing the man's horrendous death.

****

"God help us!" Christopher shouted over to Fabio only a few metres behind Beppi. Fabio was in shock while Harjit's mind graven solid, her sight fixed blankly onto Christopher's sooty blackened face. She could not look at the dead remains of Beppi!

"Allah Martyr, *ME! Not them!*" Mashir screamed out for mercy. It was strange that he felt this way and somehow accountable for the others. Suddenly he wanted to protect everyone, Mashir in judgment of himself, for bringing on this mortifying phenomenon. No one could grasp exactly what was happening, and in the aftershock of the blast, its energy jolted Fabio's body abruptly into the air and dropped him unceremoniously in front of the stone monolith.

Fabio shouted at his hard landing.

Then…

When it happened, it was not so much of a bang, but more like a loud squelching noise, a deafening sucking-in sound before the air began trembling… before an air force formed from nowhere was pulling everyone inexorably inwards for a second, when the energy ball violently imploded.

Blasting decibels at only an ear-popping distance away from the energy orb's dead zone. In a post-existence, it's last moments of glory were displayed in some sort of weird remembrance, resonating long and far through the MalisIblis Vale. Everyone moaned in helpless anguish, their exposed skin being so close, also seared red with the heat, as auditory shock waves penetrated through every organ, flesh and sinew and all this, in just a few seconds.

Shredded nerves of miscomprehension held them all strewn on the stone in a disorderly state, trying to get up like drunkards from a stupor. Each one rose, all partially blinded and deafened. Their balance askew, some staggering and falling, got up and tried again like new-born animals. Eventually, their senses slowly returned.

A lingering strong smell of nitric acid began dissipating in fast gusts of wind from the forest, seemingly like nature it tried to chase the oven-baked air away. Down below at base camp, Cesaré and Aléssandro sighed heavily as it was over. They had watched and seen it all, as the forest began breathing again.

****

"What the mother…fuck… *was that?*" Mathieson twisted his face. He shivered and wondered, *was I hit? Am I in one piece?* Looking at himself, he checked himself out. The others felt the same way, each person searching themselves for any signs of injury. Unfortunately, something else unexpected happened when an odd sound made itself present. Muttered misgivings voiced under suppressed curses and fears could be heard from everyone, blood draining from withdrawn faces. They had gone through too much already. Fearing what was happening now.

Dawn arrived.

Ill-omened sounds of dry rock rubbing together started coming from the entrance. Everyone wondered, fearing and daring to think that after all this time the impossible was now happening. Unmistakably the sounds of ground rock began grating together. Rock against rock that desiccated gritty noise, making cold shivers shoot up their backbones. Watching wearily, while the stone entrance moved steadily and unstoppably inwards, right in front of Fabio's kneeling frame, Professor Mancini's eyes watered while looking upwards in the sunrise.

****

Shining brightly onto the perfect square entrance, the morning sun suddenly lit up its ancient carved scriptures into what looked like a corridor. The sunlight's rays slowly followed the great stone doorway moving inwards, grinding itself further away from the front of the temple. Fabio stared at it and wearily got up. He stood still while watching with dazed eyes the graven dead stone travelling along deep grooves in the ceiling. The grooves were a stone channel cut like sharpened fangs for runners.

The door's granular noise kept on going, moving deeper inside and tunnelled its way through the huge outer structure. Eventually it stopped, when it stood still for a few moments. The huge block doorway began descending smoothly down below floor level, becoming flush with its surface, leaving a dark tunnel beyond with the entrance door stone scriptures lost below. Sunlight penetrated further inside and highlighted a long seamless passageway. It extended well out of sight, and into an unfathomable and forbidding darkness where it waited.

The professor gasped, looking around devastated. Observing that the energy orb had gone and almost as if it had never existed. Yet, it's after-effects had burned his exposed skin and bore witness, his beard too singed below chin and cheek, his face patched and blistered on his carbonised face and hands. The professor's clothes were partially still smouldering. The shocked professor looked on like a vagabond and began mumbling some classical history lesson at the temple. Fabio knew that he was very lucky to be alive, leaving scarred memories frozen inside his mind forever. His voice became louder and clearer so everyone could hear him. He began reciting *Homer*.

"In the twelfth book of the *Odyssey*, Homer says,

'Zeus thundered and hurled his bolt upon the ship, and she quivered from stem to stern, smitten by the bolt of Zeus, and was filled with sulphurous smoke. When beneath the blast of father Zeus an oak falleth uprooted, and a dread reek of brimstone ariseth there from, then verily courage no longer possesseth him that looketh thereon'".

Fabio continued the ancient passage, "Zeus thundered horribly and let loose the shimmering lightning and dashed it to the ground in front of the horses of Diomedes, and a ghastly blaze of flaming Sulphur shot up, and the horses, terrified, both cringed away against the chariot."

Fabio finished his near-perfect recital. Satisfied, he paused to justify his words.

"Here, rather than sulphur is the smell of ozone, and the story of Homer, I thought, seemed most apt." He softly commented while screwing up his stinging eyes.

Fabio, like the others, had been momentarily blinded by the ball of lightning. Checking his watch, the time was exactly 5:30AM and the sun had risen higher.

****

Mathieson angrily shouted from above the entrance, "Shit ma Ass man! *Are you for real Fabio!* You son of a bitch, *Beppi* has just been killed!" Livid Mathieson voiced his anger at the professor's cruel extrapolation away from death's reality. Even Mathieson's thick skin could not contain his disgust at the leader's insensitivity to Beppi's brutal death, the ranger's face summing up his complete disgust to what had just taken place.

All were witness to a catastrophic accident, a weird fluke. This was the only rational and reasonable explanation for Mathieson, he felt rotten at being so helpless to change anything. The clock wheels were turning again, and in the minds of Christopher and Mashir, alarm bells were sounding at the same thought when both eyes met.

Who had been screaming on top of the temple? There had been another man screaming above, when all this craziness had started.

"The screaming?" Christopher spoke fearfully. "My God, Mashir, who the…" He didn't finish his sentence, regarding the surveyor in compressed panic. Chris's eyes scanned everyone to see who was here and who was not. Was anyone missing – other than Beppi and seeing Harjit's distress? "Harjit are you alright?" He asked. She nodded dumbly, "Wait here," he said gauging the dazed girl's condition. Harjit sat close, "Come on guys," said Chris. "Follow me, someone up on top needs our help!"

Mashir and Mathieson broke into a quick run behind Christopher when he began sprinting up the steep steps, remembering the horrific screams of torture from the temple top. Now, there was only complete silence, it could not be good.

Barbaro Lettiere from the Official Vatican Press Office (OVPO), joined Fabio, where both men could see Harjit sitting by herself above the entrance just out of earshot, the girl in obvious shock. Everyone's faces were covered in fine black soot and smudged and appeared like ghastly apparitions. Everyone's eyes sadly met at once onto a grey black area at the doorway entrance. The ashes, that had once been Beppi, remained. It was at this silent moment that the poor man's ashes began moving and swirling around like a mini tornado. Uncannily it started blowing the particles around in a delirium of dust far into the sullen darkness, where the dust of death was waiting somewhere inside the temple. Beppi, was gone.

****

Around the top of the temple, something stank, something horrible. Disgusting putrefaction met them and got stronger as they were climbing. With dread in the pit of their stomachs, nobody wanted to see what they might find above, and when they got there, my God! What they saw was God-awful. Sitting there was a thing that defied all nature.

A spawn of something rotten was busily feeding on Dr. Boni Castiglion's limp and eviscerated body. Gasping together, the men were all horrified at the bloody site before them. Whatever it was, it made them feel like retching, staring fearfully at the massive black creature. Not what they expected; a monster! There it sat with indifference, on a blood covered altar, and on top of Boni, who now lay there dead.

Their disjointed minds staggered at what looked like something prehistoric perched onto him and decided to dig inside of the man again, a foul thing, and then pulled out its crimson beak with a deep squelching sound because it had been disturbed. Suddenly it began watching them, as their peeking heads came cautiously rising above the temple top.

The thing, akin to a hybrid between bird and pterosaur, its scaly feathers had by now grown on it in patches from when it had first appeared on earth. It already had its fill, and it would come to be notoriously known as *DEATH*. A wicked name. Where ever DEATH appeared, death would follow. The monster started stretching its wings wide, and then began angrily flapping wildly at them.

Expanding its great black wings, it started hopping off the dead corpse, bringing with it bits of flesh, some meat dropping and bouncing over the stone slab. Its quick wafting wings brought an even more awful stench, creating an olfactory overload in their direction. The men did their best holding their breath, they had no option gasping in more of its foul breath and stink. A smell so vile, it could easily make anyone sick.

It had seen them. Springing and hopping heavily down each stone step towards them, it left its perch, having already had its fill. Suddenly, it began screeching at them. Screeching a high death call. Sounding nothing like a bird or vulture and seemed more akin to a soulless mating call of a rabid dog squealing after a kick in the side.

The thing's massive bloodied beak opened wider, then wider still, shrieking hellishly in an awful arrhythmic pain, while displaying its hideous sharp razor teeth. Blood-sucking sounds were coming from its depraved beak, when a long sloth like proboscis started darting in and out, relishing the taste of human flesh.

Flapping its massive wings, it cared not for the human's appearances, its wings began to lift its gross weight up, when suddenly on a hop, its wings caught onto the rising hot air currents coming up from the lower canopy, lifting it a little, then again, when up and away it flew off. Flying from the temple, it left everyone gazing hypnotically after the filthy apparition, the huge beast defying all laws of aerodynamics, with its clumsy take-off. Seen awkward at first, but once in flight it soon changed direction swiftly and sharply, turning around flying with the flexibility of a kestrel. In shock, their disbelieving eyes trailed after a great evil, and in its wake, left them gassed in a reek so foul, its stench stroked them like rotten teeth, huge gusts propelling it further and further away from the temple. The winged beast soared in an adverse yaw around the temple, and then quickly gained the necessary speed of elevation, acquiring a higher altitude. The monster watched the men standing on top with everyone's eyes tracking its departure, and in a short minute they were far below.

Christopher and the others observed it glide off, and there had been a split moment on its lift-off when Chris reflected what he had just seen. Strangely, he thought he saw sadness in its eyes. He thought to himself, *that is no bird! But it has feathers…*

Flying then gliding more with a goliath wingspan already fully widespread, it needed only to flap occasionally to negate the sky with ease, as it began calling out deathly lamentations making the forest quake. The men stared in horror when suddenly its enormous black wings changed its course and dropped steeply, flying low and right over the temple top. They were smothered in a dead stench.

"It's biologically not possible!" Christopher yelled. "It's more like a pterodactyl and yet not that either," calling out more while his disbelieving eyes followed its foul flight-path away.

"Mother fuck... the size of that thing!" Mathieson shouted while hunching.

"Allah, it is death on wings!" Mashir screamed out as the muscle in his shoulders bunched in abomination. He could not look anymore.

"Shit man what the fuck is that screaming *thing?*" Mathieson asked. "Yuck, and it stinks! Smells like a fucking abattoir." Mathieson spat at the distant shadow but what they saw next was abhorrent to any living thing. And Christopher could only guess.

God help us! What is it, a giant condor? Chris thought, *not a condor, something else. Are we going completely insane? It is evil.* He paused in repugnance and then continued the climb towards the top. He thought more of what was ahead, *who had been shouting, what has happened? Bloody hell here goes.*

Screwing his face in repugnance and determination, he needed to know the worst. Now he was on top and taking a deep breath through his mouth, everyone breathing heavily, bending over from their effort reaching the top. Staring ahead, while trying to recover, in the sickening stench in this foul-tasting air. Now they could see a site that would live with them forever. Their eyes watered at the gutted remains of Dr. Boni Castiglion.

****

In sightless horror, and in each person's mind, his dead body stuck in an unfixed transition between reality and fantasy, while trying to ignore yet comprehend this unbelievable slaughter. Standing there stunned, everyone was completely unaware that something else was watching them.

Its emerald green eyes of malcontent studied the humans from the far end of the temple, where the beast lay there concealed behind a pillar. Growling to control its temper, its great white fangs opened and released a powerful snarl of hatred after what it had just witnessed. Stealthily observing, the winged creature narrowed its green slits, with feline-like eyes as it turned curiously, measuring the three men stepping onto the temple top. The creature, named, *Stealth,* sensed the trio's grim foreboding.

Christopher had arrived first, followed by Mashir and then Mathieson. They were intruders in these lands and yet, they had been long expected. The mortified men stood there shaking with fear and anger, their bewildered heads slowly edged towards the large stone altar, and as the creature considered their hesitation, it was not for the first time it had come here to wait, and it was also not the first time it had seen humans. To no avail it had failed, and a sacrifice was made, even though nothing could have prevented it. It had happened. The man's death was a tragic event. A sacrifice was always meant to be; always meant to transpire. Natural instincts had brought it here again trying to prevent this certain inevitability, but the prophecy, would not be denied.

From now on, unstoppable events had been set into motion, and that could never be undone. The fate of all living things would soon be held in the balance. The temple held written words only for those who could read. The time had come; these events had happened, and the creature wondered, surely at last, these were the ones?

Again, the Prophecy!

They will come first and Smite

All will shake in terror

Cold is the land

Nowhere to hide

****

"*It's Boni,* he's been attacked!" Mashir called.

"My God, my God, my God!" Christopher kept repeating, while trying to stay calm. His estranged eyes stuck onto the stone table with fear turning his thoughts, seeing this bloody butchery before them.

Twisting away in revulsion, Christopher was instantly sick at the sight of Boni lying on the large flat stone, his carcass picked apart. Crimson red and pecked tissue and bone was all that remained. His blood had only stopped dripping from around the stone edges of the ritualistic table, it had flowed and drained along small stone gutters, disappearing into the stone superstructure, leaving only red stain trails.

Standing fearfully for a moment below the altar, the men looked up and took courage ascending the altar together, the hardest part being their last final steps onto the large table. Mesmerized by this horrific mutilation, they held their breaths while the stench of the flying creature's musk still proved too much. Both his legs were pecked from the body; one had been tied and had since flopped down off the side of the table, its raw red stump was still attached to a stone table peg. It was awful.

"How could this happen?" Mathieson was clearly bewildered. "It must have been an animal that cruelly killed him or, that!" Mathieson burst out looking carefully for any signs of other wild animals and then skywards after the carrion's flight.

"Awful, just awful," said Mashir, putting a handkerchief over his nose.

"Where has that filthy bird gone?" Mathieson spat, his excellent eye-site just able to pick out a black spec, which was the creature moving quickly away from the scene of the crime, and already flying swiftly passed the great waterfall heading further down the vale and towards a blackening cloud mass.

Christopher began walking slowly as if drawn towards Beppi and closer to the altar, viewing the savage butchery. Staring hypnotically at the dead body, he said,

"This is no accident," Christopher gasped at the massacre. "Boni has no heart," he stated while suppressing a sickness in the pit of his stomach. "It's a ritualistic killing." Chris fell silent for a moment. "This is not a civilization I want any part of. It is utterly iniquitous." The man screwed his face up in disgust.

"It was that fucking big bird man! It took his heart!" Mathieson was convinced.

Mashir looked at the dead man's wrists and said, "Maybe... but I think murder would be my first guess looking at this. And whoever did it, bound him with these thin ropes, anchoring them to these stone pegs at each corner of the table, look!" They all observed the forensics of the scene.

Mashir added, "The grim deed done, his bonds were cut away by that creature." He was convinced it was murder, but Christopher believed it to be ritualistic sacrifice. There was a degree of difference, but for Boni, it did not matter.

Mashir's detective work was outstanding from his first observations and his attention to detail, which was already an essential element in his line of work. He proved his worth there. The man's bonds had fallen, sodden red as claret to the ground, his right arm then placed symbolically afterwards in the position across his chest and his left arm lay down by his side.

A fellow colleague and a craftsman, thought Mashir quietly to himself.

The dead man's face contorted in unspoken agony, his jaw was left open in one final scream from not long ago. His left breast torn open leaving blood trails drained into the stone.

"The hole in his chest cavity is where his heart should have been and was probably taken and eaten by that creature or, by whoever had killed him," said Mathieson. The ranger kept staring at the black spec, keeping track of the fowl creature just in case it decided to come back.

The cat was not the only powerful eyes looking at them. When from high above these lands, the huge beast yawed tightly in its flight path, curving over the falls, staring again towards the temple. It could see more than just mankind; it saw the feline too. In defiance, it screamed its evil intent while sailing into the darkening clouds, vanishing.

"Mother fuck!" He heard the bloodcurdling scream from the sky. "Is this place for real man?" The American felt true scepticism even of his own cognitive judgment.

"Yes, it is, *very* real my friend," stated Mashir. The surveyor stared to where the exiting wail had come from, his own rationality tested to the full at what he and the others had witnessed.

"It must be one of those mad South American Indian ceremonies!" Mathieson said, turning again to look at the dead man lying there. "Cutting out his heart and all that shit man! Remember, those native boys we bumped into months ago had warned us about this place. They told us to stay away." His grim sanity challenged even more. "Whoever did this shit man, *must still be about.*" Mathieson unblocked his throat, his eyes scanning the immediate area for somebody. Anybody!

****

Behind the altar stood a tall solid monolithic stone. High and out of reach was engraved ancient writing that could just be seen from below, the codices designed around the perfect circular black hole. The altar had been uncovered weeks ago by cutting away all the clinging vines, the monolithic structure discovered remained unblemished by time.

The large table dimensions were eleven-feet-long by seven-feet-wide by three in height. The table lay supported by four squat stone legs standing on top of a larger rectangular slab construction measuring thirteen-foot-long by nine-foot-wide and three inches thick. Its original architects had positioned an even larger base slab underneath everything, then cut it exactly twenty-four feet by thirteen in area, and was set into an arrangement of stone slabs, giving it a stepped-up high assembly to the place used for human sacrifice, to where Beppi lay cruelly dismembered.

The poor doctor's chest curved backwards, exposing his mess of what was left of his internal organs. Most had been removed by that odd-looking creature. The table position was made slightly tilted, so that most of the poor man's blood had already drained away into a thin trough running around its edges and into a hole below his feet. It had flowed to somewhere inside the temple.

Christopher saw some inscription partially hidden below the dead doctor's head. He grimaced, moving Beppi's head gently to see more. It was an engraved bloodstained coded message!

⌐⅃⌐⅃Γ⌐Γ∟⅃ ⌐⅃ ∧⅃>⅃ ⅂⅃ <⅃⌐ ⅃
⅃⌐⅃∧ ⅃⅃∟Γ⅃⅃⅂ ⅂⅃⌐⅃ ⌐>Γ<<

⌐⅃ ⅃⌐> <⅃⌐ ⅂⅃ <⅃⌐⅃ ⅂⅃⅃⅃⅂ ⅂⅃⅃
⅃⌐
⅃⌐ ∧⅃<Γ⌐Γ⅃<Γ⌐

⅃⅃∨⌐⅃⅃⅃ ⌐⅃ ⅃⌐⅃ ⅂⅃⅃ ⅃⅃ ⅃⌐ ⌐⅃⅃
⅃⅃ ⅃⅂ ∧⅃⅃⅃< ⅃⅃⅃Γ⌐<⌐ ⅃⅃⅃⅃

⅂⅃⅃ ∟⅃⅃⅂⅃∟⅂ ⌐⌐

"What's this, *the codex?*" Chris narrowed his eyes suspiciously.

"Eh?" Mashir asked.

"Yes, it's the same as yours Mashir. Yours is a copy, you know, the one that you gave me. Come on man, remember, you wrote it on that bit of paper, and handed it to me." Chris recognised the same pattern while staring incredulously at Mashir for an explanation.

"Yes, it's incredible and *impossible.*" Mashir stated. "For they are Beppi's fateful last words my friends and I believe, that they are words of power, ones that should never be uttered ever again."

****

Fact, the tall standing stone positioned immediately behind the head of the altar table, it would normally capture the rising energy of the Sun, pushing them through the hole at the top. The hole designed to take its life energies, binding them into the temple rim. The lost peoples knew how and why these elemental powers were important but now... these people were gone and their knowledge too, except... for the writings.

Fact, on any other year this sacred process of sacrifice and sun would have the magical ability to then hold and keep external dark powers at bay, and because of this, there was no access into this sacred temple.

Fact, the explorers did not realize and did not understand the significance of a new dark shadow held inside the obelisk's orifice on top of the monolith. It blocked the passage of sunshine.

Because of all these facts and events, things were not the same as they once had been. Karma was disturbed, and everything had now changed with these recent deaths.

Darkness maintained its hold inside the orifice, blocking the sun with a focused malcontent. Bad energies exuded from that black hole were being projected transparently and invisibly through the air onto the surface of the large observatory wall, where it then became visible as a dark spot. It this way, darkness had replaced the light of the sun face. With the sun face gone, only a round dark area remained and there it dominated.

Unknown to the men, the ancient temple was more complex and esoteric than anyone could ever imagine. In the evenings and occurring only at a special time, and, in full moonlight, transparent lines of power came, energies created then coming from a place called, *Nowhere.* It formed an invisible symbol that was *unseen* to *human eyes.* This magic signified, *a last resistance…* against the darkness. This year was different. Things had changed because of the sudden misalignment and slight tilt of the obelisk. It gave rise to the shadow, and so it began, a grip to dominate this world and beyond, and on to find true power.

****

The three men, Christopher, Mashir and Mathieson stood next to the altar on this fateful morning, were all unaware of what this place symbolised and what the temple's capabilities truly were. It was only now they felt its power and sensed its latent importance.

The humans could not know what the dark circle was, and a darkness still to be seen on the observatory wall, or why it even existed. How could they know why the darkness would not leave, and that the blackened orifice prevented the sun face from appearing within this hole as it had before. They had no idea or comprehension of the light's importance here, and that it had kept the balance of the Cosmos safe, until now. That balance was gone. Yet, nightly power lines on top of the temple still existed, resisting the darkness, and could only be seen by moonlit eyes, and those ones, were not human.

Again, it was the prophecy!

With the blood sacrifice complete, a vicious cycle had started, and no golden sun face would form anymore onto the observatory wall near to the monolith. The temple now waited unprotected and exposed. Time was right for the prediction to happen, and as expected, the humans had come and opened the temple. It was they, who had been the necessary catalyst for the door to open. It lay exposed, but exposed for who or for what? The answer was written again, in the prophecy!

****

The men looked around in distaste, and all they could see was the bloody butchery of a man they all knew. An ancient chronicle known long ago rumoured that some lost Portuguese conquistadores, *did* discover a mysterious temple in the deepest jungles, and that they had once stood here on this same spot. And it was also true that like those soldiers five hundred years ago, they had looked out from these remote steps towards their homes like these scientists were doing right now, wondering why they were here and what this place was all about. The only difference was, the conquistadores were *never able* to find a way inside the temple. The scientists did! In truth, hundreds of years ago, it had not been the right time to gain entry, simple as that. Time and circumstance bound by predictability and fate, and for the temple, at last it now lay open.

Completely bewildered at his death, disgusted and appalled at the bloody mess, nobody knew that from this point onwards a race had begun. It was a race to enter the temple and find its source of great power. Others would be coming to find it too; *again, this was told in the prophecy*

Would the expedition share the same fate as this man on the cold stone or would it be the same demise of those Portuguese crusaders gone before them, so many years ago? They had disappeared never to return to their homeland. Was this place to be the expedition's final justice? Five hundred years ago the temple had vanished or, so *they say*. Before the times of the Spaniard or Portuguese occupations, stories already spoke in fear about the legend and had continued to be told afterwards moving on from one generation to the next by the wise men, the Shaman.

The expedition had listened to the Shaman but not heeded their warnings, for this was the year of the Temple of MalisIblis. Once again this was a year predicted of materialization as written in grim Quipu by the Shaman, called the 'Scriptures of the Unholy Prophecies'; a story telling of its rare appearances. Was this prophecy the real-truth and the real-fate of mankind?

****

Barbaro Lettiere was from the Official Vatican Press Office and was a middle-aged man with weasel eyes and a sharp nose. His melodic voice seemed somewhat out of place and rhythmic and smooth. He and the rest of the expedition had been waiting at the temple entrance while the three men had gone to the top. The wait here already seemed too long, Barbaro restless and fidgeting with his camera eventually said to the professor, "Come on professor, let's go inside right away. I have my camera on hand and there is no more time to lose," said Barbaro, the man confidently walked towards the large entrance.

Unexpectedly, Fabio came pacing quickly from behind him, holding onto Barbaro's shoulder, hard. Anyone else may have agreed that Barbaro's idea was the best course of action, after all, was this not the moment they all had been waiting for, to go inside? But Fabio did not think so, as he was more astute than that. He understood that the Vatican official's true motives were selfish, so he stopped him in his tracks.

"Not so fast, Signor Lettiere," said Fabio abruptly. Fabio had never liked him, as Barbaro looked back in surprise at the professor.

The man from the Vatican had Velcro short hair and an unusually large head with a twisted bottom lip. Those lips were at times very persuasive, and inside was a silver tongue and like such articulate people, he harboured deceit and an ability to scheme. Ambitious yes, determined yes again. He liked it here; his talents had placed him right where he wanted to be. Fabio fumed quietly to himself. He was sure that the official was not going to take another step towards the entrance.

Another one that I never chose for my expedition is Barbaro. He is out of place. I had advised the company directors against him, but they wanted the correct coverage, and this man was very good at that! Weasel by feature and weasel by nature, no more than a promoted reporter in my mind. Blast it, I would have chosen anyone, but him. Fabio thought.

Professor Mancini disliked Barbaro intensely but the Vatican wanted the man and a full feature length edition of their exploration. Many publications of previous expedition papers had been sold because of Barbaro, so he made a lot of money for the Vatican. The Vatican was *keen* to show there would be no underhand dealings, like last time! Even though this expedition would be kept under wraps until the right moment to reveal good news of the journey.

"Need I remind you Signor Lettiere, of the *ill-fated* Tutankhamen Expedition? Those archaeologists all died because of bravado like yours and bad planning because of unknown microbes inside the structure. Microbes waiting in the stale air of the tomb killed everyone who had entered it. I remember well that it was you who covered the article in very fine detail, *did you not?*" Fabio said in numbed rage at the media man, going around him, and body blocking the press officer's access. Barbaro waited with insidious impatience.

Barbaro said nothing, and he did not have too. Obviously, he knew that to the forefront of the expedition leader's displeasure of him, was the bad press he had given to a later expedition led by Fabio's own mentor, *Professor De Luca'*. It was this man who had discovered a new chamber inside the tomb that killed the people. Professor De Luca' subsequently died suddenly from some unknown disease. Fabio was still furious at this reporter because Barbaro had complete disregard for a dead man's personal achievements and protocol. Barbaro's article tainted the dead professor and made him out to be no more than a common robber or blood sucking tomb raider.

Then insultingly, Barbaro had also taken photographs of the dead man and sensationalised them by relating this to large amounts of monies that had gone missing from the Vatican Bank, using them to finance this personal expedition. Fabio knew this story to be a total fabrication to gain publicity for Barbaro, and he threw blame from where it should truly lie, and so, the suspect Professor De Luca' had been *stitched up*. The professor suspected that the same person was probably skimming the Vatican system today.

Unknown to Fabio, this exposure would bring a young girl called Francesca De Rose into great danger a few weeks from now, *…as read in the book of Genesis,* the first story in *Gods Chain.*

In this story, a dedicated Systems Administrator called Francesca, worked inside the Vatican Bank arrived one morning like any other, and soon discovered nobody can log into the Vatican Systems. Her friend Michaelangelo had not turned up for work that morning and there had been a serious security breach in the Vatican Bank's computerised financial systems.

While trying to find out more about her friends' disappearance, her investigations would uncover deadly secrets hidden behind the Vatican walls, which would involve her in murder and assassination, and unexpectedly, launch *Operation Aequinoxium!* This was a pre-planned operation that was much more than a simple rescue mission for the scientists. It was more importantly a combat search and recover operation (CSAR) where collateral damage was to be expected. This was a *Black-Op* failover plan, concocted by Cardinal Giovanni Dalla Gassa, his guarantee to secure the fabled Reliquae. One such magical object was meant to be inside this lost temple, and, everyone wanted it!

****

Fabio suspected foul play and knew Professor De Luca' to be very fit and diligent, always taking the proper safety precautions against any contamination and yet, even he, never came back. His subsequent character assassinated by the media who for their own reasons made him a scapegoat. Fabio's attention was reflected on the injustices of life and to the mystery of what had happened to all that missing Vatican money. Someone knew because it was never recovered, and while thinking on this, his face became suddenly startled by the press officer's mellifluous voice.

"Lucky, you were not there at the time Fabio. What was it again?" He narrowed his piggy eyes into battlefield pillboxes ready to fire. "Oh, now I remember, Si! It was the Vatican Internal Audit. Ah, and it was *they* who were investigating *some missing monies*..." Barbaro mockingly placed emphasis and clear suspicion of wilful robbery on Fabio's part, rubbing it in. "They needed your statement, did they not, because your mentor had run off to his expedition *early*, and before the Polizia could apprehend him! A sure sign of guilt I would say, which set you in a bad light too."

"I was cleared," stated Fabio defensively. "*And* there was *no evidence* found against Professor De Luca' either." Fabio back peddled fast.

"Awful eh?" Barbaro paused then said, "And although some would not agree, we will never know where the money went. Terrible that our dear departed Professor De Luca' never came back to appeal and face the Internal Auditors enquiry. As you already know professor, just how tenacious they can be. The auditor's office wanted to speak with him and in my books, his absence makes him guilty as sin." Barbaro twisted a smile that became a permanent sneer feeling Fabio's grip loosening off his shoulder, the media man was the victor. Sensing the upper-hand, Barbaro began walking cockily towards the open entrance while his camera gave off an irritating automatic whirling noise with intent.

"Si! Si! Because he died out there *you Bastardo!*" The professor yelled furiously.

"Really." Barbaro stated indifferently.

"Wait!" Fabio commanded and Barbaro's shoulders hunched forward struck by the professor's authority. "Wait right there Lettiere! You will not enter first. It will be *me*, Fabio, it is my rightful place!" The Professor's voice lowered intimating serious intent to do him harm if he disobeyed. *"This is my moment, not yours."* The professor stepped forward and gripped the man's shirt collar tightly.

"Leave my collar alone!" Barbaro called out in pain, while squeezing out a piglet squeal, and unsure of what to do next. The long pointy-nosed man taken unaware by the expedition leader's vicious vice-grabbing hands.

Fabio's hold on the expedition appeared to be shaking in the balance, with first Carmello's death and here with Beppi, two people dead, maybe three. From the horrific screaming that came from above, he did not know of Boni's murder yet, but another fatality could not be ruled out. It had all gone horribly wrong except for the temple, the superstructure at last, lay open!

Professor Mancini fell into a silent resentment of Barbaro and kept squeezing the wincing man harder.

"Let me go! Let me go!" The press officer called when rationality impinged on Fabio's unbottled rage. Fabio somehow sensed Harjit's unfavourable attention, imposing on him.

"*Am I being… so, unreasonable?*" Fabio's voice quavered in anger at the man.

"*Understand…*" Barbaro's face twisted in pain while whispering best he could into his ear, "This is looking worse for you by the minute professor. Now… *let, me go!*" His throaty tone tortured by the professor's unyielding iron grip. Barbaro's eyes watered with agony looking up for help towards the girl.

"I remember your smearing articles…" Fabio's voice intense, his eyes boring into him.

Harjit could see from above what was going on, standing as a silent witness, observing the struggling man.

"If I don't get first access to the secrets inside here, and any holy treasure within it, I will make sure it does *not look good for the expedition.*" He paused because Fabio's grip crushed his neck even more. Barbaro compressed his voice in agony, but kept his resolve saying, "And your future exploits. The Holy See's will be done."

Fabio's grip loosened immediately, but kept him close, whether through threat or by clemency nobody knew. Barbaro exhaled his relief.

He rubbed his throat and with renewed caustic excitement, wielded more power over the professor by adding, "The Pope is less likely to spend any more of the Diastase collections in your direction, and I am sure your name and reputation will be forgotten forever. *I will see to it personally.*" He hissed into his ear, "They have allowed you this moment to prove yourself worthy."

"You slippery little..." A fraught look of apprehension came over the professor's desperate eyes. It was blackmail, no question. Watching Barbaro's sneering face savouring his moment in triumphal satisfaction, because he now had the professor's undivided attention.

"When we enter the temple understand this," said Barbaro, "*That I*, get the first photographs." The man's demand final. "I am sure all this unpleasantness is completely unnecessary. You are an intelligent man professor, and it is very little that I am asking of you." He started to chuckle. "I am sure it will not come to this, now will it professor." Barbaro moved again towards the entrance.

Barbaro knew the Media Man's slant on events could shut down the whole expedition. Fabio sobered up quickly, his rage gone to releasing Barbaro completely. Choosing his reply cautiously, the professor used a different tact and judgement. He knew Barbaro was a coward.

"We must be very careful Barbaro," said the Professor. "I am responsible for the safety of all the people in the expedition, *even yours.* I cannot guarantee your safety if you go ahead."

"Si, I have observed just how responsible you have been so far!" He nodded sarcastically towards where Beppi once stood. Fabio winced, blaming himself for the man's incineration. Fabio bit into his own tongue. The pain helped.

Yet the warning he gave Barbaro Lettiere had been enough to thwart him, stopping in his tracks. The man did not go any farther towards the temple, having second thoughts, looking at the professor apprehensively. Fabio smiled satisfied; after all he had a point, Barbaro thought more on it…

That shithead professor might be right, if some bacterium or virus is still inside and lying dormant, it'll be waiting for the first person to enter. I can wait, I'll let him take all the risks.

"Please, be my guest professor," said Barbaro. "*Do go first.*" His tone very deliberate and full of venom, his walk calmly settled into a sniff of forgotten urgency, Barbaro stopped casually stepping back, letting the professor walk passed him. Before the entrance, the professor stopped to stare inside.

****

Their tectonic tussle was over, so Fabio ignored any further contact with Barbaro. During his outer scan at the entrance, the men from base camp arrived and began gathering around him. A relieved Harjit held him a little as he looked worn out. The men were out of breath and all very nervous to what had happened. They wanted answers, so the professor began speaking quickly about the *accident* of Beppi while Alessandro and Cesaré who were only a scant step behind him, were drawn to the suicidal spot where the man once stood.

"I've told you everything, and you saw yourselves what happened. A tragic accident, and somehow, we must move on. I plan to go inside, but first something important. I need you to go and collect the environmental suits, breathing apparatus and bring them here. In an hour we go inside."

Resolute, the professor was determined to see the expedition through. He knew that his sole purpose was to find ancient artefacts, something priceless and most importantly something symbolic based on a Shaman's belief. It was *the stuff of legends.*

The professor suspected that inside the temple something might shake Christendom to its very fabric. Fabio's allegiance to the Pope true, and he would take all the necessary measures to secure these things for the real Catholic Order and not any other secret sect or religion.

The professor rejected the symbolic coincidences and misinterpretations made by poor Beppi and Christopher, because he had already been directed by the High Offices of his Holiness, no matter what the reporter said to taint his character. Yet Fabio could not get out of his head how much Barbaro knew about the expedition's true aims.

Fabio left the scene confident that Barbaro would not enter the temple alone; the man had no backbone. While his men headed down to base camp to collect their gear, he decided that the others on top needed him, immediately leaving the shrugging Barbaro. Super fit for his age, Fabio set out climbing and soon beheld the same macabre spectacle as the men waiting above. A scene of murder was his first thought while observing the eviscerated man. His mind reeled in overlapping thoughts.

This death is just too much of a coincidence, everything has occurred at the same time, at the same moment. The doorway is open! Fabio continued his forensic analysis; *maybe someone timed this pre-planned killing, perfectly right to each spoken word down at the entrance, but how and who? Who killed him! I need to find out where everyone was exactly at this moment. Uncannily, the entrance is open. That is what I wanted, but not this! I have strived for entry and by the looks of it, it took these deaths to achieve it.*

"It looks like we have a murderer in our camp," said Fabio. His companions Christopher, Mashir and Mathieson did not look surprised. Taking some pictures as evidence for later investigation by the authorities, these forensic photographs might be crucial in finding the murderer!

An awful job had to be done, so a little later Fabio and Mashir got the dead man's body together, grimly placing it in a bag used to hold the large army marquee tent as it would have to do for now. Tomorrow he would bury their dead colleague. At last, he could go into the temple and scout it out.

****

Kitted up and standing in front of the entrance, they looked more akin to spacemen than explorers, wearing unpleasant sealed white suits and backpacks with rations and equipment. Hoods closed around their faces, goggles with large eyed masks with a sizable front filter that felt completely alien. Arthur. C. Clarke may not be so wrong after all in his *Chariot of the Gods*. Each breath sounded laboured and mechanical as they all struggled to adapt, breathing in and out of these hot claustrophobic suits, white gloves and boots to match, all quite out of place in the rainforest. At last they were ready to enter the temple. Oh yes, Fabio had prepared very well.

Fabio, Endrissi and Christopher held battery powered torches, rope, light construction equipment, meters to gauge any radioactivity and microbe sensitivity in the environment as a precaution. The professor entered first, followed by Alessandro, Christopher, and Cesaré humming a tuneless sound; Mathieson ready as ever came next, then Harjit, unnaturally all too quiet. Finally bringing up the rear was Barbaro with a sneer. Fabio had decided for the reporter's own safety, to position him at the back of the expedition. The paper man was far from happy with this last-minute re-arrangement.

Mashir, Sebastiano Potenzia and Mykola Castrenze waved the team good luck, remaining outside to keep watch on the camp. They would be part of a rescue party and call for aid should anything befall Fabio's exploratory team.

The surveyor looked a little sad that he could not go inside with them but someone experienced was required to stay behind with the other two men, the historians whose survival skills were limited. Mashir knew when picked to stay behind by the professor, he had no choice. Studying the lost book from the mines was a rare opportunity for him to read first-hand the ways of a lost civilization. Mashir looked doubtfully at the historians. They were the weak links and their expertise in the collation of any findings in the expedition would not save them. He would be busy.

****

CHAPTER X

THE TEMPLE OF MALISIBLIS

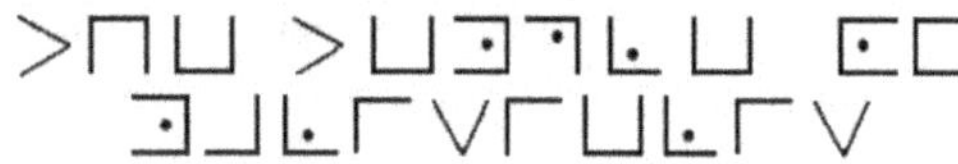

The open entrance was like a large yawning mouth that had allowed them to enter its sleepy stone interior. Fabio knew there was nothing that could prevent the great door from shutting and sealing them inside, quickly putting this thought to the recess of his mind. For him, this was an acceptable risk. Walking inside while cautiously looking upwards again, the grooves strangely reminded him of two sharp fangs ready to snap down onto anyone who dared to enter this place.

Morning sunshine followed them inside, its heat rays pushing them further along the long corridor, but all too soon the sunlight became too dim to see further, and the way ahead finally conceded into the darkness. The stone doorway that had earlier slid inside the temple and dropped out of site had since become settled and was completely flush with the floor. Their exploratory beams of torchlight began probing further into the dark tunnel. Everyone moved cautiously and slowly inwards while fanning around their powerful lights shining like *light sabres*, reflecting off its speckled inner red stone surface. The attached risks seemed acceptable. Some of them even thought that they knew the dangers; they were all wrong about that.

Walking along the corridor, the group instinctively kept close together. It seemed the right thing to do, and although nobody would admit it, everybody was nervous; it seemed surreal, stepping back in time. Wearing what looked like biological warfare suits, it made walking tough, clumsy and uncomfortable. Inside the building, it was much cooler than the surrounding jungle. Nevertheless, that did not help inside these suits; soon everything was sticky and wet.

Unseen in the professor's mind was a dark and dangerous labyrinth of routes that would lead him to other levels. Fraught looks of apprehension peered into this unchartered territory. Soon after entering, the professor stared bewildered while he studied his navigational compass. Confused, he checked and re-checked his direction of travel and shook his head in dismay, sensing fear growing in the group; they knew something was wrong as they watched him.

"The needle is way out of control," said Fabio. "And totally useless inside here. There must be a strong magnetic presence emanating from within the stone structure." Sighing aloud, he thought about his dilemma, *it's going bloody bonkers, completely haywire! It's caught in some sort of mad spin.*

Shrugging, Fabio looked apathetically at his company and resigned to a more manual approach, putting his instrument back inside his pocket.

"What do you think professor?" Mathieson asked.

"Oh well folks, the Compass served us well in getting us here." He reminisced back to their long hard trek through the rainforest to find the temple.

"Think you are still in control Fabio?" asked Chris.

"What do you mean?"

"I believe we'd have found this place, no matter what." Chris conjectured.

"Nonsense." Replied Fabio once again to Professor Christopher's rationale which seemed completely absurd.

"We have come to this place not just as a chance discovery Professor." The priest pressed him further. "You know, it is a strange feeling," he paused. "I think we have been guided here, I really do, I feel it." Christopher's tone was certain. His face was feeling super-hot, Fabio made him uncomfortable at times, like now, like a complete retard.

The expedition leader exuded confidence, which was obvious to everyone; his own ability was never in doubt. As principal and superior intellect, the professor's rightful self-destiny was unchallenged; his explicit holy orders gave him absolute authority here.

"Come," Fabio ordered.

Inside the dim temple, the small group observed that they were approaching a cross road of some kind in the corridor. Its walls were built in various sizes and shaped stones. The atmosphere felt quietly disturbing and oppressive. Soon a choice of routes was presented.

"Where to?" mooted Christopher, his voice muffled somewhat behind his mask. "Left, straight ahead or over there to our right? It all looks the same to me Fabio."

"Behind these walls must lead somewhere, man," stated the American, his twang still quite distinctive. The large whites of Mathieson's maniacal eyes stared through his large masked ringed orbitals, searching, the whites broken by thin root red blood vessels, all still quite visible; a tell-tale sign of his many restless nights of horrible bad dreams. Nightmares had been taking their toll on all the party.

In their denials, there came perpetuating lonesome feelings and yet, no one wanted to talk about these personal emotions in case they found out the real-truth, and quite frankly, they were all scared to death.

All will shake in terror; the prophecy.

Mathieson's own instincts told him to be tougher than this. His brown irises peered curiously around his murky environment and everyone seemed alien to him. It happened to everyone on the expedition at some time, the question, *is this for real man? what kind of Expedition is this? Mother fuck.* Watching Fabio who had stopped at a dim crossway. *The mother hasn't a clue man.*

"Should we split up or stick together Fabio?" Barbaro Lettiere immediately baited impatiently from behind. "Well?" The Vatican reporter observed Fabio's unusual dilemma and momentary hesitancy. "What is your decision? Which way is it then Professor?" He waited and insisted on firm action from Fabio, testing his resolve, hoping that the professor would make a wrong decision.

Endrissi Bergamaschi and Kees Acampilchtl were next to Fabio. Both men watched the professor's perplexed goggled eyes and followed the mad needle around dizzily, in time with the magnetic compass.

Looking up, Fabio began shining his torch in all directions, the light cutting a strong beam through the blackness, opening great chunks of the tunnel network. Standing still, he appeared to be waiting for some sort of a sign; none came.

"Which way is it now, professor?" Barbaro's rude voice irritate everyone as he pushed the professor further.

Fabio wanted to pull at his beard, which was something he always did when he felt perplexed. Strangely, a sudden compulsion inside the constricting confines of his environmental suit compounded his temper and honest sentiment. It was irrational but he knew it would make him feel better if he could just stick one on that insufferable official. *Keep going, rat-bag. Si, keep going and you'll not have to wait any longer.* Inside his mind, Fabio mimicked giving the man a good kicking.

Barbaro's own thoughts were that the expedition leader should have been a younger man, like him. The bureaucrat reporter from the Holy Office had just turned thirty and eager for another success. His trail of thought ended instantly when Endrissi, not looking where he was going, accidentally stumbled into Fabio, throwing the professor off guard.

"Whoops!" Fabio gasped. The unexpected barging from behind caught him. Kees, right close to the three men, tried to keep all their balances together and held onto the men's shoulders. It all looked like a crazy comedy sketch, when all three suddenly dropped out of site.

"Aaagh!" They screamed together. The others startled in disbelief and, like in an elevator, the three men descended out of site in a dangerous but controlled drop.

Endrissi, Fabio and Kees stared at the fast passing stonewalls around them, their excited eyes seeing numerous coloured hieroglyphics shooting past their blurred visions as they kept dropping. Tracked by their beams of narrowing light, each man quickly tried to cognate just how this had come about and how their survival might depend on how quickly they could learn. Kees thought that it was slowing.

"We're slowing down!" Kees shouted over the din of downward travel. It didn't stop but instead picked up more speed. Fabio stared at him with disbelief and Endrissi did the same.

After half a minute of acceleration, and with no warning, the stone platform stopped deep underneath the temple, landing on something with an almighty noise of what sounded like crushing wood or crumpling of some sort of semi-soft material that cushioned their landing. Never the less, the downward momentum caused all three to sprawl unceremoniously flat onto the floor with mellowed curses, each looking at the other all startled to be alive; at last they had arrived.

****

On top, the impossible had happened, then like a Magician's trick, all three men suddenly vanished from view. One second there, then gone. Suddenly, distressed calls of anguish were heard coming from below and an echo of reality; the three men dropped inside a large square hole in the floor before them. The remaining group watched, paralysed to act.

After a short moment of uncertainty, they ran to the edge just in time to observe the men getting further away from them, dropping fast until it suddenly stopped. Fabio's distant voice immediately called from the pin points of light.

"We're fine! We're all fine!" Fabio calling upwards.

"I suppose that this means we split up then, Fabio!" Mathieson shouted back down while chuckling loudly, the American staring over the edge in relieved humour.

The big burly and fair-haired engineer, Endrissi looked up annoyed at Mathieson's apparent disregard and flippancy.

"Fuck you, Mathieson!" Endrissi replied angrily. "We could have got killed just then! It's no laughing matter you fucker!" His deep muffled voice bellowed out from behind his protruding round mouthpiece.

The man was far too bulky for the white suit, his body appeared too ridiculous inside its pregnant seams; a terrible fit. Gathering his composure and looking away, the American's sense of humour was not funny to him. Mathieson, on the other hand, now ruptured into open laughter because he knew the men were just fine. Goggle-eyed Mathieson and the group stood together, not really knowing what to do next.

"Are you all ok down there?" Christopher called in case anybody needed his immediate help. "We will throw down a rope! Stand back!"

"You can't," said Harjit speaking softly to Chris.

"Eh?" said Christopher surprised.

"Ours is too short," she answered.

"Shit," he said quietly, his face stupefied. "Sorry it's not long enough professor!"

"Don't worry!" Fabio reassured him. "We are all fine down here! Later, Si, yes! Not just now.

I need to find out what's down here!" He confirmed this with a quick nod with the other two men. "I see an open corridor down here. I need to see where it goes. We will be exploring this area for the rest of the day and possibly tomorrow!" Pausing, he had something important to say. "Harjit, can you hear me?" He called upwards to the girl.

"Si, yes Fabio?" She answered hesitantly.

"There is another rope back at base camp, so come back this time tomorrow and we will be waiting here! Oh and by the way!"

"Si Fabio?" Harjit replied, wondering, *why does he want to talk to me?*

"I'm promoting you!"

"Fabio?" quizzing the air tentatively, *what does he mean?*

"Take charge and lead the others as far as you think it is safe to go. Be careful jumping over that small gap up there. I want you to investigate some of the interior a little further. See what lies beyond. Any sign of danger, return immediately. This is a chance in a lifetime for you!"

"No Fabio, I think you should come right back up and join us. We should not split up. I will get a rope right now. We can make a ladder and have you out safely in no time."

"Look Harjit, we will be fine. It might be easier to get out from down here anyway. If you get into a bit of a pickle, then head straight back to camp, and whatever happens to us, do not come down here. I do not want everyone getting lost.

Build a rope ladder tonight so we can use it tomorrow."

Fabio did not want to include the smaller weasel faced man in any part of his reorganization of duties, relishing the knowledge that the media man would be deeply insulted, after all, especially outranked by a Hindu and a female at that. She was level headed and that was good enough for him to take the leadership above.

"Take care, everyone!" He waved a final farewell to them from above and followed the men already making their way into the next corridor.

"Be careful boys!" The girl shouted after them. "See you all tomorrow!" She was fraught and looked around at the others for a moment. Then, with a renewed confidence and calm that settled into her nerves, she wondered why Fabio had put her in charge, considering his own personal views of women; he had seen something else in her. Smiling at the others she said, "Ok then, it looks like I'm it. We must jump this hole, it's not very wide and a run and jump should do it, but we must take off our rucksacks to do so. Mathieson, you could jump first. We will tie a rope on you. It is long enough."

"No rope for me, Harjy babe!" Mathieson dropped his pack and took a quick and easy jump, landing on the other side. "See, no problem and with room to spare!" The man in the white suit triumphantly tested her new rank.

"Not no rope, *no hope* more like," the girl countered while laughing a little. Harjit was relieved. Mathieson was the first one over!

Appearing unperturbed by Mathieson's defiance, behind her expressionless mask, was a face stone cold and unsmiling. It had been an obvious tact trying to provoke her wrath and goading for a direct reaction; *predictable* she thought. Harjit knew his game; the girl had a natural talent for leadership. "Next up!" She spoke confidently.

"I had plenty of practice running from the heat back in the States!" Mathieson bragged in continuous laughter below his muffled mask.

His depraved male hormones curiously sped through his blood stream, studying the attractive Indian girl. Even though she was kitted, he still managed to mentally undress her, peeling away her white suit.

"Right guys, throw the packs over to our intrepid explorer over there, and for you, mad boy Mathieson, I'll sort you out, Mister. It's time for you to play, *catch it!*" And without hesitation, she threw her rucksack over as hard as she could.

Her own strength indicated a hidden potential. Taking a few paces backwards, Mathieson gasped inwardly taking her pack full force. Satisfied with that, she sensed the American's grin wiping instantly away but only for a split second. He smiled again.

Two can play that game Harjy, holding that thought and being challenged, *I'm going to teach the bitch a hard lesson for that throw. Just to wind her up, it will be fun humiliating the stuck-up mother.*

Mathieson clapped his hands while waiting with open arms for the next rucksack to be launched at him.

"Ok all you mothers, throw your handbags at me!" The American demanded.

In a few minutes everyone was across safely, Harjit assumed her new leadership role. There was no time to lose and with no indecision, she led the way straight into darkness.

The others followed in silence and as they walked, each person was acutely aware that another secret shaft might unexpectedly appear and drop them too. Harjit lead the way.

Mathieson shrugged silently while bringing up the rear, shaking his head in disbelief at this new frontrunner. The girl obviously up for the challenge, *shit, she is going first after all, and I thought she would bottle out.*

****

Harjit's team kept going without further mishap, and to their surprise, they came upon two sets of wide stone stairs, built solidly and set into the walls. One began ascending steeply on their left and the other leading upwards to their right.

"It is real creepy, is it not? Which way, Harj?" Aléssandro the student archaeologist asked nervously. He just wanted to say something, anything. Breaking the awful tension seemed important.

"That way," said Harjit in no doubt, directing him with her torch. "Take your time." The boy went off quickly to the right, two steps at a time, and showed no reluctance. He had only one thing on his mind, to get out of there.

Mathieson then passed the girl following the younger man who had a zest in his steps. Harjit came next, Cesaré, Barbaro and finally Christopher bringing up the rear.

"I want to go back home!" Mathieson kidded in a childish tone, "Where is my mommy?" He jibed and laughed after the fleeing man's heels.

"Fuck you, Mathieson!" Aléssandro spat back at him. He had enough of Mathieson's big mouth, but this acknowledgement of annoyance only served to make the American worse. Mathieson was happier than ever, with this giving him another opportunity to wind him up. Harjit recognised the Americans immaturity; she had known him long enough.

What a pain Mathieson is, thought Harjit, judging the situation, *he is in high spirits and a pain, but he is a good distraction in here.* It took the men's minds away as it did for herself and her own personal problems. *Yes, he is good to have in my team*, the leader considering his contradictory moods and merits.

The temple was a formidable place, a place of strength and darkness, a place of worship and sacrifice. Unseen, something intangible was continually present, working on them all, an unexplained force increasing in strength especially the further they went in. They felt it even more since the group split. It was a festering danger like hypothermia, one that slowly crept up, working on the trance like troop. The large stone steps took a long ten minutes to climb until they all eventually manage to reach a stone landing.

Aléssandro projected his powerful and probing beam of light, blazing it around in the darkness, looking for something, a way out. But then, here it was, with his hands shaking uncontrollably, the nervous beam held focus onto a large broken entrance.

A ruination of rocks and building blocks that once made up thick stone doors lay partly wrecked and fallen around them. Bits of stone and boulders were strewn over a wide area in the surrounding darkness, while a huge mass of rubble and debris piled up high directly before them like a barrier. Huge gates had been reduced to boulders, stones and dust. The ruin was a final resting place of stone pieces graven where they had fallen, and everything caught up in what appeared to be an untold disaster. A large part of a door was still intact but badly fissured. Aléssandro stopped, acutely wary of an untold danger, not wanting to move any closer. He waited for the others to catch up.

"Look at this, guys," his tone subdued, not wanting to disturb the peace. Aléssandro swept his torch and fixed it on numerous broken rocks.

"What do you think happened here?" The others looked on, completely awestruck at the demolition site.

"A great power happened here. An explosion of incredible force and for a so-called primitive civilization, astonishing." Commented Harjit, shaking her head while studying the devastation. "How? They could not have invented gunpowder back then. What else could have caused this destruction?" Suspicious, Harjit queried her own sanity and found it wanting.

"Phew, not so primitive, I think," Barbaro felt apprehensive inside the incessant darkness. *What does this mean, who are these people?* He wondered, sensing a scoop of the century.

In the silence, Aléssandro began whistling his tuneless note again and was way off-key.

"Only a massive force could have done this, t, to, to," stammered Cesaré Padovesi. "To break this rock type. This rock is so hard, I know because I broke my diamond tipped blades on the surface of the outer structure. It did not even make a scratch! I know that is crazy but whatever happened here must have been a mighty big fucking bang alright!'

"Yeah, alright man!" Mimicked Mathieson happily.

Astounded at this wreckage, Cesaré could not comprehend what power could have caused this kind of destruction; none could. The man held onto his gold crucifix to give him comfort, fearing something superhuman had done this.

Harjit strode forward, climbing best she could to the top of the pile of debris, the others watching her efforts to stand on a precarious top position. Suddenly she faltered.

"Oops, shit and bloody crap." Cursing was very unlike her, Harjit's lips were raw with cold curses but somehow, she managed to keep her balance while stumbling through into the dark breach beyond. Her quick reflexes helped her down the rocky side, moving down like on a Scree slope, preventing injury, but other than some bruises, she would be fine.

"Watch out Harj!" Christopher called over. He hated her every step, blaming Fabio for giving her this lead role. The professor knew the risks. *Harjit does not have the experience so why did Fabio choose her to lead us?* To say something like this to the girl would only make things worse. Fabio had a lot to answer for.

"Oh!" Harjit exclaimed loudly as she took a deep breath of stale air and looked around in the darkness; she felt a deep uneasiness stirring inside her. She then felt sick, cut off like this, even though the others were not far away. Here in the darkness and alone with only a light for company, her vulnerability entombed her in fear. She could as well have been standing on the Moon.

"Harj!" Christopher shouted after her, his concerned voice calling from the other side. "Are you alright?"

"I'm through," *Oh shit*, realising what she had found, she threw semi-panicked light beams in all directions, focusing from one dead body onto another, then another; she swallowed hard. She suppressed her urge to scream alarms ringing in her head while thinking, *what is this place?*

"Harj, hang on!" called Christopher, scrambling closer.

"I'm fine, really," she replied while battling with herself. *I need to show everyone that I can take the shocks. Keep cool girl, keep cool and make the right decision. Show everyone, including Christopher, that I can lead the team. Come on girl, it does not have to be a man in charge. I must prove to Fabio and the others that I am the right choice!*

Harjit had also something to prove to herself. At this crucial moment she needed to be like iron, bottling her dread while observing the carnage all around her. *What is this place?* Rubble began tumbling down behind her.

"Fucking dead, alright!" It was Mathieson arriving first. The man gleefully confirmed the dead. Standing half a step behind her, he could almost read her thoughts and said, "Are you scared little girl? You are! This is man's work." He wound her up some more while smiling.

"Shut up Mathieson," she asserted.

"Looks like these guys have been dead for a while. Never seen the dead before Harjy?" His words were all too flippant.

"I'm a Doctor you oaf!"

"Sheeet," he got it; his smile froze. In the darkness, it suddenly struck him too, the intensity and quiet, as blackness pressed in from around and spooked him. He gawked, realising the true scale of dead bodies scattered around inside the wreckage; he did not know what to make of it either.

"This place is like a mortuary," said Harjit stonily.

"Mother, fuck," Mathieson agreed.

****

Mail clad warriors lay broken and discarded like litter everywhere. Some had spears stuck through their chainmail in deadly penetrations to where vital organs had once been. Other warriors fell at odd angles being struck in a hail of arrows, the after effects of pain vivid by their contorted positions.

Some died holding their swords while being mortally wounded by what looked like long, sharp, brown-ended, thin, dart-like needles. These could easily pass through the heavy chain links of their bronzed coloured mail.

Bones had been fractured or hacked off, evidence of a violent end in some lost battle. Only tattered leather tunics and bony skeletons remained underneath, giving the bodies some shape.

"Wow! It must have been one hell of a fight," said Aléssandro who arrived next, picking up a short sword from the stone filled floor.

He held the weapon's silver handle and rotated it slowly, his eyes rotating to behold an intricate metal design stamped onto its cross-guard surface. This unique design had been moulded by a furnace and shaped during its time of creation. At first glance, the shape resembled a holy cross in the centre surrounded by a star of David, both shapes embraced with a crescent moon.

Aléssandro found it strangely familiar. *How odd, yet so fascinating. What kingly markings are these?* On second glance, he could not even start to guess at that answer.

The double-sided blade's length was short by warrior's standards, measuring two metres and very lightweight. It was designed to be a pointed weapon specifically used for thrusting and penetrating armour or a hard-coated enemy. Aléssandro carefully rubbed the inside of his thumb lightly across the blade to judge its sharpness.

"It's razor sharp."

"I would say these big buggers got their mother fucker ass's creamed, man." Mathieson was not joking this time, no hint of flippancy in recognition of just how serious this fight must have been.

"This scene will be worth a fortune." Barbaro got busy. "What an excellent find! Exciting news for our Holy Father!" He said enthusiastically. His contorted face and greenish brown eyes considered the best angles and shots from his Nikon camera at the historical mayhem.

"These guys are really big. Look at that one, he must be between six and seven feet tall. They are like giants!" Harjit stated. Bumping Harjit a bit, Barbaro pushed forwards and flashed another snap, catching her annoyingly by surprise.

"No pictures Barbaro," she ordered firmly. "We need to press on from here. You can take photographs later."

"I must protest!" he shouted, not taking "no" for an answer and getting ready for more action as his bloodshot eyes took aim at a headless warrior.

"Get over it, pal." Mathieson jerked his shot and the camera fell.

"You idiot, Mathieson!" Said Barbaro, just managing to save it from striking some boulders.

"It's a nasty business. Whoever killed these soldiers must have been tough." Christopher began prising away a single-sided battle axe that had been embedded into a cleaved chest of broken chain mail.

"Tough and dead. These guys were wiped out after an overwhelming attack. I don't think they stood much of a chance. They must have put up a brave fucking fight, man."

Mathieson stared at one victim who had a long needle sticking through the side of his metal helmet. Shaped around his large bony skull, a bronzed lustre helm fitted perfectly. It had a small sharp pointed dagger ensign set onto its forehead and bonded onto its metal cast. The dagger point was directed upwards with a thin six-inch blade above his long protective nosepiece that could also be used as a close quarter weapon. His chainmail seemed in surprisingly good condition for its years, hard and remaining quite flexible after all this time.

"Poor Buggers," stated Chris, who had arrived too, surveying the devastation.

"Maybe they were trying to stop an assault coming into this part of the temple. It looks like a storage area for maybe food or something like that." Cesaré spoke quietly, not wanting to disturb a spectacle.

Soon they were moving along into another large hall that directed them into other rooms with large wooden drums used to contain food like flour.

The rooms had once contained a variety of food while other tanks were probably for holding water. The water was supplied from a runoff and filled reservoir coming from a much higher place in the temple. It was dry inside.

The large rooms appeared to be about thirty or forty-feet-high and would easily take up the equivalent of several of the terraced steps outside the temple. Harjit tried to gauge in height where they might be standing inside the structure.

Many more signs of a struggle were appearing all around in what looked like a running battle. Many fallen warriors had been hacked down while others were shot in a barrage of needles. They followed the killing spree trail of desolation.

"What did they want?" Mystified, Cesaré questioned these events.

"Notice something?" said Harjit, studying the victims. The others turned expectantly towards her as if to say, *whatever next?*

"What now," Barbaro asked, still disgruntled with her.

"They are not Spanish or Portuguese. These soldiers are not Conquistadores." The obvious stated, and yet nobody had taken this fact in.

"Si, and?" Barbaro replied cautiously, then he saw it too, it clicked. "Obviously you are right?" He questioned impatiently.

"Who are they?" Christopher's tone intrigued. He gripped a battle axe more tightly and began swinging it about his vicinity, its curved blade splitting the stale air with a wide *whoosh.*

"I like this weapon," smiling to himself.

"Don't you recognise them?" Mathieson smiled self-contented.

"Eh?" Christopher stopped swinging, puzzled.

"The stone figures over at the mines. These guys are the same size and appearance."

"Yes, yes, you are right Mathieson." Christopher stared at the warriors, his face boiling, annoyed at himself for not having made that conclusion first.

"Dead soldiers are everywhere! They were trying to protect something?" Said Aléssandro, speculating as the others followed him from room to room and then into another corridor.

In front of them, a set of stone stairs met their accumulated silence. The group set out, climbing it steeply. Soon they were nearing the next level when they heard an uncanny noise.

"What is that?" Said Cesaré, referring to an unusual and constant hiss. The sound permeated in from somewhere, a noise filtering down to meet them from above.

"Listen, do you hear that? I said, listen!" Said Cesaré in earnest aggravation, demanding everyone's undivided attention. "Do you hear it now?" The staleness of centuries was coming from somewhere.

Everyone followed him quickly along a spacious corridor that routed off either to the left or right, subdividing into numerous rooms or apartments. Showing no hint of hesitation or bravado, the young man was fuelled up by fear and kept going, heading onwards like a man possessed through the main passageway.

"I hope it is not what I think it is?" But his thoughts were mistaken, Cesaré had a phobia against snakes.

The darkness seemed endless, threatening everyone with claustrophobic compression. A malignant consciousness dwelt within the temple, gnawing at their willpower. In their minds, everyone battling their own demons whether in dreams or waking phobias.

The temple was a place of spells and nameless fears, where emotions were kept hidden in the recesses of their minds, a place of deep darkness and truly a test to each person's mental well-being. Time passed as they walked through more rooms.

"Look over there, I see candles! Light them quickly please."

Harjit directed her torch beam onto a table and extinguished candles. They sat in what looked like a candelabra.

The hissing noise was more definitive inside this dingy place, and until now it had been constant, with a quiet resonance each person easily got used to, and then was forgotten about, but it was different inside this room. It sounded strangely magnified, as if they were getting closer to something.

Christopher lit the golden candelabra next to a large golden goblet that had fallen on its side. He decided to move the Candelabra around in the air to locate the direction of the noise. His eyes began peering above.

A golden chandelier was located overhead on the ceiling. They could guess that the Chandelier would normally be accessed using the long chain and pulley system inset discretely into the wall.

"These people were very civilized," said Cesaré. "Consider this, an unexpected technological advance, the sounds of blowing air. Look up at those things in each high corner, they are vents to shift air inwards and expel it outwards." Each person's attention focused onto large stone grills.

"Go on," encouraged Harjit.

Cesaré's confidence grew and he moved closer to the strange sound. Even now there was a constant trickle of air flowing through some ancient ventilation system.

"There must be some kind infrastructure located behind the walls," he said, holding another candle and moving it toward the vent. It quickly blew out in a sudden puff and startled him.

"Take it easy Cesaré," advised Christopher.

"A duct system has to be behind these walls. It must be an amazing feat of engineering, a bit ropey now and erratic but still works. I can't believe it still works!" Cesaré's eyes watered from the short sharp bursts of air coming out from the stone grill.

"Look at the size of these chairs. They are really big just like all the furniture inside this place." Christopher sat on one of the uncomfortable carved wooden chairs. Its leather padding had long ago disintegrated. He sat in his white suit with its tiny light emitting diodes of flashing lights pulsing reassuringly on green; each light an indicator of health.

"It must have been very claustrophobic living here," Harjit advised. "I would hate it. Cooped up like this with no natural light, oh dear. Maybe it was only on special occasions or in times of ritual ceremony. Looking at this place, it might serve to help during a siege too, and could be a place for protecting their aristocracy. I don't think this place was just for anybody though," she speculated.

"Yes, you are right. This place is..." but Christopher did not finish his sentence.

"Don't worry Harj," Cesaré interrupted while sitting down heavily, obviously relieved that no snakes had surfaced from those sounds.

****

The team continued onwards, systematically moving from one room to the next, and much evidence of the living-quarters remained as a ghostly reminder of those ancient days. Time seemed to be slipping away, and with no natural light enclosed inside, here was what might be called a prison. Their body clocks guided them by hunger and reminded them to stop.

"Why don't we have a break and have something to eat? I am starving!" Cesaré complained.

"Good idea," Harjit said, agreeing with him. Like the others, she had been too preoccupied. "Let's make something to eat. Do not drink anything other than from your own canteens and remember to use your own rations."

"Fantastic, only one thing wrong Babe." Mathieson smiled behind his mask again. They all turned. What might he be coming out with next, "This is a lovely outfit we are wearing, yes?"

"Come again?" She moved her head, a little annoyed at this random statement.

"How do we eat with these mother masks on then Babe? And something else?"

"What?" Her mind worked on the problem.

"And, I am ready for a crap," he stated bluntly, sending a muffled chuckle coming from the others; Christopher was not one of them.

"Mathieson!" Said Harjit disgusted at his bluntness. Her eyes fixed frostily onto the American. "And stop calling me Babe!" she called, mixed in with more chuckles from the others.

"Mathieson has no decorum Harj, that is true." Said Christopher, "But he is right, how are we meant to do our needs and have something to eat?' Half-smiling at her and seeing the funny side, he looked up at the others, "Oh, give it a rest you lot!"

"Should we take this mother fuck off or not?" Mathieson was not kidding.

"We have only been able to drink using those sealed bottles that plug into the sides of the mask, remember?" Barbaro pained the point. "Absolutely nothing is going to happen to us." The man was delighted to be able to add to her consternation.

"These are awful suits and they stink, and I need to go now! Nothing's happening down here," referring to his electronic LED lights. "Man, come on!" The American exasperated.

"We are all on the green Harjit." Cesaré confirmed, intimating their environment was clean and healthy with no harmful microbes.

"Cesaré is right. None of our indicators have displayed any warnings." said Barbaro, the man seemed instantly willing to make life easy gauging his own indicators and then the others, "Cesaré is correct in his observations." He said, then quickly glancing at Aléssandro's numerous small meters. "Everyone is just fine."

A semi-permeable membrane allowed absorption of the outside atmosphere to contact an organic meter, and no further. This is where all the tiny light emitting diodes were located and pulsed regularly on the green. Green for good, signifying no gaseous toxins or harmful microbes present in the air.

"There are no gaseous toxins or bugs indicated. Well it is a question of reducing the risks, and obviously we have our needs. Try to keep yourselves as little exposed as possible," Harjit spoke in a mono-toned voice. She was not happy juggling his rudeness with reason while cutting him an icy stare through her round goggles. Mathieson loved the agro.

"Ok, I'm going in that room and don't follow me in Harjy! Oh, and after my crap, expect everything to go on the red Babe!" Mathieson walked off laughing loudly while the others tried their best to suppress their boyish giggles, listening to the black man's banter.

"It's your risk mister piss artist, so breathe deeply you son of a black ass mother." The girl recognised his particular brand of humour and got her own back. The others were completely taken by surprise, Mathieson too.

The amusement in the group could not be contained after that. Jovial laughter resonated throughout the corridors at Harjit's blank awkwardness. There was no getting away from it, so she dropped her embarrassment seeing the funny side of their predicament. "Anyone else?" looking slowly around, as everyone exploded into more fits of laughter. Harjit smiled.

"Me."

"Me too!"

"Hey Mat, you've got company!" the girl calling at the American.

"Man!" Mathieson shouted while clapping in hilarity, laughing even louder on his way out, while calling back to her, "Never thought you had it in you Babe!" He smiled behind his mask. At that moment there was some mutual respect between them.

Their convivial sounds of combined hilarity floated through the ominous darkness. They were in good spirits, laughter unheard inside this place for millennia. Lighting another long candle, Harjit then saw another door way. It was covered in a layer of thick spider webs, the girl was intrigued a little more, asking them to follow her for a short distance through it. It led into a different living area where lots of furniture lay broken and vandalized; no sign of anyone, dead.

Bits of wooden legs and seat tops laid scattered around with everything left as debris by senseless marauders. Picture frames, dishes, and broken crockery also lay on the dusty floor tiles. Everyone scanned the room with care and unease. They had seen inside many similar places and all had been systematically plundered and spoiled. Long curtains were hanging in tattered decay on the walls and a large dingy tapestry laid fallen into a dusty heap; time had taken its toll. Clearly, some catastrophe had overcome this ancient people.

The group rested here for about thirty to forty-five minutes. Harjit insisted that they keep their masks on. Always the rebel, Mathieson kept his off because he wanted the controversy, it was his awkward nature; a senseless risk but Harjit could not stop him.

Back on track, and this time they used lit candles. They moved on slowly while observing the surrounding carvings cut into stonewalls. The temple seemed full of stairs and everyone climbed again. Unexpectedly their route bent around in a curve.

Making excellent progress, they soon reached a larger stone platform above. A much larger area with some purpose, maybe built for a central meeting point because they could see that there were many other smaller sets of stairs coming together here.

They could see that any way up was steeper. Stone columns were set at regular intervals on both sides of the steps giving the place a rich and colossal feel about it. Each column had a glassy stone lustre and was translucent like quartz, extending up from step to ceiling. The height of the columns being thirty-three feet or more giving the stairs an airy hidden depth about them.

At regular intervals a sizable niche had been cut out in each pillar to hold an oil lamp, each placed about shoulder height. The lampshade made of a translucent crystal stone that reminded Harjit of a princess's tiara.

Lamps were inset and sitting behind a thin stone horizontal curved bar, functioning as a barrier to prevent an accidental knock when anyone walked past. Nobody had walked this path for a very long time.

Moving along, their way was hindered by annoying sweeps of spider webs becoming gradually worse. Each person forced to fan ahead sweeping light threads away from their facemasks. These webs had been here for a very long time because there were no spiders, only their silky memories.

"Light one," Harjit instructed.

"Eh?" Aléssandro asked.

"Light a lamp, please."

"Sure."

Mathieson quickly volunteered moving past the young Italian. When lit, the illumination unexpectedly filled the whole column with a calm soft light that intensified a warm presence from naked lamp light, it was an ultimate of ultimate's in lamppost design.

"Shit, my ass man!" Mathieson cursed in complete surprise jumping backwards at this weird discovery.

The other's mooting sounds of incredulity as well at the mysterious luminosity of pillar light added to their awe of this civilization. Moving on through, they opened the immediate area to a wider field of vision.

Their environmental white suits had been covered and coated in filth with sticky cobwebs. Walking through rubble had also exposed them to copious dust clouds. Their way here was much easier in this new light as they lit more candles.

"Who could have made such a thing?" said Harjit wondering.

"What a place this must have been when all these columns were lit." Cesaré tried to imagine the columns of light in their heyday. Mathieson seemed more excited than ever at the prospect that these new discoveries would make him rich.

This new founded light source highlighted and extenuated all the fine detail on the massive inner walls with an unnamed esoteric artistry and strange elemental codec wizardries.

None of them were sure what it meant but they could see many hues of rich reds and beautiful blues, misty whites and glorious green tones that had all aged to an extent into some places drab with shades of grey and jaded pastel colours, yet despite its age, it remained beautiful.

"This place is much older than I first imagined. How can this be?" Christopher's perplexed mind whispered estranged thoughts of dismay.

From top to bottom, huge walls displayed massive mosaics, telling of a struggle of epic proportions and of odd-looking creatures and wild scenes. Artwork of an ancient people had been drawn, they had been or were still living in another land at that time. It was a land much different from here. One with far-reaching green pastures and trees, places drawn of where there were once great cities. These detailed designs were highly intricate with complex staccato patterns that must have taken decades to create.

"They liked their stories, did they not?" Aléssandro surmised.

"Si, maybe these are a chronicle." Christopher remembered he had seen similar style, but the ones in the mine-works were macabre murals, while these were lighter and happier scenes except for certain creatures.

"No, it's like a story book, look at these horrible creatures, they are not real, they can't be! They cannot be true, probably made up grisly fairy tales." Aléssandro's tone was not convincing anyone. He was scared, plain and simple.

"More like an oversized imagination. In fact, this might be some weird religion or maybe, a fear or possibly a nightmare or..." Harjit felt something stir, thinking to herself, *or a warning.* She said nothing else.

Around the area, there was more desolation. Many weird macabre shapes cut out of solid stone, some were figured gargoyles that seemed to guard the passage with stony stares, hard and certain, and as if real watched over the dead.

Chainmail links left on the chipped steps and bits of bone from bodies parted were all remains of a quick and decisive massacre. There were many warriors lying over on the cold hard steps, their Helms and Shields all lying close by. Eyeless skulls stared openly within their open-faced chainmail head-guards. Once mighty warriors, these Goliaths had fallen in a different age, long ago.

"What were these people like?" Cesaré asked.

"Did you not see their images? A bit like us, except bigger," advised Christopher.

"Come on this way," Commanded Harjit. "And take that lamp too and be careful. Let's go." She did not want to stay any longer, time was precious and something intangible had spooked her.

Aléssandro took the lamp and detached it from the long column that instantly dulled until it went out, leaving only light in the lamp fuelled by a limited reservoir of oil burning in its lamp base. They could move on and conserve their torch batteries.

"Weird," said Cesaré staring at Aléssandro regarding his silhouetted appearance against the lamp. He seemed out of place. *Lord protect us.*

"Everything about this place is odd," Christopher agreed while bringing up the rear. The biotechnologist's own appearance was also lit up uncannily by lamp light. Moving carefully between the dead soldiers, he left them once again in timeless darkness.

Up seemed best, the group climbing with no fixed destination, only up. Harjit hoped to reach the top of the next landing and the next level. What they saw there on reaching it made them gulp.

A set of large black pointed arched gates stood before them, with the middle in the most dominant position. The door construction protruded three or four feet out in front of the others and was cracked and chipped but still intact. It had seen the rigors of battle. The smaller wrecked doors stood partially, with some ragged chunks stuck in their original closed position. Most of the stone remnants had been subjected to great forces.

A row of fierce looking stone gargoyle heads stared down on them from above the pointed stone arches sculpted out of rock waited to fend off evil spirits. Their horrid stony faces appeared to be watching them approach.

"Weird," said Aléssandro. "Here take this," handing the lamp to Harjit, while switching on his torch. Aléssandro knew what to do. The man just wanted to get their exploration over with and get back to base camp. Without asking, he purposely moved once more, directing his beam towards the left doorway. Harjit nodded silently and he went through.

"Be careful Alé," Harjit felt fearful, *this is getting risky,* she thought. *I might be pushing them too far.* She felt that maybe it was time to go back. Harjit began to think they had gone far enough.

The possibility of the area collapsing whilst watching him pull and squeeze cautiously through the larger section of broken doorway made her cringe, realising that for a big man, there was not much room. In he went, making it and was suddenly out of sight.

On the other side, his torch light stopped directly in front of his face and he was confronted by an opaque greyish curtain. The stuff spread widely across his range of vision and the torch light varied over its opaque surface, highlighting different depths to it in a strange grey blanket showing a cheese-like patchwork consistency. It moved lightly when touched and stuck fast to him, spider webs.

Unable to see clearly with tacky webbing matted over his eyes sockets that were glued thickly onto his mask in a snug wrap all over his face, the young man regretted his up-front bravado. His heart started to race.

"Yuck!" he said in disgust, knowing that he would have to go further inside now. *I cannot turn back, I do don't want to look like a coward! I'll have to keep going now.*

"Are you ok, Alé?" she asked with a deep sense of dread.

"I can't see!" shouting back. "Some shit is all over me!" Aléssandro's voice was shaky, fear washing over him as he erratically rubbed away the web around the plastic orbitals of his high-tech mask. Unable to see his life saving indicators, the young man panicked. He swiped his face again and luckily his vision cleared. He heard Harjit shouting again.

"Come back, Alé," Harjit could tell from his tone he was not happy.

"Phew, thank God," his panic attack recessed, and he began to breath rhythmically once more.

Above his head and on the walls of each side of this dingy place, were sets of angled metal holders with thick bars inserted about three feet long, made of whitish translucent feldspar or granite. The walls inside were tiled with complex geometric designs.

"Yuck! This place is filthy!" His voice called back. The others looked carefully inside and could see him wiping more of the webs from his eyes. He pretended, "There must be lots of creepy crawlies in here Harjit. I hope you have brought your fly spray!"

"Fly spray does not kill spiders, Alé!" Harjit bantered back. The others said nothing, lost between deciding whether to enter or not.

"This place has not been occupied for God knows how long." He swung his torch left and right, pulling more of the long sticky web like candyfloss. The light was absorbed by this grey black web, making it quite impossible to see any great distance beyond this point. If there were spiders here, then there would also be flies but there seemed to be neither.

"Hard to see anything inside this shit." His arms were like windscreen wipers.

"Do not go too far ahead." Harjit scrambled inside behind him. Christopher came next, then the others, all hurrying like children because nobody wanted to be last or alone in the darkness with death surrounding them.

Torch in one hand and sword in another, Aléssandro swept slow swathes of sticky sheets away with his blade, using a double-edged sword that he had acquired from one of the dead warriors. Even so, the web material floated stubbornly around, trying to catch onto him.

Mathieson came through last, and unusual for him, he was not cursing or swearing. His head was still uncovered so he could see better.

"Look man, I am taking off this bloody space suit. A little bit of spider shit don't put me off. I can't move inside this gear man!" He hid the fact that this place was getting to him, he was beginning to crack.

"I do not think that is a good idea Mathieson, keep your suit on, any microbe could be inside this place." The girl attempted to persuade the American to stay protected.

"Nothing's happening babe. We have been in this shit-hole all day now, and all my meters are still on the green, nothing is happening and nothing's going to happen, Harjy."

"What is that up ahead?" The press officer asked because through the dusty web, Barbaro had made out the shapes of some stone pillars.

Mighty pillars in matted shadows could be seen towering high above them, holding up the lofty ceiling, all arranged in parallel rows and columns. Each carved pillar was spaced out equally inside this great chamber giving the structure solid support.

"Come on!" said Aléssandro wanting to go. His torch beam was not powerful enough to sway a light path through the misty web work, it was a bit like driving through fog with full headlamps on. The glare dazzled against the webs, restricting their view and yet, at times they could make out some clarity further inside.

For centuries, maybe longer, spinning spiders had previously created these silk tapestries with soft weaved sheets, much of it torn away and left floating stubbornly in the air. They teasingly stuck to them and anything else that passed, tearing and creating gaping big honeycombed cheese-like holes that opened and exposed sizable hollow pockets of stinky stale air and dust.

The troop walked onwards through the foggy grey blanket and caused more large gaps and holes to appear, which helped them negate a series of large empty spaces. Their dirty silk edges dropped slowly while wafting around like ragged clothes.

In time, they had lost all sense of direction inside this place, and soon nobody could tell the difference between east and west, their compasses suffering the same disoriented spinning effects that Fabio had experienced earlier. It all seemed endless.

"This place smells," said Aléssandro grumpily, the man annoyed and frustrated from not having a clear path to follow.

"It's worse than the jungle," commented Harjit. "Come on Chris, Cesaré, Barbaro and Mat," said Harjit, turning backwards and stretching her neck to the point of pain; she could not see him. "Where is, Mathieson?" Her eyes hardened, and her visage became rigid because Mathieson was not there. The American had disappeared.

"Eh?" Christopher was taken aback too.

"Mathieson! Mathieson!" Harjit called fearfully. There was no reply. Suddenly, drapes of web started tearing away, abruptly sweeping open near to her face, when the American suddenly appeared at her side.

"Nervous, are we?" said Mathieson in a soft jokey voice into her covered ear.
His voice jovial, because it was a gag, the man back to his old tricks again.

"Mathieson don't do that!" called Harjit, the girl automatically jumping backwards, repulsed at his rude webbed appearance, saying in a crossed tone, "That was really a stupid thing to do!"

"Harjy!" Mathieson said, laughing apologetically.

"Shut up and follow me," Harjit was completely pissed off. She ordered, "Ok everyone keep-up! Aléssandro, you and I can make a proper path this way."

"Stick together, Mathieson," Christopher tried to lighten the situation but saw Matheson's intoxicated expression and knew their exploration could not go on much further.

"Good choice of words Chris," said Endrissi. "It looks like that is just what we are doing. Look at Mathieson, he's covered top to toe in this web crap, and that's what I call really sticking together!" Endrissi saw the funny side and everyone laughed, except Harj.

Cesaré kept swishing his machete some more and Mathieson and Christopher patiently did the same, slicing continuously, slowly from left and then right.

"Men, watch those swords would you!" Harjit's tone hardened, becoming more assertive. The situation was deteriorating with more web wrapping around them.

Not a breath of air in here, the ventilation system had not worked in this chamber for a very long time. Web floated harmlessly around them, waving its gluey blankets as they moved through. Something obscure came into view at a far distance, it was becoming partially visible. Barbaro's greenish brown eyes lit up behind his mask and a smile twitched in the corner of his breathless lips, *it's a pulpit*, he thought.

Torch beams reflected off a precious silver-gemmed wall set above the stand. It had gilded silver bands ascending on its edges on a small set of steps leading upwards to that holy place. Incredibly it resembled some sort of holy stand with metal steps all matted in web. Each step protruded and extended half way up the east wall; it appeared to be made of solid gold.

Mathieson turned his head to his right and could just see that in the corner of this murkiness there was what appeared to be a larger set of narrow stone stairs. The American felt hot and sticky, he had been like this for a long time. Extremely agitated, he had had enough. Then without warning, he began impulsively pulling off his synthetic white suit, leaving him wearing his usual white round neck, short-sleeved shirt and shorts. All his garments were soaked in sweat. Thirst taking hold of him, Mathieson gulping copiously at his canteen of water from his backpack.

"What are you doing Mathieson?" Harjit called out, her stress levels mounting. She tried to understand, realising that he was losing it, mentally. Mathieson did not answer her and suddenly began running towards the wall where he saw the narrow stairs and set to climbing them with the speed of a cheetah.

"Mathieson!" Harjit shouted at him. *He has lost his mind,* she wondered. Harjit wanted to avoid panic, her eyes tracking his run like a guided missile. She needed to know where he was going for his own safety.

The steps inclined steeply upwards at sixty degrees from the side of the smaller entrances, just about where they had entered. In seconds, he had reached the top of this perfectly squared chamber. The chamber spanned the whole of that tier within the temple. Where he was running to had no barrier in place. Once more, this was an accident waiting to happen.

A fall could easily occur from the platform to the floor below. The American had to be very careful, Harjit was watching him anxiously while he continued his sprint energetically over on top of the platform that encircled each wall below it.

"Hey ya all!" An excited Mathieson called down to them. "There is some sort of lever up here!"

He had seen it at the end of this platform. It was an elongated bronze metal lever with a shaped grip. The dark-skinned man attempted to use all his strength to pull it down into himself but did not have the weight.

"Eeeyaaaa!" Mathieson screamed out in effort. First, he pulled and then pushed at the lever exerting as much force he could muster. It did not move an inch.

Mathieson was fit, very fit, but he had no real weight behind him. His physique let him down quickly as he shouted to the others for help.

Instantly, Cesare and Aléssandro obliged by springing into action and soon joined his renewed efforts. Their joint body weights and strengths gradually began to move the lever downwards. The lower it became the more smoothly it continued to move until finally it clicked firmly and securely into a fixed position at their feet.

Relegated to be only spectators, Harjit, Barbaro and Christopher looked up with waiting anticipation; anything could happen now. At last, the men finished struggling with the lever when a low grinding of stone on stone began to make its presence felt. Listening to the dry and gritty noises all around, the physical mechanics set numerous crescent shaped windows to open within the platform walls. The men on top were getting excited from looking through the spaces as they appeared. They had forgotten just how good it was to see outside when the grinding stopped.

"Look!" Harjit gasped. To see daylight through the newly formed crescent windows was a wonder of sunlight streaming in to meet them.

"The Sky!" called Christopher, "I see it!" smiling, his spirit lifting at even a glimpse.

Ironically, in minutes being at the Equator, everyone knew that this would be short lived as it was late in the afternoon and daylight could disappear any moment.

The *holy-stand* on the East wall for the moment was forgotten, except by Barbaro, the Vatican Official tip-toeing away and then speeding quickly towards it unseen by the others. Heading for the golden holy structure, he would be there in a minute.

"I can see the high tree tops in the distance across from the temple, I can almost touch them, man!" Triumphantly, Mathieson called down, adding to everyone's exhilaration.

Cesaré held the sides of the window and stared eagerly outside, then called to Harjit.

"Yeah, we are also about three hundred feet up above our campsite. It is just in my view and no more. There is a direct drop of thirty feet outside here!" He stared outward. The sides of the vale and surrounding jungle mass dwarfed the temple.

A rush of warm humid air could be heard clearly all around. It sucked inside, starting a mass movement of all the light cobwebs inside the chamber. The breeze quickly became stronger, wafting rhythmically through and channelling oxygen and life-giving air throughout the colossal structure. It felt good.

There were many unpleasant places deep inside where the rudimentary ventilation system travelled.

"I can just see the edge of camp!" Aléssandro shouted with renewed hope, the urge to escape from here intensifying inside him. He Stared outside like a prisoner in solitary confinement, ready to break out of jail through one of the crescent moon windows.

Others that had joined Mathieson were taking off their own white biohazard suits; they had enough too; dehydration would cause collapse.

"What will be, will be," said Harjit, watching helplessly and understanding because she too felt quite unwell inside her own suit.

"There must be other openings, come on!" Cesaré gestured to the other men and said, "Look over there, more levers!" Two at each end. "Let's go along all the walkways."

Jogging quickly around the distant walkways, they managed to open the second set of curved windows on the right half of the wall of the temple, this action allowed two open semi-circles to come miraculously together, forming a perfectly round window about twenty-one-inches in diameter!

"Fine idea, man!" Mathieson swept long strands of remaining web away as the men opened each of the other sets of windows in turn.

The men's higher vantage points and extra illumination did not help much in trying to gauge the immensity and magnitude of the chamber that was all covered in web, making them quite obscure. They could not see it all, the place below was in complete shambles. Inside were many parallel long rows of wasted and hacked up stone sitting benches. The benches all lied in ruins, and oddly, the cobwebs were vibrant and shaking in the incoming moist breeze.

Solid stone pillars held the ceiling up and were secured high above them. It was not easy to observe between the swaying web. The airflow caused their changeable vision and could see the distant holy stand over on the east wall.

Mathieson watched, *that little bastard Barbaro is running over there!* The ranger saw him getting completely covered in sticky web and darting away from the group.

In the foreground underneath them lay a shattered and broken front row of seats, once used for an assembly of some kind. It was too difficult to see clearly because moving blankets of cobwebs kept obscuring their view in every direction.

With only minutes to go before sunset, the Sun's profile shone inside through a flawlessly formed round stone window into the temple. This window was formed by the creation of two half-moon shapes that had joined ritualistically in union of sun and moon, and as the last embers burned through in deep orange, its roasting tone shined in parallel through every other window and lit the chamber.

In those closing moments, the light unexpectedly cracked open and sunlight split apart, instantly separating into its component frequencies. This split light transcended seamlessly through the temple's weaved webbed curtains, showing it as an amazing symphony of fine rainbow colours. Their eyes stared widely in amazement at this effect and its beauty.

During the light works display, the outer stonewall window acted like a mask or a filter letting in only God's last rays of sunlight, creating many singular split beams. It seemed like magic, when the sun-moon beam shapes began forming into many small energetic crescent moons, all seen floating, some waning and others waxing and all moving smoothly in time and inwards towards the holy stand to the east.

Watching with awe, everyone's faces looked utterly astonished, their disbelief grew at this grand paradox of extraordinary proportions created in a lunar display of sunlight. What a vision! What a spectacle!

Mixed in between the myriad of colours, a display of numerous moons began being strangely generated into hologram-like entities with lunar surfaces, all floating in the chamber space like fleeting ghosts. Watching them going in and out and drifting through the dusty webs, it all seemed too crazy to take in. These moon spirits converged with a fatal sense of purpose over at the pulpit stand, and began swirling about this intricate shaped holy place. Its short steep steps lead up to a large illuminated silvery disc.

At this moment, sun-setting light kept streaming in through the geometrically positioned central moon window, and when the setting sun had lined up perfectly, it shone through into the temple. Its deep orange sunglow energies touched the silver disc, beginning to transform it into a molten mix of metal of silvery-orange kicking off a chain reaction. Holding their breaths, everyone watched it with glued eyes, seeing its magical molten fluidity all contained inside the illuminated disc.

Impossible, the people were completely stunned witnessing this. *Alchemy! What a wonder! What a Godly design!*

"My Lord, what is going on here, this is all too impossible!" Christopher was mesmerized looking at the media man standing right next to it. "Barbaro, what's he doing over there?" His tone drifted in suspicion.

Like the soulless paparazzi media machine, Barbaro had already started taking copious camera shots of the rainbow moon crescents merging and becoming a whole entity. Where white light intensified, it magnified its energies onto the close by precious, silver orange disc.

"It must be an optical illusion," Barbaro said speaking to himself, his breathing laboured with camera excitement, taking another and another, snap, snap, snap!

No sooner had his words of disbelief been spoken from his twisted lips, the molten disc burst into unexpected life. The disc was holding inside it a pure raw energy, and like a build-up of magma reflecting its energies with the anger of a Volcano, it was ready to blow.

Suddenly a jet of roaring flames came blurting out of it, jetting forward in a violent stream with short ragged edges like a huge flame-thrower, quickly roasting a straight path right through the chamber in an unstoppable tunnel of fire, instantly disintegrating any web mass in its path.

Everyone shouted and jumped back in surprise. The group wondered what was going on as the surrounding web drapes near the flames immediately caught fire, melting them into separate floating fires and long draping tatters.

The webbed veil melted so easily, and opening like a hot poker passing through candyfloss, its putrid smell of denatured protein burned while its deadly flames kept clearing a relentless path. Reeking smoke trails of webbed wipe out all seen and smelled by everyone, the flames left havoc in their wake. Then the flames suddenly stopped, and the violence was over. Strangely, Harjit thought it looked like an escape tunnel.

"Shit ma black Ass, man," Mathieson stated bluntly in monotone, the man surprised, his face a picture, as he and others with him could only watch the silky ignition.

Barbaro was so close to the focal conflagration and dangerously too close to danger that the flames blasted past suddenly, stopping him from taking any more photographs and stunting him into inaction. Falling backwards away from the intense heat scorching over him, his expensive camera dropped hard and slid across the floor.

Pity that, smiled Mathieson.

Besides seeing the horror of the spent flames and its path conflagrating everything, the already amazing light display inside the chamber began to create a new phenomenon, projecting a circle of rainbow colours onto the northern wall. This action highlighted another mysterious area with a pointed archway set into it. Another complete enigma! Then, nothing about the temple of MalisIblis seemed in harmony. An unbalance of nature seemed everywhere, and everything inside it was an extreme.

"Chris, are we delirious?" asked Harjit while watching the spectacle. "Is it really happening to me, *to us?*" Harjit questioned her own sanity and reality. "If this is not true, then have we been drugged? Maybe there is something floating inside the ventilation system, a hallucinogen?" Harjit replied lost between the choices, "My God, the masks, we should have kept them on." Shocked with a dawning dread, her words remained a verdict. Harjit's mind tried to work it out.

That's it, but the symptoms presenting themselves are beyond imagination. The vector, the transport agent...is the dust and air moving inside the ventilation system? Possibly a microbial infection! The girl debated quietly to herself. *Unlikely, simply because we are wearing these suits, our masks, and yet it is still possible if the particles are smaller than bacteria, this, whatever it is, is able, to pass through the mask filters... it's a Viriod, it must be! And yet, everyone is seeing the exact same hallucination!*

"This place is awful, we have to get out."

Christopher was about to speak more, but she cut him off, the girl intent on a logical explanation.

"A Virus, or, maybe a human Viriod like hepatitis B," Harjit spoke aloud while analysing their common symptoms, focusing on this more than what was really happening. Christopher listened closely to Harjit's paralyzing fears, "These masks would keep out Bacteria, yes, but, not... not," the girl stammered. "Not a Viriod! That must be it! My God, Chris these suits are useless."

"Steady Harj, I do not believe it. These masks would keep out anything. And listen to me, we still have ours on."

"A Viriod Chris! It is a fucking Viriod! Smaller than a virus, usually affect plants but it is possible some affect humans, those could penetrate these filters. I'm sure of it!" Harjit's voice cursed in a muffled lament.

"If this is true then why do we all see the same goddamn hallucination? I tell you Harjit, what you are witnessing is all too real!"

Sensing her impending panic, the girl's mind was set to overload at all the impossibility around her. Chris watched her confusion in helplessness and hopelessness. It touched his heart seeing Harjit's tears welling inside her round goggles. Deeply concerned for her, the young man held onto her arm, squeezing it gently.

****

Everyone re-focused their attention onto this new development at the north wall where rainbow colours were forming and highlighting a pointed archway. They cumulated into a brightening halo.

It was obvious to them now that an arch was located there, realising that it must be another place of sacred prayer, a *mihrab*!

"What a place! What a wonder!" Aléssandro shouted, overawed at the holy site and chain reaction of events. The phenomenal lighting effect produced by this mysterious halo materialised around the *mihrab*. Unbelievably, all this creation took only a few seconds!

When all these reactions were happening, everyone watched and were incapable of any decisions. Barbaro was transfixed, frozen in fear, lucky to have lived, reminding him of the ill-fated doctor's demise. He might have suffered the same fate of his dead colleague Beppi Genovesi, the man who had been sacrificed at the temple entrance; he had simply burst into flames!

Barbaro feared being the next victim, being so close to the conflagration passing en-route to the illuminating disc. His body began shaking, yet he had no intentions of suffering like Beppi. Barbaro tried to control himself, struggling up to his feet.

The fierce flames lasted only seconds and had scorched past him only a metre or two away, leaving the web-wrap melting off him, his skin instantly heating, and his sooty white suit smouldered too. Getting up slowly, he staggered away, yet, rather than bolt from here in mindless retreat as if touched by some derangement, Barbaro did the opposite by picking up his camera and, unbelievably, taking more pictures. Like a man possessed he wanted evidence of this magnificent manifestation. Only one problem.

"Look at this...it must be God's work," whispered Barbaro to himself and clicking his camera. *"Oh no, its broken!"* The man realised and said loudly, his temperature rising while fumbling and attempting to turn on his spare camcorder. Barbaro gasped, desperately moving its switch which, using ill-fitting gloves, was not an easy task. Suddenly, he heard a solid whirring noise as it sounded into action.

"Si! Si! Here goes!" His eyes lighting in excitement, shouting over to the others. "Would you all look at this?" He turned and saw them on top of the platform. He had worked hard to capture this unique lighting exhibition when, the whir had stopped. His heart dropped. "God, no!" He instantly knew his video recorder was dead.

Electronics were not suited for harsh environments like these, especially inside the temple. Barbaro's face was mortified. The man cursed profusely because the scoop of the century would all come to nothing.

"Now, there is a nice picture," commented Mathieson, grinning gleefully.

"Christ, it is ruined," Barbaro growled under his accursed breath.

****

Keep it together, thought Harjit, the girl digging deeply to find renewed strength from within her shredded nerves of miscomprehension. It had been Christopher's warm touch. She steadied herself and was good.

"Phew! This is something else, Christopher," said Harjit, observing the reporter's strange antics in the distance, *is he going mad* she wondered? Harjit held onto her sanity and felt her responsibilities return; others needed her. "We must leave here, right now."

Barbaro, embroiled in the middle of these unnatural events unfolding before them, watched the man run blindly, panicking from being all wrapped in new webs.

Barbaro spoke in gasps, "I do, not, like this." Something inside him halted; a sudden instinct that changed his messed-up mind. He lost it, screaming, "This is beyond God, it's the Devil's work, it can only be… *il demonio!*"

Suddenly, survival became instinctive. Barbaro started running away and was almost blinded in webs, but alive, he re-joined Harjit and Christopher, but her attention moved from him to another event taking place over in the great hall.

Their eyes became hypnotically transfixed onto it, the north wall where the halo started changing its appearance.

"Awe," Chris groaned. "How can this be?" He said, fearing something new.

"Use the rope," ordered Harjit. "We can get out, use the rope." Her tense tone drove her logic of simple escape.

"Eh?" Barbaro looked up desperately at the windows above the platforms, disaster foregathering in his mind. To him, the windows were the obvious choice too.

"We can get out from the window, come on!" Harjit called and led the group.

When unprepared, the sunset ended, plunging the forest into complete darkness and stopping them in their tracks. With no natural light coming in, the mysterious floating moon shapes disappeared too. Yet, the craziness never stopped, it changed and got crazier.

Over at the north wall and in defiance of natural law, the halo grew brighter by the second, its importance drawing their undivided attention over to it. Its aura increasing out of control. To their utter horror, this unexplainable power began pulsating like a beacon, when unexpectedly the pulpit began blaring blinding luminosity outwards to warn them.

Their escape stopped to take stock of what was going on. The energised chamber had become so complex, because now, there were multiple places of energised holiness; to the east, the pulpit, and to the north, the mihrab. They all knew this was no random occurrence either, it had to be gearing up for some cataclysmic event. At this moment the pulpit seemed esoterically super-active.

"This is real! It must be real! It is happening, Harjit! Are we too late to get out?" Asked Christopher, speaking in an accelerated tone and his hope fading fast. He knew something bad was about to happen. They needed to leave by some other way.

The other men joining Harjit, Barbaro and Chris. The whole group watched, horrified together, seeing all these colours unquestionably.

Tightening their sore eyes staring at the furious flames. Each nerve seemed severed, each brain cell fried and every neuron flat-lined into paralysed axiom inactivity. Stunned, their brains tried to make sense of the impossible.

Their choices were slim, stuck between reflex and self-preservation. Helpless to stop anything, each person was acutely anxious to what might happen next. Everything seemed so hopeless and any run for the moon shaped windows was already too late. There would be no escape.

****

Minutes before the onslaught of pandemonium, and as the last rays of sunlight burned brightly, a quiet fear subdued the rainforest. The land waited on the verge of something major. Nothing stirred, leaving an eerily and unsettling silence. Outside the temple, only the high waterfalls could be keenly heard through the trees. At this moment, the MalisIblis Vale became the loneliest place in the world.

When night came, Mashir had remained at base camp in preparation and planned a possible rescue of Fabio and Harjit's exploratory teams. Sebastiano and Mykola had not gone inside the temple and had felt a dread, sensing something was not right on the terraces.

Casting their distrustful eyes over its black shadows and murky shades of stone, somewhere up there, an unspeakable terror lurked. Its steep walls threatened everything, its structure dwarfed everything, and imposed its dominance onto everything, the temple's consciousness affected, everything.

Walking anxiously along the treeline perimeter path, the two men sensed something following them, and no matter how many times they turned to check, the feeling remained. With not much else to do but circle the temple and think, they questioned the merits of those who had gone inside to explore and those who were already dead, while their fearful eyes flicked in between stone, shadow and tree moving from one threat to the next. Totally spooked, danger seemed everywhere.

Heading back to base camp, they felt the dark shadows following them, the men's silent thoughts of deep doubt and regrets were lost between threat of danger from the temple to the trees. Surrounded by the unknown, fear fragmented their minds into shards of lunacy and despair. Their aimless conversations made little relief, each one not the first to think it, *was this how the insanity began?*

Restless excitement nipped at their exposed nerves, the men knowing that their companions were still inside that place. Tense as a scream, they hoped that a new dawn would come quickly, and with it, new hope. The others would return. Troubled doubts told them this would be a long night. Wearied and forlorn both men felt the same unabated and unnamed fear, listening to this hushed silence. The forest was waiting for something. The last rays of sunlight had just gone, leaving a land of darkness.

Sebastiano stopped. Mykola stopped too. Sebastiano's muscles stiffened, his face the same, wooden.

Mykola swallowed thickly, his eyes fixed firmly onto his companion.

It was then they heard something that defied nature, something unmistakable; the sounds of sucking air coming from somewhere that were strangely felt from above. Suddenly, air movement started all around them. The jungle's outer perimeter's trimmed edge gave the men no feeling of safety or sanctuary; they were caught between the untamed and unexplained.

Feeling the atmosphere pressing directly onto a pressure point below their ears, their heads turned uncannily to look upwards at the temple, as if it wanted them to see it. Their blood pressures began pumping like steam engines and both men knew something was badly wrong. Then at that second, everything transformed.

In an almighty explosion, orange light shaped moons curved by the open stone windows were sent blasting outwards from the high walls of the temple. Orange moon beams were seen instantly shot in a line into the jungle in a weird spectacle like an apocalyptic rock show and erupted. What they were witnessing conflicted against all nature.

"God, what is happening?" Sebastiano crouched, trying to hide.

"Only the Devil knows this," said Mykola.

The jungle instantly reacted when suddenly birds started taking to the wing and sent themselves launching away in terror. Manic monkeys began screeching and jumping about as their own madness took hold. Whole communities of animals wailed and screamed at this spectacle. Nature vented its pain.

The curved moon beams shot with laser precision, suddenly and simultaneously angling upwards as if directed into the equatorial night sky; the first sign that something new had happened. How could this be?

All hell let loose when a mass of cataclysmic animal activity ignited. Unseen feral noises abruptly deafened them from all around, the men staring wildly at the savage jungle, not knowing where to look next.

"This place is fucking nuts. Wow, look at that!" Screamed Mykola, taking another pace backwards, not quite knowing whether to run or hide.

"What have they done?" Sebastiano reproached the missing exploratory team, "What have those fuckers been getting up to inside there to have caused this?"

"We must go and let Mashir know what is going on. Come on!" With panic in their paces they started running. Mashir would know what to do. Rounding the corner of the temple, they could see base camp. Dismay gripped their hearts and the closer they got, the more dread they felt because the campsite was unexpectedly in complete darkness.

"That's fucking odd, we have only been away a couple of hours." Said Sebastiano. They had left to take measurements around the perimeter leaving Mashir praying. Mashir prayed a lot.

"What is going on at camp?" Asked Mykola.

"Unusual, the campfire should be burning and the lamps on," Sebastiano warned, while breathing heavily. No warning required, both men's suspicions were raised and they dread that something else had happened.

"Surely he hears all this commotion? Must have! Shit Seb, something is seriously wrong!" Said Mykola, catching his breath.

A few minutes more and they had arrived, and a complete and quick search revealed nothing. There was no sign of the surveyor anywhere. Base camp was deserted.

"Mashir! Mashir! Where are you?" Mykola called out against the jungle din. "Fanculo," he cursed. "Where is he?" said Mykola. Like a magician's trick, Mashir had disappeared. "Where has he gone!" Mykola's face was sharp with urgency.

"I know! I know! Look around, I'll check his tent!" Sebastiano said, as a lack of self-control became imprinted on his face, while his head shook quickly. A minute later, Seb spoke nervously to Mykola.

"Well?" Asked Mykola.

"Myk, his kit, his rucksack, his clothes, boots, everything, are all gone!" Sebastiano's staggered speech held unease, while wiping away the sweat from his brow, the man bewildered.

"What do you mean gone, gone where?" Mykola was baffled.

"Gone, I mean gone, completely gone!" Sebastiano irritated with Myk's stupidity.

"Ugh?" He made a noise as a nervous itch sunk in, moving from Mykola's head to his bristle moustache.

"Deserted," said Sebastiano making the sign of the cross. "God help him if he has wandered off. No one goes just wandering into the jungle at night. People get lost only to be found dead miles from safety. What are we going to do now?"

"Well, Mashir looked perfectly calm earlier on when I saw him. Maybe he developed jungle fever by himself. You know, the same thing that took hold of Carmello? He went Cuckoo."

"No wonder, look! Those mad lights coming from the temple. This place is crazy!" He gasped for breath again. "Maybe he got scared and that's why he ran off leaving the camp unprotected? Or he's been taken." Sebastiano contemplated the worst.

"Taken? You mean, kidnapped?" Gasped Mykola.

"No. Remember, there is a murderer at large," said Sebastiano, his eyes studying the wall of darkness next to him.

"Head hunters!" Mykola said, raising his voice over the jostling of foliage and flapping in the gathering breeze.

"I hope you are wrong, I really do," said Mykola. "Mashir is fanatical about praying. He does it at least five times a day. Maybe he's gone up there, you know, up to the temple." Nodding his head to the floodlit monstrosity, his face portrayed a certain degree of insanity. Watching as this weird rock-show continued above them, its unnatural light erupted from the temple like a gigantic lighthouse or beacon! Its purpose was unknown. For all they knew, the temple could have been a colossal light flare to be seen from the stars or a warning from the past.

"My God, look at that!" Called Sebastiano while pausing for breath yet marvelling at the craziness. "Yeah, Mashir would do that! He would go it alone. I know it, I know him. That mad Bastardo is foolish enough. A hero type and nothing like a bloody surveyor!" Sebastiano's eyes were glued onto the temple's mayhem.

"It does not make sense, none of it, and to go it alone. Christ, nothing in this forsaken place makes sense anymore," said Mykola, his head nipping with uncertainty.

Mykola was jealous of Mashir, holding some secret resentment because the Iranian was a man that he could never be. Mashir was fit, smart and had a sense of courage, or was it more foolhardiness? Mykola was not too sure but the man had qualities he would never come close to and the last thing Mykola would admit to was that he needed him.

"Shit...remember...that's it!" Sebastiano called out. "He mentioned it before! He said that he wanted to pray inside that bloody building." An agitated Sebastiano scratched deep into his thick wavy hair. Insects buzzed around his face, annoying him even more and with a beaten feeling of helplessness, he said, "I wish we were not here, Myk." His chipped front tooth was exposed in an awkward smile. "Ouch!" He said, while swiping furiously at the airborne pests.

"It is not exactly Kaaba in Mecca is it? And how the hell a Muslim got on this trip, is anyone's guess!" said Mykola, attempting to make the leap of faith to conceive the basic idea that Mashir might even think to treat the temple like a mosque. He always suspected that Mashir did have some weird ideas.

"What kind of a temple does that anyhow? If he is up there, look at the place, its lit up like a fucking firework! I don't fancy his chances much. It can't be a temple, or not one as we know it." Sebastiano stated grimly.

"What is it then?" Mykola's face was drawn in fear. "And what about the others, what about them?" His tone accelerated.

Staring up to the entrance high above, their eyes were greeted only with darkness and light, both looking stupefied and with inconsistent curiosity, twisting their faces at it with dread. Minds reeling at the craziness, the deaths, the hopelessness each man suspected that Mashir would not return. One other question remained, what had happened to the others?

****

Back inside the temple, they must escape. The sun had not long set. The men who had been on the overhead platforms were together with Harjit and the others. Noticeably, everyone breathed heavily with exertion while staring around, madness filling their fraught minds with sickening apprehension. They wanted to live. They wanted to survive this impossible ordeal, but fate or luck would depend on a tumble of the dice.

The group looked distantly towards the Mihrab at the north wall, a place of sacred prayer. The Mihrab lit differently, its pulsating halo transforming as one with a single large beam of solitary moonlight shining and coming in from outside through the central moon window.

Each person stared at the brightly lit place of worship. It had much more to give, containing a potential unspent like a lit fuse on its way to explode or maybe give an answer to its purpose.

The moon had risen into the black sky above the superstructure, casting a subdued silvery shimmer over the rest of the rainforest. Its atmospheric influence could be felt near and far. Its lunar surfaces peeking above the treetops and building, everything outside alight in a spectral shine.

The temple moonlight dominated, and apart from the uncanny light effects beaming out from its windows, it sent its magical light energies over the facing forest and into the sky seen by those sheltering in the campsite. This mysterious light from the temple suddenly and sharply angled steeply upwards away from the forest and into the heavens.

Scientifically, moonlight did not normally transmit the same light energy as the Sun. Its brightness was normally only a reflection. Absolutely nothing was normal about this place, nor the single beam of moonlight shining its lunar light energies onto the Mihrab at the north wall.

Harjit felt a warning inside her, she instinctively turned to look and narrowed her eyes in the hope of seeing better, when the moon started transposing miraculously and transforming its lunar light onto something else, a new creation that was slowly formed into a haunted image of a full moon with its crater pock marked and its face staring directly back at them from the Mihrab. The light intensified in luminosity. The group watched the spectral moon face blending in and out the round surface of the Mihrab's golden disc, reforming it into a final image, and what they saw now, defied all laws of physics. They could not believe it was coming face to face with a fable.

A large golden skull!

"Is this true! Is this for real?" Said Aléssandro calling out. "Oh my God, it is the lost seven rays!" Aléssandro stood aghast. He knew it instantly. Fabio had described it so many times to him, Brazil's inheritance, its rightful legacy, *the key of the gods of the seven rays* had returned.

"This is impossible," Harjit said, witnessing the evidence appearing before them.

"The professor has been right all along!" Confirmed Aléssandro with renewed vigour and confidence in his mentor's teachings.

"Take a picture Barbaro! Quick!" Aléssandro shouted aloud but the media man was inconsolable at another missed opportunity because, as fate would have it, his camera was broken.

Here for this moment, and after all these centuries, *the seven rays* were found again. Unmistakably seen with its skeletal deep eye sockets and jaw right in front of them, a legend had become reality.

"My heavens," said Christopher, nearly speechless. The chamber around them energized with untamed raw power. Everyone beheld the truth that in the Temple of MalisIblis lay the key to the gods!

"From Peru to this temple, here the legend ends." Aléssandro could not hold back, and called out, "So, it is true, it is real!" Aléssandro's eyes were more alive now than they had ever been. "I wish Professor Mancini were here to see it!"

"I wish he were too," said Harjit solemnly, stating her admiration for the professor's knowledge.

"This disc, as legend would have it, is an escape route and conduit to the world of gods!" Said Aléssandro, his voice thrilled to bits.

"Pity, and I thought it would be made of gold," said Mathieson disappointed, thinking more of a world of riches.

"Look we need to get out of here right now," said Christopher desperately staring around and at their deteriorating predicament. Everyone else was watching this awesome spectacle. They needed to move.

They could see that the thick curtain of web among the clouded chamber had been severed, giving them a direct escape route. They had been permitted to go to another part of the chamber. It appeared that there were powers at work inside the temple. For an unknown purpose, the key of gods by design, had allowed this possibility of escape, to where? Nobody knew, but it was their fate to find out.

The prophecy would be fulfilled.

Salutations from God gone, it was time to get out of here! God's key was not enough. In these quiet few seconds nobody spoke, everyone listened to unsettling sounds coming from inside the chamber. At first, there was a rumour or a suggestion of a sound, not quite there, not quite audible but yes, there it was again.

Unnerving noises came from all around and were very difficult to hear but it was their path, unmistakably soft rustlings heard by all, reminding them of long water reeds or grasses swishing endlessly back and forth in a summer's breeze, calming and yet inside this place, unsettling. What could it be?

Sighing gently, the group wanted to get away, yet they needed to know more. Everyone waiting transfixed and almost willing for nothing else to happen. Hoping against this quiet menace that it might only be in their imaginations, and who could blame them? Watching each other with unspoken solace, and maybe, just maybe, this time nothing else would happen; sadly, they were wrong about that.

When sounds came to them, noises like leaves rustling in a light breeze through bushes began drifting more throughout the webbed spaces, and a hushed movement could just be detected, wafting gently throughout and disturbing the unnatural peace. Their eyes looked upwards in dismay, Harjit watching circumspectly, fear flickering awkwardly between her and the others, then fixing onto Christopher's. Multiple movements and badness headed their way, reminding them of something unknown, a danger not seen before would not remain hidden much longer. Still, they wanted to forget and ignore it, but knew they could not. And, there it was again! It had not gone away.

Unquestionably, everyone knew something unseen was approaching and now self-denial was not an option, not anymore. Yet without saying so, they wondered questionably what to do next and their panic-stricken eyes anchoring onto their leader Harjit. The girl also looked for an answer, and if there was any doubt...*there, it was again!* The noise came again, stronger and clearer and closer this time. Within earshot there was a disturbed quiet stirring across the whole of the chamber. An invisible menace moving inexorably against them.

"What is that?" Barbaro fearfully looked around. "Mathieson, can you hear that noise?"

"Steady men," Harjit's tone was firm and clear, controlled.

"Calm yourself B," ordered Mathieson, not looking at the media man who was also struggling to keep a level head, the ranger's bravado face failing and falling short, his crazed eyes scanning directly above him for danger.

Something was about to happen and of that everyone was in no doubt, the humidity inside intensified, the temple challenging nature once again.

Harjit knew this location was too vulnerable. She sighed hard knowing that they had to leave here right away but instinctively, she waited staring like the others, upwards, when her face began twisting in revulsion.

The girl could not see the stone ceiling above, due to an uncountable mass of dark fidgety shapes moving all over the web folds stretching across the entire expanse of the chamber!

The copious web drapes above them had been unveiled from the darkness by being exposed in this weird illumination, but not the multitudes of undefined shapes inside it, mainly hidden within the smoky clouds of webbed candyfloss. On the move, swathes of vague shapes were busily creating numerous opaque shadows in mixed-up masses that were becoming more and more defined, an increasing mass of crawling things, all moving over each other.

Then, without warning, some started jumping and swinging crazily behind the veils closest to them. Creatures hectically knitted new nets at incredible speeds. In a short moment, the blanket had dropped substantially lower towards them and Harjit realised that very soon it would capture them all.

"Look up," her voice tightly controlled, watching them heave closer above.

The others suddenly gripped in paralysed fear as they watched these small horrors, about the size of flattened tennis balls, dropping further down the web. Many swung and extended loosely on long elasticated webbed strands, uncountable others crawled up into a heavier part of the webbed honeycomb where something else was happening.

Horrified, the group identified a moveable madness going on above them as more and more bodies seemed to be pouring out from somewhere and sinking into the shadowy veil. The web cloud was quickly getting heavier and more pregnant as its weight and mass increased, bulging its volume. Their black bodies blotted out the bright Moonlight from outside the temple, breaking the explorer's only hope with reality.

Simultaneously the holy seat started losing its energy, dulling down. Alarmingly, unless they escaped, it would all end here. They had walked right into a trap. Their mortified faces were stuck in horror, the group seeing millions of what looked like spiders purposely crawling downwards to get them.

Uncannily, these minions seemed to wait for a moment, almost hesitating as if thinking about it, before moving again and again, weaving and scurrying around before stopping to cognate or maybe even question at their quarry and then again bursting into fervid over-activity. Every time like a heave, in a sudden motion, each time getting closer, and at this rate, Harjit reckoned that they would be completely smothered in a few minutes.

"Look at their long fat bodies," said Christopher surprised. "They are breathing rhythmically as one, all in time and tempo, breathing like one large organism. That is so odd. Each individual is in complete communication with the other!" Christopher's mind was working, trying to understand.

"Oh my God, are those things intelligent?" Barbaro exclaimed.

"They seemed to be planning," Chris agreed.

"Bloody spiders' man, masses of the mothers!" Stated Mathieson, watching the peril. His head and body were already covered in parts with this dark grey sticky web from cutting screeds away from the walkways.

As a tough boy and from Detroit professional guide, spiders were an everyday occurrence to him. These ones he had never seen before and knew they were not indigenous. How Cesaré would react, was anyone's guess.

Mathieson knew that these were also likely to be poisonous.

Some had already reached the floor by now and were quickly crawling all over the entrance from where they had entered. The girl was unsure what to do now, realising there could be no escape back that way. Cut off, these spiders kept on coming in waves, their bustling bodies dropping all around and onto the floor, running crazily or springing towards them.

"Right, follow me!" The Scotsman called at the group. "Over there! Over there!" He shouted desperately, "Come on, head for the light over to the north wall!" They all looked at him a little hesitantly not quite knowing what he had in mind. Nobody moved.

"Follow Christopher if you want to keep breathing!" Harjit said, commanding their obedience.

What choice did they have? Already multitudes of hairy bodies were overflowing off the overhead platforms and onto the floor, and some were precariously swinging already too close to their heads.

Oddly, they swung like clock pendulums using their tiny legs to catch or attempt a *monkey jump* at them, so strange that flying motion appeared, which allowed the spiders to travel great distances. In the short time since their first whisper of presence, the chamber was overrun with bristling bodies.

Everyone suddenly spurned into action, moving quickly, hunching awkwardly as some of these menaces detached which forced them to duck and dip to avoid the hunters' nets!

Christopher began running on while swishing furiously with his sharp double-edged sword, the blade cutting any remaining parts of the old webbed canopy not destroyed by the hot fireworks. But this silk cloud above was beginning to descend above the long and scorched pathway. Unbelievably these creatures were attempting to bar their escape. The others right behind him full-pelt sprinted towards the Mihrab, believing somehow that Christopher must have seen another way out. They knew that he had a plan.

Christopher's route was clear and open in his mind, passionately slicing with his sword on his way, continually cutting in smooth sweeps where any new web formation had reformed. It was tricky and dangerous, but his smooth motions began killing lots of spiders.

Their strange bodies popped in contact with the blade, instantly disintegrating them easily, while releasing a light powder or dust off from its outer casing while bursting out a gutsy black fluid and disgusting odour.

All the time, multitudes of Spiders inexorably chased after them. Each on them like a heat seeking missile hot on their trail.

Driving on, each person shouted crazy warnings to each other, their danger magnified when those pests began firing a thick smelly liquid at them! These spidery creatures with ugly yellow striped bodies, were all pulsating and rippling with a hateful excitement. Each with peculiar deep evil blue eyes watching them, all hungry to feast.

It was more difficult in the darkness like this but battle axe-wielding Mathieson, his face set with purpose and like a man possessed, kept moving forward faster and was now in front of Christopher, thrashing wildly at the spiders that were blocking their escape.

"Aaaagh!" Matt screamed defiance, popping and bursting them, left and right, up and down clearing the way. Already it felt that this fight for survival had gone on forever, but really it had taken only a few minutes to get to the far north wall.

Once here, it found them all standing directly in front of a ten-foot-tall pointed solid archway and richly coloured Mihrab. Its solid silver styled banding trailed around the high arch with gold metal staccato markings covered within its silver tramline. Fraught looks of misgivings suddenly dawned on everyone, each with a crazed bewilderment. They had made it. Right in front of them was *the Key of the Gods of the Seven Rays*, its golden disc and skull face in moonshine staring creepily back at them. Everyone stood desperately looking at its mystery and looked for the way out. There was none.

Dead end…

What were they to do now? They had reached this enchanted place and could see nothing and nowhere to go. With no way out, everyone turned and stared at Christopher, wondering, *why?*

The flames had gone out, allowing their run to get here, and the only light inside the chamber now came from its own sources of godly illumination and the rapidly diminishing moonlight.

The net closed in with multitudes of these menacing creatures scurrying and getting nearer to them, then quickly running over their boots. Some began sticking like glue onto their ankles and legs. Everyone kicked out in horror, panicking and breathing heavily with exertion. They couldn't kick them off. Soon it felt like standing in a fast-flowing dark river of crawling insects.

Mathieson started screaming.

Harjit began screaming.

Cesaré and Aléssandro screamed too.

Barbaro screamed loudest!

All screamed at each other. Their minds could not take much more, all becoming giddy in the surging flow of bodies. The whole chamber heaved with these unholy creatures.

"Shit, don't let any those mother's bite you, man!" warned Mathieson, who had already had taken off his protective suit earlier, feeling more vulnerable.

"Where are we to go!?" Barbaro shouted out, the man petrified but the closeness of newly created web damping down his voice.

"Wooooah!" Mathieson called out, his face sharp with urgency, while he looked around the area as his keen sharpness became blunt in recursive dismay. There really was no escape. Questionably, he darted a quick look at the Scotsman, "You brought us here mother, now get us fucking out!"

"This is a place of prayer," Harjit spoke fearfully, her frightened eyes peering back into the dingy darkness.

There was nothing back there, except for the heaving masses swinging on newly formed web drapes. Their situation grave, with the last energy of light coming from the eastern pulpit, the holy stand. Web already blocked any return, the pulpit only a vague shape made out through the newly webbed tapestry, with its solid gold metal steps sticking from the wall, the holy stand remained to be seen, and gave off some energy. In the semi-darkness, they felt hairy bodies crawling onto and over them. Everyone shrieked. It would be over soon.

****

"What next? You told us to follow you!" Said Cesaré shouting, while slapping spiders away. He would not stop calling at Christopher like a crazy man, "My God, you really have no idea!" He saw Christopher's confusion, "Why, Chris why?" but the scientist had no answers. "Chris, I am speaking to you!" Exasperated, he got no answers, fearfully turning to look for guidance from the others.

In the terrifying torch light, nausea came over him as their blank faces confirmed there was no hope, when suddenly Cesaré started screaming and jumping uncontrollably about from spiders running up his back. Cesaré's phobia of spiders terrorised him! Never the less, their end would all be the same, when like some insane red Indian war dance, everyone began yelling and stamping madly on top of the scurrying vermin! Harjit's expedition was overwhelmed, everyone was trapped.

Christopher thought frantically, he could not understand his urge to come to this place. *Why have I run here? Why here, I do not know. Lord, where else do I go? Help us Lord,* and in his shredded mind, he remembered his old friend Mashir's favourite quote:

"*All is as God wills it, my friend, even unto death*".

Christopher knew already that they could not have stayed where they had been either, it had already been engulfed. If they had stayed there, they would be dead. This run had given them a valuable second of extra life. *Why Lord!* They stood here at an impasse with nowhere else to run. He had bought them that extra time, not much, but maybe just enough.

Being judged by the others, his involuntary action had spurned him to take that leap of faith to get here with their predicament being critical. Yet, something told him that they still had a fighting chance. What about God's key? Why had it appeared? He needed to know the answer, but he could not think!

Without warning, Christopher aimed a slap at the screaming Cesaré, striking him with a light smack at the top of his head, its impact bringing him out of his madness. Cesare winced and instantly stopped screaming at this unprovoked attack. He could not believe that Christopher had slapped him.

Is he insane? Has he flipped! Thought Cesaré, hurting and raising a fist in retaliation. They were now fighting amongst themselves, it was all falling apart.

Harjit snapped, "No, Cesaré! He hit that spider off your head!" Cesaré looked at her shocked, then down at the little horror.

Suddenly Cesaré became unhinged, the man's legs trembled and screamed at anything and hit out at everything. It made no difference because more and more of the yellow striped bodies began falling off from his wiggling shoulders.

Unseen by Christopher, a spider came swinging on a long length of web straight at him. He turned too late. The biotechnologist could not avoid it because simultaneously two others were flying in on either side of his head.

"Aaah!" Chris screamed out, the two went passing only inches from him. He then saw another coming right in front with its vicious little mandibles opening. Unexpectedly, a swishing noise came down right in front of his face, blurring his vision, and instantly taking the vermin away.

"Gotcha mother!" Mathieson's battle axe had swiftly cut the small flying creature in mid-flight, its horrible fluid bursting over Christopher's goggles. The heavy blade missed him only by a few inches as the fast axe head travelled past him in a downward curve!

"Shit," Chris cursed, yet relieved. His life was saved by the American.

"Come on you bare arsed Scotsman! You got us in this shit-hole now get us the fuck out!" Mathieson demanded more from him.

"Si, you idiot Christopher, do something quick!" Barbaro screamed while glaring spite at the scientist. Barbaro felt two things, anger and hatred towards Christopher. The media man dwelled on him…*it is not meant to happen this way!* Barbaro started kicking four or five spiders away that were crawling on his boots and legs, knowing that the newfound wealth inside the temple was slipping quickly from his grasp. His material thoughts of gaining everything were gone, his mind festering more, *bloody killed in a forgotten temple! No one will ever know or find me. I am never going to be powerful or rich after all! What a fool I've been too trusting of that idiot, Christopher!*

There was no doubt, Barbaro held deep resentment towards the priest, bitten to death in his moments of life.

Anger welled inside Christopher too, but even that seemed as pointless as hope. Chris ignored the insults coming in at him from all angles. Right now, he had more to worry about than dodging insults. Christopher knew that his life was on a timer and on a countdown; he began a silent prayer.

Staring hard at the golden skull inside the Mihrab within its open mouth, Christopher observed something vague. He was not quite sure what he saw within its shifting holographic silvery moon face, images moved in and out of dimensions when at this second of ethereal transposition, there inside its golden jaw he could clearly see something definitive. Swallowing hard, he dared to believe.

My God, something's in there? Yes! Christopher's heart missed a beat, hoping with lifted curiosity, *what is it? Lord, is there enough time to find out? I beg of you, Lord, please give us your help again.*

****

Strangely inside the keys mouth he could see a mysterious message.

My God, my God, my prayers have been answered! Christopher's eyes lit up, *it's a short scripture, it's there, scribbled inside the key's mouth.* Chris encouraged himself at this last lifeline. *Come on man, God, I need more time!* Desperate to read this enchanted holographic illusion, he saw its ghostly scripture as if scratched on the metal surface but not quite there; he quickly scrutinized its fine details.

Sweat lashed off him, with all sanity aside, his battle to stay calm was impaled by his gathering nerves to understand its deep secrets.

It had been several minutes from the first indication of infestation around them, and now the spiders were everywhere, crawling over everything. Terrified, Harjit's eyes pleaded with Christopher's, the girl urging him to finish the job.

"Whatever you are going to do, do it now!" Harjit compressed her panic-stricken voice.

"It's a puzzle?" Kick starting his mind in a final effort for Harjit's sake. "I know what it says, but shit, what does it actually mean?" Chris went on his natural instincts, scanning the symbols, missing nothing when it suddenly came to him, as if it were something he had always known, a miracle. Christopher instantly interpreted the symbols and read them out fluently.

"What is it Chris!" She knew they had only seconds left to live.

"I have a gift from God." Chris realised that God had really been listening!

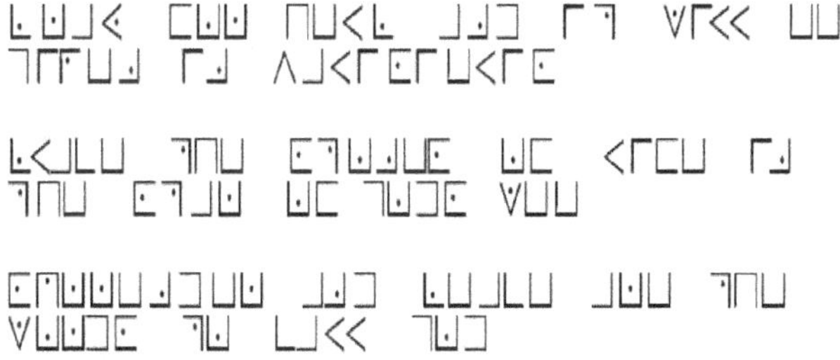

This is going to be close, his thoughts were desperate, brow dripping. The Scripture said:

Pray for help and it will be given in MalisIblis.

Place the stones of life in the star of God's web.

Surrender and peace are the words to call God.

"Give me the stones Barbaro," said Christopher sharply to the reporter. The man either did not hear or chose to ignore him. "Give me the fucking stones!" Christopher demanded immediate obedience. He stretched out his shaky hand towards the smaller man, *does he want to die?* Christopher thought? God's web was right behind them and full of undulating bodies.

"What stones?" The man's reply was muffled from behind his mask while giving Chris a hidden sneer. Barbaro felt threatened at losing something that was his, growling epithets under his breath as another second had gone.

"Bullshit man!" Mathieson exploded. "Give him what he wants!"

"The stones, you little shit head!" Christopher commanded. "The ones you picked up at the entrance to the temple, fool! Remember when *Beppi* died! Don't you understand? You will be next!" Christopher's eyes burned malice, he could not make it any plainer.

"Oh?" Barbaro's uncertain face changed, realising that hiding them was suicidal. Barbaro sighed hard in protest grudging Christopher's demand, he really wanted to keep the stones secretly for himself; he paused as precious seconds passed.

"Those stones you have are moonstones and Beppi's life! I need them now!" Chris yelled at him.

"I was watching you pick them up, mother," said Mathieson. "Give them to me. Right now, motherfuck or I'll shove them up your a…" The American was cut off, when Christopher leaned over and grabbed the slim reporter by the collar with both hands and pulled the man to him. Barbaro staggered, almost falling forward while fumbling inside his pockets for the stones.

Unexpectedly, his eyes almost burst out of his peculiar large head in shock, when a yellow streaked soft ball dropped softly onto his shoulder; the man screamed in fear.

"Aaaagh!" Barbaro shrieked in quick revulsion while instantly swiping at the odd-looking spider with his hard fist already clenching the moonstones.

Christopher instantly ceased this opportunity, grabbing the man's clenched fist and turning it, quickly holding Barbaro's arm and prying each finger apart, almost breaking each of Barbaro's fingers.

"Aaagh!" Barbaro screamed in pain, his prize taken by force, and with one smooth movement, Christopher swept his hand over to the skull, placing the sacred stones into a carved hole inside the centre of its jaw.

In the middle, a small star-shape was positioned inside the spectral moon image where the stones now rested. Christopher knew exactly what to do next. He shouted loud and clear, "Surrender and peace!" He called boldly, expecting himself to burst into flames and join poor Beppi! "Surrender and peace!" He called out again for a blood sacrifice.

Beppi's image scarred his mind. The dead man's pitiful agony that he had seen when his flesh was bubbling, his body engulfed in a conflagration of fire. Now it was his turn and he fully expected to sacrifice himself, holding his breath. Finally, his fear was conquered by thoughts of Harjit, calling a last time, "Surrender and peace!"

Staring at her with a hazy mind, Christopher recalled her brown eyes through her tarnished and matted environmental suit, remembering her silky black shoulder length hair sitting perfectly curved as it always did around the natural fine features of her face. His last thoughts were of her, his secret love slipping away when he really saw in her eyes something more, glinting sharply at him. Through her round goggles, Christopher could see she was frightened too, realising she was also ready to die to be with him for this end. *God no, no, not yet,* he begged into himself. He did not want it to end this way, not now, not for her, not ever. Yet the words he spoke seemed to do nothing.

Harjit, beautiful Harjit, smiled back at him, her love and sadness hidden behind a mask, and yet her eyes conveyed this sincerity. A smile of knowing love. She was frightened yes, but there was a peace also, a settlement in her mind and of belief of eternal life.

Sensing her despair, Christopher gently pulled her strongly into him and held her, the girl crumpling into his arms. There was nothing else he could do as the spiders energetically overran this last safe area. It was finished.

"Hold on to me, Harjit!" Said Chris, as both people gripped each other in a last second of passion. Everything around them was forgotten and whatever expectations they had, had failed, and sadly there was no final escape, and nowhere to run.

Gravid fears took over the others, mixed in lost looks of despair, watching blindly at the surrounding black masses. Nobody was interested in the couple's embrace. Forgotten, the priest had done his best and failed as the hunter's net enclosed. Each person, utterly spent, all struggled to keep the horrible things from biting them. Each person tried to come to terms with death and one's own longevity and finally, *to die?* Death grew huge and heavy, it was going to be bad. It was going to be horrible.

****

The waning and waxing crescent moons on the north wall were not visible anymore, and although the full central moon was still seen on the Mihrab, its last faltering energies began to extinguish too. They stared hopelessly at a heaving onslaught that engulfed them, when without warning something else happened. Something quite unexpected. Suddenly and miraculously, a tall slim stone door opened forward from behind the moving Mihrab.

The Moon's unsure embers were held there by some higher power of light and had taken a hand in a battle against the darkness. Those precious last moments they had made for themselves were crucial, providing a *time lock* in life, that had held the darkness at bay giving the light they needed now to escape. Impossible as it all seemed, everything was too much to take or comprehend. They all stood there motionless and relegated to being stunned spectators in shocked immobility.

With only seconds to leave, the doorway was held by a time lock. They all watched in dumbfounded disbelief and almost detached from reality as they stared anxiously at the opening doorway. *What was this? Was it really an escape or another illusion?* Yet, there it was right in front of them and for the taking, a way out and life.

"Come on, this way!" Harjit screamed at everyone, breaking away, running with renewed vigour leading her men to safety. The girl nimbly dodged the swinging Mihrab, going through the doorway behind it with Christopher, and the others quickly followed, all swiping and stamping and shouting their way out.

Behind them, more layers of spider webs were being rapidly remade as the whole area regenerated again in silk weaves throughout the chamber, just like it had been a long time ago. The skull image grinned above the holy seat, happy that it had defeated the darkness and then finally it too faded and simply disappeared. God's key was gone forever.

When the key vanished inside the chamber, a hidden and unseen force began slowly pulling the levers back up into place, shutting the doorway tightly behind them. The stone windows of the temple closed in unison, as the chamber plunged once more into complete darkness, waiting for anyone who might be so foolish to come this way again. The chamber entering another *dark age.*

Hearts pounded like pistons and the group fearfully expected a chase from behind, everyone drilling their eyes frantically around and onto each other, checking for an unseen enemy. In the dingy light, reassuringly they could see that the tall thin doorway was shut tight.

Visibly shaking from head to toe, the team was caught in a mixture of emotions while more adrenaline kicked in through their bloodstreams. Heartfelt relief and exhilaration was felt, some laughing hysterically while Cesaré began sobbing like a child, the man overwhelmed, so glad to be out; they were still alive.

Revulsion of what they just witnessed took its toll, each person busy cleaning off the sticky mess from their web coated suits and clothes. Minutes passed and with the adrenaline wearing off, it found them exhausted and relieved to be alive. They began looking around, becoming more aware of their new surroundings, inside a long slightly inclining narrow corridor running parallel with the north wall.

Aware of a pale illumination, a light emanated from inside this strange corridor, that gave a luminosity of about a thirty or forty-watt light bulb. The yellowish diffusion extended along the corridors vague distance.

Battled by stress and bewilderment, they had already seen too much. Everyone hoped their nightmare was over, but they still had their doubts.

Cesaré stamped on three or four of the spiders that had slipped out before the doors shut.

"Si, take that you little mothers!" Using his heavy leather walking boots, he crushed them mercilessly, stamping hard, listening to the satisfying popping and squelching underneath. He swept his weapon left and right, missing and cursing after them, some got past and quickly crawled up onto the walls and ceiling and disappearing somewhere. It was payback time. One near to Barbaro crawled upwards and lost its grip and, timing it perfectly like a footballer, he viciously kicked it away, impacting onto the red sandstone floor and exploding instantly to his great delight.

Mathieson, not to be outdone, got a few other stragglers that tried to escape down the corridor, dutifully halving them with his trusty battle axe.

"Come and sniff on this you little mother fuckers." The American shouted his challenge. "Hey, I'm getting to be a real expert at rubbing out these spiders, bring it on!"

"Everyone ok? No bites or scratches?" Harjit wanted to check for any rip, tear or bite. "Chris, your environmental suit indicators are on yellow."

"Yours too, Harj"

"What the hell happened back there?" Asked Cesaré.

"Fuck knows, man."

Matt pissed off, staring towards the location they had appeared from and shook his head in relief and guilt.

Humiliated, the American knew that at the end, he too had panicked, and lost his nerve, showing a weakness to them and to himself. This was something he had never experienced before. Inside the chamber, he had come face to face with his own vulnerability, judging himself too hard and as a man who had lost control. *Cowardice,* Mathieson was ashamed of himself.

Barbaro stared condescendingly at everyone, measuring their resolve while twisting a smile. *Amateurs, would be explorers.* From behind his mask, he sniggered quietly, harbouring his twisted private thoughts; sensing Mathieson's shame, he began focusing his own sadistic pleasures onto the black man's personal humiliation.

The Vatican reporter knew that everyone here was expendable, each person only a pawn in this expedition. His cesspit psyche would never change because of his own personal racial and religious beliefs.

Lost your bottle inside big boy, ha! You're not so big now are you? There should be no other foreigners on this mission let alone a black American Jew! For God is my witness, I still can't believe it! A Muslim, a Hindu, a Jew and a Scotsman, all together on one expedition! What is the Vatican thinking? Now a woman in charge! She's not Catholic or worthy! Fabio has a lot to answer for and I will see to it that he sinks with all the others before the end.

"Ha, ha, ha!" Barbaro laughed loudly, his happiness almost complete, fuelled by disdain and conceit. These people were everything he hated in his brooding bigotry, something he so cherished.

"Happy are we, Barbaro?" Asked Christopher in a matter of fact tone. The man sensed something not normal, unaware what Barbaro was contemplating. Barbaro's body language appeared too buoyant, too lively, especially after what had just happened to them. He watched him suspiciously, wondering, *what's he up to now?*

"Si, Si, very happy. We live!" Barbaro shouted at him while sneering more behind his mask.

"Are you alright Barbaro?" Harjit observed that the little man's mind appeared in shock. "You need to get out of your suit, its breached."

"Ugh, infected?" This news wiped his sneer away.

"If it were infected, your LED's would be on the red. There is no contamination, you're fine. The suit is torn and punctured, useless. You can take it off."

"Those little swine ripped all our suits somehow but still, it gave some protection, I think." Christopher wiped away the horrid black fluid splashed across his goggles.

"I'm just glad to have got through this, thanks for your help Chris." Feeling Harjit's unseen smile, *what were those magical stones all about?* Harjit thought to wonder, *how did Christopher know to use them?* She did not probe further, fearing an answer. That might be too much to handle, her brain was already on target for overload.

"Si, Harjit, just a bit glad to be out of there, that's all." The man from the press office interrupted the girl. "I'll gladly take this off." He pulled away his head mask, twisting his lip again in a weird smile at her.

"By the way, mother!" Mathieson strode quickly towards Christopher with intent, his angry voice snapping at the priest. Harjit stiffened, taking a quick breath in, powerless this time to interject. She was shocked but held her anxiety; trouble had been brewing between the two for days.

"Yes?" Replied Christopher cautiously, instinctively turning towards the oncoming threat, staring from his round goggle vision. He knew it was important to stand his ground, their fiery eyes meeting explosively an inch apart.

Chris waited. The others stopped, watching this powder keg ready to blow.

"Thanks, you son of a mother. You did alright in there." The ranger nodded. "You really did it, man!" Mathieson smiled uncontrollably, extending his hand out, gripping and shaking the younger man's shoulder in comradeship. Matt grinned, showing the spaces between his perfect white teeth.

"Thank you Mathieson." replied Christopher, totally relieved.

"Homme and take off that white suit! God-damn man, stop being a mother!" Mathieson began laughing and clapping his hands in total happiness. *The Scotsman did just fine.*
Mathieson was full of admiration and newfound respect for Christopher, their differences were sealed. Christopher's shoulder hurt from the grip but he manned up.

Taken aback, Chris gulped awkwardly and felt embarrassed at the American's unexpected display of respect for him. Friendship might be too strong a word, *a truce, I'll settle for that,* he thought. Both men shook hands firmly. How long the armistice would last, time would tell.

"Cool, man." Christopher took off his mask and smiled back. Harjit breathed a silent sigh.

"Christopher," Harjit whispered. "Don't tell the others but have you had a close look at these hairy little guys?" She whispered in a low tone. A blank expression was his answer, "Mmm no?" She continued, "Well this little chap here is squashed but have a closer look. What do you see?" She waited, "Count its legs." Harjit watched him as his slow realisation awakened and was seen in his astonished eyes.

"A spider has eight legs and an insect six, this creature has twelve, and out of those two had tiny retractable hooks that look as if they're specially developed for swinging or grabbing and cutting." Christopher acknowledged that this was not a spider. "Funny looking thing, eh Harj?"

"Hilarious," She replied in monotone. "These are not spiders. Let's get out of here."

"Where to Harj?" He felt that they would not last much longer without rest and he waited for her orders.

Harjit quickly investigated the distant darkness, checking both ways up and down the corridor. She needed to get them moving and make the right decision right now. Oddly there were no signs of where they had come from. The opening shut tight and seamlessly sealed, the doorway was completely gone.

The walls were made of the same sandstone found throughout the superstructure. Unexpectedly, deep inside the sandstone crystalline lattice, there was a type of potential energy in it. She watched it change using an energy growing in potency. Each crystal transforming kinetically emitting tiny amounts of light. The light sources began increasing the overall luminosity within the corridor. The overall effect was dim, but good enough for an ancient power system by anyone's measure.

Now they could see the complex mosaics covering the walls and all lit up casting complex shadows into the darker passageway. A star symbol appeared inside the wall and the illumination there was greatest. Light focal points like these were set in at regular points along the corridor.

"This is incredible. Long before we discovered electricity or invented appliances, it's truly amazing!" Barbaro said while thinking and thought, *how wonderful this place is.*

"Where is this light source coming from?" Asked Cesaré. "Where is the wall-lights getting their energy, have they a power station hidden somewhere inside this temple?" The young man was awestruck.

"These are like street lamps, just weaker," Christopher acknowledged.

"You don't get it, do you Cesaré?" Mathieson was annoyed at the young technician's simplicity. "This mother is a big battery. The whole fucker, ancient or not is a big fucking power station!"

"No, it is you my friend, who is a little crazy," replied Cesaré in a childlike voice. "Electricity did not exist four hundred, let alone ten thousand years ago." He completely disagreed with the American's sweeping statement.

"How do you explain this then?" Mathieson pressed the technician while studying Cesaré's face, seeing a man on the verge. Mathieson recognised this same expression as the one he saw on his friend Carmello and decided to lay off the young man.

"Hey! Leave him alone, Americano!" Aléssandro spoke out in Cesaré's defence, "I put money in the electric meter!"

"Yeah Mathieson, give it a break." Christopher was furious at Mathieson's idiocy.

"We must go back," came her soft voice. "It would be the best thing for us all and the safest route is to go back down and out of here. This place has become far too dangerous to continue our exploration. I am responsible for everyone's safety. That way leads to where we came from and back towards the temple's entrance." She pointed her finger down towards the sloped corridor, waiting tentatively for their response. Blank faces simply stared back at her. This move would gauge her leadership.

"That was a close run just then, I agree with Harj." Christopher was disappointed about returning but had to side with Harjit. He smiled softly and felt strangely close and personal to her, while reminiscing their embrace in those last dire moments inside the chamber. He knew he would return here sometime later and be better prepared.

"We go on! There is too much time lost already! Too much still to discover and the Vatican needs to find out what this place is. His Holiness needs some answers!" Barbaro shouted in protest, his large head shaking with disbelief at the girl's cowardly leadership. "We go on, I insist!"

"Go on, Harjy babe, you go. But going your way we do not have a clue what is down there either! Fifty-fifty. Go on up and see this thing through, that's what I say." Mathieson was convinced and influenced by his natural exploratory traits, danger and excitement pulled him onwards. "Things cannot be worse than what we have been through. Come on, get a grip Harj and grow some balls, there is no point in running away." His words remained like a verdict.

"It was just some fluke of nature," said Cesaré supporting both the American and Barbaro but remained uncertain and in denial of his own fears.

"We must Harjit. Fabio would have expected it of you. There is much to learn and if we get hurt trying then it's our call, babe. We all knew the risks coming here."

Aléssandro pressed her more, his mind stepping up to the mark, after all he wanted to gain Fabio's respect once more thinking of some historical explorers he had read about.

Maybe it will be me, I will be the next John Lloyd Stephens or Teobert Maler, and not the professor! Fabio might even recommend me to lead the next expedition! Aléssandro smiled at his self-made dream.

Harjit quickly considering their wishes; this was a pivotal moment for her, knowing this decision would be crucial. She had not signed up for this kind of danger or responsibility. Harjit could never have envisioned this, after all she was only a student medical doctor and not an explorer. She doubted herself, questioning, *what would Fabio do?*

"Ok, good, and now that everyone has their suits off, I have come to my decision." She paused as the others waited. "I do not agree with you, Aléssandro. If what we have been through is anything to make judgment on, it's likely we're in for a rough ride from now on." The girl paused again for a serious last moment of contemplation and timed it perfectly, just before Mathieson was about to butt in with something derogatory, Harjit used a small hand gesture to shut him up. It was obvious to her from their comments and postures that the men wanted to continue with the exploration, "Yes, Si, we go on."

Remarkably, she changed her mind, knowing there was no safe guarantee whichever way they chose.

"Nice one, babe." Mathieson's face lit up.

Harjit looked at them all, "Is everyone up for it?" They all agreed, nodding keen affirmations. "Last chance to change your minds." They all shook their heads. "Ok then, everyone be very careful, this will be dangerous. Let's go."

I hope to Vishnu the Sustainer that I have chosen wisely. I wonder how Fabio is managing? For us, I fear this is the wrong way. Her face was set dead ahead. *Oh, let it not be Shiva the destroyer that we meet.*

Feeling peril in her bones, Harjit walked first and the others followed. There was no sense of triumphal satisfaction going along through the dim passage with only grave thoughts for company, they had all decided.

****

CHAPTER XI

HUMAN SPIDER

Fabio and his small band of explorers set off wearing their pristine white environmental suits, walking quickly along the lower tunnel, leaving Harjit and her team above. Each man packed sets of short lightweight poles on top of their rucksacks that were useful for helping negate simple obstructions. These extendable scaffolding poles were made of a very light and strong plastic. Synthetic poles, especially those telescopic in design and constructed correctly, could hold up extraordinary weights. Fabio decided to put his recent fatalities furthest from his mind, concentrating on the job at hand, to find a place that would make this journey special. Undaunted and re-energised with youthful eagerness of adventure and discovery, Professor Mancini was once again in his element! Endrissi and Kees went ahead of the professor, each man determined along a dim claustrophobic passageway to where nobody knew.

Everywhere around them was built using a sparkling solid red-stone rock, all cut and arranged into a perfect square tunnel. They moved onwards and after a while, this unique red-stone assembly changed dramatically. The men cautiously used powerful torches beaming brightly, shining through this enclosed tunnel system, and highlighted just ahead of them a dazzling pure white rock.

"Look at this transformation professor. What do you make of this new type of stone?" Kees asked staring at the startling stone difference from red to white.

"It is the stone from Endrissi's earlier description. This suggests it has come from the seam in the mines," said Fabio whispering as if in a library. "Endrissi?" He asked the man for a second opinion, their eyes straining from looking at the direct brightness.

"Indeed, it is a rare stone, although we are far below ground level and I am not sure if this is simply a continuation from the mines or cut, processed, constructed and placed here into seamless position. It is strange to say the least, but it is the same stone, without question." The geologist blinked rapidly between eye water and nerves, trying to come to terms with this new and unexpected change. The pure white crystalline structure felt smooth and highly polished as they cautiously scanned ahead, their torches beaming ultra brightly inside the white stone corridor.

"I thought you would know a bit more than that, Endrissi." He sighed long and hard, annoyed at the geologist's shortfall.

"This stone must have come from a rare rock seam indeed, somewhere deeper in that complex of caves," said Endrissi ignoring the professor's stark rudeness. He took out his geologist's hammer and began tapping away for a rock sample while ignoring the professor for a moment, much to Fabio's consternation. After half a minute, Endrissi stopped. He examined the rock closely where he had struck it with the hammer point. There wasn't a mark.

"It is weird, but the transition is seamless," Kees agreed.

"This stone type is much harder and denser than any rock I have ever come across, it's unearthly," added Endrissi quite bewildered.

They then observed strange long horizontal parallel lines deeply grooved into the walls, like a track and made for some forgotten reason that they could not even guess at. Maybe it was a simple décor? The men had no way of telling.

Walking on again, they were unaware of descending in a long slow spiral, the curvature was negligible but the wide corridor gave the illusion of being completely straight. By this time, the team were quite close to the outer perimeter of the temple base and albeit already well below ground level.

"This tunnel is going on for ever Fabio, it's as boring as hell," said Endrissi, mumbling inside his mask. Kees yawned in sympathy because by now, they had been walking for what seemed like hours. The explorers in their white suits appeared camouflaged against the crystal white walls. Tiny flashing LED health indicator lights on their suits gave them away, reassuringly they were all confidently blinking on green.

Endrissi was at least six-foot eight inches, large and strong. For his twenty-eight-year frame he felt old and clumsy inside his tight suit. Kees was also big; both men made Fabio look quite small standing together.

Behind Endrissi's mask, his full-bodied wavy fair hair had flattened, becoming spring loaded. His jaw was broad on short stubble shin, giving him a handsome smile. The man, with a PhD to boot, had studied in geology, building technology and architecture at the University of Rome, an excellent choice for Fabio's team, despite Fabio's immature views.

"Si, it is becoming a bit of a hike, is it not?" Said Fabio who could not deny the tedium.

"I can hardly move with this pack on my back Fabio," He grumbled to the man in charge, "Just as well, these tunnels are much bigger than the ones inside the pyramids of Egypt."

The professor reminisced to his previous expedition studies in another continent. That time he had observed how the ancients constructed such monuments to their gods and pharaohs.

"Come, come, my dear man, please stop complaining. You are about to discover an ancient way of life, a civilization between fifteen to seventeen thousand years old. One that has never been seen before!" There was something else Fabio wanted to say, he held their attention for a moment; both men felt it.

"Is there something else, professor?" asked Endrissi.

"Signore's, can I draw to your attention something that you both have missed. Examine where we are walking. In a low decline, Si? It is also easy not to observe what is happening, but I did expect you to see more," Fabio was disappointed waiting for a response from the two baffled men. "What am I talking about? And you pair might ask? Oh, and what is that noise" he stated sarcastically. "Listen, Hear them, oh Si! Yes! It's two brain cells, yours and yours." Fabio shook his head in boorish resignation and at their lack of awareness.

"But…" Kees thought of biting his tongue, *cheeky Bastardo.*

"Sorry, professor," Endrissi winced at Fabio's open ridicule, *superior asshole* he thought at the man's rudeness.

"Since you both obviously haven't a clue, we are moving inside an integral curve and it is becoming more and more curved inwards as we progress in a decline, like a cone."

Both sub-ordinates were being treated like children, the men corkscrewing their eyes towards the walls and, he was right enough! Both men astounded tucking in their tails in at the Archaeologist's super-keen and flawless attention to detail. This was something they had been completely unaware off.

Here it comes, thought Kees, *the usual, Fabio's one-upmanship. Unfortunately, the*

*Government listens to him so I must do the same, one real pain in the...*the professor interrupted his thoughts.

"May I remind you both that I am the archaeologist among us and albeit quite a good one. You Endrissi, are an Engineer and Kees, a government official and surveyor to trade, yet between both of you, nobody spotted this complete change of direction and decline and attitude! Signores, I did expect better!"

"Throw us some slack Fabio, it is not exactly easy to find our way around here." He breathed curses at him and thought in vain while watching the professor throw his hands in the air. Their eyes were wide, and they began smiling with self-satisfaction slapping that gauntlet onto their red faces. Their embarrassment was hidden behind their goggle-eyed masks. Fabio was always ready to put anybody in their place.

They should be more aware of a change to the structural environment, thought Fabio. The professor knew there would be danger ahead and a little ridicule now might save their lives.

****

They continued walking in an indiscernible arc, and it was not until sometime later when the corridor curved measurably more into a tighter twist, the radius within the temple becoming closer together. Both men quietly regarded the older man thoughtfully because it was obvious to them that the professor was enjoying himself.

I've got them like jumping beans, Fabio bemused knowing that he was in complete control. That was the way he liked it, on edge.

Endrissi's right leg was giving him nagging reminders of his younger days when he played football. Having already walked quite a distance, the man began limping heavily in front of his colleagues when quite unexpectedly, he smacked head long into something solid.

"Oooo!" He shouted out in agony. He came to an abrupt halt with a sudden jolt running right through his body, the impact sending him sprawling and falling backwards. The man was off balance, "Oh! Ouch!" He called out in pain, hitting the unforgiving floor. "Bloody hell, what the..." said Endrissi cursing. The geologist was down and lying like a legless giraffe. "Ouch man, it bloody hurts." His brown eyes dazed and he, rubbed his swelling forehead. The other men moved quickly to help him, shining their torches into his mask to see his eyes.

"Are you ok, Endrissi?" Fabio was concerned but also had become aware that some kind a vague solid wall was protruding in the nearby shadows, sticking directly out at right angles to the main passageway.

Endrissi looked upwards from his elbow props, and with a quick flash of light, he highlighted an odd-looking walled section sticking out in front of him, which was a continuous part of the surrounding corridor.

"I'll survive, could do with a pain killer though."

"Take this, it is an anti-inflammatory." Fabio brought out his emergency kit while checking the dangerous protrusion.

A quick examination of the protruding wall was featureless. Barely visible before impact, its surface was identical with no distinguishing marks blending seamlessly in with the surrounding environment. Fabio hadn't seen this protuberance, so what chance did they have?

"Endrissi, let me give you a hand up. Can you stand?" Kees bent over the man and helped him to his feet. "Are you alright?" the man began to laugh.

"A bit of a bang," said Endrissi wincing while rubbing his head.

"You'll live." Kees looked at Fabio with a grin.

"Hey, it's not funny!"

"Course not, you're fine. Now, take your medicine." Fabio was all smiles seeing the funny side too.

"Prego. Where the hell did that bloody wall come from anyway?" Endrissi could not believe it, the man moved over in the dimness and felt the jutting wall about half way across the corridor from the right.

Kees took a turn to do the lead walking, this time with a bit more caution. Another ten metres further on found another similar protrusion sticking out, this time from the opposite side. This pattern soon established repetitive weaving onwards. Their minds conjectured many times on how there could be such a construction like this, and its existence seemed impossible. Why have this crazy wall system? It all seemed so out of place.

Kees could not directly see the others behind him. Occasionally, where the wall should have been, there was now an opening leading into another part of the temple complex. Where these went to was anyone's guess. He and the others kept on going along the main passageway.

"This place is like a Warren!" Kees shouted back. The others quickly caught up with him in what looked like a mad game of tag, Endrissi took over lead again.

"Stick to the main channel, Endrissi! Keep going downwards and do not stray into the other areas or you'll get lost for good." Fabio could not have been more serious.

"There's plenty of hiding places down here. I have never come across such a building in my entire life. It is a maze," said Endrissi, understating its enormity, knowing that there must be thousands of tonnes of weight pressing down onto this honeycomb structure. Its design would give it a fundamental inherent strength that would enable it to take massive compressions. Fabio was clueless as to how deep they had descended; Kees estimated it to be about six hundred feet as the tunnel twisted downwards in a right-handed helix.

"Fabio, it is getting much steeper now," said Endrissi while turning and shifting his balance, the man moved into the next section while still ahead of the others.

"I wonder if there is anything beyond the walls around us. I always knew this was a mammoth superstructure but coming across this makes it even bigger!" Kees extrapolated.

"It is colossal," Fabio added. They continued more carefully. The wall surfaces were brightly reflecting extra light from their torches and hurting their eyes, giving them a sense of *tunnel vision*.

Each person could hear the other's laboured breathing behind their masks. Tired and slowing to a standstill, their purpose was no more than a forgotten urgency. The explorers had been inside too long already, yet time seemed unimportant down here where no light came in and there was nowhere different to look at. Their exploration had become a complete slog.

The men suffered from the same overheating problems as Harjit's team above, and it was becoming more impractical for them to sustain this much longer. They would soon pass out, unless...

"Ok, you can take them off. Take the suits off. It is risky, however if we want to go on Signore's, we must be prepared to take a few risks," said the professor.

Fabio sounded a bit disappointed compared to the applauded grunts from the others. Progress was made from then on and the route became easier, having dumped their suits and, despite it not being a direct route, there was a continual weaving and zigzagging motion. It was going on forever. Any attempt to travel faster was next to impossible and dangerous. It seemed like miles tramped under foot. Deflated and demoralized, the men sat down heavily and discussed what to do next over some light refreshments.

"This shit is going on forever," Kees said, stating the obvious. "What do we do? Go on or go back professor?"

"No question. We go on!" Said Fabio firmly.

"We have come this far. If only I could get a sample of this rock, I could get its age," stated Endrissi.

"Not…when this place was built!" Kees intercepted.

"Correct, when this place was constructed is something completely different to its geological age of the stone, smart-ass." Said Endrissi, miffed off a little at being interrupted. "And as I was about to say we could use uranium-lead radiometric dating," which is the oldest and available technique to find the age of stone."

"Yes, I agree." Fabio understood where Endrissi was taking this practicality.

"It is one of the most highly respected methods and has been refined to the point that the error in dates of rocks is about three billion years old, with a tolerance of no more than two million years out. It is quite accurate."

Endrissi stroked the smooth wall surface and blinked rapidly with excitement. "Getting me so far?"

"Oh, really," Kees nodded his head, his bored tone hard to disguise, and pissed-off with himself that he had asked about going back in the first place, tried to look interested. *Shit, he is going on and on and on...*

"Considering the Earth is roughly four point five billion years old, I think we will not have a problem. Uranium-lead dating is usually performed on the mineral Zircon that forms multiple crystal layers during metamorphic events. Much more accurate than other methods you would agree. *Do you go with this?*" the geologist considered the scientific possibilities.

"Sure," Kees yawned a little.

"Signore's, let's drive on. It is getting later. Unfortunately, you know that we will be spending the night down here. We will try to get a little further on before we stop and rest."

Fabio relished the idea of staying a night in such a place as this, steeping himself in its ancient aura; the professor was keen to go further and much deeper than anyone else! Endrissi got up and began slowly leading the way, the atmosphere inside the temple and sensory deprivation was most unpleasant, it continually wore away inside their minds. The quest subconsciously took its toll, when unexpectedly someway off, they heard a noise.

****

"Look out!" Endrissi screamed. He stopped abruptly and tried to stagger backwards from nearly falling over a sheer drop, but the others caused him to go forwards.

"Ooof!" Fabio gasped, shunting into him.

"Wait, hold it!" Endrissi stood, arms wide apart holding the others from going past him. "Hold it I say!" He steadied his balance firmly, on the very edge of an unfathomable precipice.

Endrissi began inching backwards like a crowd steward, restraining his comrades shining their eager lamps into this total blackness. They could see nothing.

"Where's the floor?" Kees heart hammered against his chest. "My God, what the…?"

"I think you are very lucky to be alive." The professor held the engineer's shoulder just in case. "Now be very careful and let's all come away from the edge."

"Funny Faib, and I thought it was I, who saved you just then," Endrissi retorted. Endrissi's eyes hardened as they stopped.

"Fanculo! Look down, Fabio." Kees pushed an inch closer, angling his powerful torch downwards as the light beam opened into a massive chasm; a gaping black hole that seemed endless.

A deep shaft presented itself and a silent danger; a menace cut out by someone or something. Whatever its purpose, it had been crafted this way by someone using something of incredible power. A power able to dig and slice through this rock type was unimaginable. What story did it tell?

"It is really deep, I feel it. There is no way of telling how far down it goes." Fabio appeared a little shocked at the scale and yet he was already contemplating his next move. The problem was, how? Fabio, for once in his life, was beaten.

Taking a deep breath, Fabio racked his mind. *I did not come to the ends of the Earth to turn away, and to turn back!*

"I won't have it!" The professor shouted a challenge at the barrier. The others just looked silently at his enraged frame.

The stone underneath ground level was the same crystalline white rock found in the corridor. To him the problem was not totally unsurmountable, nothing had really changed except the floor in front of him was gone.

"What do you think?" Asked Endrissi.

"It is a shaft for a lift," answered Kees. "Similar to how we got down here in the first place, except in this case, the elevator has not returned. Look at those horizontal and vertical grooves, maybe runners of a sort. By the way, what time is it?"

"What time? It will be just about dark outside, though it does not matter down here now does it?" Fabio replying rhetorically. "I think you are incorrect about this being a defunct lift. I think more accurately, that it is a trap or barrier to prevent people from gaining access to whatever lies beyond this point. A transport mechanism would not be stuck in a dark place like this."

"It could be both. There must have been a platform here at one time. Maybe there is a lever or something around the next corner that may make it appear, like a bridge?"

"My good Endrissi, it is more likely that whoever was on the other side would not be coming back out for a while." Fabio smiled at the man's simplicity. "It's more like sealing a tomb, the Egyptians did it. No one expected anyone to be coming out once sealed inside. The place is full of mantraps too. We must be doubly on our guards."

"Next idea?" Kees' dull tone bantered with a grimace.

"It is going to be risky. I do not expect anybody to follow me." The professor smiled and paused at their injudicious glances.

"You are not seriously going on, are you?" Endrissi was surprised.

"Si! No question." His eyes scanned theirs. "And I am going to need your help too." He meant it, turning and looking wildly over at his next trial.

****

Their environmental surroundings lit up in torchlight semi-darkness. Visibility was far from perfect, but Fabio, undaunted and energised, was soon standing on the precipice. His physique was excellent for his age, he was quite slim and fit and wore his spider monkey mountain boots; he always kept them handy in such expeditions. He switched on his headlamp with a clear click. Around his waist hung a limited number of quick draw wall nuts on wires and karabiners for rock climbing. He was stripped to his shorts and vest; the *human spider* was ready to go.

"Signore, I'm prepared. I cannot hit or tap anything into the wall. It is far too hard and dense for that. I will wedge these wall nuts into those tapered grooves that go around the walls as far as I can."

"Oh," Kees gulped a swallow.

"You can see them above and below running along the walls. The vertical grooves are useless, can't see me using those much."

"Hmm," Endrissi didn't say much more, he had his reservations about the whole climb and especially that last bit. He knew that the professor would need all his tenacity.

There were a few facts about Fabio. He was an accomplished climber in his day, and his idea of a good time was visiting Scotland on holiday and fitting in a climb. Glencoe's Rannoch Wall was something he really enjoyed.

Yet there was something more unusual about him, for all his humanly failings, climbing became metamorphic. He changed from pompous professor into a younger and more youthful man in his prime. With a new born enthusiastic innocence, untainted by the yolk of life, here he stood against nature and was determined to reach his end goal.

"All you big guys must be ready to take my weight," his tone was steady, watching them look at him more unsure, but he was joking. "And stop me from dropping off that ledge. It doesn't get any simpler than that." He watched their quizzical nods reluctantly coming towards him and felt reborn, holding a renewed confidence. It was essential to trust them implicitly.

"A ledge! A ledge! Fabio, it is hardly that! There is only about two inches of grooved wall if you are lucky!" Kees was mortified at the site of those parallel running lines, one about head height and the other to stand on. "They may go all around the structure, we do not know. You must be insane professor!" Kees was exasperated with Fabio's latest adventure. Whatever it was, it was the spark inside him, and this sort of danger that really made Fabio tick.

"It is easy, I'll wedge my monkey boots into the bottom ledge and use my hands to move and place a wall nut periodically along it. It could not be simpler." Confident, if not a bit too flippant about the matter. Fabio was not a fool, he knew there would be danger and no room for error. One slip and he would be gone.

"Don't do it professor," Endrissi warned.

"I hope the end is only around this blind corner. Once I get to the other end, we will use the ropes to transfer things across, then construct the scaffolding later. Just for now I will go alone."

All joking aside, Fabio was willing to move towards the deadly drop, his concentration now firmly fixed and focused.

"You will not be going alone Fabio," Kees encouraged, while thinking, *he may be a pompous big-headed pratt most of the time, but he is one brave bastardo.* He showed his respect by shaking the professor's hand. "Hang tight, we will be coming with you once you find the way. Good luck."

Fabio smiled warmly again, he had always been unsure of Kees' slightly strange grip. "Do not worry, this is nothing. I climbed Annapurna, the tenth highest mountain in the world when I was in my early thirties!"

"Careful now prof." Endrissi looked worried, as dark shadows gibbered in their torchlight.

"The rope is good for another two falls at least," the professor joked again as his fearful followers watched him go. "I cannot think of better anchor men than your own good selves." His confidence implied peril.

The men were not laughing, their eyes looking down into the abyss of dark shadows. Feeling a renewed sense of importance, they knew that this is as serious as it gets. The ropes were designed for about eight falls at 8 KN stress, but the stress put onto their brains might break before that.

"God go with you." Endrissi's brown eyes anxiously stared after Fabio, the professor placing his first karabiner into the groove.

Kees held his breath for a moment, extremely nervous as the expedition leader began stretching out his long arm, watching him feeling it first then gripping into the top groove.

Holding the rope, the men held their breaths too, their climbing gloves would ensure extra grip. Remembering Fabio's words of warning, *if I fall be ready.*

The men fed out the slack as Fabio began pulling himself onto the narrow straight horizontal ledge and swung immediately around the wall, his karabiners dangling and chinking at his waistline; the jangling of metal on metal sounded like distant church bells. Fabio's slender fingers pressed down tightly into the narrow ledge, forming white bony knuckles that shined through the tight skin taking his own weight. He pushed out a few quick sharp breaths of air from his lungs. He was on track and moving fast.

The human spider's fingers speedily touched inside the groove and away again, with just enough time as though feeling thoughtfully back and forth like a pianist, then moving on. His musical moves held his passion and sure grip inches above shoulder height was good because any higher would cause him to lose too much energy. His climbing height was just about perfect.

Sliding easily along like a professional climber, each move was timed with perfection. His feet moved accurately with the delicacy of a ballet dancer, the toes of his boots fitting snugly into the lower horizontal ledge. Maintaining his upright position, his smooth reach was unnaturally long almost like a primate's giving him that natural climbing ability.

Fabio's hairy forearms and shoulders rhythmically bulged then relaxed with each short manoeuvre. Thighs and calf muscles strained with effort and slackened to rest. His face touched and was almost kissed by the flat rock, his expression hardening instantly with surprise, cursing a warning into himself. He could sense that something was not right.

I cannot move, Fabio thought and began awkwardly pulling on the rope. *Auch, I'm snagged and slipping.* His face was set with purpose, calling out a warning.

"Give me some slack, for Christ's sake!" Fabio shouted sharply, expecting nothing less than complete obedience. The rope eased instantly. Fabio was on the move again and like a tightrope performer, he readjusted his position and balance, while his mind worked out his next move. This time he continued unimpeded.

Very athletic in his tight green vest, he adhered to the wall. His supple body tensed, and his pace quickened considerably, reaching the first corner. He stopped for a moment to observe his new right angular surroundings as his headlamp shone brightly onto the walls, spreading the beam widely.

Each time the rope stopped the others stared silently into the shadows after him, willing him on. Both men were already distraught knowing he would be standing precariously in the indented horizontal line, and that each second would sap a little more energy from him. Frustrated, they were helpless and could not see anything other than a reflected profile on the opposite wall.

With nerve tingling precision and perfect balance, Fabio looked confidently at his next challenge, gauging the distance to be long. He knew that this section needed speed.

Tensing his legs, they became quite rigid and unmoving like a plank of wood. Fabio immediately let go of the grooves above him and held his line, perilously balanced there for a moment, unsecured. Only his muscular rigidity held him in an upright position with his boots giving him the correct feel and rigor inside the groove. He looked frozen to the spot with wooden muscles and this, a balanced technique he had used before.

He sweated profusely, carefully placing a wall nut into the corner, making another main anchor, slowly securing the metal karabiner and then began feeding his climbing rope through its ring.

Done. Relieved, his body relaxed with protection assured in case he fell, *that should hold,* he thought, tugging on it securely with one hand, with the other holding onto the top groove. Fabio immediately measuring the way ahead, trailing his eyes to his right where the others could not see. His head torch cut a path through the darkness that allowed him to calculate the distance to his next target. He could see further beyond this, noting another wall presenting itself on a blind side.

Fabio soon reached the corner; seeing further now, he was mystified to observe another right-angled wall, resigning himself to assume that the rest of the climb was likely to be the same. He started sliding carefully around the next phase of his climb. Pit dark surroundings enclosed him; he was alone and out on a limb. The void below beckoned to unfoot him at any opportunity. Even now, a distant incantation seemed to weave wizardry from nowhere, burrowing uncertainties through his mind.

Why worry, it said softly to him. *What's it all for?* The dark charm goaded him some more. Fabio listened numbly, staring firmly ahead into the torchlight dividing darkness. The blackness around him looked so comfortable, so easy to give up and fall into, then there would be nothing.

Nipping his lip with his teeth brought his consciousness back from his dream. *My God, a waking dream! What happened? It's this place. Get a bloody grip!* The professor fought himself. He focused again and double checked his footing. He knew his survival depended on a steady equilibrium between nerves and imagination, a balance linking doom with success rested right now on him having a calm mind.

Phew! That was scary, game on! Taking a deep breath and holding it, he exhaled slowly and steadily pushed his obituaries away. A coolness and confidence settled into his nerves, his mind urging him still, *do not look down, do not look down.* Some nerves remained; Fabio took another deep breath in and looked down.

He was back in control, the darkness waited but his mind ignored the murky calls from the pit; Fabio breathed out and moved with the fluidity of quicksilver.

"It is a long way down boys, anybody got a parachute handy?" He was happy and in high spirits again, his voice echoed through the quiet space back to the anxious men.

"What is happening, professor?" Endrissi called back.

"The gap continues! There is still no floor anywhere to be seen!"

"Be careful, professor!" Kees bellowed his support as Fabio carefully shifted his position bit-by-bit. The men felt nausea in their mouths and in the pits of their stomachs, they could not take more of this suspense.

Fabio continued traversing methodically, placing wall nuts into numerous groove positions and increasing his pace all the time. He was acutely aware of his limited energy resources to finish the job. The next section of hard graft would be very tricky.

Negotiating around another protrusion, his climb continued with its square edge, quickly turning a hundred and eighty degrees. No other light could get through except from the sharp headlamp strapped onto his forehead. The wall opposite him ran in parallel and he moved on into the dark bastion. The climb so far had taken fifteen minutes and was much tougher than he had first anticipated with its zigzagging walls, the route resembled the edges of a giant stone zip with many teeth.

"Professor, how are you getting on?" Kees called out, him and Endrissi feeding more of the spirit rope to the spider already edging around another precarious outthrust.

And as much as the professor did not want to admit it, he really hoped that around the next corner would be the end of his climb, imagining that the floor would appear and continue somewhere ahead. His climb in the darkness had a completely unknown quantity. This could easily end up as a one-way trip with no floor at all.

Fabio moved like a blind man, warily taking his time and partially feeling his way along. He could not see around the next obstruction and past the narrower wall face. His heart beat faster because the protrusion stuck treacherously outwards.

Taking a few deep breaths, he decided to go for it. The bold move immediately proving awkward to negate. Sweat poured off his brow, dripping and stinging into his eyes that made this section particularly dangerous. He caught the groove with his right hand while moving his leg over and stretching it, when his left hand slipped off.

"Ah!" He said in a low short shout, losing his grip and knocking his breath out. "Ooof!" Fabio grunted, while automatically holding on with his right hand, his arm socket stretching out in pain. With extra effort, Fabio began moving his body weight and swinging more like a monkey let alone a spider around the outcrop. In that split second, his momentum slapped his body hard onto the wall and he found himself glued face to cheek onto its smooth surface, kissing unspoken curses to the dry rock.

"Grip it!" He said, his tone deep and guttural while his eyes bulged and grimaced in protest. His slender piano-like fingers gripped into the narrow-channelled groove, instantly tensing. His shaking arm was locked in extreme effort, with this manoeuvre suddenly turning into a one armed pull up and with his legs, scuffing them off the polished wall to generate friction. He then lifted himself just enough to get his legs to catch into the lower groove. With his toes inside, he began pushing on them more, unbearably levering himself back up. His other hand quickly got hold, and to his relief, he began balancing again with an equal grip by pulling himself up flush with the wall.

Fabio had managed to get around the right-angle outthrust, heart pounding to bursting point with this forced manoeuvre leaving him hugging the wall and muttering curses; his muscles screamed for oxygen.

His long reach, wiry joints and extreme effort saved his life. Fortunately, the others were completely unaware that he had almost fallen into the pit because the rope had still plenty of slack. *Ignorance is bliss,* he thought. His muscles shaking with the continual stress of being in tension, he stood in the groove and could not go on. There was no time to lose other than to catch his breath. Fabio dug deeper and had just enough stamina to go on.

"Phew!" Fabio sighed. *Thank God, I am around it, more difficult than I expected.* A silent prayer opened his eyes quickly to check his immediate confines, which were clear as anything.

The floor! My God, I have made it and only about four metres to go.

****

"Fabio how are you getting on?" a distant voice anxiously called to him. It was Endrissi's echo from the darkened silence.

"I am fine! I have traversed the most difficult section." Fabio placed another wall nut tightly into position. "I can see the floor!" His stressed voice stammered with exertion, the floor so close to him, almost within touching distance. "I can see the floor! We are in luck men!"

Fabio's beam reflected off the white surface of the floor and simultaneously highlighted the bare blank walls enclosing a connecting corridor. The professor deliberately fastened a karabiner into the wire loop end of the nut, heard the click and fixed in securely. His confidence was supreme pulling on his rope again when quite by chance, Fabio fumbled and awkwardly slipped losing his footing.

"Aaarrrr!" He screamed loudly, with no time to think, plummeting into the darkness.

"Twang! Rrrrrzzzz," the rope ran fast. The human spider looking up helplessly, falling down the shaft out at a frightening pace. All he could do was listen to the high-pitched friction noise coming from the rope.

Accelerating at a frightening speed, the wall nut held its anchor point. There was no time to think, only time to panic; hysteria held his horrified mind.

"Rrrrrzzzzzzzzzzzzzzzzzzzzzz," the rope heated up, zooming through the metal loop like a high-speed train running unimpeded for seconds. The line of wall nuts and karabiners pulled down heavy and tight.

Instantly the rope tightened, stretching and then unexpectedly stopping dead, jerking him hard then catapulting him upwards.

He felt like he was on a trampoline, and his mind the same. There were many points of potential failure.

His eyes inspecting the wall nuts, karabiners and rope along the distant line. *Will they take the stress? Will they hold?*

****

At the far end, the heavy anchor men, Kees and Endrissi, both gasped when the bombshell blew. The rope pulled tight running fast. Shock mixed with panic as there was no doubt in their faces; Fabio was falling!

Fabio's sudden screams came to them from the distance, echoing his warnings of imminent doom and death. Each man looked at each other, startled. The rope already whizzed through their hands. This could easily have happened at any time, yet nothing could have prepared them to its sudden gravity.

The simple swiftness of physics, even with Fabio's light frame, made his weight at speed feel much heavier. The rope whipped past them like a shot, their arms reflexively pulling back, taking the strain like a tug of war. Instinctively bulging eyes were drawn onto the straight rope as they took the torturous strain. It had all seemed too quiet, too simple, and now their traumatized features squeezed into furrowed fears of sweat and panic.

The rope pulled firm and then slipped as if greased, sprinting off again through Endrissi's gloved hands. Without thinking, he gripped it harder but was unable to hold onto the spiteful lifeline because his palms were heating up fast. Endrissi shouted out in anguish and pain. The rope cut into his leather gloves and he knew that the pain would soon become unbearable.

"Mmph! Aaaghhhhh," Kees called with the same hot rush of friction.

"Shiiiit!" Endrissi shouted, resisting.

"Aaaagh it hurts!" Kees gripped harder, forcing more agony into his hot palms. The thin rope bit through his gloves and made his face grimace in pain.

"Hold him!" Endrissi said, demanding more help, his face sharp with urgency as the rope rasped through his gloves. The rope suddenly stopped and slackened a few times then set taut as the men held it firmly. It had only been a few seconds, the strain on their faces tighter than the rope. Sweat poured off the men, each agonisingly tugging, using incredible strength; it was obvious that their effort could not go on for much longer.

"Pull him!" Endrissi insisted.

"I, can't," Kees said, his hands blistering.

"Hold him!" Endrissi's gritty voice struggled.

The rope tensed tighter than a stretched bowstring as both men anxiously stared into the darkened depths as respite seemed a-far-cry from Fabio's lifeline. Somewhere down there they knew he would be dangling. The problem was, they could not pull him any further, he was stuck.

The men competed with failure, staring at each other in angry denial. They were out of ideas and in the end, gravity would win, and Fabio would fall to his death.

"Fabio, Fabio! What is happening?" Endrissi called desperately through the darkness. Nothing came back, no answer.

"Professor, can you hear us?" Kees shouted next, both men unclear if they had heard Fabio's fraught voice replying like a distant echo in the reality of darkness. Their strength ebbed like flour through a sieve. Fabio was doomed to die.

****

The professor's body bounced stupidly around like a marionette. His puppet arms and legs flailing uncontrollably in mid-air below the level of the floor. He found himself dancing to the tune of yells from his struggling colleagues and caught between helplessness and desperation, but his reflexes were still trying to catch a grip of something.

The rope stretched and jerked hard onto his arched spine, shooting a sharp pain through the full-length of his body, hurting him while springing back up like a trampoline; his horizontal body unexpectedly righted into a better angle.

Luckily, the rope held. Fabio refocused his thoughts to escape, his head thumping in pain, blood trickling down his forehead; he was missing his climbing helmet. Peering up urgently above, the expedition leader had no idea why he had fallen. Right now, that did not matter, but living did.

Bloody hell! He thought. *Climb! Grab anything, now! The guys are big, thank God, but they will not be able to hold me for long.* Fabio's mind raced like his heart.

"Hold on to me men!" Fabio called out in the darkness. "I am dangling about fifteen feet below an indented ledge!"

"We hear you professor!" Kees yelled back.

"I don't have a good grip yet!" The professor's voice echoed through the chasm as he battled against gravity, trying to lift his outreached arm.

It felt heavy, very heavy, Fabio struggling to stretch upwards with his muscles screaming with lactic build up. The effort needed enormous strength as his tentative fingers touched the vertical rope.

Uncannily it moved away from him, like similar poles of a magnet. Fabio gave it another try, this time more determined while speaking into the darkness.

"I'll get it..." talking to himself. He didn't. *...this time...* "Mmmph!" but he was wrong about that too!

Fabio groaned curses then screamed pure hatred at it. "Aaagh!" He shouted angrily and dug deeper, his spirit defying failure. The man stretched out like on a torturous medieval rack and challenged his hour of darkness.

Blood pumped his propulsion forward and his fingers shook, all adrenaline was charged, and he touched the rope; this time he was lucky.

Fabio caught onto the climbing rope, and instantly began pulling himself vertically using both hands. Hugging the rope tightly like a lover, he quickly wrapped his legs around the rope and was on the move again. Upwards he went, his body expanding and contracting, worming rhythmically and getting higher.

Each movement took seconds with his knees up, compressed, then extending and pushing. His crossed legs and ankles allowed him to stand up perpendicular. Fabio was going for glory, with his men still holding his lifeline with each second seeming like an eternity.

The professor's keen eyes waned apprehensively, when without warning the rope slipped awkwardly and dropped him a few feet and sent him into a wild spin.

Shit! The men are losing. His primal fear had become literarily touch and go.

Kees sensed Fabio's alarm.

"Faib, are you alright!" Kees shouting Fabio's nickname. The men felt Fabio's desperation with each tug of the rope. "We will hold you!" Kees confirmed.

Fabio did not want to die, but realistically, Professor Mancini knew it would be only a matter of minutes before he would fall to his death. This set panic into him, the man unleashed his last energy reserves climbing at a superfast rate, bursting his mortal bounds.

"I can't." said Endrissi faltering.

"Come on, Endrissi. Hold him! Kees squeezed out his voice, using extreme effort to hold the rope. "You're slipping again, hold him, come on!" His veins stuck out, blood pulsing hard at his neck and forehead. They both had to do better.

All the time, Kees stared hard at Endrissi, gritting his teeth and breaking the pain barrier while his rope continued to dig into his blistered palms; sweat lashed out from every conceivable pore while pulling like a locomotive.

"I hope those wall nuts hold." Fabio spoke out to himself for reassurance. The chances of the men taking an extra strain on a failed anchor point did not bode well for him. He was high enough to reach out. "Uugh!" He groaned and gave it all his exertion. "Si!" He shouted out and got a hold of the outcrop on the wall.

He felt the white rock formation underneath, rough like crystalline and unlike the polished upper part where he had been traversing. This property had been fortunate because it gave him enough friction and foothold he needed. The lower groove in the smoother part of the wall was now just above his fingers.

The wiry professor was flexible and strong and forced his mind and readied his body.

One last go, God, and I can make it! I will not fail! His mind screamed into a last supreme effort, *I will not! I will not let the Holy See down!*

He vowed in an echo, his total loyalty and commitment bursting from him.

"I will not fail!" Fabio called loudly, and bolstered with such determination and willpower, pulling fiercely on the rope using his left hand and quickly joining it with his right.

Fabio projected his arm upwards as high as possible and was rewarded. His long arm stretch enough, catching onto the foot ledge. He gasped hard and gulped in a lungful of air but did not stop. With a superfast set of body movements, he generated enough pull for his right leg to get into position at an extraordinarily odd angle, one only those who are double-jointed could manage.

Fabio – the human spider, lifted higher, his left hand pulling simultaneously with the right in a breath-taking manoeuvre. Finally lifting his leg, able to position tentative toes inside the ledge and body lifting more, believing in himself. *And now for the other leg!*

His feet rested in the perilous groove and finally stood up straight once again, his chest heaving, muscles screaming between spasms. Instant relief washed over him, he was up at last.

"I am safe!" He shouted through the darkness. His relived voice echoed his safety.

"Thank God for that!" Kees replied instantly, "Si, and merda, don't let go again!"

"Not far to go now!" called the professor. He prayed silently but still had to finish the climb. His newfound calm encouraged him.

His face turned to the right and his body hugged the wall, edging closer to the finish line. *Just a few metres to go…*He made it! Fabio stretched out again while lifting another wall nut from his belt to finally secure him.

"Whoops, Fanculo!" Many climbers had died this way. Fabio was too relaxed and let his guard down. "Merda!" It was too late. His last reach was a little bit too far this time. His arms began to shake uncontrollably. Another drop would break the rope for certain. And now he was going to fall again. *Oh no, not now!* Fabio's hands shook nervously under this immense strain.

"I have got to make it!" Inserting his last wall nut just in the nick of time.

Once again, he stood on a solid stone floor, breathing hard and turning around with only his shredded nerves for company. Readjusting his headlamp, he cut its light through the narrow tunnel, fanning it to spread out the gap and the grooved wall he had traversed.

"I'm on the other side! I've done it!"

The feeling was like no other, an ultimate euphoria. His heart pumped pure adrenaline; he had been very lucky.

The rope dropped limp and Fabio sat down heavily with a well-earned sigh of self-satisfaction. Here he would relax for a long moment. Dreamily he began to remember years ago and back to a better time, a better day and another climb to Sgurr Alistair from Sgurr nan Gillean, South East Ridge in the Cuillin range in the Isle of Skye. Long ago he had smiled in triumphal satisfaction after that successful climb and as one man next to God.

This was no such place. He sat quietly inside the enclosing darkness with his legs dangling over the ledge. He looked with a sightless stare into the dark void below; God had no place to play here. An unsettled calm closed in. The Temple of MalisIblis was a far cry from the free mountain range thousands of miles away. Unlike the misty Isle of Skye, this was no scenic view and had no sense of oneness; Fabio felt its paradox. It was a great achievement and a great loneliness. His lone light looked down into the unimaginable Abyss below; it would be so easy to fall and forget everything.

****

He rested there for a while and it regenerated his sore and tired muscles. Professor Mancini's mind mended too. *What was that?* He heard a distant calling which awakened him. He stood up carefully, holding his stance steady and confidently pulling the rope tight; this was necessary for Kees and Endrissi to begin the construction of a temporary bridge.

"Fabio!" It was Endrissi's voice.

"Si!" Fabio replied.

"I had to dress Kees injured hand."

"Bad?"

"Si!"

"How bad?"

"Bad."

"I'll be fine, Fabio," Kees cut in. He was too proud to admit the seriousness. "I've taken pain killers, let's just get on with this construction job and get the hell out of here! Si?" Kees swallowed a groan.

"You both know how to use the telescopic poles, we have practiced it often enough!" The professor shouted. "Build it using the wall grooves."

End to end, Fabio had calculated the distance using the length of rope and the number of poles required. He was relieved that the team had brought enough for the job.

Orders were given and it would take a few hours to build and test. The lightweight extending poles came in small sections easily linked to each other with adjusting lengths to fit. Time passed while the men worked hard reaching the far end of the first section of the wall. Endrissi and Kees used their specially designed ratchet tool to fix both ends firmly, making the horizontal pole flat and as firm as steel. This the basic building blocks of an unmovable scaffold construction safe enough to take their weight.

These super plastic designed poles were positioned inside the grooves, forming the first complete straight section. The men meticulously checked and rechecked each pole position until all sections were securely in place. It had become a unified structure ready to use. The climbing rope remained at about chest height, giving more balance, with each man having his own safety rope just in case. Kees and Endrissi patiently took turns fixing the next section of the pole construct. Eventually, the men were able to work around to where Fabio had previously negated.

****

It had been several hours before the interim construction had been made safe enough to cross over, however, even now they all could speak to each other from the closing distance when they turned the last corner. Endrissi saw Fabio's torch beaming towards him; the Professor was waiting for him.

"Endrissi, it is good to see you again!" Fabio helped the geologist with the last part of the pole construction. At last, both Endrissi and Kees stood safely on the solid floor with the professor.

"Well done men, a great effort putting all those poles together." Fabio's relief was obvious.

"Fabio, it is great to see you in one piece! We thought that you were a goner." Kees spoke with a new mark of respect for the professor's self-achievement and courageousness.

"Let me see your hands Kees?" Fabio retrieved a bandage and cream from his first-aid kit, taking off his dressing to look at Kees sore palms.

"I'll live." Kees winced as Fabio removed his makeshift dressing.

"This antiseptic cream should help and take these strong painkillers. You will have to take good care of this wound. In this climate it could easily turn septic in a few hours. Harjit will give you some antibiotics when we get back to base camp. Hopefully we'll get out of this place by tomorrow morning."

"I'll be fine, Prof." Kees did not want to make a fuss.

"I am in your debts, Senores," Fabio said, expressing his gratitude. "Thanks to God, we all have made it across."

They waited for a short time and ate and rested, gathering their strength for the next leg of their journey into the unknown. Ready again, Fabio's face firmly fixed on the blackness beyond.

"Leading the way Professor?" Endrissi asked tentatively.

"Follow me." Fabio smiling confidently. Everyone wore head torches and their beams burrowed sharp channels through the blackness ahead. "I did not go any further than here, remember, we stick together." With a firm nod, Fabio was proud of his team and set off, the others following.

Doggedly, the route followed a familiar zigzag pattern, and after a short while, the corridor descended. Since crossing the Abyss, everything looked laboriously the same; even Fabio, like the others, lost all sense of progress.

Oddly, another slow change began and the passage gradually brightened. Progressing more, the light diffused from inside the horizontal wall grooves.

"Strange." Fabio's eyebrow raised an inch. *I knew it! The grooves had a purpose after all.*

"How can this be?" Kees was anxious seeing this uncanny phenomenon appearing around them; it seemed impossible as the light got brighter.

"The light source is emanating from inside the crystalline structure within the grooves."

The air was as still as a held breath in this melancholic semi-darkness. Now there was enough light that it spurned them to switch off their headlamps.

"You look awful Faib." Kees expressed his open thoughts, not realising that they all looked the same way.

"I could have been doing with this light an hour ago. However, let us be thankful for small mercies, Senores. This is a bonus, we have light!" Fabio spoke enthusiastically while looking at his watch, 11:30 P.M; it was late.

"How is this light produced? Do you have any theories professor?" Kees touched the wall and asked Fabio what he knew. The professor said nothing.

"Strange there is no heat from the walls," observed Endrissi.

"I would have expected something?" Kees was more puzzled than ever.

They twisted along this pedantic route and the men continued in and out like before.

Fabio seemed to be in deep thought, when quite unexpectedly the stone pattern stopped. Suddenly artificial illumination emanated from every part of the stone structure. The light blasted out from everywhere and the stone crystal walls pulsated rhythmically and in unison, its intense oscillations making everyone feel giddy.

"I have never come across such an ancient civilization like this one. Extraordinary it has a source of real power," said Endrissi, who wanted to say more about the discovery, but Fabio beat him to it.

"The ancient Mayan civilization had no such knowledge of electricity. We must be thankful for the published work of *Treatise De Magnete, Magneticisique Corporibus* on the magnet by William Gilbert in 1600 A.D. Then Benjamin Franklin in June of 1752." Fabio lectured them, and he was just warming up.

Kees suppressed a desire to yawn.

"Si, I remember," agreed Endrissi. "He performed his famous kite experiment, charging a Leyden jar from a key at the end of the string and drawing down electricity from the clouds." It was Endrissi's turn again, "And what about Thomas Edison, in 1879 using lower current electricity, a small carbonized filament was able to produce a reliable, long-lasting light?" Endrissi joined this riveting discussion, offsetting another long sigh from Kees.

"Now this light phenomenon which we have here is apparently quite different. Obviously, we have made an astounding discovery, Signores! Inside this temple, we have discovered a light source that is incredibly still operational after all this time. I would guess it's been here since our own recent history. We must ask ourselves the question, is this source electrical? I think, sooner than later all our questions will be answered."

"I do not entirely agree with you Fabio," stated Endrissi. "This building was built when our ancestors were hunting and living in caves, not in 1879!" The man smiled and said smugly, "*Do you go with this?*" Endrissi critically re-evaluated Fabio's light theory.

"I wonder how Harjit's team are faring tonight, I think their exploits will be a little less hazardous than this one."

Fabio was beaten, and changing the subject, he fed more to the master of Academia, Endrissi.

"They'll probably be drinking coffee and singing by the campfire by now." Kees thought how he would like to join them even more now than anything else.

"I would not be too sure about that," countered Endrissi. "They must have come across some obstacles inside here too, it's a massive superstructure, and I am convinced it has many other hidden secrets to spring on us."

"I hope they are outside, I really do. This place is too dangerous," Fabio concluded.

"All temples are unique, I just hope they have been careful," Kees said, also concerned.

"She knows to leave if it gets too dangerous," said Fabio. "These new discoveries truly knock Christopher's idea of freemasonic influence right on its head."

It was so bright here that sunglasses would not have been out of place. Fabio walked forward preoccupied with a semblance of a smile, his all knowing opinion rearing its ugly head once again. He was completely unaware that his keen observational skills had deteriorated.

The floor was dead level, it had been that way for a short time and in this growing light made their eyes water. The passageway opened into a perfect square tunnel. They were progressively getting much closer to the source when the area expanded massively in front of them. Inside, the place was like a giant cube, its walls all spotlessly clean, virgin white and extreme with brilliant brightness blaring out off the walls from everywhere. Everyone strained apprehensively inside, daring to think, this was it. Each man was silent, having arrived at their final destination.

Directly above them and going around the entrance, there was a reddish opaque coloured border with strange codices extending along into a hallway. The entrance was a perfect seven square yards, although its planes were almost indistinguishable from everywhere else. It was the border that made the difference. They could see a distant wall facing them and although they did not know its dimensions, it was forty-three-yard square if measured accurately.

The most striking object was a strange golden sun face set into the opposing stone wall. The object was positioned at centre and two thirds up, where its gleaming face stared. Strangely, it gave the illusion of being suspended magically in mid-air. All three explorers stood quietly, wondering whether to walk inside.

"Were here," Fabio spoke softly. "Follow me."

The professor stepped inside, and it was like walking into a white stone box. Taking a deep clinical breath, Fabio stared with excitement. The others looked on unsure.

The men cautiously approached the facing wall, but their eyes could not perceive from this distance the several double etched grooves cut deep into the walls. Deep grooves ran downwards from below the top two corners of the large square wall, extending like a cone or wedge-shaped triangle, and tapering to a point below the level floor plane.

The men kept walking forward, getting closer to the far wall and its sun image, holding them with hypnotic traction as its gaze strangely pulled them further inside.

At the point where both grooved lines met together below floor level, a second grooved wedge cut upwards from there, extending in the opposite direction towards the ceiling. The men got closer, the inverted apex below gradually coming more into their strained view.

They felt awkward and apprehensive about the purpose of this near featureless place. Its design resembled a large star shape, the *star of David;* how incredible, how impossible!

The grooves seemed to almost vanish and their eyes became more accustomed to this place; their perception became less keen, melting into one. Their blank visions were too difficult to define in this whiteness and intense illumination. Everything here blending seamlessly together, the grooved geometry only perceivable until close.

And all this time, the facing wall of the golden sun face kept staring at them. The floor finished in white, and if it were not for the entrance and codex border, a person could easily loose themselves and become disorientated in this bright place where perception challenged intuition. They approached the golden sun face, its shining and gleaming effects being their main-focus, its aura attracting them like a honeypot towards it. They should have been warier in this almost featureless place, the danger was unseen and straight ahead. The white floor was bland too, it was like walking in a dream-like state with everything the same. Each man walking forward to certain death.

****

Fabio stopped with a jolt. It was as if someone had slapped his face, which shocked him into spotting a deep drop only a few metres in front of them. Panic rippled through their bodies, seeing what appeared to be a crevasse cutting across their way from one end of the wall to the other. It had been there all along.

"Watch out!" Fabio shouted. "That's a bloody sheer drop right in front of us!" Fabio's sharp sense of awareness and ever so keen eyesight had seen a slight difference in tone at the drop. Their feet set like cement from being so close to an almost transparent ledge; everyone took a few steps back, their powers of observation catching up.

"It's geometric," Endrissi stated glibly, aware of many lines assembled into shapes, one running horizontal to the floor bisecting both tapered lines that joined on the far side of the gap just underneath the floor level. He made out other identical lines like a mirror image above, both together creating a shape similar if not identical to a huge Godly symbol. Endrissi thought, *My God. It looks like the star of David.*

"Here we are Signores! This is the place we have been looking for. It is our final destination." Fabio's face lit up, hardly able to contain his glee.

"What exactly have you been looking for professor?" Kees eyes hardened, with rightful suspicion that Fabio had been holding out on him, not telling the truth. His government should have been pre-warned of the importance of this place.

"I see the simple geometrics and cut grooves on the facing wall look more like the Star of David! So, what do you mean Fabio?" It baffled Endrissi too, Fabio knew much more all the time, especially about this place.

"Si, this geometry has been used by other civilizations and not only Jewish. This place is where the real entrance exists." Fabio smiled sanctimoniously while believing, *I Fabio, have discovered the eighth wonder of the World!* The Professor thought in triumphal fulfilment, *"Here lies the real temple."*

"The real temple!" shouted Kees very annoyed, his eyes opening wildly with warning. He could see there was no doubt in the professor's mind about this place. The government official realised that this was what the professor had been searching for all along.

****

Fabio and the others' sore eyes were glued to studying the huge facing wall beyond the drop. They could clearly see that inside the upper apex of this geometrical shape, it held the three-dimensional golden sun face set into the white illuminating stone. A sun face with seven wavy flames was the most significant artefact in this large mysterious area. Each golden flame displayed the effect of a ray of sunlight, and no doubt in their minds, it was all made of pure gold. This iconic design impressively looked down on them; it commanded their respect. The men stepped cautiously nearer to it and towards the edge for closer inspection, wanting to know more.

It became more evident that this deep chasm at their feet was a longitudinal gap cut away, the drop running parallel and separating the floor from the wall. A wall-to-wall barrier was set between them, displaying another mind-numbing precipice thirty-two foot wide. The gap was completely impassable. Weirdly, the surface sloped closest to them like a slide before plummeting into a sheer vertical and bottomless drop.

"Is nothing ever simple?" Kees said, fed up with the expedition.

"Not again, Christ!" the geologist cursed while looking desperately down into the white crevice, gauging it. "How far does it go?" He wondered. They all plainly saw that there was no way across.

"Makes life more interesting, does it not Endrissi?" Said Fabio while looking at the drop from a few paces away. "Surely you did not think that whoever built this place would only have one little obstacle for us now, did you?" He humoured a little too quietly while surveying the dangerous chasm. "It's too difficult to see down because of this slope in front."

"I'll give you that one," Kees agreed.

"If it had been dark inside here, we'd be dead. This is a trap. More than just a barrier, it is a death moat. I think it will prove to be ultra-deep, based on previous experience. If you step on this slope, you will not be able to scramble back up because of the steep angle and this polished surface, so no chance."

"Who said an explorers' life is a dull one." Fabio smiled. "Look at those interesting codices within the pentagram."

The professor and the others began to refocus on many of the strange looking complex shapes. The professor considered these implications, wishing secretly for once that he had asked Christopher to come with him.

Endrissi's eyes blinked rapidly, his head shaking in disbelief, studying these numerous lines and how they met together at the apexes. He observed the overall symbolic design and thought, *what a sign!*

As if on cue, he threw aloft a small handful of coins he had in his pocket. Everyone watched them turning almost in slow motion in mid-air before quickly dropping and disappearing into the gaping white trench.

They waited and listened but there was nothing but silence; no sound at all and the moment passed.

"I wish you would stop your school boy pranks." Fabio seemed more anxious than irritated. He also wondered where the shower of coins had fallen.

When they least expected it, eventually to their disquiet, the silence was broken by an echo of tiny chinks striking something at a very great distance.

It was very deep, and the chinking noises became increasingly distant and eventually went out of earshot. Endrissi remembered something he had wanted to forget. Without consideration, a silent memory was stimulated, followed instantly by a haunting visage of Carmello. Endrissi's lips quavered in tune with his damaged mind.

"I would say maybe two hundred feet or more at a guess," Kees said rubbing his head.

"Nonsense," Fabio replied, looking at him as if he were stupid.

"No, much deeper. You could not imagine. I cannot even guess at it," Endrissi stuttered and sensed some wrong doing, wishing he had kept his coins.

Immediately the brightness around them began strangely fading as if its power was draining like melting ice from the crystalline stonework. The whole chamber drew dimmer and dimmer as the men stared around helpless to stop it.

"Great idea you had their Endrissi! You caused the light to go, so what is going on? What are we going to do now?" Kees spoke angrily to the geologist who had triggered their apparent demise, "That was your bloody fault Endrissi!" He said, snapping at him in a conceited voice. Endrissi could have cried then; he looked dreadfully sorry and dreadfully afraid, his eyes rolling and blinking uncontrollably.

"Sorry, sorry, sorry," Endrissi kept on repeating his apology.

"Quiet," Fabio demanded, there was something else he had heard from underneath. He turned his ear towards the trench, trying to listen more clearly. He felt an intense dread at something mysterious happening, something he had not calculated. A creaking or moaning sound came from deep inside the trench. Then a quiet calm settling for a moment followed again by that sound.

"There it is again!" He involuntarily called out while watching the others. The two men were looking at each other alarmed because they heard nothing at all.

"Apologies professor, we do not hear a thing," Kees stated with a blunt face. Endrissi nodding robotically in agreement while watching Fabio questionably.

Fabio needed to know if he was losing his mind, *is my imagination getting the better of me? I have been down here too long.* For the first time, Professor Mancini doubted his own sanity.

Meanwhile, the light energy was going fast, waning more until it was completely gone. Absolute darkness took hold of their hearts and minds and in under a minute, the men stood in blackness with sightless expressions, each fighting delirium and decision.

"Get your torches on!" Fabio's nervous voice seemed dampened inside this black void. Sudden sanity and survival fought to win, his amnesia killing his thinking processes. Fabio suppressed his growing panic. To lose it now would be suicide, he was only a few fatal steps away from the abyss. "No!" Fabio shouted out sharply as voices inside his head played with him. The reality of his own voice stopped his mind from walking through the void and gripping onto his frayed identity.

Endrissi suffered from this delirium too and in the darkness his uncertain mind started to crack at its edges but his logic told him they were all still there together. The geologist suffered too, he could hear their heavy breathing and Fabio's crazy shouting. Endrissi felt a deep dread, suspecting his mind was unhinged in fear, and thought he heard somebody walking.

Step...step...

"Come back!" Endrissi yelled fearfully, his courage lacerated. The blackness was an asphyxia that was absolute and all encompassing. Endrissi struggled to speak while breathing heavily, sweat expressed from every pore, chest tightening and his head giddy. He held his chest as if it was going to burst, and in the blackness he suddenly gave up, sitting down heavily. *My God, I am having a heart attack!*

Click! There was light!

"Oh!" Endrissi called out, totally surprised at seeing Fabio's torch-lit face lighting up spookily, his body cast in shadows looking down at him. Endrissi was unsure of his own whereabouts and could not take much more. His battle-fatigued brain tried to grasp reality once again.

"Steady," the professor said, his calm tone reaching down to the man's sanity. Fabio understood that Endrissi could not last like this but the light settled him a little.

In this new light, they looked for solace in each other, trying to find it anywhere. In this limited illumination, one light suddenly became three; Kees and Endrissi had switched on their torches too. Scarily, all three men were aware that they were far too close to the sloped edge.

****

"Step back from the precipice men," Fabio's tone commanded. "We need to have a rest and something to eat, follow me."

"Si, Si, that would be very good!" Endrissi got up and retreating to a safe distance with the men back from where they entered the cubed chamber.

"Now that we have found this place, we could return and continue this exploration another day." Kees hoped Fabio would see sense. His hand throbbed with pain.

Roaring gas stoves soon began heartening them, although the noise seemed to drop dead in the complete blackness. It was like sitting in a sound booth; the loneliness was unnerving. In a short time, their muffled voices held a fear that was stifled in claustrophobic silence.

The temple was a beast of a place. Its subjugation completely overwhelmed in any scale of measurements, threatening to engulf their very being. Yet, hope remained. After a while their enthusiasm began to rekindle and from staring at the blue flames of the small camping stove which gave them a sense of comfort. They all laughed loudly and pretended to be hundreds of miles from where they were sitting right now. Heads turned and faces brightened when Fabio pulled out a large bottle of Limoncello.

"I think we all deserve a little well-earned break Signores!" Fabio grinned.

"Ah Limoncello, manifico Fabio!" Endrissi shouted cheerfully.

"You do surprise us!" Said Kees astonished.

Fabio twisted the bottle top that cracked loudly and sent a cheerful echo around them.

"I think a celebration is in order Signores." He poured the lemon liquid into their tin mugs. "We rest here tonight then decide what to do tomorrow morning. To us!" Fabio toasted, raising his salute.

"To us!" Spirits were high and everyone chorused together.

The bittersweet Limoncello reminded the professor of the baking hot Italian orchards back home, bringing thoughts akin to near tranquillity for him. He had stashed two bottles for this occasion and soon they were all quite merry.

After a while, Fabio rifted loudly while staring at them blankly. They looked at each other before suddenly rifting in unison. The men unexpectedly burst their sides.

"God bless you Faib! Both men chorused for a third time.

"You know." Kees opened up a bit bothered. "I do not fancy waking up in the darkness, this place creeps me out."

"Here, this will help." Fabio handed him another mugful.

"Molto bene Faib, thanks." The Government official polished off another nightcap.

Without thinking, Endrissi took out some large candles from his own backpack and proceeded to ritualistically position and light all five of them. The others watched quietly without asking; it looked like part of a ceremony. Nobody thought to question him, especially if it made him feel better.

He sat them meticulously around their sleeping area, taking his time with what looked like semi-unconscious deliberation. His sluggish movements were the result of the most welcome alcoholic beverage. He hoped this circle of light might give them shaman-like protection.

The light from the candles illuminated the cubed hall around them as the enclosing darkness threatened its magical aura. There was just enough light for them to switch off their torches and they settled down for the night. Endrissi estimated that the candles could easily burn for a few days.

"Night is like day in this place." Kees gathered closer to one candle for comfort; its warm luminescence attracted him to it like a moth to light.

"What will we do next Fabio?" Endrissi slurred some more.

"I have found the place we seek. However, our resources are now so depleted we have no other option other than to return to base camp."

"Phew!" Endrissi sighed heavily.

"Brilliant!" said Kees, relieved.

"We can begin a fresh assault in a few days concentrating down here with a larger more penetrative group."

"Fabio, there have been so many unusual happenings inside this place. Where did that mysterious light come from and why did it disappear like that? I keep thinking that something else is in here, with us. I feel it, this place is evil."

"I really do not know what you are talking about Endrissi," Fabio lied.

"Something is listening. Watching our every move."

"No, we are quite alone." Fabio tried to bring a stabilising influence on his colleague's uninhibited ramblings. "I assure you there is nobody about. A lot of unanswered questions, Si, but this is why we are here.

"But..."

"But nothing, it is impossible for anyone or anything to be watching us. The light source we experienced is unique and quite unexpected. Maybe it is a renewable source of energy, a natural resource inside these rocks, and I am sure we would all agree this is a discovery that may change the world's energy needs!"

"I have not come across anything like this rock type ever before," Endrissi agreed. "You are right and in all my years, it's unnatural."

"This place is ancient," Kees said.

"Given time we will find there is a reasonable and logical explanation behind all of this. Signores, this is a fantastic discovery and that my friends is our game. This is what we live for!"

Fabio continued to speak for a little while longer to himself, the drink helping him talk and the silence too. Even the government official was sleeping soundly. Endrissi loosely twitching in a disturbed slumber but something else was bothering Fabio, it was that unnatural noise, a worrying sound of something elemental; a sound from the pit.

Fabio tried to put his thoughts at the back of his mind, but his drunken state made him remember them instead. Lying alone, he thought, *Endrissi just might be right.*

The professor closed his eyes and was unexpectedly asleep in an instant. The search, the climb, and all the stress had really taken its toll. His unconscious state quickly translated out of this world, listening to haunting dreams calling on him. Once more like every other night, everyone's souls were floating in a spirit world, all spirits mixed up in the *ether,* until found.

The temple was a dreadful place, where spirits were chased by demons. It was a disturbing place to be lost in, and a dwelling not so different to where Giovanni Dalla Gassa, the Cardinal, visited each evening. To where he too began a cat and mouse game between spirit and demon, a place of parry and pursuit bursting all mortal bounds. There was a link, there always had been. This was a place where time and distance meant nothing, with no physical confines of the world.

Inside the temple, in the dreamland, it had become a living hell for everyone in a war that had begun millennia ago. The physical evidence was seen by the expedition all around them and they were now a part of it too. In this place of living nightmares, their own war was about to begin.

The psychological evidence was experienced every time they slept, finding themselves in a battle, forgotten next day. Leaving them with only an illogical sense of foreboding and a feeling of dread they could not explain. What was happening to them? Unknown to them, what was coming their way would be much worse.

In the semi-darkness, they all laid exhausted and asleep on portable foam mats, using rucksacks for makeshift pillows. From above, their positioning was curiously shaped into a star; with their heads close together at its centre, their legs pointing out towards a candle. Inside the cubed hall, the air stood motionless with five flames burning high and steady. Each candle illuminated five circular areas evenly around the star. At the end of each flame, a tall slender shadow had appeared standing sinisterly outside the star, watching them sleep.

****

Hours later, Fabio was disturbed by a dark dream of black clouds and a dark flying creature. Remaining outside the star, a slender shadow drew closer towards him. Still unaware of its presence but it startled him out of troubled vision. Fabio instantly opened his eyes widely staring straight upwards into darkness. His heart was thumping. He didn't dare move, lying frozen in fear, because something felt really bad.

Fabio could not explain it, but he felt scared to move, except for his eyes already scanning the high ceiling. *What's wrong?* Nothing seemed different yet his mind was on edge. The candlelight projected a large weird shadow from another source. It was then he became aware of the dark shadow that was of a man projected onto the ceiling. His heart began pacing harder in panic.

Disorientated, he took a few slow seconds to comprehend where he was. *I am in the temple*, he urgently turned his head towards the shadow and saw what it was, and it was *not* the tall mysterious figure that had been watching him. It was the shadow of Kees. A pinprick of reality stabbed Fabio's mind, the professor instantly sat up alarmed.

"Kees?" He was not next to him. Fabio swung sharply around to see where he had gone. *Is that really him over there?* Straining his eyes, he saw a man's dark shape standing holding one of the candles. *My God he's standing above the precipice.* Fabio tried hard to make sense of the looming catastrophe.

Instinctively, Fabio wanted to shout a warning, but he didn't want to startle him over the ledge. He got up and walked quietly towards him until he stood behind Kees.

"Kees." Fabio spoke in his soft steady voice, gently holding the man's shoulder. Sweat lashed off his forehead, clearly under pressure. The professor's calm tone drifted in the darkness. "I wouldn't go any closer my friend. You know it is quite unsafe over here. Come back with me." His voice articulated authority and stability.

The large explorer did not to hear his words. Kees appeared to be in a trance, and he began coughing uncontrollably. He stood there shaking then fell hard to his knees. He held his throat gasping for air with one hand and dropped his candle. Fabio reached out to hold him when a torchlight began shining on the struggling men.

Endrissi was already running towards them as the candle started rolling away down the short slope, its illumination falling into the chasm, then was gone.

"What's going on? What's wrong with him?" Endrissi arrived to help half-awake, trying to comprehend the impossible.

"Kees was going to fall down there." Fabio pointed to the chasm. "What the hell he was doing here, is anyone's guess. Come on Endrissi give me a hand with him."

They laid the semi-conscious man onto the floor, and loosened his belt, making sure there were no obstructions to his breathing. Around Kees' neck hung a gold chain and small pendant, one that he always wore; a pendant of a large letter G.

"What does the G symbol mean?" Endrissi asked.

"One God." Fabio replied with no hesitation. Kees stopped shaking and began opening his dream-like eyes. "Are you alright Kees? Take it easy now.' Fabio spoke softly. "Have a small drink of water."

"What happened?" Endrissi nervously asked Kees.

"I, I am not sure." Kees bewildered face explained nothing. "I was dreaming of, of, something, an opening, and of shadows, all engulfing me. And *I think* they were *strangling* and *pulling* me. Strangely I seemed to be going further into the temple. *I forget the rest!* I do not know now, it's gone. What the hell, it was only a dream."

"Your dream almost killed you. Why did you not tell me?"

"Tell you what?"

"That you sleep walk!" Fabio was concerned.

"Sleep walk? I 've never done that in my entire life, I don't do that kind of thing." Kees face went from bewildered to the realisation of his near-death experience.

"You do now." Endrissi spoke, thinking of the similarities that befell Carmello.

My God it's bizarre, Endrissi thought, *Kees could have gone the same way as Carmello. I know it, he was in a trance and by himself too when he died.* Endrissi felt heavy guilt.

"*Gracias, grazie molte!* I think that is what you would say in Italian, professor." The Brazilian was very grateful to Fabio for saving his life.

"We need you Kees." The professor smiled quietly. *Poor Kees, it has all been too much for him, and Endrissi too. I cannot trust him anymore. A grave incident averted si, but the cause might be claustrophobia and, the Devil's work. Unless we get assistance, only a few of us will make it out.* Fabio's conscience was without falter. *My goal is the same, my mission is very clear. I knew this journey would be perilous.*

The professor reminded himself of his holy mission, and inwardly began justifying any human expense, including his own.

"Thanks professor," said Kees.

"Let's get you back over to where the rucksacks are." Fabio had come to a decision. "We will get ready to leave once you feel well enough."

"I'm more than ready now professor." Kees' spirit lifted while Fabio assisted him back onto his feet. Returning to the circle of candles, Fabio wanted to mark today.

"You know signores, it's the 1st of October."

"Oh, really?" Endrissi was not interested in the date.

A short time later the men had breakfast, their rations depleted substantially. Water was also in short supply, but the way back would be much easier. Having packed up, everyone was ready to go. Kees wrapped his bandage again around his wounded hand, swallowing some more painkillers.

"It's getting worse Fabio. The quicker we get out of here, the better. Harjit will be able to fix me. I will need some antibiotics for sure, it's now infected."

Fabio took his hand, looking at his wound. He applied a fresh clean dressing.

"Sure, she will that's her job." Fabio could tell that speed was required. The professor was last to leave the cubed chamber.

At the entrance above him it was bordered with large red sandstone blocks protruding out from the wall surface where codices were inscribed.

He had to stop to look back inside once more. Fabio's torch beamed again onto the sunstone, its Godly image shined out powerfully, chasing the mute shadows to vanish. Fabio felt unsure. He began turning nervously and was soon gone with the others leaving these slender shapes to wait there for their return.

Hours later, the men were once again standing where they had descended the previous day. It was late morning and as luck would have it, they found them standing and staring straight up the shaft. No rope? No ladder either!

"Why worry?" Kees said, he resigned himself to their disappointment.

"Where is Harjit? She should have been here." Endrissi moaned.

"Harjit! Harjit!" Fabio called up, anything could have befallen her as he looked bedraggled hunched down heavily next to his crumpled companions; no water or food, everyone exhausted resting hard against the walls. Even for the "Human Spider", Fabio shook his head at the shear polished walls above him. A free solo was out of the question, the shaft too high than he had the energy for. This would be their end, left to die in this dinginess at the bottom of a pit. Their fate soon to be a pile of rags and dry bones.

****

CHAPTER XII

SHADOW OVER THE SEA OF TRANQUILITY

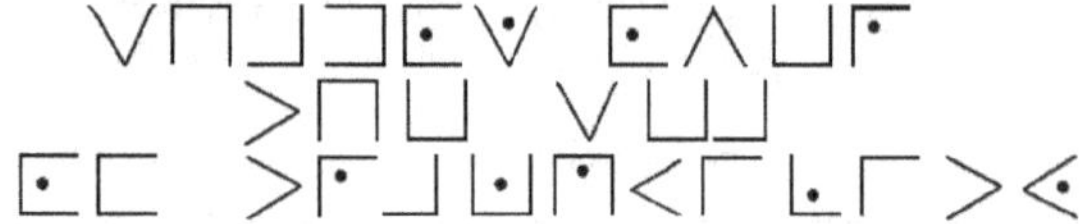

Inside the temple and long before it found Fabio sitting at the bottom of the shaft, Harjit had begun the chain reaction inside creating a myriad of illumination effects, sending them bursting into the forest through its moon windows.

Unknown to them, it was *they* who had been the essential catalyst for these cataclysmic events to be seen beyond its bounds. This was the same crazy moment taken over in mayhem just when Mykola and Sebastiano arrived back at base camp and quickly realised the camp was empty. Suddenly the men saw a rainbow of colours deluging the forest edges and without prelude, it all suddenly stopped. Without transition, the moon's illumination began whitewashing the temple in fear.

With base camp deserted and with Mashir's disappearance unexplained; it scared them. Only moments ago, the temple had been lit up like a giant firework. Maybe he got spooked and made a run for it, which might explain why he was not tending the fire and keeping a vigilant eye on their campsite.

It was wrong; there was no trace of him. If it were a group of drug traffickers casing the camp intent on kidnap, this might seem most likely. Yet, the death of Doctor. Boni Castiglion, with his limp and eviscerated body on top of the temple, defied this theory. Fearing the worst, if he was captured by headhunters, he was dead or soon would be. Searching around the immediate perimeter, they found nothing. There was no sign of a trail. Like children, the men felt vulnerable and alone. Mashir's belongings were gone too with no struggle. All signs suggested a secret departure. Logic seemed out of place. They believed that those same murderous natives *had him.*

"I think he's bolted." Seb suggested. "Must have seen these fireworks going off at the temple, had enough and was off! Lost his rocker and simply made a run for it."

"Not his style Seb," said Mykola shaking his head. Let's at least go up to the entrance and see if there's any sign of Fabio and the other guys. Maybe Mashir is up there too." Mykola held onto hope.

"Si, maybe, we'll see," Sebastiano shrugged.

"We just can't stay down here doing nothing. We must try and find out if the others are alright." Mykola's tone conveyed desperation. Sebastiano said nothing.

"Some crazy happenings and now this shit with Mashir. No matter how you look at it, it's bad and I don't want us to be next." Sebastiano watched the forest fearfully. The trees made strange unearthly noises swaying wildly in the strengthening wind.

"Me neither, I don't want my head shrunk. First, they dart you, and then, *have their way.*" Mykola's mind textured the intimate process of head shrinking.

"*Have their way?* What do you mean?" Sebastiano grimaced.

"It's an art form for some tribes."

"*Is it?*" Sebastiano's face stiffened.

"When you are alive, they prepare your head by sewing your eye lids shut *and then your lips* so you cannot scream. Then come the ointments, *before.*"

"*Shut up!* SHUT UP!" Sebastiano shouted.

"Listen to me, three people killed!" Mykola blurted. "Freaky lighting effects came out from the temple. An ancient building that lay dormant for countless centuries *and now* it's turned into some kind of bloody volcano! And to cap it all off, Mashir is gone! Picked off by a *headshrinker!* The civilization that once lived here *is dead* and it looks like our expedition is next in line to become extinct!" Mykola suddenly stopped talking realising that he had said too much.

"We cannot leave here, and we cannot get word back home." Sebastiano's weak resolve finally cracked. His abnormally large knuckles tightened with tension.

Calm settled into Mykola's raw nerves.

"Sorry, accept my apologies Sebastiano. I do not know what came over me." Mykola's medium frame seemed to crumble and shrink as if broken.

"Listen." Sebastiano replied softly. "It's my fault too. This place is not healthy for any of us. It has a mind of its own. I feel it working on me too, *don't you?*" In a solemn tone he asked, "Do you believe anyone will return?"

Above them, the moonlit temple was lit up in light-dark greys of dappled shadows, its massive rock face casting mystery against the blackened forest. Its rocky presence bearded a malign personality to all those who beheld its visage. Feeling lonely, the men were staring up further into the night sky, when something horrible appeared in the distance and set against the moon.

Seb and Myk both tried to say something, but nothing came from their dropping jaws. Each man hoped to believe that what they were seeing was part of a horrible dream. Instead the moon as if attracted to the edge of the world in some outlandish optical illusion, seemed to be drawing its bright surface closer to the earth. Its orbital lunacy transfixed their primal fears when unexpectedly an odd shaped flying creature appeared flying around its haloed edge.

Seen up there, an unnamed thing soared on invisible eddies, a forlorn and enigmatic form like that of a colossal pterodactyl yet not quite that either. Long ago extinct, it could not be. The two men questioned their eyes but what else could it be? The winged beast seemed to be squeezing on their hearts, unable to tear their eyes away from the mysterious apparition.

Breathing harder and heavier while watching it glide like a phantom across the bright lunar surface, their eyes screamed at the fiendish apparition. The monster was held for a moment as a distinct silhouette, suspended against the lunar light and frozen on its moon's surface called, the *Sea of Tranquillity.*

Without warning, the beast of the night began screeching at a great height letting out a foul sound. It began effortlessly twisting in the warm air while turning slowly on the wing, sensing its dominance.

The moon watched the world as the beast got closer. Its sounds became worse; calling out like a hyena being kicked repeatedly yet much worse than that. With each arrhythmic breath the monster inhaled, the more it screamed out wretchedness.

"What is it?" Sebastiano asked.

"Death on wings." Mykola whispered fearfully.

The creature was known by different names, but here in this world of mankind, its common name would come to be known as, DEATH.

"It's black." Sebastiano tracked it hypnotically. Moving off its lunar perch, it was harder to see because of its natural camouflage. It was on its way, descending fast in their direction. "Do you think it knows something we do not? Shit Myk it's coming for us!" Sebastiano was ready to run.

"Wait, its flying into the darkness!" Myk said. The devilish site quickly dipped below the trees, breaking his trance.

"Thank God, it's gone." Sebastiano sighed.

"I can't see it! Do you know where it went?" Mykola hysterically shouted.

"Gone below the tree-line and under the canopy, I think." Sebastiano was soaked in sweat. The shadow had vanished.

Myk whispered cautiously, "I don't think God has anything to do with a creature like this. It has more to do with the Devil."

Both men began quickly crossing themselves for divine protection.

"Fabio's in trouble." Sebastiano stared at the temple. "Ok we go in. Our friends need our help."

"Let's get our kit." Mykola agreed. Both men held each other's shoulders while looking at each other for solace. Their time here had become simply one of survival.

Their exploration would at least take their minds off their immediate dread of headhunters that might be lurking behind every tree and bush.

Organising themselves, they quickly collected all necessary equipment for the temple.

Swiftly gathering rain clouds rolled in from the south making the air feel heavy. A lonely screech could be heard in the distance and was a telling reminder that the creature named DEATH was ever present. The unnatural shriek scared off a nearby flock of night birds and caused other animals to stampede off. Those that heard it knew not to return.

The air rumbled with deepening thunder over the canopy expanses, growing in potency, its supercharged turmoil began to chase away the last of the bright stars in the heavens. Myk and Seb were already standing in front of the temple's entrance.

Massed vines were growing around the entrance, some stretching inside the open corridor and in places spread out in spaghetti madness. Each historian was kitted with their backpacks and no environmental suits. With torch in one hand and machete in the other, both men were ready. The temple appeared dead and that's what scared them. Taking a deep breath, they entered.

Behind them, thunder clattered its violence and urged them on to meet their fate. The sounds of the heavy pitter-patter of raindrops started striking on top of the stone-terraces. A sheet of white lightning flashed brightly, flaring up their scared faces. The men were blinded momentarily and knew no safety would come from outside.

Looking to where they had come from, the entrance mouth flashed again blinding them and lit everything up like an incendiary device. It felt that their quest was becoming as uncertain as vapour, automatically switching on their torches giving them relief once more, their bright beams spearheaded into the darkness. There was nowhere else to go. Not far away lay panic; leaderless, their sanity would not hold for much longer. They shook their heads regretfully. Going back seemed as pointless as hope.

****

Walking through the oppressive passageway, a fearful atmosphere seemed to be welcoming them in. They were no longer able to make out the heavy rain coming from outside, leaving it all behind in a rumour of muffled thunder.

It was not long before they found the deep gap in the floor, the same place where the corridor crossed itself. At this level it was the centre of the temple. The temple felt hot and airless. Standing above the vertical shaft, they wondered which way Fabio and the others had gone. The historians knew nothing of what had befallen the earlier expedition and were oblivious to their previous method of descend by cleverly concealed mechanics, unusual sets of pulleys and lever systems and power that lay hidden behind the stonewalls.

"Did they *really* go down there?" Sebastiano shone his beam into the deep drop.

Troubled, he turned the beam back along the straight tunnel where they came in.

"Unlikely, they just needed to jump this gap and then could have gone any way." Mykola said. Both were unsure what to do next. They were oblivious to the fact that Fabio's group had descended on a type of elevator to below ground level.

"Down would be more Fabio's style; the harder the better. But there's no rope? Did he not say that he was a climber or something?" Sebastiano asked.

"That's right. So, I guess somebody held a rope here, then after this, split up? Or not, *Christ*, I'm not sure anymore." Mykola was frustrated.

"We need to make a rope ladder."

"That will take hours!"

"We have no choice and the sooner we get started, the quicker we can return home. We need to get the stuff from outside again. *Come on let's go!*"

Through the rest of the stormy night they worked hard taking turns; one man knotting the longest vine they could find, estimating the length to be long enough to reach the bottom of the temple. The other man on guard; they had been in the rainforest for months, so Sebastiano knew how to use a rifle.

Next, a secure bridge would be needed to cross the gap by binding small tree trunks together and using cut vines. By morning, everything was ready.

Prepared once again, they soon assembled the rope ladder construct over the gap, securing it onto the wooden poles on their bridge. Mykola cautiously sat on top of the gap while at the same time edging himself over, bit by bit, precariously reaching the centre. Dropping the vine into the darkness, he waited, when unexpectedly a voice boomed out from below.

"Oi!" A voice shouted from below. Mykola almost fell off his perch. Sebastiano began standing at the edge of the shaft looking underneath. "Oi!" It came again. Seb began shining his torch down while holding onto the tree bridge. "Oi! Up there! Do you hear me?" The voice called harder this time.

Suddenly beams of bright torch light appeared shining straight between the two men's legs coming from below. Bewildered, Mykola's face told it all. It was as if he had seen a ghost.

"Hello?" He answered.

"That's right, it's just us! And I see you've been quite industrious with our natural resources! I'm very impressed!" It was the professor alright.

"Fabio is that you?" Mykola asked.

"No!" The professor laughed loudly. It was him alright, with his unmistakably smug voice. "Glad you could make it!" He was relieved.

Soon, all the men had ascended the rope. Exhausted and relieved. The two historians were quick to relinquish their responsibility of leadership back onto Fabio. The professor quickly lead the way back to base camp to rethink his tactics. He needed to plan a rescue to find Harjit and the others.

****

Eight o'clock in the evening, the storm continued. Tent poles kept rattling under the strain, the material stubbornly resisted the battering. The forest canopy gave some additional wind shelter. The storm had built up into a frightening scale with bits of branches flying randomly about the camp. Around them, trees were bending in the wind and some already collapsed outside the safe perimeter. The campsite waited it out and against all odds of nature, the tents stayed fixed.

The tent walls of their large ex-military marquee abode were smacking wildly, as the men sat at the table eating their meals. A few swinging hammocks with mosquito nets raised off the ground helped ensure their safety from any perils from the forest.

Unexpectedly, a large branch suddenly fell through tearing the heavy material.

Other sharp and broken branches began sticking through too, shredding the green cloth in several places. Yet, the ingress of the elements seemed somehow less important as mankind's grip on the forest slipped. Mending it would have to come later because nature was not finished. She would have her say.

Seeing the immediate destruction, the men looked too relaxed drinking caffeine laced with alcohol, easing the storm inside their minds. Even some laughter came after discussing their exploits inside the temple, but was short lived against such a reality.

"Mashir, gone? It's suspicious to say the least. You came to look for us, Mashir did too and got lost. Fabio spoke slowly while deliberating the surveyor's whereabouts.

"That is quite likely Fabio, Mas going off to search inside like that, then following Harjit." The alcohol warmed Endrissi's fuzzy mood. "He's the hero type," he said.

"The last time we saw him, he was looking up at the temple and feeling annoyed for being left behind. He should be with the others." Mykola nodded.

Sebastiano agreed uneasily. "For a while we believed that headhunters might have captured him." His eyes darted over to Fabio for reassurance.

"We cannot rule out that possibility," stated Fabio. The historian gulped down more alcohol. It was obvious to Fabio that the man was frightened.

"What about that gigantic bird thing? What about that, it's a monster! Sebastiano brought up the subject they all wanted to forget.

"We first saw that strange creature on top of the temple before we frightened it away." Fabio withheld the grim details and the fact it lifted off with no regard for them. "It's an oddity, a new species of bird unknown to us. I think it's a peculiar type of super vulture indigenous to only this area. If we can snap a shot of it next time, we will be in Discovery magazine!" The excited professor said.

"I don't want there to be any next time!" Sebastiano raised his voice fearfully.

"Seb's right I saw it too and its massive, it's a monster! It's *death* on wings." Mykola swallowed hard staring at Sebastiano, nodding at him...

"DEATH it is then," said Endrissi glibly. That's the name it should be called."

"Just great, just fucking great!" Kees snapped at him. "You have no idea Endrissi." Kees changed the touchy subject. "I need to do something about this hand Fabio, it's getting much worse. Can I look in Harjit's supplies?"

Fabio nodded, seeing his swollen wound. It had become deeply red. *We will need Harjit's help soon* thought Fabio, then realised the men were waiting for his guidance.

"The temple is a real mystery is it not signores? We were all quite surprised to discover last evening that the temple has a unique source of light inside, next to the inner temple. This would appear to be about the same time you both observed those strange lighting effects coming from the outer walls?" Fabio asked.

"No idea." Kees said disinterested. "I'm going to look for medical supplies." He left as his hand throbbed in pain. "I'll take first watch, can't sleep anyway."

Fabio watched him go, knowing their own medical skills were very limited. Finishing off their coffee, soon were staggering to their own sleeping quarters.

****

Morning arrived, and the storm had not abated. Overcast clouds mixed around in the wailing winds, its powerful force moving Brazil nut trees and Awara palms to sway briskly around; the forest making incredible noises as masses of wet foliage kept slapping in mad urgency. Animals had already taken shelter where they could. Far off in the dimness and over to the northwest of camp, the high waterfall could be seen coming over the distant cliff edge, dropping heavily in grey white streaks down from its lofty heights. Its roar and violence all appeared as a swollen mass of overcapacity. This tumultuous load was seen striking below explosively where the wild water kept on going, endlessly moving in the unstoppable deluge.

The lively stream had been transformed into a river, rushing on for half a mile or so close-by the mega-stone structure. Without end, its fresh waters were continuously smashing off riverbanks and breaking them up. On its way, it went into the gulley and mineworks further down the vale and eventually found a path into the rainforest beyond. The temple dominated the lush green vale, a place of howling noises created by the wind shearing over its primal rock terraces and high voodoo like obelisks. It was not a place for humans and there was no escaping the disorder and desolation here. The men felt that it could only be the Devil's place.

At this moment, the Satellite was overhead.

Inside his two-man tent, Fabio waited behind his yellow stained mosquito net, as his tent rattling wildly by the wind. Sitting with his laptop, he read the onscreen instructions flashing at him; **UPLINK READY**. The professor logged on.

He had managed to connect to one of the few *uplink connections* and was now able to communicate directly with his superiors. Transmissions had been intermittent in the location due to some unexplained interferences and at best, it was unreliable! Fabio understood that the strange magnetic interferences occurring was due to the South Atlantic Anomaly, whether this was the same experience he could not be certain.

His weekly transmission could be lost in an instant inside the vale, and the *uplink* lost without any warning. The non-communication usually suited Fabio because he really disliked his commercial overlords, the Company but now he needed their help.

The mission details were highly privileged and sensitive, the company and Vatican decided there should be no vision or voice data, even though all data was encrypted. Only text and still digital images were allowed for transmission. His portable scanner transmitted the data from a few extracts from the book from the mines.

Fabio had to balance the information he fed them, *the Suits*, the *Stakeholders* and the *Vatican*, carefully ensuring that his messages did not alarm them. He made the call.

Professor Mancini of the Universita Degli Studi di Messina had uncovered many things that would inspire certain individuals back home. This was the place told by the old manuscripts, it all made sense. The professor sure that some of the extracts from the book matched theirs and this would make one reader back home particularly interested.

I cannot tell them everything that has happened. Any mention of unexplained accidents and low morale will never do. He thought to himself. *Tell them what they need to know, nothing more and that everyone is in good health. No mention of any disappearances or deaths.*

He quickly typed his message.

```
MISSION SUMMARY
======== =========
Initial Reconnaissance of Temple
======= =============== == ======

All is well.

I have discovered an Inner temple.
Returning to new excavation site
tomorrow. Require immediate fuel and
food replacements.

Status - Everything is back on
schedule.

        Arrivederci.

        Professor Fabio Mancini.

        UPLINK LOST...
```

That was all. He needed to gather more facts from the temple.

The Mission is back on schedule. The professor grimaced to himself because this would be his last communication with civilization until he found what he wanted. Lives had been lost. *I need to find Harjit and her team.*

****

GOD'S CHAIN'S spellbinding sequel continues inside the next story.

DESTROYER OF WORLDS.

Finding the temple proved to be truly magical! The Professor's expedition was back on track. His expectations higher than ever to locate an ancient artefact inside its enchanted walls. He was determined to find, the Key of the Gods. Ancient powers had allowed a doorway of the temple to open. It had taken the ultimate, human sacrifice.

Harjit's escape from the deadly spiders was a taste of many dangers to come. Her team might as well have been on another planet as they moved precariously through the upper temple. In the shadowy light, broken stone and shattered bone lay all around them as they tried to find a way out.

In the darkness of night, a military search and rescue operation arrive at base camp to discover an armed guard on its walls. Probably mercenaries, deducing that the civvies were imprisoned inside or dead. Why? What for? The prophecy held the key.

DEATH, that named flying beast from another dimension had been born on the wing and storm. Evil incarnate, it had come as a spearhead of wickedness and where DEATH flew, death followed…